THE HEADMASTER

Book 2 of
To Serve Them All My Days

A novel of youth spanning two generations who fought in two World Wars, surveying their values, their ideals and the country they served, it sees the period 1918–41 as a cycle of years in which the enormous changes of the twentieth century first became apparent. The whole theme is expressed through the eyes of four hundred growing boys at a remote public school in Exmoor and of their teacher, David Powlett-Jones, David is a miner's son, who emerges from the horrors of Passchendaele to find a new identity as a bridge between the Victorian–Edwardian generation and the post-war generation seeking new freedoms and new values. From an unqualified history teacher, he ultimately emerges as headmaster of Bamfylde School, and in 1941 finds himself in exactly the same position as his predecessor who lost nearly a hundred of his Old Boys in the 1914–18 conflict.

This is a school novel which develops fundamental questions about the real purpose of education, a novel of social change in the twentieth century, of compelling strength, and a plea for British standards of character and conduct which will find a strong echo in many hearts.

The Headmaster

*Book 2 of
To Serve Them All My Days*

R. F. Delderfield

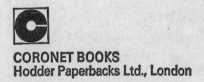

CORONET BOOKS
Hodder Paperbacks Ltd., London

Copyright © 1972 by R. F. Delderfield
First published by Hodder and Stoughton
Limited, 1972
Coronet edition 1973

Printed and bound in Great Britain for
Coronet Books,
Hodder Paperbacks Ltd,
St. Paul's House, Warwick Lane,
London, EC4P 4AH
by Hazell Watson & Viney Ltd,
Aylesbury, Bucks

ISBN 0 340 16709 2

*Dedicated to my friend and colleague
of the book world—*
ROBIN DENNISTON

A QUALIFIED DISCLAIMER

Almost every writer of fiction inserts the obligatory disclaimer in his work and some, I suspect, do it with tongue in cheek. The truth is, of course, no one ever *invented* anyone. Every character in fiction is an amalgam of factors drawn from the author's memory and imagination and this is particularly true to *To Serve Them All My Days*. No character here is a true portrait, or caricature, of any master or boy I ever encountered at my six schools and one commercial college, between 1917 and 1929, but aspects of people I met are embodied in all of them, and I have even used nicknames I recalled, as well as several scholastic backgrounds. To write fiction in any other way would be to divorce oneself from reality and what kind of book would emerge from that? In using, say, an average of six schoolmasters and six boys for every one between these pages, I intended no slight or criticism, only to portray life at school as I saw it up to 1940, when I had entered my twenty-ninth year. I was glad to leave five of the six schools but there is one I still regard with the greatest affection. I leave it to the reader to sort the wheat from the chaff.

R.F.D.
February 1971

Chapter One

I

Looking back on the period of his life that he came to think of as 'the impasse years', David Powlett-Jones could never be sure of the precise moment when the shadow first touched them, when he and the rest of the rump became unpleasantly aware that one era had ended and another, stormy and cheerless, had begun.

It must have been during the last few weeks of Algy Herries' reign at Bamfylde, between his first formal handshake with Alcock on the day of the appointment and the final night of term, when he sat below the dais in Big Hall helping Skidmore, the senior prefect, with the presentations at Algy's farewell supper.

It was then, looking directly up at the new man sitting on Algy's right hand, and noting his impassivity during the farewell address, that he finally acknowledged Alcock's implacability, for no man, he reasoned, could be completely unmoved (as Alcock obviously was) by Algy's valediction, a subtle and wholly unselfconscious blend of pathos, humour, gallantry and profound resignation. But there might have been earlier indications of what lay ahead, for he recalled a curious incident in Barnaby's study, a day or two after he and Carter had finally buried the hatchet—'a couple of rejects here to console one another' as Carter had put it, and very handsomely David thought, considering the bitterness of their feud over a stretch of more than eight years.

From the start there had been a mutual antipathy between the starchily correct war veteran, who had never seen service overseas, and the miner's son who had arrived at Bamfylde still in a state of shell shock. They had come into head-on collision over the erection of a war memorial in 1919. Carter, allying himself with Alderman Blunt, the chief donor, had insisted on adhering to the traditional idea of a

stone cross; whereas David had led a campaign with the Old
Boys to provide new buildings for a peacetime generation of
boys. It had become known in Bamfylde history as 'the
War Memorial Spuddle' in which Carter was the victor.

The bitterness between the two men simmered on until the
year of the General Strike when Carter, now housemaster of
Outram's, nicknamed Havelock's 'the Kremlin'. David, prepared to explain his left wing allegiances to the Sixth, was in
no way prepared to accept this insult to his passionate belief
in democracy, or the insult to his house. Quite out of temper,
he levelled at Carter the accusation so long suppressed, that
Carter's knee injury had been nothing more than a cowardly
excuse to avoid active service. Into the ridiculous scene that
followed in Carter's study, with his two younger housemasters flailing at one another as in a bar room brawl, Algy
Herries had injected a little peace, a little reason, and im-
posed an uneasy truce.

Both had accepted Barnaby's invitation to partake of 'real'
coffee in his quarters, at Nicolson's on a day that school
ended at eleven a.m., in honour of the match with the
Devonshire Dumplings. Barnaby, a ritual coffee-maker,
scowled down at the common room brew and said, "With
important visitors about the place other ranks can be
moderately sure of a bubble-and-squeak lunch. Come and
fortify yourselves. Everyone invited."

Irvine and Howarth had joined them, and all five, housemasters apart from Irvine, sat around talking shop before
Carter raised the subject that was in everybody's mind.

"What do you make of this chap, Alcock? Oughtn't we to
begin trimming our sails?" An innocent-enough remark one
would have thought, hardly calling for Howarth's testy,
"Trimming is more in your line than mine, Carter!" whereupon, anxious to demonstrate that their peace treaty was
more than a gesture, David said, "No, Howarth. Carter's
right. We ought to have sized him up by now, he's been
mooching about the place ever since he was appointed. Has
anyone exchanged more than a word with him?"

Nobody had, not even Carter who, as they all recalled, had
been the first to congratulate the incoming head. Irvine said,
with an uncharacteristic touch of malice, "He's been living

with Algy. Powlett-Jones is the only one with a direct line to the Head. Hasn't he leaked anything to his protégé, Davy?"

"He hinted that Alcock was short on humour. Nothing more. I'd say he was a pedant, and will act like one until the place takes him over," whereupon Carter said, flatly, "It'll never do that, old man. Never!"

He sounded so emphatic that Barnaby raised an eyebrow. "What makes you so sure of that? It managed to mellow everyone here, didn't it? Not much but somewhat. Even Howarth," but then rendered the gibe harmless by winking very solemnly and refilling Howarth's cup.

"Call it a hunch," said Carter and then, with a nod at Barnaby, that might or might not have been an acknowledgment of his hospitality, he slammed down his cup and stalked out.

"Hallo, hallo, hallo? What brought that on?"

This, from Irvine, whereupon Howarth growled, "Pique. Plain, unadulterated pique. Carter has been given the cold shoulder and wants us to restore circulation."

It was not often that David ran counter to Howarth and never had on Carter's behalf. He said, carefully, "You might as well know, all three of you, that Carter and I have settled our account."

"You might have settled yours, my friend," Howarth said sourly, "but don't bank on Carter paying up. You should have learned by now that common room feuds never heal. Invariably they fester."

"Well, this one won't," David said, and recounted Carter's confession of nerves, which amounted to a peace treaty, as they awaited their interviews by Bamfylde's Board of Governors, as rivals for the headship. David smiled when he repeated the first joke he had heard from Carter's lips, "When I get in there I know just how I shall feel. Like that smug little brute in the picture, 'When Did You Last See Your Father?' As for Carter being the first to shake hands with Alcock, why read anything into that? I'd have done it myself if I'd thought of it. My impression is Alcock is difficult to classify."

Howarth yawned, indicating that the subject bored him,

but it was one of these infelicitous occasions when everyone makes the wrong remark at the wrong moment. Irvine, always baffled by abstracts, said, "Tell you something else. There'll be no more bonus free periods like today's, for cricket or rugger. Man isn't interested in games. Probably never played anything but croquet in his whole life."

"That raises him a notch in my estimation," said Howarth, and went out before Irvine could protest, and although Howarth's contempt for games was a long-established school joke, David could see that the bull-necked Irvine, whose tireless coaching had made Bamfylde the most formidable school side in the West, was upset.

He said nothing, however, but followed Howarth out, so that David had an uncomfortable suspicion that the arrival of Alcock might mean a reshuffling of common room alliances. For a moment he was tempted to explore this thought with Barnaby but thought better of it, remembering that Barnaby made a point of never quarrelling with anyone and would explain why when he could find anyone to listen. Trudging across the moor on one of their hikes he had once said, "A man can't teach Horace and Cicero all day and fall to bickering between times. It's all been said before, P. J. A long, long time ago."

He continued to think about it from time to time, however, inclined to dismiss the notion that a stranger, not yet in office, could introduce new tensions into the place, and yet, it did occur to him, as the last weeks of term ran out, that the Lent tight-rope was making an unseasonal appearance in high summer. It could only be, he reasoned, the impending departure of Algy, whom everybody liked, and most of them revered. Halfway through the head's farewell speech he changed his mind again.

Algy was not rated high as a speechmaker, an after-dinner speaker that is, where the neatly turned phrase, and the gilded platitude, is almost obligatory. He was, however, a breezy chatter-up and today, somewhat to everybody's surprise, he excelled himself. He seemed, almost, to be voicing stray thoughts and deductions rather than saying his official goodbyes, or acknowledging the gift of silver tableware, inscribed with his name and dates. Instead of addressing himself to a rambling tour of something over sixty years of Bamfylde history (a speech that everyone present felt his due) he preferred to present a potted *raison d'être* of the profession, illustrating his theme with all manner of sly jokes at the expense of boys, staff, Governing Body and himself. Mostly himself, for Algy appreciated a joke against himself above all others.

". . . Occasions like these are free gifts to the professional windbag . . . I could keep you here until rising bell, telling you Bamfylde stories, most of which would qualify as thrice-baked chestnuts . . . Things I have seen and experienced, since I came here as a scared little toad of eleven. By Christopher, I *was* scared too, now that I think of it! Oblige me by passing that on to the smallest and scruffiest of your September intake, Mr. Alcock. Who knows? It might cheer him up a bit."

But Alcock, legs neatly crossed, arms carefully folded, did not so much as blink.

". . . I could spin yarns of long ago, when anyone with more than six mistakes in Sunday dictation was flogged by that brute Wesker. God, in His supreme mercy, endowed me with an ability to spell. But I was caught on 'rhododendron' and had them rooted out when I came here as head. I could spin yarns of Wesker's time and yarns of the day before yesterday, when I overheard something to my advantage while seated on Mount Olympus, otherwise known as Spyglass Hill . . ."

For half a minute he paused to allow the laughter to subside. Almost alone, among those crowding the hall as far as the kitchen hatches, Alcock was ignorant of the fact that Mount Olympus, otherwise known as Spyglass Hill, was not to be found on any local ordnance map but was the head's privy, with its stained-glass Judas window, opening on to the quad. The man could be forgiven, perhaps, for looking bewildered at the immoderate reception accorded this innocent-sounding remark but not, David thought, for withholding a token smile when Algy went on to say that he overheard one boy tell another how he had managed to gouge ten shillings from his father to add his name to the farewell gift subscribers' list. "He then contributed a mere five and was gracefully complimented by the head boy for his extreme generosity.

"No matter . . ." and here Algy picked up the silver tea-pot, lifted its lid and glanced inside, ". . . I wouldn't like to give anyone the impression that I'm complaining. It is indeed a very handsome reminder of my twenty-three years here as headmaster, and the subscriber in question—no names, no penal drill—can always salve his conscience by slipping across the parish boundary on the first Sunday of Michael-mas term and dropping the missing coins into my offertory plate."

Not a muscle of Alcock's face twitched. He might, David thought, have been listening to a lecture on bimetallism, so that Carter's remark—what was it?—the man's inability to identify with Bamfylde, suddenly had relevance, and the laughter, renewed and prolonged had no power to cheer.

He had missed a quip or two by then but Algy was now ambling towards his climax, with his audience silent again as he tried to explain what he saw, what he had always seen, as the true function of a headmaster. "It isn't an instructor. Any reasonably staffed school should have plenty of trained in-structors on hand. And it isn't an administrator, either, or never has been in my case. Anyone here will tell you that, judged on my paperwork alone, I wouldn't qualify for a remove every other year. No, no, I've seen myself, latterly at all events, as a kind of co-ordinator of all the aims and im-pulses that keep a place like Bamfylde alive and useful. Education, in the generally accepted sense of the word, has never rated very high on my list of priorities. All that the best of us can do is to teach boys how to educate themselves between their time of leaving here, and their time of crossing that Rubicon, that comes, for most of us, at about twenty-five, when the memory sponge is getting soggy and we tend to read and forget.

"I've had plenty of first-class scholars through my hands since 1904, but I can't claim much credit for their academic successes. They would have been achieved at any school, given the same material. But helping to equip two genera-tions of predatory males with the qualities of patience, tolerance, good fellowship and the ability to see someone else's point of view—qualities I see as the keystones of democracy—that's something else. I'll pipe down now—did I catch a gusty sigh of relief from the back? But let me close with a final anecdote, one that came to mind when I was riffling through the Old Boys' register this morning, in search of inspiration for this interminable valediction.

"It was a very trivial incident but it must have impressed me at the time. Why else should it have stayed in the mind for nearly twenty years? It concerned two boys, Petherick and 'Chuff' Rodgers who accompanied me over to Barcombe by train, when we were giving a charity performance of that year's opera. It was Christmas time, of course, and the train was very full. We finally secured seats in a compartment where a young woman was nursing a baby. Within minutes of starting out the baby was dramatically sick . . . I remember poor Petherick's expression well, as he took refuge behind my copy of *The Times*. Upside down it was, but a thing like that wouldn't bother Petherick. He was one of our sky-rockets, and went on to become president of a famous insurance company, and collect the O.B.E., or whatever they give the cream of insurance brokers. But I wasn't thinking so much of Petherick but of Chuff. Always unlucky, he had been sitting alongside the mother, and was thus on the receiving end of the business. I didn't know what to do but Chuff did. He whipped out a handkerchief—the only clean handkerchief I'd ever seen him sport—leaned across, wiped the baby's face and then the mother's lap. And when I say 'wiped' I mean wiped. It wasn't a dab. It was more of a general tidy-up, all round. After that we had a tolerably uneventful journey, with Rodgers making soothing noises all the way to the junction.

"Now some of you might think that is a very damp squib to conclude the regular fireworks display we have had here tonight, with so many kind speeches, and the giving of such splendid farewell gifts, but it isn't, you know. It's very relevant, to me at any rate, relevant to what we've all been engaged in up here on the moor all these years. For Chuff Rodgers, bless his thick skull, never won a prize or a race in his life. Neither did he find time to do the only thing he was equipped to do—raise a family. He was killed at First Ypres, but I still remember him. Rather better than I remember Petherick. As a matter of fact, when I came across his name this morning, I thought of him as one of our outstanding successes.''

He may have intended saying more but nobody gave him the chance. After a dithering moment he sat down and reached for the beaker of water. Because the story was so typical of Algy it touched an emotional spring in his audience that could only find surface in applause of the magnitude no one had ever heard in the Big Hall. David, joining in, forgot to notice if the armour of Alcock's implacability had been dented but then, suddenly remembering him, he glanced that way again, and was momentarily certain that Chuff Rodgers' handkerchief had achieved what all Algy's jokes and nudges had failed to achieve. Very deliberately Alcock unfolded his arms, uncrossed his legs and bent towards the floor. It was only when he straightened up that David realised he had been fooled. Alcock's head came up like a stork's, neatly and tidily, as he replaced the table napkin that had fallen when Algy lifted the water beaker. His long fingers busied themselves straightening the creases and then, as he refolded his arms, his expressionless eyes resumed their neutral scrutiny of the middle distance.

David thought, with an inward qualm: "Carter was right. He'll never identify,'' and cast his mind back to his arrival as a convalescent and the warm welcome of the Herries, the general atmosphere of noisy good cheer and warm comradeship which had brought him back to life as war ended. He thought of the contrasting solitude of the moors beyond Bamfylde, features which had strengthened and mellowed him and Carter and Howarth and generations of boys and staff.

He would never lose the nightmare vision of Venn's lorry careening down Quarry Hill, smashing into the small three wheeler and killing Beth and little Joan and injuring Grace. Neither would he forget Howarth's support, young Winterbourne's practical aid and Chad Boyer's persuasive arguments, involving him in the life of his house and the school, and restoring his sense of purpose and belonging in the black days of his early widowhood.

Now, looking at Alcock, he wondered what the near future had in store for everyone cheering the tubby little man in the centre of the stage.

II

Before half-term he had acquired a variety of nicknames. It was held at Bamfylde that a nickname, even when the bestowal was derisory, none the less implied absorption into the family. Alcock was the exception to this rule. The very nature of his nicknames signified his separateness, rare even for an instant failure, or a boy or master who had never rated a nickname.

Howarth, the one member of the staff who did not appear to be rattled by the man's remoteness, called him The Mandarin. Barnaby, paying his usual tribute to the classics, called him The Stoic. "A Stoic of the woods, a man without a tear," he quoted, and there was something stoical about Alcock's detachment, as though he had set himself a task that absorbed the last dregs of his nervous energy, leaving absolutely nothing to spare on the units of the school as people rather than pieces of a jigsaw puzzle to be contemplated from above and ultimately, one hoped, allotted their proper place in his neat, tidy mind. Always, they came to realise, his mind. Never his heart, providing he had one under the trim alpaca waistcoats he wore.

He had been widowed, it was said many years ago in Africa, but no one could be sure of this or, indeed, of anything out of his past. Alcock's personal life was double-padlocked against them all. His degrees, which were impressive, and his educational achievements in the Dominions, were there for all to see. Beyond this nothing. Nothing at all, so that communication with him, from the first day of his first term was reduced to a kind of sign language. "Of the kind," jested Barnaby, "that a cautious trader might use to barter with a native despot of unbelievable taciturnity."

Grudgingly, as the weeks passed, they conceded his few good points. Under him, in a matter of days, the administrative machinery of the school achieved the smoothness and impersonality of a heavy turbine engine, tended by a dedicated engineer, who had identified every nut, bolt and piston of its composition. He had the knack, also, of maintaining an awed and hushed discipline, without raising his voice, and he achieved this with his eyes, quite expressionless unless he had occasion to stare anybody down. When this happened, as it frequently did, the eyes were those of a man fanatically involved in himself. Steady, penetrating and terribly chilling. His face, if one happened to study it without meeting his gaze, was at odds with his personality, in that it was slightly puckish, with deep creases on either side of the prim, contained mouth, topped by a clipped moustache. But instead of softening his eyes the creases had the reverse effect, converting what might have been sardonic humour into an icy impatience, so that one was left with the impression that Alcock believed himself to be living in a world peopled exclusively by fools of one kind or another.

His administrative expertise was effortless, that of a Trappist monk with a high spiritual reputation. He seemed to solve day-to-day problems without giving them a fleeting thought, but although his decisions were effective, inasmuch as the problem was solved on the spot, there was about these snap decisions the neutrality of a mathematical equation. One had a feeling that all they need in the way of a signature were the letters 'Q.E.D.'

This first became apparent in his marginal involvement in games. It seemed that he approved games, always providing that they were pursued as a means of exercising bodies. No more and no less, deserving no more prominence in the curriculum than, say, a bi-weekly hour of Swedish drill. His first time-table was a masterpiece of precision, with not a minute of anyone's day wasted. His review of the school diet and re-organisation of the kitchens produced startling gastronomic improvements, welcomed alike by staff and boys, who had muddled along for years on lumpy porridge, burned toast, tough beef, doubtful stews, semolina puddings and strips of treacle tart that the boys called dry-dock wedges. Under Alcock even the fabric of the old place took heart. Surfaces, dull and scarred for a generation, began to glow, and the sun found its way into long-forgotten corners. Scuffled coconut matting was banished from the central aisles of the dormitories, replaced with fibrous material that looked exactly like congealed oatmeal. The boys soon found a name for it, calling it 'Donkey's Breakfast'. Out-of-the-way windows, some of which had not seen a leather in months, lost their ribald slogans, written in ancient dust, and down at the church scores of laboriously carved initials disappeared overnight under thick coats of pew varnish, the smell of which was capable of materialising the new headmaster the moment a head bowed in prayer.

For that was Alcock's way. He was never once present as the actual agent of these changes and transformations. Nobody ever saw him perform or initiate them. They simply happened, and whenever they did one or other of the senses proclaimed that Alcock had been there. Alcock had heard, seen and decreed.

He took the modern Sixth for advanced maths and here, it was claimed, he occasionally emerged, if fleetingly, as a man rather than a force, using symbols as a lesser mortal might use a quotation, or a piece of apparatus in the laboratory. But once the bell had clanged he withdrew into himself before he had so much as stepped down from the dais and they were left with the familiar enigmas; who was he, and why? What secret forces kept his batteries charged? What did he think of them as people and of Bamfylde as an institution? Was he dismayed or satisfied with his results so far? Was his withdrawal due to a terrible shyness, or was it a personal preference? Did he like the job or did he regard it as a penance, stoically performed? Nobody knew the answer to any one of these questions.

Here and there, as the term unrolled, he left a clue, as in the case of his silent assault upon the sanitary system, and the clue indicated that he was a fastidious man who had been appalled (justifiably, some thought) by prevailing conditions down at the Bog.

Nothing effective had ever been done about the Bog. Under Algy, as under his predecessor, it had remained medieval until, presumably, Alcock had stumbled upon it by chance, at once summoning an army of plumbers who transformed it overnight. Under its heavy coats of whitewash, and sporting its shining array of copper cisterns and pipes, it suddenly assumed the aspect of a twentieth-century privy in a small,

well-administered township. There was no question now o
flushing fugitive new boys into the open by the time-honoured
ruse of a 'fireship', that is to say, a bunched-up newspaper, set
alight and launched downstream. The cubicle partitions
were raised by more than a foot and, as was inevitable, all
the entertainment value of the walls disappeared under the
whitewash. It was now a sterile, featureless place, and even
the sanitary-minded regretted its passing.

It was the transformation of the Bog that brought about
David's first brush with the new man, touching off a series of
smouldering rows that had the effect of changing the system
by which David had measured time over the last decade.

In Algy's day every season had a focal point, some of them
disagreeable, but a majority associated with sparkle of some
kind. Now this was changed utterly. Weeks merged into one
another, starred only with head-on collisions, and he could
never be sure when one of these confrontations would occur,
or even how some of them began. They were bracketed, in his
mind, as a series of 'times'. The Time of the Missing Edict.
The Time of 'Stoker' Monk's Pipe. The Time of the Stoic's
Statute of Limitations, and so on, a long period of ding-dong
strife, ending in an eruption that tested his staying power to
the utmost, and set him examining and re-examining all the
underlying reasons for withholding his resignation.

The very first of these clashes stemmed directly from the
facelift at the bog. As usual, it came out of an indifferent sky.

The boys, they learned in the common room, had yet
another nickname for the new head, a tag that puzzled
everyone, even Barnaby, mintmaster of nicknames. They
called him 'Noble', and the word was so much at odds with
Alcock's image that the staff pondered its origins unceasingly,
Barnaby claiming that it cost him sleep. Questions in the
form of hints produced no satisfactory answers from the boys.
The boldest evaded the query, the timid declared it was
outside their experience. David stumbled on the answer one
lunch-hour when, on his way up to the pavilion, he popped
into the Bog when all its official patrons were in Big Hall.

The first thing that attracted his attention, aside from the
transformation, was a large official notice, presumably prepared by the headmaster's secretary, Miss Rowlandson, for

it was professionally typed on foolscap and pasted on the angle of the wall sub-dividing the building into two unequal halves. It was a typical Alcockian decree. Boys would refrain from clogging the drain with refuse. Every effort would be made to trace culprits who persisted in this disgusting practice, and so on, and David glanced down it until his eye stopped at a pencilled addendum to the typed surname under the signature. Someone had printed, in bold capitals, 'AND NO BALLS', after the word 'ALCOCK', so that it was clear how the nickname had originated. It was obviously a codeword for the addendum. He removed the notice and hastened to put Barnaby out of his misery.

Barnaby was very impressed. "It shows a certain dignity, don't you think? It makes its point, while masking its basic vulgarity. There's logic in it too."

"Logic?"

"Yes. I imagine they think of him as a eunuch. I'm not suggesting he is, of course, but you might look for that terrible separateness in someone who has been castrated, wouldn't you say?"

"Are you implying that Alcock is psychologically frustrated, and that accounts for his detachment?"

"How do we know? What do any of us know of his childhood, boyhood or ancestry for that matter?"

"Freudian cock," David said, "and you know it, Barnaby. You're just playing with words."

"But of course," replied Barnaby, swiftly. "Do I ever do anything else?"

"No, you don't," growled David, "and apart from Carter —of all people—no one here seems alive to what might happen to us all under that bloody cipher."

"Cipher? Well, that fits too, but I see him more as an eccentric, an eccentric with a strange knack of getting things done, P.J."

"Howarth made the same point but it doesn't console me." He tore the notice into small pieces and dropped them into Barnaby's wastepaper basket. "Fine. He gets things done. The grub improves. The Bog is rebuilt. The church pews are revarnished. But what's happening to the *tone* of the place? The real Bamfylde, *Algy's* Bamfylde? This used to be a lively, noisy, happy school. Alcock has subdued it in a matter of weeks. What might he do in a year or two, sitting up there on his bloody private Olympus? All right, maybe Carter and I are especially anti because we were passed over, but I for one never expected to land that job. Damn it, Barnaby, you're a pretty discerning chap most times. Can't you *sense* a creeping paralysis?"

"I can smell dust raised by a brisk new broom. I wouldn't put it higher than that. And, even if you're right, institutions of this kind aren't frozen. They like to prattle about tradition but change is at work all the time, and the pace has speeded up appreciably since the war. You'll join me for coffee, I hope?"

"Not today, thanks," David said, for the man's neutrality irritated him, equating, as it did, with Howarth's on the same topic. Only two days previously he had had an almost identical discussion with Howarth, and had been surprised to discover that Howarth had drawn up a balance sheet as regards the new man's innovations, deciding that Alcock emerged with a small credit balance. He had said something else, too, doubtless aimed at dispelling David's misgivings. "Why worry? He'll spend himself in a term or two. That kind of chap always does. Bamfylde isn't an old foundation, as schools go in Britain, but it's old enough to slow his gallop," and when David denied this Howarth said, spitefully, "Then go and mull it over with Carter, your new friend. You and he are in cahoots now."

It was an overt display of jealousy on Howarth's part. A little of the cordiality that had developed between them during his feud with the Outram housemaster had been dissipated by the armistice and this retort proved that Howarth was no more proof against the occupational hazard of schoolmasters than the next man. As for the feud, it struck him as absurd that he could have maintained it for so long, for now they were on the best of terms, drawn together less by their shared failure on the day Alcock was appointed, than by a common distrust of the new man and his methods. Twenty-four hours later David had a chance to assess Alcock's uncanny grasp of the minutiae of school life.

When the boys assembled by houses after morning school,

preparatory to dispersal to Big Hall for their midday meal, the head emerged from his quarters through the door opening on the quad and took over the parade from Heffling, the duty prefect. He said, in his quiet, carrying voice, "Before you disperse—a small matter, but one I require to be cleared up before lights out. A day or so ago I caused a notice to be posted in the latrines, regarding the disposal of litter. This notice has been removed by some unauthorised person. I require whoever removed it to return it, with a written apology. He will be admonished, no more. If he has insufficient moral courage he may return it to me anonymously. That is all. Carry on, Heffling."

Heffling, somewhat taken aback by the terms of the ultimatum, called the parade to attention, and dismissed it. The boys streamed off into the corridor and over them, like a swarm of bees, buzzed a cloud of speculative guesses. For here was an unusual use of the traditional code of honour that was supposed to apply to a situation of this kind. It had, in effect, been turned inside out, for while, from time to time, appeals for culprits to own up and face the consequences had been made by authority, it was only resorted to in cases of grave breaches of discipline, usually involving clashes with outside personnel, farmers, tradesmen and the like. Judy Cordwainer, a perfect example of the old style dominee and Carter's predecessor at Outram's, had, David recalled, been a great believer in extracting confessions by a threat of collective punishment, but Algy rarely employed the device. David could even recall what he had once said of it: "Germanic! Don't care for it. Has the smack of the hostage system, and it's damned lazy too. Our job to catch the burglars, without holding a pistol to their wives and families."

Forty-eight hours passed before Alcock launched his second ultimatum, appearing through the same door at the same moment in the school day. This time Winterbourne was duty prefect, and David could have sworn he winked in the direction of the knot of housemasters, waiting, as by custom, for parade dismissal before going into their own lunch.

Alcock said, in the same reasonable tone, "Er . . . pertaining to that missing notice. No one has come forward. No one has returned the document anonymously. I have therefore no alternative but to take steps that will involve the innocent. Unless that notice reaches me by lights out today Saturday's half-term holiday will be cancelled."

There was an involuntary buzz at this, loud enough to cause Alcock to call for silence, before handing the parade back to Winterbourne. Barnaby said, as they passed through Fifth Form arch, "Here's a how-de-do. P.J. What now, I wonder? Do you keep mum, and inflict injustice on the least of us, or volunteer for six of the best from the Noble Stoic?" but David, profoundly irritated, derived no compensating humour from the situation. "All that, over a damned litter warning! Doesn't that highlight the idiot's inability to communicate? Algy would have made a joke about it, posted another notice, and threatened the hide of the next boy who removed it."

"Ah, so," said Barnaby, "but Algy was twenty years threatening to rebuild those latrines. It was fortunate I concealed the source of my information concerning the euphemistic 'Noble'. As it is, what the devil can you do, without sacrificing your dignity?"

"You let me worry about my dignity," and he moved up to the staff dining table, choosing a seat between Bouncer Acton, the genial divinity master, who had not been present when the ultimatums were issued, and old Rapper Gibbs, who never spoke at mealtimes. Fifteen minutes before the bell signalled the first of the afternoon periods he made his way to Alcock's study.

He had not been in here since Algy left and was stunned by the changes. The place had always looked a regular tip, with papers spilling from every chair, books from every shelf, and every inch of wall-space covered with group photographs of Bamfeldians in operatic or athletic costume. Now, he mused, it looked like a specialist's waiting-room. Every book and paper was in its proper place, and the walls, freshly distempered, were quite bare. He wondered what Alcock had done with all those yellowing groups, including the one Algy had pointed out the first afternoon he stood here—Bamfylde's Fifteen of the 1913/14 season, the names of all but two inscribed on the cross outside. Alcock was at his desk, writing.

He even had the look of a specialist, an exclusive and very expensive specialist, very scrubbed, very clinical. His manner, without being friendly, was polite.

"Do take a seat, Powlett-Jones. I won't keep you a moment," and he wrote an address on an envelope and used a sponge to seal it. "He would," David thought, "licking would be out for him," and as Alcock raised his head he said, "It's about that litter notice, Headmaster. There's no occasion to cancel the holiday."

"You have identified the culprit?"

"In a sense I have. It was me."

"*You* removed that notice?"

"I had a good reason."

"Of course. What was it?"

"It was defaced."

"You mean you caught someone defacing it?"

"No. Everyone was at lunch when I found it."

"I see. You kept it, I hope?"

"No, I didn't. It was scrawled over and if I could make a suggestion, Headmaster, I should advise replacing it and leaving the matter there. It won't be interfered with again, they've had their warning."

"I rather think that's a matter for me to decide, Powlett-Jones."

"Yes, of course. I was offering a suggestion."

"It's good of you." There was a moment's silence, Alcock occupied in lifting and clasping his hands, as if in prayer. "Damn it, the man doesn't even doodle," David thought, "he probably did once and cured himself of the habit." Then, from Alcock: "I made my first appeal two days ago. You seem to have been reluctant to tell me. Was there a reason for that? Possibly you suspect a boy from your house?"

"I haven't the least idea who it was. In the circumstances, however, I think you'll agree that any member of the staff would hesitate to admit that he had removed a notice posted up by the headmaster."

"I really can't see why."

"You don't think he would have found it embarrassing?"

"That depends on the nature of the defacement. Just how was it defaced?"

For a moment David was almost inclined to tell him, and see what he made of it, but he thought better of it. He said "Nothing particularly obscene, if that's what you're thinking. Just a piece of schoolboy mischief."

"In other words, you refuse to tell me in what way the notice was interfered with?"

"Yes, I do. The main thing is that you now know that a boy didn't remove it."

"I don't think that's relevant, Powlett-Jones. The main factor is surely that one of my staff, and a housemaster at that, refuses to co-operate with me in the maintenance of discipline."

"I'm sorry, Headmaster, I still think it's best forgotten."

He had expected some reaction but there was none. Alcock had himself completely in hand. The familiar empty expression had returned to his oddly puckish face. He said, standing, "Well, then, we shall have to leave it there, won't we? Regretfully, on my part, I may add."

He nodded and David moved out into the corridor, leading to Big School. He had a strong sensation of having been dismissed, or having narrowly escaped a thrashing for some silly prank, of the kind Boyer had perpetrated when he was in the Lower Fourth. There was no victory here for either of them, just stalemate, leaving their relationship, an important one for Bamfylde he would say, precisely where it had been before he tampered with that damned notice. He mooched off to take the Upper Fifth in his favourite nineteenth century but there was neither pleasure nor profit in the period. Gilroy, still stuck with the name 'Strofe', on account of his mispronunciation of 'apostrophe' years ago, remarked to Fogaty, as second bell rang and David moved off, "What's eating old Pow-Wow these days? He's been moody all term, hasn't he?" and Fogaty, who missed very little, replied, "He isn't hitting it off with Noble. Wouldn't surprise me if he didn't pack it in after a term or two."

"I hope to God not," Gilroy said. "We could do a lot worse than Pow-Wow. At least he can make a period pass quicker than some of them."

III

It did, in fact, occur to him to start hunting up another job
during the Christmas break, but time passed swiftly when he
took Grace to his old home in the Welsh mining village to
visit her grandmother. The small terrace house was filled
to bursting for the Christmas celebrations with his sister
Gwynneth and Ewart and their noisy brood. Then it was
time to visit her other grandparents, Beth's people, in
Town, before the onset of the tight-rope term. He realised
that resignation, at this stage, would be an empty gesture he
would live to regret. He had small hopes of learning to live
with Alcock, as all but he and Carter seemed able to do, and
apart from that silly business of the notice there had been no
open conflict between them, only a dragging sense of im-
permanence and disarray that hung over the school, as
though he and everyone else were experiencing everything
second-hand. It astonished him that only Carter, whom he
had always regarded as a very insensitive man, shared this
sense of strain.

Then, towards the end of the Lent term, the 'Stoker'
Monk crisis was upon them, reducing the litter-notice tiff
to insignificance.

* * *

Monk was a seventeen-year-old in the Upper Fifth, whose
addiction to pipe tobacco had earned him his nickname as a
Third Former. Returning from a visit to Austria he startled
the hard core of Bamfylde's smokers by squatting on a trunk
in the hideout above the covered playground (the smokers'
favourite retreat) and puffing away at a huge, ungainly pipe,
with a bowl carved in the shape of a Tyrolean peasant's
head.

The addicts had laid bets that Monk would throw up in
something under three minutes, but he did not. On the contrary, he seemed proof against the fumes of the strong Long-
shoreman's Flake he was using, and henceforth refused anything less lethal, declaring that a cigarette was a little lad's
smoke. Soon it was rumoured that Stoker got through two
ounces of pipe tobacco every week. He was caught on three

occasions, twice by prefects, who beat him, and once by Carter, his housemaster, who lectured him for the better part of forty minutes and beat him into the bargain, but at least Carter refrained from carrying out his threat to write to Monk senior. Stoker, a quick-witted boy, pleaded that Monk Senior had a serious heart condition, and hinted that a letter home might lay Carter open to a charge of man-slaughter.

Beating and lectures notwithstanding, however, Stoker refused to be parted from his pipe, replacing the three that were confiscated by a fourth of equally extravagant design. Apart from his incurable smoking habits, he was an amiable, law-abiding boy, and his academic progress better than average. Somewhere along the line he had acquired the habitual pipe-smoker's habit of cool reflection, and could digest everything he imbibed in class. He thus sailed through exams and trick questions held no terrors for him. He could sniff them out, he said, in the phraseology they employed.

His end-of-term reports were spattered with commenda-tions. He was living proof, his contemporaries declared, that the warning alleging the habit caused dire shortness of wind was a load of codswallop. Monk made the Junior Fifteen while he was still in the Upper Third, and the First Fifteen a year later, where he played as scrum-leader throughout the season Bamfylde never lost a game. He was also a long-distance runner, and came close to winning his running colours last season, so that Carter, himself a non-smoker, was baffled by Monk and through bafflement came to conceive a deep respect for the boy. Perhaps he saw him as a medical phen-omenon, to whom ordinary rules of health did not apply. At all events, he made him a house prefect and looked the other way if he had reason to believe that yet another pipe had replaced the one with the negro's head, now reposing in the Outram repository of confiscated items. He was heard to say, on the last occasion Stoker's name came up over common room coffee, "He's going to have quite a collection of keepsakes when he leaves. As well as three pipes, all made in appalling taste, there are two catapults and an air-pistol, dating from his pre-smoking days. I suppose we should rejoice that the Stoker took to the weed. Harmful it may be but only to Stoker." They deduced from this that Monk qualified as one of Carter's favourites.

David's first knowledge of the crisis at Outram's came when Carter stopped him in the quad after morning school one gusty March day. He seemed extremely agitated and the signs were so obvious that David enquired if he was ill. "Not ill," Carter said, breathlessly, "but more upset than I can remember being since the day those asses appointed that brute over both our heads. Will you oblige me by stepping inside a moment, P. J. ?"

David, mystified, followed him up the steps into Outram's, remembering the occasion he had gone there to complain of Carter's snide comment on his political sympathies. It seemed a long time ago. Already the benign reign of Herries was receding into history. Carter closed the door and stood with his back to it, still breathing very heavily, and looking dazed and distraught.

"You won't believe it, P.J.," he spluttered at length, "nobody would who really *knew* the old Stoker. It's clear against the rules. Everybody knows that. But in every other way Stoker's a brick, an absolute brick! Besides, he's due to sit for matric in June. Why the devil did he have to do it *there*, of all places? Why didn't the idiot stick to the plantation? That's where they go since we rooted them out of the covered playground, isn't it?"

"You aren't making much sense. Do I gather Alcock caught Monk smoking one of his gaudy pipes?"

"In the coke-hole, after prep. He should have known the wretched man is always poking about in premises that were always left to the maintenance staff. And now he's been sacked. Sacked, you hear? And without so much as a reference to me, if you please! I wouldn't have known a thing about it if the boy hadn't made a direct approach to me."

"Alcock sacked Monk for smoking? Is that what you're telling me?"

"I said you wouldn't believe it. Hang it, if every boy caught smoking had been expelled over the time I've been here, we should have been reduced to a handful of prep school boys by now. You know it and I know it! Everybody knows it except that . . . that iceberg over there!"

"Have you tried to talk him out of it?"

"Good God, man, of course I have but I didn't make the slightest impression. I pointed out that Stoker was a splendid type in every other respect, and that no one had ever been expelled for smoking, but he kept insisting that Monk was a previous offender and he was going to make an example of him. I begged and I pleaded. Practically grovelled before him, but the man has no human feelings, P.J. I even suggested a compromise, that we let Stoker stay on, take the exam in June, and leave in July, but he didn't take kindly to that either. Now old Stoker is packing and that brute is putting him on the four o'clock train. How did he know Stoker had been caught once or twice in Herries's time?"

"He probably keeps a dossier on everyone, us included. But what did you think I could do about it, beyond sympathising?"

Carter looked evasive, then said, with a rush, "You're . . . you're very popular here, P.J. More popular than any of us, I'd say. You get along with people in a way I never could."

"Good of you to say that, Carter, but I'm less popular with the Noble Stoic than anybody. If you want someone to intercede, and I don't think it would do any good, why not approach Barnaby, Howarth or both?"

"I mean to," Carter said, knitting his sandy brows, "but . . . er . . . *through* you, if you follow me, P.J."

"I don't, but I'll do anything I can to help."

"Well, then, suppose *you* tackle Barnaby, Howarth and some of the others, and get them to add their names to this. They'd do it for you. I don't think they would for me," and he took a paper from his 'in' tray and thrust it under David's nose.

It was a sheet of letterheaded Bamfylde notepaper, rubber stamped 'Outram's', and closely written in Carter's neat, legible hand. It said:

Sir, We, the undersigned, respectfully request a reprieve on behalf of C. J. Monk. We do this in the hope that you will reconsider three factors, all of which we regard as extenuating, viz:

(a) We have all known Monk since he first came here

four years ago and can testify (corroborating the opinion of his housemaster) that he has proved a great asset to the school; socially, academically, athletically.

(b) No previous warning has been issued to the effect that smoking carries a mandatory penalty of expulsion. We feel one such warning should be given.

(c) Monk is due to sit for University Entrance in June. In our view he is certain to gain exemption from matriculation. Dismissal now would have a disastrous effect upon his career.

Signed,
T. S. CARTER, M.A. (London).

"Good God," David exclaimed, "this is a bit of a belly-crawl, isn't it?"

"Yes, it is," said Carter, readily, "but that's the point. An appeal like that, signed by all the old hands, will be a feather in Alcock's cap, even if it means him climbing down. If that petition is in his hands before Monk's train leaves, I've got a feeling he'll act on it, in his own interests. It isn't blather, either. The old Stoker is aiming for the F.O., and expulsion would put paid to that, unless he could bring some powerful influence to bear. I happen to know he couldn't. His father is an ironmonger. Will you do it, P.J.? For him, and for me? I can't tell you how much I'd appreciate it."

It was not only Carter's pitiful earnestness that prevailed but David's curiosity concerning the reaction of Alcock and the staff to his extraordinary petition. Especially, now that he came to think about it, that of men who had been his own and Carter's colleagues for more than ten years. One assumed that one got to know people very well in these confined circumstances, but clearly this was taking too much for granted. Why if Howarth, Barnaby and old Rapper Gibbs were friends, was he quite unable to predict in advance how any one of them would respond to a move that would diminish them in the eyes of Alcock. There were several unknown factors here. How much loyalty and comradeship existed between them, now that Algy had retired? How many would be likely to put themselves in Carter's place? Or in Stoker Monk's place? How much dignity would, say, Howarth, be prepared to sacrifice in the cause of Carter and Monk? Answers to these imponderables might be interesting.

Tucking the letter into his jacket pocket he said, "I'll give it a try, Carter. I haven't got much faith in it working but you'd probably do the same for me."

"I would, I would, P.J."

"Maybe you'll have to, if things don't take a turn for the better," and to by-pass Carter's gush of gratitude he hurried out, crossing the quad and making his way up the staircase over the Fifth to Barnaby's quarters.

*   *   *

It would be best, he thought, to start with an easy one, and Barnaby was by far the most congenial man on the staff. Aware of the need to cut corners he explained the situation in a few sentences, then produced Carter's plea, having added his own signature before knocking on Barnaby's door. At least one man was predictable. Barnaby, regarding the thing as a huge joke, signed without hesitation.

"We seek tears from the Noble Stoic of the woods? I think the hope is vain, P.J., but I should be delighted to be proved wrong. Whom will you tackle next? Howarth? He'll refuse, shooting quills in all directions. Come to think of it, I doubt if he'd sign a bleat like that for you, much less Carter."

Bouncer and Rapper both signed, the one gladly, because he agreed with Carter that the sack for smoking was 'a bit much'. His standard punishment, four penal marks, would have been more seemly, he thought. Rapper Gibbs, the music master signed reluctantly, and after a good deal of persuasion on David's part.

"I'm not doing it for Carter or Monk," he grunted, "but because you've got yourself mixed up in it. Seems to me I owe you a favour or two, Powlett-Jones, but maybe you've forgotten."

"I'm afraid I have. What favour do you owe me?" Rapper sniffed and rubbed his long nose, a habit he had picked up from Algy during the countless operatic rehearsals they had shared over the years. "Well, not you, exactly," he said, "your wife."

"Beth?"

"I was very fond of her, did you know that? Best leading lady we ever had, and the easiest to coach. No sulks and no temperament, just hard graft, ending in a rattling good performance, even when she was carrying those twins of yours." He looked glum for a moment. "They were the salad-days, Powlett-Jones. We aren't likely to see their like again under him. This is the first year since 1904 we haven't produced a Gilbert and Sullivan. *He* thinks they're frivolous, you know. So what did we have to cheer us along last Christmas?"

"Excerpts from Molière."

"Ah, yes. Lot of piffle. Who the devil wants to listen to a lot of French gibberish? Nobody, save that rackety chap, Molyneux. Place isn't what it was, is it?"

"If it was I wouldn't be standing here asking you to put your name to a document of this kind," David said, and Gibbs signed, advising him to try Molyneux next, for Molyneux and Carter had 'once been thick, hadn't they?'

If they had the relationship must have cooled, David had never been close to the man who took Ferguson's place as French master. He was well up to his work, they said, but difficult to know, another who seemed unable to identify with Bamfylde, in the way the Old Guard had before and throughout David's time. He had private means and drove a red sports car to and from his lodgings in the village. He was also reckoned a highbrow, on account of regular visits to town and Bristol where he patronised obscure productions in club theatres. Molyneux got along reasonably well with the new man and now confirmed as much, refusing to co-operate in any way. "Ridiculous gesture," he said, returning the petition. "Damned surprised at Carter going to these lengths, and even more surprised at you and the others abetting him. Kind of thing that belongs in the Lower Third, doesn't it?"

"We don't think so. Carter has a point about the effect it might have on Monk's career."

"Monk is Outram's pigeon. He certainly isn't mine. Try Howarth, and see what change you get from him."

But David went first to Irvine, where another shock awaited him. Irvine also refused to sign, on the grounds that Alcock would interpret his signature as a climb-down regarding the disputes between them concerning the amount of emphasis to be placed on games.

"But that's ridiculous," David argued. "This has damn all to do with games."

"Indirectly it has. I've stood up to him about free periods for training, and I mean to tackle him again when the cricket season opens. This would give him the edge on me and, in any case, what the devil has Carter ever done for any of us? He's always had his eye on the main chance."

David left him and made his way up to Howarth's study, where Howarth heard him out, his expression even bleaker than usual. He said, "Can't understand why you're trotting about the place pulling Carter's chestnuts out of the fire. I realise you and he had signed articles, but Carter is still Carter, isn't he?"

"I don't think he is," David said, voicing a persistent thought that had kept recurring to him since he quitted Carter's study. "Something odd is happening to Carter. He seemed to me almost hysterical. He's been brooding a lot about Alcock over the last two terms, mostly about Alcock taking house decisions out of his hands, but he's not had a direct confrontation as I have. Or not until now."

"Let me see that silly petition again."

Howarth took it, adjusted his pince-nez, and read it very carefully. "Well, there's a hint of hysteria here," he said, and then, shrewdly, "I hope to God it isn't rubbing off on you, P.J."

"I'll survive it," David said. "And survive Alcock too, I wouldn't wonder. I suppose the truth is we all had it pretty soft under Algy. He was my sole experience of a head."

"He wasn't mine, and there's no tyranny like it if you happen to strike it unlucky." He pondered a moment. "I'll sign the damned thing. Monk has potential, and who the devil am I to penalise a boy for smoking? If you denied me my forty a day they'd soon be calling for me in a plain van."

He took a pen and signed with a kind of snarl and David thanked him and withdrew. "What the devil is happening to us?" he asked himself, moving down the steps and recrossing the quad to Outram's. "In spite of occasional bickering we used to be a team. Now everybody's pulling a different way."

IV

Carter's hunch was correct. Within an hour of receiving the petition, signed by Carter, David, Barnaby, Acton, Gibbs and Howarth, Alcock relented, if that was the word. The reprieve was granted on two conditions, both, to Carter's way of thinking, harsh. Monk would be allowed to sit the examination and finish the school year but there could be no question of his staying on after that. He was also required to submit himself to a public dressing-down in Big School that night and concerning this Carter had misgivings.

"Even Alcock can't beat a man in the Upper Fifth," he told David, and when David suggested that he might make an exception, Carter shook his head. "He's against corporal punishment. I know that from something he said during our discussion."

"Well, that's at least one thing we have in common," David said, "for you all know my views on it. It's always seemed to me a miserable confession of failure on our part. So what else can Alcock do but jaw?"

"I don't know," Carter said, gloomily. "We'll soon find out."

They soon did. Immediately before prep bell all the boys, including the juniors, were crammed into Big School, and Alcock swept in with Monk in tow. There was just the faintest suggestion of a sigh when they appeared, prompted perhaps by the tacit implication that the old Stoker was seen as a heretic about to be burned at the stake. David noticed then that Alcock was carrying the Stoker's fourth pipe, the usual monstrosity, with a curved stem and a bowl of impressive proportions, again carved in the likeness of a negro's head. He held the ungainly thing between his finger and thumb, so that Howarth muttered, "Looks as if the dam' fellow is handling a rattlesnake. Why the devil doesn't he throw it in the wastepaper basket and be done with it?" But Alcock had more ceremonial intentions. Standing well forward on the rostrum, with the abject Monk slightly behind him, he held the pipe aloft for everyone to see, and began: "I am probably correct in assuming everyone present knows why we are assembled. It is to draw your attention to a disgusting habit practised by the wretched boy you see beside me, a boy I happened to catch indulging himself on school premises, with this so-called symbol of manhood in his hand. You are aware, of course, that every school has strict rules against smoking. Apart from a health hazard, it is generally regarded as a grave infraction of discipline. Yet Monk saw fit—indeed, has seen fit on previous occasions—to set the rule at defiance."

He paused for a moment, an actor getting the feel of his audience. Then he continued, "It had been my intention to expel Monk forthwith. The fact that I had second thoughts is due, solely, to an urgent intercession on the part of his housemaster and some of that housemaster's colleagues. All stressed the fact that I had issued no specific warning concerning the automatic penalty for smoking, adding that Monk was due to sit an important examination in June. Those reasons, although not strictly relevant, had validity. I was moved by them. I took them into account. However, you may take it as read that *no* extenuating circumstances will influence me in the future. Any boy caught smoking, or found in possession of a pipe, or cigars, or cigarettes, will be sent home within the hour, notwithstanding his age or the circumstances. In the meantime, however, in order to underline this example, I propose to destroy this implement in your presence," and to the amazement of everyone present, including Monk, he reached into the folds of his gown and produced a claw-hammer.

David had the impression then that Alcock had quietly gone mad and was about to use his hammer on Monk as well as the pipe, but then his attention was deflected by a movement of the head's right hand, as he laid the hammer aside, raised his left arm high above his head and snapped his fingers twice. At the signal, Potter, one of the junior kitchen staff, made a self-conscious entry carrying a tin tray, of the kind in daily use in the dining-hall. Setting it down on the desk he retreated wordlessly, stepping down from the rostrum and disappearing as unobtrusively as he had appeared. Alcock placed the pipe on the tray, picked up the hammer, tried it for balance, and then delivered his first shattering blow on the bowl, smashing it so effectively that fragments

shot across the dais and ricocheted from the panelling.
Five other blows followed until the pipe was in small splin-
ters, the clang of each impact shattering the silence of the
big room. As the final clang died away a loud buzz of
exclamation arose and under its cover David murmured,
"He's dotty! He must be . . .!" but Howarth said, "Not in
the least. In his way he's an artist. It will add flavour to
every cigarette I light from here on . . ." But by then Alcock
was calling sharply for silence and at once a sense of anti-
climax descended on them all. From the rear of the big room
somebody was heard to smother a laugh and the sound was
so distinct that everyone's head turned, trying to identify
the culprit. Alcock said, crisply, but still without raising his
voice, "Will the boy who finds this amusing step forward?"
and there was a stir among the two ranks representing the
Sixth as Sax Hoskins moved out into the central aisle and
stood there, nearly six feet in height and not, David would
have said, as shamefaced as he should have been.

"You, Hoskins?"

"Yes, sir."

"Would you mind telling us all what prompted you to
laugh?"

"I . . . er . . . couldn't help it, sir."

"I see. You couldn't help it. That is *all* you have to say?"

"Yes, sir. I'm sorry, sir."

"I'm glad to hear it. You're a prefect, I believe."

"Yes, sir."

"Next term, under normal circumstances, you would have
become head boy of the school?"

"Well . . . yes, sir."

"You are no longer a prefect, Hoskins. Prefects are expected to co-operate with the headmaster in the maintenance
of discipline. That is all. You may dismiss."

They rose as Alcock descended the two steps to floor level
and swept out. There was no point in anybody making the
least attempt to stifle the loud buzz that followed his exit.
Everyone, masters as well as boys, contributed to it, and the
only two present who had nothing to say were Carter and
Monk. The first sat beside the radiator looking stunned. The
other moved closer to the desk and looked down at the small

heap of debris in the tray. The rest of the staff moved out in a body, turning, by common consent, into the quad where Maxton, the third official bell-ringer David could recall, was already swinging his handbell for prep.

Barnaby said, "I like to think we have just witnessed the compulsive act of a throwback. That was almost an exact reproduction of a medieval book-burning, the kind of thing Tyndale might have been called upon to witness before being burned at the stake. Interesting, don't you think?"

"No, I don't," snarled Rapper Gibbs. "It was the silliest piece of cheap melodrama I've ever had to witness. The man is a complete ass."

"Howarth doesn't agree," David said. "You don't, do you, Howarth?"

"Not entirely," said Howarth, ostentatiously lighting a Gold Flake, and inhaling deeply. "You don't have to like him in order to concede his originality."

But Gibbs had drifted off, and Barnaby began to elaborate his throwback theory, so David turned back towards Big School and was just in time to see Monk cross the quad with Carter. The housemaster's gait was jerky and in the half-light it looked almost as if Monk was assisting him. He hurried across and caught them as they were mounting the steps to Outram's and Monk, turning aside, said, "Mr. Carter told me, sir. I'd like to say thank you, if I may."

"It was your housemaster's idea, Monk. I didn't have much confidence in it." And then, "For God's sake, man, stay well clear of the head until the end of next term. I wouldn't like to see that little scene repeated, would you?"

"No, sir," said the Stoker, seriously, "it was a very good pipe, sir," and David felt a tide of profound irritation rising in him, not merely with Alcock but with youth and youth's ability to slough off emotional involvement in all manner of things, not merely an idiotic pipe-smashing ceremony but the stupidity of the entire human race. It was a very disquieting sensation, carrying him all the way back to a time when boys not much older than Monk were exchanging facetious jokes within minutes of walking into a curtain of shell-fire. He said, curtly, "Cut off, Monk, and try and stay out of trouble," and as the boy withdrew he glanced through the open door of Outram's, wondering whether he should go in and console Carter. He decided against it. The episode was finished and already, he supposed, absorbed into Bamfylde legend, to be passed from generation to generation until it became apocryphal with Alcock portrayed as a mountebank, chasing Monk up and down Big School with a hammer in one hand and a gaudy pipe in the other.

He climbed the stairs to his own quarters, wondering how Grace would take the summary demotion of Hoskins, perhaps the only one among them with a true sense of proportion, and was not surprised to see Sax awaiting him on the threshold, holding a record in its cardboard sleeve. He, more than anyone else in the school had helped Grace to overcome her limp. It had been Sax Hoskins, himself an accomplished jazz musician and dancer, who offered to teach Grace to dance, to help her overcome her limp, when she finally left the convalescent home. David was often gladdened by the sounds of music issuing from his quarters at Havelock's and never ceased to feel warmth towards the boy who injected so much fun into his daughter's young life. Sax said, cheerily, "Evening, sir. I was on the list as duty perk to take prep, but as I'm reduced to ranks that'll be out, won't it? The head does like us to keep to the letter of the law, doesn't he?"

"I believe he does, Hoskins," David said, and suddenly felt immensely grateful to the boy. He thought, "Maybe we can all learn something from him," and said, "Is that a record for Grace?"

"Yes, sir, came this morning by post. A peaches and creamy number, sir—'Carolina Moon'. Good rhythm, tho'. Harry Roy's orchestra, playing 'Button up your Overcoat' on the reverse side. Would you give it to her, sir?"

"Give it to her yourself," he heard himself say, "we all need a bit of cheering up, Sax." And then, as they went in, he called to Grace that Hoskins was here. "Did anyone else laugh, Sax?"

"No, sir. They were all too concerned for poor old Stoker. I think it rattled 'em a little, sir."

"It obviously didn't rattle you."

"No, sir. To be honest, it just struck me as . . . well . . . the funniest thing I had ever seen happen here. I mean, walloping away at poor old Stoker's pipe with a hammer. And that bit of stage-dressing—Potter coming in bang on cue, with the tray. I don't mind about the demotion, sir. In a way it was worth it. I mean, you could wait around a long time before you saw anything as funny as that."

The near-despair he had experienced a few minutes ago turned itself inside out, so that now he saw youth's resilience as a miraculous restorative, capable of reducing everything to a laugh. He marvelled at Grace's recovery, her enthusiasm for life in this all male preserve, her devotion to himself and the boys in his house. These now received her love and concern, filling the void left by the death of her mother and twin sister Joan. But her favourites would always be Sax, her dancing master, closely followed by Spats Winterbourne who encouraged her painting. Strange how the bond forged between the runaway and his housemaster should have extended to Grace. For it was Winterbourne who had seen David roaming the storm swept hillside and led him to his hideout, a cave deep in the valley, and there warmed and clothed him. The self-possessed Third Former had set aside his own emotional problems and, hearing the story of the accident, had suggested that the child now struggling for life after the fearful crash might need David's presence above all other.

He thought, "That's how it's been from the very beginning, since the day I first came here, looking and feeling a total wreck. Self-pity was out from the moment Algy collared that boy on the way in from the playing fields . . . Who was it again? I remember, Daffy Jones, with news of a last-minute recovery by Nicolson's. And then Nipper Shawe appeared, swinging that bell, and I felt . . . renewed somehow. I hope to God that's how it'll always be, with someone like Sax Hoskins around to remind us that nothing matters much. Except the ability to laugh at ourselves now and again."

Grace had dashed out of her room, welcoming an opportunity to abandon her homework, and in a moment they had the record turning. Sax was right about 'Carolina Moon'. It was a peaches and creamy number, but soothing to the nerves in an odd sort of way. He smiled across at them and went into his study, closing the door on Alcock and all his works.

CHAPTER TWO

I

He saw it, throughout the summer and autumn of that year, as a cross-country ride on a half-broken mount, a succession of jolts, swerves, slitherings and punishing jog-trots, interspersed, every now and again, with a head-on collision, incidents like the lavatory notice row, and the last-minute reprieve of Stoker Monk.

Looking back on his ten years under Algy, his life seemed, in retrospect, to have been unbelievably smooth, even allowing for occasions like the Havelock's dormitory fire, the Carter feud, Winterbourne's disappearance, and his own personal tragedy. Now, with the staff divided and distrustful, the boys bored and bemused, and everyone isolated from the methods and policies Alcock adopted, he was more often out of the saddle than in it, usually, he would have said, just about holding on in hope that some dramatic improvement was around the corner. And yet, for all his misgivings, he never thought seriously of throwing in the sponge and leaving Bamfylde to run itself into the ground.

The summer up here had always been especially welcome after the frost, wind and rain of the Lent term. Year after year the weather was predictable in May and June, although it sometimes deteriorated towards the end of the term. It seemed settled enough now, after their reassembly in late April, and he made a resolve to enjoy it in spite of Alcock, immersing himself in his day-to-day schedule, and dividing his spare time between work on 'The Royal Tigress', and excursions beyond the school boundaries, where he could put the school out of mind.

But then, confronting him in much the same way as the two previous eruptions, the Hislop crisis loomed up and within a few weeks of that the certainty of Carter's withdrawal and almost total isolation. And after that, towards the end of the succeeding Michaelmas term, an uncompromising declaration of war, that could only end in outright victory for one man or the other.

*   *   *

Hislop was the leader of The Lump, a cadre now trapped in that traditional repository of rascals, the Lower Fourth, where one always looked for the originals and (providing one was lucky and patient) promise of better things to come once the natural leaders had moved to the Fifth. Boyer with his phoney epileptic fits and his foray into the local pub, disguised in smock and false beard, Winterbourne and Sax Hoskins had been of this ilk, incorrigible at fifteen and sixteen, but worth their weight in gold once they had sobered down and been given responsibility.

Hislop was a boy who could go one way or the other; towards a modest fulfilment, or to perdition, like Ruby Bickford, now, it was said, spending his father's money in the Argentine, and living the life of Old Reilly according to ill-spelled letters to former contemporaries.

Hislop's father was a publican, a heavy, florid man, with a sharp little wife, said to bully him unmercifully. Hislop got up to all the usual pranks, including the placing of a plaster cast of Aphrodite in Barnaby's bed when he was absent, then spreading a rumour that there was a corpse on the premises. He had averaged, in Algy's time, about one hiding a week, but he never minded that, viewing authority, and authority's visitations, much as the old lag regards arrest and an occasional stretch in gaol. It was this attitude in mind, of which David and other old hands were well aware, that made his admission so surprising. One would have thought that, given the circumstances, he would have swallowed his loss, and gone about his business, without taking a course that was bound to lead to one hell of a row.

Havelock's had been troubled, of late, by an outbreak of petty thieving, not unique in David's experience, for once or twice, in Algy's day, there had been trouble of the same kind. Small, personal items had disappeared from lockers, rarely anything of value but enough to promote an orgy of padlocking, enquiry and surveillance, involving domestic staff as well as boys. Then, one day towards the end of May Hislop presented himself at the door of David's study and reported the theft of twelve pounds, fifteen shillings.

It was the size of the haul that staggered David and he questioned Hislop closely as regards the source of money that had been stolen, according to Hislop, from a bedroom slipper kept in the laundry basket that lived under every boy's bed.

He said, appalled, "Nearly thirteen pounds? Taken from a slipper in the senior dorm? But that's ridiculous, Hislop. Apart from having that much money, what on earth possessed you to hide it in a slipper?"

"I thought it would be safer there than in my locker, sir. Anyone can open those padlocks on the dormitory lockers. Gage's was opened a week ago and a fountain pen stolen."

"I know all about Gage's fountain pen. He reported it at the time. But that was worth five shillings. What were you doing with twelve pounds, fifteen, anyway?"

Hislop looked evasive. Unlike most of The Lump he had never been a good liar and David's experience told him at once that he was hoping to gloss over the source of the money.

"Well? You'll have to tell me now you're here."

"It was from my aunt," Hislop said. "She was going to live abroad and gave my Guv'nor fifteen pounds for me when he came over for Sports Day. I was supposed to bank it in my Post Office account but I didn't. I spent some on a binge at Ma Midden's, and was saving the rest towards a motorbike."

"And you were daft enough, knowing that there was a thief around, to hide it in your slipper?"

"Yes, sir. I see now it was crazy but it seemed a good idea at the time. I thought he wouldn't be likely to look there, among stuff awaiting to be collected for the wash. I stuffed it into the toe and kept it there with a ball of newspaper. It was there last night, sir, and it couldn't have gone during the night."

"Why not?"

"Because I put the slipper under my mattress and took it out again in the morning. I didn't check then but I'm certain it was still there."

"And then?"

"I nipped up during break to get five bob to blue at the

tuck-shop. The ball of newspaper was still in the toe but the money was gone."

"Well, that seems to be that. Unless you have any bright ideas."

"I know who took it, sir."

"You *what*?"

"It was Cricklade. That new chap, who cleans up in Havelock's."

"You saw him take it?"

"No, I didn't see him, sir, but I've got proof. I asked around, and Trubshawe, in the kitchen, said Cricklade was the only one who had been up there since breakfast. So I . . . well . . . took a chance, sir."

"You challenged him?"

"No, sir. I knew that wouldn't do any good. I got Gower to tip him to go into the village for cigarettes. While he was gone Gage and I went through his room, sir."

"My God, that was a risky thing to do. Did you find the money?"

"Thirty bob of it, sir. He must have the rest on him. We found Gage's pen, too, sir, and Harper's postal order that he hadn't cashed."

"Apart from the postal order and the pen how do you know his thirty bob was part of your money?"

"It was three ten-bob notes, sir. One had been ripped across and stuck with transparent paper. Another had an ink blotch on it, shaped a bit like a thistle. I know they were two of mine, sir, but . . . well, I would have kept mum about it if it hadn't been for the postal order."

"What do you mean by that?"

"Well, sir, it was that that decided Gage and me to go through his room. Gage didn't care about the pen, and I wasn't that worried about losing the money, but Harper's just a kid, and that four-and-six meant a lot to him. He hasn't got a father and his mater's pretty skint—not so well off, sir. He doesn't even have tuck money, just the Wednesday sixpence for pocket-money. Losing that postal order worried him. He was blubbing about it."

It seemed conclusive. Two identifiable ten-shilling notes, Gage's pen and Harper's birthday postal order, lost five days ago. He said, thoughtfully, "Cricklade is new here, isn't he?" and Hislop confirmed that he had been taken on during the Easter break. "Couldn't we—just, well, collar him, Gage and me, sir? He's only a little squirt and we could give him a going over between us. Maybe he'd cough up the rest."

"Don't you do any such thing! This is a matter for the police, or if the head wants to keep it inside the school, something he and the bursar can attend to. The head will have to know right away in any case."

Hislop looked alarmed at this. "We didn't reckon on that, sir. We reckoned it was Havelock's business, and that you'd tackle it on your own."

"I can't. Cricklade will have to be sacked, and I can't sack him."

"You could frighten him into leaving, couldn't you, sir?"

"Not even that. He's obviously a cool customer, and if it came out that you and Gage had searched his room God knows what counter-charge he might bring. I'm sorry, Hislop, I'm glad you came to me, and even more so that you made a clean breast of it because of the thieving element but I've no alternative but to tell the head. You see that, don't you?"

"I suppose so, sir," he said, glumly. Then, "Are we likely to catch it hot, sir?"

"Not if I can help it. In a way you've done us all a service, as I see it. But you have to admit you went about it very unconventionally, and I daresay the head won't care for that part of it. How about Harper's four-and-six?"

"You don't have to bring him into it, sir. I made it up to him and kept the postal order. I've got it here, sir," and he handed it over.

"I'm afraid I'll have to borrow those ten-shilling notes, Hislop."

Hislop shrugged and groped in his pocket, coming up with three notes, two of them disfigured as he had described. Lunch-bell sounded then and they went down together, parting in the quad where David said, "Both you and Gage will be wanted after lunch. In the meantime, keep your mouth shut about this. That's an order, understand?"

"Yes, sir."

He slouched off and David spared him a sympathetic thought. It was interesting, that reason he had given for searching Cricklade's rooms, and not all that improbable either. Hislop, although a young ruffian in many ways, was popular among the Lower School urchins, possibly on account of his openhandedness and reckless attitude to authority. He decided to see Alcock at once, letting himself into the head's house by the quad door and catching Alcock just as he was going to his own lunch.

"Could I have a word with you, Headmaster?"

Alcock glanced at his watch. "Now? I was about to have my lunch."

"I'm sure you'll agree it's urgent."

"Very well."

He turned and led the way back to his featureless study, motioning David inside and taking his customary place behind the desk. That was one of the many irritating things about Alcock, his way of reducing every interview to a confrontation between headmaster and erring pupil. David told his story factually, exactly as he had heard it from Hislop, and Alcock, his eyes on the strip of moor seen through the narrow window, heard him in complete silence.

"Is that everything, Powlett-Jones?"

"Everything I learned from Hislop, and I've no reason to suppose he was holding anything back."

"I'm afraid we differ there."

"I don't follow you, Headmaster."

"You don't? I think you should, after eleven years as a schoolmaster and, what is it, five as a housemaster? Wouldn't you say it was extremely unusual for a boy to possess that much money? Even a senior boy, and Hislop is not a senior."

"It is unusual, but not unique. Some of the parents are generous about pocket money and Hislop's father is that kind of man. Breezy, and a little . . . well . . . loud. Apart from that Hislop is an only child."

"You're telling me you believe that story of his about his aunt?"

"Not entirely. It's probably a cover story."

"'Cover story?' What is that, exactly?"

"A half-truth."

"Concealing what?"

"I don't know. How could I know? Some personal trans-
action, conducted during the holidays, possibly. He's saving
for a motorbike. He might have made a sale that he wouldn't
want his people to know about. Frankly, sir, I don't see the
source of the money as important. Surely the important
thing is that Cricklade should be seen and questioned."

"That will occur, naturally."

"You intend reporting the matter to the police?"

"I might. Then again I might not. I'm afraid that's a
decision you must leave to me."

"Of course. But it happened in my house, and naturally
I'm very concerned."

"I should be surprised if you were not. Kindly ask both
boys to report to me immediately after lunch. That's all,
I think."

It was another of his curt dismissals. Not for the first time
David restrained an impulse to insult the man, to shake him,
pinch him, anything calculated to smash through the glacial
screen of his self-sufficiency. There was nothing to be done,
however, so he nodded and went out, wondering why successive events continually contrived to bring him into collision with a man of Alcock's disposition.

He told Hislop and Gage to report and noticed they were
still absent from class when he took the Lower Fourth for
last period. By the time tea was over he could endure the sus-
pense no longer and went in search of them. Neither was to
be found, so he entered the headmaster's house from Big
School passage and knocked on the study door. He was still
there, awaiting the summons to enter, when Rigby, the
aged butler Alcock had inherited from Algy, came out of the
kitchen and said, in response to David's question. "The
headmaster isn't back from the station yet, sir."

"What's he doing down there, Rigby?"

"I'm afraid I couldn't say, sir. He went off about an hour
ago, with two boys."

"Hislop and Gage?"

"I couldn't be sure, sir. My eyesight isn't what it was. I only
caught a glimpse of the car moving off. He's sure to be back
for dinner. Any message, sir?"

"No message." He went through the tiled hall into the forecourt, standing at the junction of the twin drives and wondering what Alcock and the two amateur detectives could be doing down at the station. It seemed likely they had gone there to catch and confront an absconding Cricklade.

He was conjuring with this and other possibilities when Alcock's Morris Oxford swing in the east drive and ran between the beeches at its statutory twenty-five miles an hour. Alcock had a reputation for excessively careful driving, a subject for the school wits to work on. Hoskins had laid a wager that he could beat him to Stone Cross and back on foot, providing he cut across the cricket-field. Rockingham Major, who owned a Douglas motorcycle that he rode in the holidays, said the Noble Stoic had never learned the difference between the accelerator and the footbrake, and drove by Braille, using his big toes. The car drove up, made a cautious half-circle, and was backed carefully into the parking alcove. Alcock and Gage got out but Hislop was nowhere to be seen. With mounting curiosity David followed them through Big School arch and into the quad, where they parted, the head going across to the bursar's office, Gage making for Outram's.

There was no point in asking for developments in front of the bursar so David went after Gage, catching him halfway up the steps to Carter's house.

"Hi, there! Gage!" and the boy turned. He looked, David thought, as though he had been undergoing considerable strain.

"Sir?"

"Where's Hislop?"

"Hislop?"

"Yes, Hislop, man. He went with you, didn't he? To the station in the head's car?"

"Yes, sir, but . . . well, he caught his train, sir."

"Train? What train?"

"The train home, sir."

"Are you telling me Hislop has been sent home, Gage?"

The boy now looked completely bewildered. "Yes, I am, sir . . . I thought . . . Hislop thought . . . well, that you must know, sir."

"Know what?"

"That he's been sacked."

"*Expelled?* Look here, Gage, are you pulling my leg?"

"No, of course not, sir. I was there when he went. His things are being sent on and I've got to tell Matron. But first I've got to report to Mr. Carter, sir."

"But why? For heaven's sake, what did Hislop do or say to get himself expelled? If it was for searching Cricklade's room that's an outrage and how is it that you're still here? You were with him, weren't you?"

"Yes, sir, but it wasn't for that. It all came out when the head telephoned Hislop's pater, sir. About the money, I mean, how he got it in the first place."

"How did he get it?"

"By . . . by making a book, sir. On Sports Day. He cleaned up, especially on the steeplechase."

"Hislop got that fifteen pounds making a book?"

"Yes, sir."

"Laying odds on the races?"

"Yes, sir."

"And the head found out about it?"

"Yes, sir. Mostly the senior events. The head phoned and Hislop's pater blew the ga . . . told him it didn't come from an aunt, sir."

It took him so long to absorb this that Gage began to fidget. "I . . . er . . . have to report to Mr. Carter straight away, sir. I'm not even allowed to go into prep tonight. Can I go now, sir?"

"Yes, yes . . . and I'll see you don't get into more trouble for telling me. Tell Mr. Carter I'd be obliged if he'd come over to Havelock's after prep."

"Yes, sir," and Gage scuttled off just as the prep bell began to clang and the half-empty quad erupted with boys hurrying to and fro under the arcades.

He pushed his way through them, too stunned to notice the occasional collision, or heed the lighthearted apologies. Hislop sacked. For making a book on Sports Day. In other words, sacked because he had been sharp enough to use his wits about tracking down a persistent thief, then honest enough to report his loss to his housemaster. Blind, unreasoning fury rose in him as the probable sequence of events took shape in his mind. Alcock's relentless questions concerning the money. Hislop's reliance on a fictitious aunt and a telephone exchange that had disposed of her. And then, his alibi in ruins, a confession resulting in a second phone call to Hislop senior, and a final trip to the station.

"Good God!" he blurted out, reaching his own quarters, "that bastard didn't mean me to know until I missed Hislop at callover, and came running to him! Damned if I don't deny him that little triumph . . .!" but standing there he heard the phone ringing and force of habit projected him across the room to the study. Grace was already answering it and said, "He's here now. It's one of the parents, Daddy, I didn't catch the name . . ."

"I'll take it. Go out and shut the door, Grace."

She slipped out and he heard Hislop Senior's gravelly voice say, "Powlett-Jones? That you? My boy's housemaster?"

"Yes, this is Powlett-Jones. I've only just this moment heard about it. I'm going down to see the head now. Do you mind if I ring you back?"

"Wait—listen—this is a damned outrage! The boy explained everything, tells me he was robbed . . ."

"So he was, and reported to me at once. I repeat, I've only just heard what happened. The head didn't see fit to consult me. Is your boy with you now?"

"Yes, he is, but . . ."

"Would you put him on, Mr. Hislop?"

"What good would that do?"

"I want to explain my side of it. Then I'll see the head, ring back and tell you what happens."

There was a pause. David heard himself breathing hard. Hislop Junior spoke into the phone. "You, sir?"

"Listen, Hislop. I got the story from Gage and I'm going down to see the head right away, but I thought you ought to know this is the very first I've heard about you being sent home. I think the head is seeing the bursar about the servant in question. Don't mention the name on the telephone and try not to worry too much. I mean to do everything I can. And, as I said at the time, I very much appreciate you coming to me in the first place."

"Yes, sir. Thank you, sir."

He rang off and helped himself to a drink, a stiff one. Then, leaving a message with Grace where he was likely to be, he went down and marched along the passage to Alcock's study.

Alcock must have recognised his step on the flags for he called, clearly, "Is that you, Powlett-Jones?" and David went straight in without answering. This time he was standing by the window, perusing a small file of carbons. He said, absently, "Cricklade's references. They seem in order. Probably wrote them himself."

"Hislop's father has just telephoned me!"

"Indeed?"

"He's very angry and I think he has a right to be."

"He'll cool down when he gets my letter. So will you, no doubt, when you know the facts."

Resentment at the man's majestic calm rose up and almost choked him. He made a tremendous effort and succeeded to some extent in controlling himself. "I don't understand . . . it can't be right to take advantage of the boy's straightforwardness . . . in his coming forward, voluntarily."

"His straightforwardness? That's a curious word to use regarding a boy who sets himself up as a bookmaker on the precincts of his own sports field. I assume Hislop Senior told you why I sent him home, as soon as I had confirmed the source of that money?"

"But don't you see none of us would have known about the bookmaking if he hadn't reported the theft. Most boys wouldn't have. They would have realised straightaway that it was certain to get them into serious trouble."

He had at last succeeded in astonishing the man. Alcock's head came up slowly. "What on earth has that to do with it? You don't seem to appreciate the enormity of his offence. *Bookmaking!* Taking bets from other boys, on school premises! It's the most reprehensible thing I've ever heard of."

"More reprehensible than breaking into lockers and stealing money and goods?"

"They are virtually one and the same, aren't they? Both acts of complete irresponsibility."

"What Hislop did was wrong but it was really no more than an extravagant lark—he's that kind of boy and always has been. And what about all the boys who placed bets with him? Are they exempt? Half the school must have wagered if he showed a profit of fifteen pounds."

"I should be equally severe with them if I could trace them. Obviously I cannot, so I must make an example of the one I have caught. Apart from that, do I take it you approve of boys breaking into a servant's quarters and searching his belongings?"

"In Cricklade's case? Yes, I do. If it had been left to us Cricklade wouldn't have been caught. Or not until we had a real problem on our hands. But even that isn't the whole of it. Hislop's action was disinterested."

"You say that? With all his money stolen?"

"He didn't care about his own money. He told me, and I believe him, that he was encouraged to do what he did on account of young Harper's money. Doesn't that put the whole thing in a different light?"

"I find it irrelevant. Even if it's true, which I beg leave to doubt."

"Very well. Let me try and explain it from a personal angle. I came to you within minutes of Hislop coming to me. I came in confidence and trust. But you dealt with the matter summarily, without even consulting me, making nonsense of the tutorial system we've practised here since the school was founded. Boys are encouraged to trust their housemasters. What kind of trust will they have when it gets about that I was the means of Hislop implicating himself? Even Cricklade, if you catch him, will be warned that anything he says might be used in evidence against him. Try and put yourself in my place, Headmaster."

Alcock was silent for a moment, drifting over to his customary vantage-point behind the desk, so that David thought, "He needs that barricade . . . without it he's just one of us . . ." and the thought encouraged him to add, "Under these circumstances we might just as well abolish the house system."

It seemed then that he had scored a point, an insignificant one perhaps, but at least Alcock paused to consider. Then he said abruptly, "I agree. It has occurred to me more than once that it serves no useful purpose. An institution can only have one source of directive. It is sometimes confusing to have half a dozen. However, that's something else, and I would want to give it a serious thought before I introduced an alternative system."

David stirred but Alcock raised his hand, indicating he had more to say. "You asked me just now to regard this on a personal level. I'm very willing to, Powlett-Jones. Sometimes I ask myself if you and I can ever hope to work as colleagues. Why? It's quite clear you resent me, have set yourself against me time and again, and you encouraged Mr. Carter to make me act against my better judgment as regards that boy Monk. Now you seem determined to provoke an open quarrel over another flagrant breach of discipline. It won't do, will it? Am I to expect your resignation?"

He said it almost casually, as if he had been talking about a laundry list or a parcel notice, but in a way this helped.

"My resignation? No, Headmaster, you may not. Not now, not any time."

"You don't agree we are likely to prove incompatible?"

"I think that's so, but it's not going to scare me into re-signing. You can try and get rid of me, as you got rid of Hislop, and tried to get rid of Monk, but I'll fight and I'm in a position to fight hard. I'll fight like the very devil. I've put years of my life into Bamfylde, and it owes me as much as I owe it. I don't mind you knowing I disagree with your entire policy here, and I'm at a grave disadvantage, but while making things very uncomfortable for me it doesn't frighten me. Tell the Governors anything you like, Headmaster. Then I'll give them my side of it and leave them to judge. Neither of us would come out of it with much credit but that can't be helped, can it?"

He was encouraged to note that Alcock seemed the tiniest bit rattled. He was toying with his paperknife, and even this was a concession. Perhaps twenty seconds ticked by. Then Alcock said, in the same infinitely restrained voice, "Very well, Powlett-Jones. We'll leave it there, shall we? I don't think we can have anything more to say to one another just now."

"Is it too much to ask you to reconsider Hislop's case? To suspend him until the end of term and give him a fresh start next term?"

"Altogether too much, I'm afraid." He got up, crossed to the door and opened it. David went out, wondering who had had the best of it this time and thinking, possibly, that it was honours even.

II

Carter was waiting for him, unable, it seemed, to contain himself until the end of prep. It was a very different Carter, however, from the semi-hysterical man who begged his help over Monk in March. He seemed confident, almost jaunty, having, it appeared, had time to absorb Gage's story, but he raised his eyebrows when David told him about Alcock's mention of a resignation.

"I'm glad he didn't put the same hint to me," he said. "I should have been very tempted to throw the damned job in in his face and that would have been a little premature on my part."

"You're thinking of resigning?"

"Well, let's say I'm thinking of promoting myself. I've got a bit put by, quite a bit as it happens, for I've been careful, and lucky with my investments. I want my own school and I mean to get it. As a matter of fact, I've got my eye on one, and if I made an offer I should want a partner. We behaved like a couple of bloody fools for long enough but that's all behind us. I'll never forget your attitude over Stoker Monk last term, and we seem to be the only two here who have faced up to the fact that Alcock is in a fair way to ruining this place. Suppose I come up with a proposition, would you be interested in buying in?"

"That depends on all kinds of things. What sort of school, what sort of money you'd want."

"It's a good-class prep school, in Kent. About a hundred boys so far, but we could soon double that. I believe we could work together and, frankly, I'd sooner take the gamble with someone I know and trust than a stranger. As to the money, you could give me a hint. How much, in round figures, could you raise if you had to?"

"Not more than a couple of thousand, and I should have a job raising that. I've saved, and I've never touched my gratuity, but I'm still responsible for my mother and I've Grace to think of."

Carter tapped his teeth, a habit of his. "Well, no point in pushing it further now, but this last business has helped me to make up my mind. You didn't persuade that bastard to give Hislop another chance, I suppose?"

"No, and there's no point in another round robin. That worked once but it wouldn't work again. I've promised to phone Hislop's father now."

"Then I'll shove off, for there's nothing I can offer but sympathy, old man. You know that, I imagine?"

"Yes, I do. And thanks, Carter."

They shook hands and Carter let himself out. For a long time David sat looking at the phone. It required a considerable effort to pick it up and ask for Hislop's number. When he did Hislop's wife answered and her voice had a cutting edge to it.

"You're *sure* he won't have second thoughts?"

"Quite sure. He never has second thoughts about anything."

"There's the possibility of legal proceedings. It wouldn't do the school much good, would it?"

"No, Mrs. Hislop, but it wouldn't do your lad any good, either. He'll be going on to another school, won't he?"

"If we can find him one, after this."

"I think I could help there."

"How?"

"By setting out the facts as his housemaster, and presenting a case in writing that any intelligent headmaster would take into consideration."

"You'd do that?"

"I'd be glad to. Your boy isn't a bad boy. He's very popular here, especially with the juniors. How does he feel about it?"

Her voice had mellowed a little. "Well, naturally he's shocked, but in a way he's also relieved. To be out of the man's reach, I mean. He tells me things aren't at all the same since Mr. Herries retired. Is that true?"

"Quite true, unfortunately. All the decisions are taken out of our hands. The new man is a law unto himself and I'm only saying that because I feel I don't owe him loyalty."

There was a pause, then she said, "Will you write that letter? Something I could enclose in an application to a headmaster?"

"I'll write it now. Tonight."

"Good. Then I don't think you need worry about legal proceedings. Don't tell that awful man as much, however."

"Madam," said David, "I wouldn't tell Alcock the time of day," and it was a pleasure to hear her laugh.

He replaced the receiver and was surprised at his own calmness. Whatever it was something had been resolved, and that was an improvement. He took a pen and began to write, reflecting as he did that he had never improved on 'Moderate' in any report he had compiled in respect of Hislop, king of The Lump.

CHAPTER THREE

I

It arrived in the form of a housemaster's circular, a few days before the end of summer term. A brief crisply worded directive, couched in terms that were, David decided, so typically Alcockian as to qualify as a self-parody. It was more of an edict than a statement of policy. There was nothing in the least consultative about it and it had the surprise side-effect of rallying them, temporarily at least, under a single banner. Barnaby, mulling it over, said it would have looked well under the signature of the Emperor Caligula. In their long association David had never seen the amiable Barnaby show that much resentment.

The edict announced: "It has come to my notice that a number of sentimental friendships appear to exist between senior and junior boys. I do not think I need be explicit as to what this presages. I have therefore decided that steps must be taken to suppress such friendships as, at best, undignified and, at worst, extremely unhealthy. I look to all housemasters to co-operate. Signed, J. D. Alcock, M.A. (Lond.)"

It referred, of course, to the custom recognised as 'ninging', and it was manifestly clear from Alcock's tone that he had completely misunderstood the traditional Bamfylde approach to the practice. David did not blame him for this. He himself had taken time to adjust to it and it was to be expected, he supposed, that a new man, with little or no experience of British schools, should take a very prejudiced view of an association between boys of different age and status. It was one more example of Alcock's failure to communicate.

'Ninging' was a verb that Bamfylde appeared to have appropriated to itself round about the turn of the century. In the view of Algy, and other old hands, it had its approximate equivalent in every public school in the country. In general terms it was no more than a personal attachment between a boy in Upper School and a boy who was working his way through the Lower School. What Alcock overlooked at Bamfylde was its comparative innocence.

In his very earliest days on the moor David had half-concluded that ninging was a polite euphemism for a positive homosexual relationship, of the kind common enough in the army. Soon after settling in, however, and guided by the prescient Algy Herries, he had seen it for what it was, a combination of hero worship on the part of the younger boys and what he could only describe as a status charade on the part of a senior boy, advertising his improved position in the school, a traditional, if bizarre, example of throwing his weight about, much in the way he might flaunt newly acquired school colours. Sometimes it showed itself in nothing more than a beefy patronage towards his fag, or some other junior. Occasionally it progressed to the stage where the younger boy was the recipient of teatime extras or minor privileges.

In his Grammar School days he had heard very sinister rumours of the kind of friendships said to exist between seniors and juniors in all English boarding schools, and had thought of them as yet another instance of English decadence. But under Algy, and particularly when he had a house of his own, he had seen these associations for what they were, at least on the spot. In Wesker's time, again according to Algy, he might have had good grounds for suspecting the worst but as the tone of the school improved in the decade leading up to the war, Algy's policy of tolerance had paid an unexpected dividend. Algy's approach to ninging, like his approach to many aspects of school life, had been unconventional. David recalled him saying, on one occasion, "Drive this sentimentality underground and every now and again you'll encourage it to develop into something positive and dangerous. Let the nippers have their hero and the seniors their sounding board and admiring private audience and you take the steam out of it in ninety-nine cases out of a hundred."

David had asked him what he did in the hundredth case and Algy said, with a shrug, "You sit on it within the hour.

Not forgetting that it was slackness on a housemaster's part for not spotting it from the beginning."

He had never had occasion to question Algy's precepts. Not once, in his time as housemaster, had a friendship of this kind merited intervention on his part.

It seemed, however, that Alcock had other views. Possibly his experience in schools overseas was that much wider but if this was so why didn't he say so?

"That's asking altogether too much of the idiot," Carter announced, when the matter was being discussed over coffee in the common room. "We should have learned by now that the man is constitutionally incapable of communicating."

But Alcock wasn't, or not altogether. To everyone's amazement he suddenly presented himself in the common room and addressed them as a body, just as if they had been a group of monitors training for promotion to positions of full prefectship.

He said, distantly, "Touching that letter I sent to housemasters. It occurred to me later that I should have addressed a copy to every member of the staff. I take it you have had time to discuss it among yourselves?"

Irvine, not a housemaster, growled that they had, and went on to demand, with his usual bluntness, what, if anything, he was expected to do about it.

Alcock said, mildly, "Why, sever it, Irvine. On the spot. And then report to me, in order that it can be fully investigated."

Barnaby spoke up. It was the first time he had ever challenged the new man but he did it without preamble.

"There's nothing of that kind in my house, I can assure you of that. Friendships, yes, but perfectly harmless ones, believe me."

Alcock lifted one shoulder. "I should like to, Barnaby, but none of us can be sure, can we?"

"I can," Barnaby huffed. "I don't speak for anyone else."

Alcock seemed to consider this for a moment and then, when nobody followed it up, nodded and withdrew. Barely was he clear of the threshold when the bull-headed Irvine exploded.

"Bloody man's a nut-case! First he cancels free periods to

watch important matches, then he starts sacking left, right and centre, now he confronts us with a thing like this! How the hell is a man supposed to investigate a ning without risking a snub? Aye, and a bloody-minded parent's letter into the bargain! Bound to make a fool of yourself, however you tackle it," and he went on to provide them with what David thought a very fair illustration of his point. "I see Skelton, pacing round the plantation boundary with young Grattan, deep in conversation with him. Now *I* happen to know that Skelton regards Grattan as the likeliest kid among the juniors to captain that new Colt's Eleven I'm bringing on. Boy's going to make a first-class bowler, providing he keeps at it, and where the hell would he look for coaching if he's got a ha'porth o' sense? To the captain of the First Eleven, wouldn't he? And that man would have us believe they were madly in love with one another, when the damn fool has never watched a match in his life!"

Barnaby, having recovered his equanimity somewhat, resumed his favourite role of verbal *agent provocateur*. "They might, of course, be using cricket as an emotional bridge, Irvine."

"Cock!" roared Irvine, who had never adapted to Barnaby's gentle leg-pulls. "I *told* Skelton to coach the kid! What does that make me? A pimp?"

It became known, when discussions on the subject widened, as the Stoic's 'Statute of Limitations', an attempt to draw an arbitrary line between seniors and juniors. Among the boys it acquired a less dignified title. They called it 'Noble's Three N's, or Non-Ninging Notice', and this is how it was referred to years later, when Old Boys reminisced round the bar at Whitsuntide reunions.

But at the time it soon ceased to be a joke, especially after Alcock launched his follow-up, demanding of each house-master the imposition of a virtual ban in association between the two groups. It was then that Howarth scored for the staff, following a demand for a personal report on two of his boys transgressing the Statute of Limitations. Replying to Alcock's enquiry concerning the relationship between Dobson, an Upper Fifth rugby colour, and Vesey, a first-termer in the Lower Third, he produced a letter written from Vesey's

father, then serving in the R.A.M.C. in India alongside
Dobson's father, whom he happened to outrank.

The relevant quotation was passed from hand to hand as
proof that even the Stoic was vulnerable to Howarth's irony.
Vesey *père* had written,

> *The kid is sure to feel a bit low, seeing that this is his first trip*
> *home, but Captain Dobson happened to mention his younger boy is*
> *in his fourth year and asks me to ask you to put in a word with young*
> *Dobson on the kid's behalf. I don't want him coddled, mind you,*
> *but it was a great relief to his mother to learn that Dobson's boy is still*
> *with you* . . .

"You see the supreme wisdom of keeping files," Howarth
said, savouring his triumph, "for I've come to believe that
chap takes nothing on trust." Then, glancing around the
common room he added, "Not that I blame him altogether
when I regard you lot."

They conceded Howarth his gibe for by then the Statute of
Limitations had crystallised the opposition in a way that no
previous act on Alcock's part had. Yet it proved something
of a false dawn for David, who soon found himself in a position of virtual isolation. By the end of the following term
wickets were falling fast. Howarth had once again withdrawn into himself, Irvine and Rapper Gibbs had resigned,
and Carter had made his move.

*   *   *

Rapper's retirement came as no surprise to anyone. He was
sixty-four but had let it be known that he was prepared to
soldier on indefinitely. He was a widower without children,
and Bamfylde had been his life since before Herries's time.
He had no stomach for a man who was not only tone deaf
but seemed to regard housemasters as palace spies. For him
the Three N's was the final straw. He gave in his notice and
shuffled off to do for himself, and his two Siamese cats, in a
cottage adjoining Gatwick's farm north of the village.

Surprisingly, Alcock offered Irvine Gibbs's house, Camp-
bell's, and even more surprisingly Irvine rejected the offer.
Even in Algy's day Irvine and his attractive wife had been
restless, Irvine seeking a more prestigious school, where his

talents as a rugby and cricket coach could expect greater scope, and his wife Phyl could look for more sophisticated leisure. Secretly, it seemed, they had gone about their prospecting, and Irvine had finally landed a new post in a well-known Eastbourne prep school.

David was sorry to see them go. Among them all Irvine was the only man on the staff who had shared his army experiences in a time that sometimes seemed as distant as the Crimea, and both man and wife had been close to Beth. The time was approaching when no boy, and few among the staff, would remember her. Irvine, breaking the news, urged him to join them in a move, but David said, "I'll stick it out a while yet. It can only get better or worse. If it doesn't improve then I'll take your advice. Meantime, Carter is still around and since Howarth went back in his shell he and I have been getting along extremely well."

Phyl Irvine said, shrewdly, "Is it Bamfylde or Beth that keeps you here, Davy?" and he replied with a smile, that it was a little of both, plus the occasional visits of young men whom he had taught in the Second and Third forms. There was a grain of truth in this. Almost every week one or other of them zoomed up the east drive in a jazzy sports car, or astride a powerful motor-cycle. The trio he always thought of as The Reprieved—Cooper, Fosdyke and Scrubbs-Norton, boys who had been in the Sixth when he came here early in 1918, and were saved by the Armistice the following November, were frequent visitors. All doing very well, he noted, for two of them were married, and Cooper was the father of the boy he had visualised that summer day when Algy had surprised him reading the news of the breaching of the Hindenburg Line.

Another regular visitor was Boyer, who was up at Cambridge and had decided to teach if he got a good degree. Taylor, the Latinist, was making his mark at Oxford, and Dobson I, who once won a history prize by cribbing, had struck oil in an expanding radio firm and appeared at the Whitsuntide reunion driving a Rolls-Royce. Of the others he had come to like, Skidmore, embryo martyr, who as a new boy had refused to bow to the founder's statue on religious grounds; the two Kassava brothers whom he and

Boyer rescued on the night of the Havelock dormitory fire, Nun Stratton-Forbes, who had brought him news of Beth's twins, Ruby Bickford, broke and home in disgrace from Brazil, and many others, some put in an occasional appearance, others wrote. Possibly his most regular correspondent (and an unlikely one at that) was Paddy McNaughton, who had threatened his persecutors with a rusted revolver at the time of the Irish Troubles, and who now had a tourist office in Dublin, and was assembling material for a documentary film of the Irish troubles. He kept in touch with more than a hundred of them all told, and a very few of the cream, like Spats Winterbourne and Sax Hoskins, were still here, so that he was able to salvage something of the family spirit of happier days, sensing that their loyalty was to him rather than the school. Whether this would survive the departure of the very last of the boys here under Algy he was not sure. Probably not, in which case he might well take Irvine's advice and make a change.

A fortnight before Christmas it got around that old Bouncer, the last survivor of the veteran quartet that had included Judy Cordwainer, Rapper Gibbs and Ferguson, David's predecessor at Havelock's, had been pressured into resigning, ostensibly, Doc Willoughby told him, on account of deafness, but this was not the real reason. Ever since David could remember Bouncer had been deaf, but he could still teach, and even keep order with his volleys of penal marks. It was rumoured that Alcock had overcome Bouncer's reluctance to resign by getting at the Governors.

That left only Howarth, Barnaby and Carter of the originals, and on the final day of term, when everybody's mind was on Christmas, Carter cut another link, appearing in his quarters while he was helping Grace to pack for their biennial trip to the Valley, and announcing that he had something important to say.

David left the rest of the packing to Grace and took Carter and the whisky decanter into the study. Carter was buoyed up, he noticed, more like the man he remembered from their feuding days than the jaded housemaster of recent terms. He said, accepting a whisky, "Fill your glass, P.J. This might be to us."

"You've decided to go ahead with that prep school idea?"

"All settled," said Carter, beaming. "Got a phone call from the agent in the lunch hour. Now it's up to you."

"Come again?"

"You said you could chip in two thousand, remember? Well that still goes as far as I'm concerned."

"You mean, it depends on my putting up money and coming in as a partner?"

"Well, no, not exactly. I mean the offer is still open if you want to accept." He looked, David thought, slightly embarrassed but then, swallowing half his drink he added "I won't hedge with you, P.J. I've got all the money I need. As a matter of fact, I can raise two thousand by private loan if you turn me down. I ... er ... prefer not to disclose the source at this stage. What's it to be?"

"Let's get this straight. If I join you, and bring in two thousand, we're partners. If I don't, then you can still go ahead by borrowing the amount I should contribute?"

"That's the picture, old man."

"Not quite, or not what I would think a fair arrangement, Carter. You told me some time back you would be paying five thousand plus for fabric alone. That would make you the senior partner, wouldn't it?"

There was a rather uncomfortable pause. Finally Carter said, carefully, "That was my idea when I proposed it, back in the summer. But, as I said then, I think we could work well together, and I wouldn't lay down any conditions about seniority. Regardless of stake we should start out level pegs."

"That's damned generous of you, Carter."

"No, it isn't. To my way of thinking it would be the only way to ensure harmony. Well?"

"I couldn't accept in those circumstances. I don't doubt your good faith for an instant, but if I came in now it would have to be on the basis of a junior, with a possible option to buy equality later, if and when I could afford it."

"And that doesn't appeal to you?"

"No. To be honest, I can't see myself ever possessing five thousand pounds, but neither could I work under anybody."

"Damn it, you're having to work under that brute, aren't you?"

"Yes, I am, but on ground I know much better than the brute. It makes a difference. You must see that."

"Yes," Carter said, thoughtfully, "I see it, partly because I like to think I've come to know you pretty well, P.J. What you're really saying is, as regards Bamfylde you still hope?"

"Yes. And I'm backing myself to hold on, even with you and most of the others gone."

"Then it's 'no', old man?"

"Regretfully. Have another drink. Let me drink to your school. What's it called?"

"St. Magnus. Bloody awful, don't you think? It's got a bloody awful motto, too. '*Facta Non Verba*' I intend to change that, however."

"It would suit the Stoic. He performs all the deeds and we have to get along on his words. No matter, here's to you, Carter, and to St. Magnus, and I'll add something to that. One of the more intelligent things you and I ever did during our time was to bury the hatchet."

"Yes, it was," Carter said, "but it makes leaving you in the lurch that much more difficult."

"I'll cope."

"I bet you will."

They finished their drinks and shook hands, David seeing Carter down the steps and across the quad to Outram's, where they shook hands again.

When he retraced his steps he heard the whine of Grace's gramophone, backed by thumps and squeals of glee. She and Hoskins were dancing to the rhythm of Sax's latest record, a convivial number called 'Happy Days are Here Again'. He thought, sourly, "Not for me, they aren't. With Carter gone, I'm more or less alone, for I can't look for much support from Howarth and Barnaby. One seems to be going stale, and the other has no real feelings for the old place." He went in and Sax grinned at him over Grace's dark, bobbing curls. "And there's another of them," he thought, "Old Sax will be leaving at the end of next term. I'm beginning to feel like Crusoe up here." He crossed to the study and glared down at the pile of manuscript representing the latest draft of 'The Royal Tigress'. Beth had encouraged David to embark on this historical novel about Margaret of Anjou during the long winter evenings in their cottage at Stone Cross. His account of Owen Tudor's rumbustious wooing of the young widow had always been a high spot in his history lessons with the Lower School and his return to writing had been his salvation during the sleepless nights after the accident on Quarry Hill.

II

He was on the point of leaving the following morning when Howarth appeared, the inevitable Gold Flake between his lips, and an expression of bafflement that David recognised as the forerunner of a confidence of some kind. Howarth found every confidence a great embarrassment, irrespective of whether it was given or received, so that David thought, "I hope to God *he* isn't packing it in! He's been more than usually crusty of late but I'd miss him more than any of them." He said, "Is it about keeping the Sunsetters occupied?", and Howarth said no, he could cope with the Sunsetters for a week or so, and was here to confirm that Carter had not talked him into that prep school venture.

"You knew about that?"

"Good God, of course I knew about it. Have you ever known anyone pull wool over my eyes?"

"No," David said, grinning, "I don't think I have. I turned him down, although I must say he made me a very generous offer."

"I'm glad you showed that much sense. If you hadn't my little backstairs strategy would have gone for nothing. Have you got a minute or two?"

"Half an hour. The taxi is due here at eleven. Will you have a drink?"

"Not at this hour of the day." He drifted over to the gramophone table, picked up the record Hoskins had left in the turn-table, scanned the title, grimaced and put it down again. "Funny thing, that," he said, "I got it into my head you'd welsh on us. Must be slipping."

"You haven't exactly given me the impression you were over-concerned who stayed and who left. I'd come to believe you'd opted out."

"Sidestepped that guerilla war you and Carter have been waging with Alcock? Well, you're right. It irritated me. I never thought Alcock was worth it. However, we owe the fellow one thing. He got Carter out of the way."

"What are you driving at, Howarth?"

"What's in it for you—and the school. That's what I'm driving at. I know you and Carter formed an unholy alliance, and that annoyed me, for I never did trust the chap. He'd have let you down in the end, you know. If you had gone in with him you would have lived to regret it."

"Is there much to regret at the moment?"

Howarth gave him one of his bleakest looks, of the kind he reserved for boys who shattered the silence of a classroom by dropping a desk-lid. "The present has very little to do with it. This place has had bad men in the past. That sadist Wesker was one of them, if you believe everything Herries told you. But Herries pulled it up in no time at all and you could do the same if you had to. One thing is for sure. You wouldn't have had the chance if you had sunk every penny you possess in that venture with Carter. Why don't you look ahead a little? Alcock isn't forever. He's older than I am, and looks to me like a man who drives himself. Anything could happen in the next year or so and if it does, who will those fools on the Board look to for a rescue operation? Don't tell me you haven't thought of that."

"Oh, I've thought of it, but I can't see myself sticking it indefinitely with Alcock breathing down my neck. He could easily stay on as long as Algy did."

"I can promise you he won't," Howarth said.

"How can you possibly say that? You're not in his confidence any more than I am."

"I can promise it, none the less. I give him two years, Probably less. How old will you be at, say, Christmas, 1932?"

"Thirty-six."

"Just right. So my advice is to stick it out, and do what you can to chasten that damned Welsh pride of yours in the meantime. You and Carter and Gibbs, and even Barnaby, have all been behaving like Second Formers lately. I say nothing of Irvine. He was always poised for flight, with that flipperty-gibbet wife of his."

"Damn it, Howarth, you can't say we haven't been provoked."

"Not madly provoked. Show me any job without stress. Pinpricks shouldn't induce hysteria in a man who stuck it out three years in the trenches. As to Alcock's ultimate impact on the school, I think it'll be negligible. A new head, who had his finger on the pulse of the place, could achieve a turnabout in a month."

"Then secretly you've sided with us all the time?"

"As regards him? Up to a point. He's not interested in the school as a school, only as a source of power, and a stage for his ego. Somewhere to strut, like a ham actor. He'd behave in exactly the same way if you put him in charge of the regional gas board. That shows you how much degrees are worth. Most people, including parents, still regard schoolmasters as desiccated imparters of fifth-hand information, but you know and I know that they're more than that if they're any good. What applies to one school doesn't necessarily apply to another. You wouldn't administer a Crown Colony the way you run the London County Council, would you? Besides, we've got something out of the silly ass. He's improved the fabric, and his window-dressing isn't so bad. We needed a spring clean and an academic hoist. And the numbers have remained fairly steady, haven't they?"

"The tone isn't the same and on your own admission that's what is important."

"You can adjust a tone. Those new latrines of his will last us a generation. I wouldn't be talking this way if our waiting-list had suffered but it hasn't and it won't, until the blight sets in."

"What blight?"

Howarth glared at him again. "What blight? Great God, man, I thought you were a political animal! Can't you see where we're all heading?"

"You mean the Wall Street crash?"

"Among other things. The 'thirties are going to be a bloody difficult time for all of us, especially for places like this, that aren't buttressed by inherited wealth and a snob reputation. By this time next year numbers will have fallen by ten per cent. And by the year after that by thirty per cent.

Many of the parents we rely on won't have the cash to keep
boys here, and as soon as the barometer falls Alcock will go,
you see if I'm not right."

It was a point of view, and one he had never thought about,
perhaps because his continual collisions with Alcock had
obscured what was happening outside, where the unemployment figures were mounting month by month, a minority
government was running the country, and a gale was blowing through the treasuries of the world. He wondered if
Howarth's prophecies were relevant and decided that they
were. Alcock was not a man who was equal to a challenge of
that kind. He was too dedicated to rule of thumb, too self-
assured, too set in his ways. He said, "What was that you
said about your backstairs strategy, Howarth?"

"Oh, that?" He gave one of his thin smiles. "That was
masterly, though I do say it myself. Did you wonder where
Carter got that private loan he talked about? It was from
me. I advanced him three thousand, at a rate of interest he
wouldn't get from any bank in the land. Almost interest
free, you could say."

"You did that? To prevent him roping me in?"

"Why not? I can afford it, as you well know. Buying the
man off seemed the best way to go about it, although I
misjudged him in one respect. I didn't really suppose he
would offer to take you in on equal terms. I suppose even
Carter has his own interpretation of the word 'loyalty'. Well,
I'm not here to apologise for it. Go off and enjoy yourself
over Christmas. I daresay you'll find things seething in the
Valleys, and come back here with a crated guillotine. That
could lead to another display of fireworks, I suppose, but I
never minded fireworks, providing a professional was lighting the fuses." He nodded and stalked off, Grace appeared
from the bedroom, saying, "Will you fasten the straps,
Daddy? The trunk is too full for me to manage," and he
said, absently, "Yes, dear, right away. Go down and watch
for the taxi. We've cut it fine if we're after that eleven-
thirty train."

CHAPTER FOUR

I

Howarth was right about the mood of the Valleys. David could not recall a time when there had been no talk of militant action and when the names of families drawing royalties from deep and dangerous seams were mentioned without a curse. But now, with a sense of crisis that recalled the long dragging strike of 1925/6, the mood of the mining communities was one of blazing anger and frustration. "A Socialist government is in, isn't it? A Socialist Prime Minister has plumped his arse down in Number Ten, hasn't he, boyo? Then why the hell doesn't he do something about unemployment and nationalise the whole bloody industry?" All the miners he met, including his brothers-in-law, Ewart and Bryn, talked this way, rejecting the argument that MacDonald was only holding on to power by the skin of his teeth, and could do little without Liberal support. For years now they had seen their own salvation in Labour's promise that the industry would be taken over by the government, and the fact that Ramsay's victory, in the spring of 1929, had not achieved this by December, implied that they were going to be betrayed yet again.

Some of the older men, pillars of the local constituency parties since pre-war days, were already toying with Communism, and a majority of the youngsters were casting around for Communist candidates, swearing that nothing would improve until capitalism was confronted with the demand of a majority to wrest power from the hands of the few.

He was able, nowadays, to regard pit politics objectively, and it struck him at once that the miners were being unfair to men like MacDonald, Snowden and Jimmy Thomas, the jovial ex-railwayman. Against every forecast, and with the minimum funds at their disposal, they had emerged from the last general election as the majority party. It seemed to

David uncharacteristic of the long-suffering Welsh to expect an instant solution of tormented domestic problems in the face of international depression. Local Labour stalwarts were fighting back, however, and he attended one of their meetings, addressed by a fiery Doncaster speaker, called Routledge, whose co-speaker was a young woman, a lucid platform speaker and clearly a person of education. Enquiries established that she was an Economics graduate, with an Honours degree gained in Manchester.

She received a good, if ironic hand from the men when she sat down, after talking for twenty minutes on the Labour government's present difficulties, and when the meeting dissolved into a dozen argumentative groups, and tea was served by the women workers, Ewart, the husband of his sister Gwynneth, offered to introduce him. Routledge, the Doncaster man, had spoken at previous meetings in the area, and Ewart knew him well. The girl, he said, was travelling about to gain experience for a bid at the next election, and her name was Forster, Christine Forster, a Yorkshire lass well in with the party executive. "Not that I give her a dog's chance whereffer she stands," Ewart added. "She's sharp enough, and can talk the hind legs off a donkey, but why waste deposits on a lass at places where even a man like Routledge couldn't dent the Tory majority?"

He introduced Davy, using the reverent voice the uneducated miner habitually reserves for someone wearing an educational halo. "My wife's brother, Davy Powlett-Jones—schoolmaster he is, at a big college, in England. But he hasn't forgotten where he comes from, have you, boyo?" After which, slapping David's shoulder, moved off and joined the group surrounding Routledge.

Ewart's implied dismissal of her was not lost upon Miss Forster, who smiled and said, "Your brother-in-law is very proud of you, Mr. Powlett-Jones. But he doesn't give a slice of streaky bacon for my chance of getting elected. Neither does anyone else in the Valleys."

She looked far more personable down here on floor level, away from the yellow glare of the footlight bulbs. She had thick brown hair, lighter than Beth's, sharp green eyes and an exceptionally clear complexion, as fresh and pleasing as a flower. She had a long, thinnish nose, that some would have said spoiled her looks, but David decided suited her figure, the exact opposite to Beth's figure, he found himself thinking, with no well-defined curves but long, elegant legs. Her accent was what these people would call 'posh', but he could detect a trace of Yorkshire in the broad vowels and clipped consonants. She seemed to know what she was about, and had come to terms with the prejudice against all women candidates among constituency workers.

She said, politely, "A college, he said. What kind of college, Mr. Powlett-Jones?" and he replied, smiling, "Every school bar a red-brick council school is a 'college' to Ewart. He has the Celt's veneration of all educational establishments. My place isn't much to write home about, a small public school, called Bamfylde."

"Bamfylde? In North Devon?"

"Why, yes. You've actually heard of it?"

"Heard of it? I've visited it! One Sports Day, several years ago, when I was still at school myself. One of my cousins went there. His name was Ridgeway, my mother's sister's eldest boy."

"The Ridgeway who was there in 1925, A tall boy? A first-class miler?"

"He did win the mile that year."

"But of course I know him. He was head boy of my house, just before I took over. He put up a first-rate show the night we had a bad fire, and helped me get the boys out. I'm delighted to meet you, Miss Forster. How and where is he? I don't think I've had word of him since he left. That would be in 1926," and as he spoke he realised why the girl's strong features had seemed familiar as she had advanced downstage to speak. With so many faces imprinted in the memory, however, it was difficult to compare one with another when a coincidence like this occurred. Now that he had a chance to look at her closely he could see a resemblance to Ridgeway's bone structure, particularly as regards the nose and jaw.

"I believe he's in tea-planting in Malaya," she said, "but I can't be sure. We've lost touch lately. All the older members of the family are true-blue Tories, so I'm cut off from family chit-chat. A case of 'Turn-Christine's-face-to-the-wall', you could say."

He laughed, liking her wry sense of humour, and remembering how it would have appealed to Beth. Whenever he met a young woman he caught himself comparing her to Beth, and measuring her by Beth's standards. It was morbid, he supposed, after four-and-a-half years, but there it was, an instinctive reflex that time was transforming into a habit.

He said, offering her sugar, "I think it's encouraging, a person like you, with a good degree, coming over to us," but she replied, "Nonsense! No one who thinks and observes, could do anything else in present circumstances. The majority of my University set vote Labour, and two are nursing constituencies in the North. I took my time waking up to what was going on. Five years ago I was a snooty little bitch from a *nouveau riche* family, who regarded myself as a cut above most folk."

"I can't believe it, but what changed you?"

"The General Strike. That was in my second year at Manchester and Manchester is a good place to see what goes on below stairs. Almost as good as here. The textile industry up there is in a terrible way, and unemployment is even higher than in the north-east. But I suppose Bamfylde is true blue, isn't it?"

"I'm afraid it is," he admitted, cheerfully, "but I'm chipping away at it. My subject is history and that gives me an advantage."

"In what way?"

"Well, think of the ammunition at my disposal. The Peasants' Revolt, the Civil War, the Industrial Revolution, the Chartists. Not to mention the Tolpuddle Martyrs, Peterloo and the Mutiny at the Nore. What chance does a Tory philosophy stand among young animals who spend their entire lives looking for ways to overthrow authority?"

"Do you know, Mr. Powlett-Jones," she said, "you're putting heart into me. I can't recall meeting a schoolmaster of your type. Certainly not one from 'an English gents' college'. Look, I'm speaking at an afternoon rally in Newport, on Saturday. Could I persuade you to attend, and sit in the front row? I should like one sympathetic face in a dozen rows of blanks."

He said that he would come gladly and meant it. Her enthusiasm reminded him vividly of Beth when she was riding a hobby-horse, but when, later, he told Ewart of his promise, the miner echoed Christine Forster's own doubts about her ability to help Labour in a way beyond service behind a tea-urn, or selling raffle tickets.

"Pretty little thing, she is, and means well, I daresay. But women and politics don't mix, Davyboy. No woman elector will cotton on to a lass, in the way she will to a pair o' breeks. Besides, folk in the Valleys don't trust anyone outside their own class. If she was a scholarship lass she might cut some ice but she's not. According to Routledge her folk are stinking rich, boy. Doesn't add up, to my mind."

"That's the most prejudiced summing up I've ever heard in these parts, Ewart, and that's saying a hell of a lot. She's got a quick brain and the party ought to be able to use young women with her qualifications, who cross the floor on account of deep, personal convictions!" But Ewart only grinned at David's sister, Gwynneth, saying, "Sounds like Davy's started looking for consolation in his old age. She's bonnie enough, I'll grant you, but too skinny for my taste," and to illustrate his preference he slid a great horny hand over his wife's behind. "What did you think of Routledge?"

"Not much. He's too platform-conscious. It was like listening to someone reading from a radical pamphlet and an out-of-date one at that. It's time you chaps dropped your nineteenth-century slogans and started persuading the floating voter that a Socialist isn't a home-grown Bolshie. I'll go over to Newport and tell you what line they're taking in a city. I hope it's a bit more sophisticated than here."

* * *

He found a seat in the middle of a row of empty chairs in the fifth row, although even here he was well exposed, for the meeting, so close to Christmas, was thinly attended and that by the converted, judging from the ritual 'hear-hears'! every time a speaker made a point.

He found himself studying Christine Forster objectively,

not merely as a speaker, or even as a prospective Labour
candidate, but as an attractive woman, with a pair of shapely
legs that tended to get between her and her theme. She reminded him of Julia Darbyshire, the pretty young Second
Form teacher who left the school before young Blades's
romantic attachment to her should cause a public scandal.
She had found the all male school a lonely ordeal in her
grass-widowhood, while her husband, a casualty of the
Flanders gas, coughed his life away at Netley. David had
been impressed by her honesty and courage and when they
had stumbled across one another in London, an affair had
sprung up and blossomed so suddenly and joyously that
David had hoped to find in her a second wife and a mother
for Grace, with whom she had immediately formed a firm
friendship. But Julia, when asked, was clear sighted enough
to realise that she could not spend her life contentedly as a
schoolmaster's wife. She warned David that she might
come between him and a future headship. Instead she had
accepted the independence offered her by her wealthy
American suitor, Hiram Sprockman.

The letter which told of her marriage had aroused pangs
of loneliness and jealousy in David, but he had thrown himself whole-heartedly into Bamfylde life again by day, and
filled the lonely hours of night writing his 'Royal Tigress'.

When the speeches were finished he joined her in the
committee room behind the stage and, without giving the
invitation a previous thought, "Why don't we go in search
of something stiffer than stewed tea? Would you care for a
drink before you catch the train to Cardiff?"

"I certainly would," she said, without hesitation, "but
I'm not much of a drinker. Two ports and lemon have me
giggling. Three are enough to start me singing 'The Red
Flag' solo."

"Try beer or shandy," he said, and she told him, smiling,
that she wouldn't, for the smell of beer made her sick. "It
must be an ancestral hangover," she said, "I come from a
long line of chapel teetotallers. Even port, in our house, was
always called 'medicinal', so I came to that in stages."

She arranged to meet Routledge and other speakers at the
station at seven o'clock, and they found a pub called the

Prince of Wales that looked less seedy than its neighbours. He ordered port and lemon for her and gin and tonic for himself, and they carried the drinks over to a table under the frosted window of the saloon bar. She was the only woman present and one or two early drinkers gave her disapproving glances.

"I'm sure they take me for a tart chatting up a client," she said. "Wales has that much in common with the North. Women aren't any more welcome in the pubs than they are in the pulpits."

"Tell me a bit more about the North," he said, "your area particularly. I've never been there, except to pass through in my army days."

"You were in the war? You were old enough?"

"Don't I look it?"

"No, you don't, David. You mean, you actually *fought* in that awful business?"

"Yes," he said, "but as we've only an hour I don't intend boring you with trench stories. Tell me about Sheffield. That's where you come from, isn't it?"

"It's where I was born, but my people moved out when I was fifteen. Father could afford to by then. He cleaned up during the war, though we were terrace-house before that. He had a tiny foundry, employing two men, in 1914. By 1917 he had seventy on the pay-roll and was turning out shell-casings at about a hundred pounds a shift. Profit, I mean. It still sticks in my gullet."

"I don't see why it should. Somebody had to make shells to throw back at Jerry."

"Not at that price. It's odd, really, I never thought of myself as lucky in those days, just special, in the way second-generation Victorians thought of themselves if their fathers made a pot of money in a mill or a factory. It never occurred to me that, if the cards had fallen differently, I would have been one of those kids whose fathers were killed out there, and whose mothers were left to bring them up on a pittance. When I did realise it, I felt guilty. I even used to tell girls at school my father 'worked for the government', implying that he was in the Foreign Office, or something of that kind. Later I decided to do something to . . . well, pay back if you like, using the education his money had provided to even things out a bit. It sounds frightfully smug put like that but I don't know how else to put it. As a matter of fact, I've never admitted that much to anyone else."

It was good, he thought, to hear her say that. Like Christine Forster, at this stage of his life, he was in need of encouragement and somehow she did encourage him. He said, "I don't think it's smug. Honest, maybe, and the kind of thinking that's rare these days. What are your plans now?"

"I'm on the roster for a candidature, but that doesn't mean much. The party needs candidates, God knows, but a constituency would have to be pretty hard up to choose a woman of twenty-six. I've been on a short-list once or twice, and there's another in the offing, but I haven't much hope of being selected ahead of an eligible male. Deaf and dumb he'd stand a better chance than me."

"Now it's you who are letting prejudice take over. The party will soon get around to shedding its sex bias. It'll have to, to ride out the weather we're headed into."

She said, hesitantly, "There's another thing."

"Well?"

"Technically I'm a Roman. I'm married, you see. Separated from my husband, but still married. And because he's R.C. likely to stay that way."

He could think of no reason why this totally unexpected piece of information should hit him like an umbrella handle, jabbed in his stomach, but it did, and the fact that it did made him so nervous that he stuttered.

"M-m-mmarried! But when? . . . I mean, you only got your degree a year or so back, didn't you?"

"I met Rowley at University. He was a don, frightfully brainy, and the youngest member of the faculty at the time. I imagined I was in love. I probably was and still might be if he hadn't been the person he was, and I hadn't been the person I was; or became. Oh, I'm not blaming him. He was born a Roman, and their values are different from ours. Not better or worse, just different. It was a disaster almost from the beginning." She stopped, swallowed what was left of her port, and said, "I'll risk another, if you want me to go on."

"You don't have to."

"I'd like to. It's too long since I talked about it to anyone."

He bought her another drink and returned to the table. She was applying lipstick with the aid of a tiny handbag mirror and he found himself noting the movements of the long, supple fingers shaping the cupid's bow. Her hands were as elegant as her legs, with finely tapered fingers, and perfectly formed fingernails. He also noticed, for the first time, her backward-curving thumb, an invariable sign, in his experience, of a strongly independent nature.

"Rowley was thirty-three when I met him. He was what my mother would have called 'gentry', before she began to think of herself as belonging in the same class and moved to Harrogate. That, in a Yorkshire terrace-house, means class. Yorkshire folk aren't taken in by second, or even third-generation wealth. His father owned a big estate in Northumberland. I still can't figure out why he married me. It might have been to forestall his father marrying him to a neighbour's daughter, with legs like those on that billards table over there. He was a rebel in those days but first-class at his job. We were lovers for nearly a year before we married, but I didn't put pressure on him. Maybe someone else did. Somebody senior to him might have found out he was bedding one of the students, and passed it on to the vice-chancellor. I never did find out, and now I never will. Anyway, he proposed and I jumped at it. We were married in his church —he's a very good Catholic—and naturally I was expected to go along with it all the way. Before and after marriage. It was the after bit that we came unstuck on."

"Children?"

"The certainty of having a string of them. I lost the first, stillborn, and it was his attitude to that that produced the first drip of acid. He wouldn't even discuss using any form of contraceptive, or practise birth-control other than their rhythm system. Not even the first time we made love, a few days after I came out of the clinic. We began rowing over that, and it soon led to other rows, over all kinds of things, silly things mostly. We said unforgivable things to one another and after a final, blistering row, we parted. He took the initiative, actually, and went to Quebec. He must have planned it in advance, for he'd not only given notice at the University but made arrangements for my allowance to be paid through his family lawyer. He wasn't mean about money. That was one of his good points, and he didn't have many when I came to reckon them up. I've never set eyes on him since. All that was two years ago."

"You wouldn't ever consider giving it another chance? Over there, in a new country?"

"Quebec wouldn't be a new country to him. It's more Catholic than the Pope from what I hear. Not that I've a thing against Catholics as Catholics. Sometimes I envy them very much. They've got something to hang on to, and that's more than you can say of us heretics. Besides, his people were kind, in spite of the fact that they were opposed to the marriage. I can go there any time, and be sure of a welcome, but I don't take his money. It's still accumulating at the lawyers for all I know."

"What did you do after that?"

"Your job. Teaching at a girls' school in Lancashire, but I was no better at that than keeping a man. I know what I want to do now and nothing is going to stop me. I'm hoping to get into that male club at Westminster and say my piece. On behalf of the working-class in the North, and on behalf of so-called liberated females everywhere. I don't care if it takes me twenty years. Or maybe that's just the port and lemon talking."

She jumped up, pointing to the clock that stood at ten minutes to seven. "What's special about you, Davy? I'm a very punctual person and you almost made me miss my train. Are you going to walk me to the station after confessional?"

They went out into the street, meeting a light flurry of snow that was beginning to lie on ice below. She took his arm, explaining, half-seriously, that she was obliged to with two-inch heels and a glacial pavement. She said, as the station lights came in view, "All that, and you haven't told me a thing about yourself. All I know is your name, your profession and the fact that you taught a cousin of mine who took off for Malaya."

"We'll have another chance, I hope."

"I don't know when. I'm not likely to get to Devon, except

on a charabanc trip, taking in Clovelly and the Doone Valley."

"You will," he said, with a strong inward conviction, "and before the tourist season begins. Your platform is five, isn't it? Mine's two. I can catch a local five minutes after your train." They stopped at the barrier. Beyond it he could see the stocky figure of Routledge, beckoning. She said, "Wait, Davy . . . can you tell me one good reason why I should un-load to that extent on someone I've only met twice?"

"Yes," he said. "It's a fallacy that professional school-teachers are just talkers. If they're interested in the job, as I am, they have to learn how to listen. I must be progressing."

II

The letter came when he stood in most need of it, when he had reached a new low, despite his good resolutions on returning to Bamfylde at the start of the tight-rope term.

He had renewed his resolve to concentrate on his subject, and on his book, with the intention of keeping well clear of Alcock, and going out of his way to avoid a clash. He saw himself as a kind of Perrin, in the schoolmaster's cautionary tale by Walpole, *Mr. Perrin and Mr. Traill*, that had been a subject for common-room jokes since it had passed from hand to hand in the early 'twenties. Like the wretched Perrin he had found himself repeating; 'It *will* be better this term . . . it might be different this term.'

But it was not. He did succeed in finishing the book to his satisfaction but by late February, when the moor looked its dreariest he came to the conclusion that Bamfylde, Algy's Bamfylde that is, was dying on its feet. Not academically, and not from a numerical or economic standpoint, but inwardly, as though Alcock had petrified it.

The rhythms within rhythms that had been such a com-forting feature of the place were shattered and he doubted if anyone would ever be capable of restoring them. Something of the national mood of flatness and political stalemate had invaded its draughty corridors. The Choral Society was all but defunct. Carter's beloved O.T.C. was a ritual exercise, performed every Wednesday afternoon. The Debating

Society had wilted under rigorous censorship. Entertainments, uninhibited in Algy's day, were now limited to classical plays that even Howarth thought a crashing bore. The emphasis was on work and exam-passing, so that the gulf widened between the clever boys and the slackers, one group exulting in their exemption from compulsory games, the other becoming bored and listless, so that even the occasional flash of mutiny showed as no more than a ripple. The rugby and cross-country enthusiasts missed Irvine's stimulus. Molyneux, who lived off the premises, was no substitute as games master, and David had not been offered the job, although he still went out on the runs as whipper-in, and played an occasional game in the senior scrum. Alcock kept mostly to himself, the remote, austere abbot of a monastery where all the monks were at odds with themselves.

It was difficult to put one's finger on the major cause of the decline and Howarth, Barnaby and himself, who clung together these days ('Like three old drunks going home in a storm', Barnaby jested) occasionally searched for it over a bottle of gin in Howarth's quarters. Barnaby may have touched on a root cause when he said, "Place reminds me of a Regency rake who has undergone religious conversion. He's much more likely to pass the Golden Gate but he's damnably poor company at home." Howarth had another analogy; "It's getting to *smell* like a grammar school in a red-brick town. Well-scrubbed and antiseptic, but me? God help me, I'm nostalgic for the smell of damprot and boiled greens, of Herries's days."

Then, one dull overcast morning, he found the letter on his hall table, the envelope addressed in strange, flowing handwriting very legible despite the fact that it looked as if it had been dashed off in a hurry. The postmark was 'Taunton' and he opened it unsuspectingly, thinking it must be from someone's mother, making enquiries about a new boy's winter cough or a supply of underclothes.

It was from Christine Forster, announcing triumphantly that she had been adopted as prospective candidate for the South Mendips division, a rural constituency where Somerset, Wiltshire and Gloucestershire merged, for the most part agricultural but with several small industrial pockets, including one small coal mine, a glove factory, and several leather-processing centres. "It really is a forlorn hope," she said. "The Tory majority here is over fifteen thousand, and they've never even elected a Liberal, although one came close in 1911. It means starting from scratch, because they've never had a Socialist candidate, but the Trade Unions have got their foot in the door at two or three of the factories and there's potential in the farm labourer's vote. The Liberal candidate seems a colourless chap and his vote has been dropping steadily since the 1918 election. We could even run second, if we put our backs into it, and that would encourage the party to field more women candidates. What I really want to know is, will you be a dear and come over and support me on the platform at my adoption meeting next Saturday? It'll be a very modest affair in the Church Institute, at Bilhampton, the constituency capital (pop. 2,301) but you wouldn't have to speak if you didn't want to, although I'd be very flattered if you gave us a blessing. Wire me if you can come. If you can't, I'll understand and write again, sending on press cuttings, providing the press bother to report it. One other thing that I thought you might like to tell Bamfylde. My cousin *is* in Malaya, up-country on a rubber plantation. (I said 'tea', didn't I?) The poor boy lost an eye a year or so ago in a hunting accident but the other wasn't impaired and now he has a glass eye that he turns to unique advantage. He has persuaded the poor devils who work under him that the eye can see them whether or not he has it in. He puts it in a glass of water and leaves it on the bungalow steps when he goes off for a drink, declaring that it keeps the helots at work when his back is turned. The feudal tricks you Bamfeldians practise in far-flung outposts!"

She signed it, 'Affectionately', as Julia Darbyshire had signed her letters. Warmed, and excited at the prospect of seeing her again, he dashed off a reply saying she was to look out for him on Saturday and ran down to broadcast the story of Ridgeway's glass eye. It might cheer the old hands who remembered him. There were still four or five of his contemporaries, and a story like that was certain of a place in Bamfeldian lore.

He told Howarth and Barnaby about Christine that same night, mentioning that he was attending the adoption meeting, but saying nothing of her invitation to sit on the platform. He knew that Howarth despised all politicians, and that Barnaby had voted Liberal all his life, but they had all grown accustomed to his party loyalties by now. Barnaby agreed to stand in for his one Saturday period.

He set off in high spirits early Saturday morning and soon after midday caught the branch line train to Bilhampton, a pretty, sleepy, red-roofed little market-town at a junction of two sluggish rivers. He had not expected to be met at the station but there she was, looking very spruce in a navy two-piece, and a short ocelot coat, a scarf over her brown hair. She called, gaily, "Welcome to Rotten Borough!" and kissed him on the cheek, and then, smiling, "I know precisely what you are thinking—that this ensemble doesn't fit the party image—but you're wrong, you know. Cloth caps are fine for the lads, but this place needs a boost. The Member's wife is a frightful frump, despite her husband's seat on God knows how many boards, and the Liberal is a bachelor who trots around in tweeds and a pork-pie hat. It was nice of you to come, Davy. I appreciate it very much. Now let me give you lunch at the Bull. It's a nice old pub and you can meet the troops."

It was, he reflected, a very different Christine Forster from the disconsolate girl he had met in Wales two months before. Selection, over the heads of three young men, had boosted her self-respect and it seemed to have done something for her appearance too, for she had obviously made a favourable impression on the middle-aged men composing the constituency committee. More than that, there was no question but that she meant to be boss down here, and was unlikely to let herself be regarded as a kind of mascot, the impression he had got watching her in the company of Routledge and the Valley stalwarts.

The adoption meeting was a great success. Unlike so many of these occasions it had dignity, and a sense of purpose, and perhaps it was this that encouraged him to call her aside during the coffee-break and take her up on the offer to speak.

She said, eagerly, "You mean it? Well, that's fine, Davy!

But will you let me give you a hint? Cut the flannel and say
something factual, on the lines of what you said to me that
first time we met. About your job as you see it, and the
ammunition you feed boys."

"But that's ridiculous," he said laughing, "this meeting is
about you. You're the star here tonight."

"Maybe, but I've got my reasons. This is Monmouth
country. In that market-place out there nine local weavers
were hanged for their share in that uprising."

"But it wasn't a popular uprising in that sense. Monmouth
was a royal bastard, and a feeble one at that."

"It was a case of the people versus the others, and that's
good enough for me. Moreover, it's a local banner, so why
can't we wave it?"

He had a conviction that she was hedging, that her in-
sistence on reference to a local revolt two-and-a-half centuries
ago was based on instinct, an instinct that rested on something more subtle than an attempt to highlight Bilhampton.
It was a woman's attempt to establish that the Socialist
cause was attracting intellectuals and here was proof of it,
a schoolmaster, who taught at a public school, but was ready
to champion her in public.

He took her advice. Years of dominating The Lump, on its
long haul from Second Form to Sixth, had disposed of any
inhibitions he might have had addressing an audience.
He spoke authoritatively and lucidly, giving the town its
place in the history of the Englishman's struggle to wrest
power from the hands of narrow, sectarian interests, and
prepare the ground for real democracy, and because the
Bilhampton victims of Jeffries' Bloody Assizes were local,
whose family surnames were still familiar to his audience,
he made his impact. "They died in what we should think of as
a poor cause," he concluded, "but it wasn't as poor as all
that. The men who came out to fight for Monmouth, in that
wet summer so long ago, were responding to an impulse that
has brought the Englishman into conflict with local tyrants
down to this day, a determination to have a say in how he is
taxed and governed. Sometimes, his leaders have been
demagogues, or opportunists, but that did not keep him at
home, making do on the leavings tossed him by entrenched

privilege. He came out, generation after generation, often dying for a principle, and today we are privileged to hold the torch. Not only with a vote but under trained leaders, of the calibre of this young woman, whose educational qualifications could earn her a thousand a year if she had an eye on the main chance. My advice, for what it is worth, is lend her a hand. And when the time comes to vote for her, in the certainty that she cares deeply for the descendants of men Kirke's dragoons hanged from the end of a rope, at the command of a pedant in Whitehall."

The weight of applause astonished and embarrassed him, so much so that he took small heed of the rest of the proceedings, not excluding the speech of a minor Cabinet figure Transport House had sent from London. But afterwards the politician set the seal on his success by singling him out saying, "Ever thought of politics as a career, Powlett-Jones? You might do worse, with your natural feel for an audience. I've no doubt we could find a constituency for you to nurse," and while David was wondering how to reply to this, he caught a glimpse of Christine's flushed, smiling face over the politican's shoulder, and she answered for him, saying, "Leave him be, sir. He's far more help to us where he is, preaching the gospel in the tents of the Philistines. Isn't that so, Davy?"

"It's what I'm better qualified to do, enjoy it or not," David said, and momentarily his mind returned to Bamfylde under Alcock, and he wondered if, since Algy's departure, he could claim to have preached the gospel in the way she claimed on his behalf.

III

He stayed overnight and on Sunday morning, having borrowed the local Secretary's Austin Seven, she drove him round the constituency. About noon they stopped at the summit of Coverdale Beacon, dominating the plain and giving a view, in clear weather, of the three counties.

It was a fitfully sunny day, with the very first hint of spring in the wind, and great masses of cloud casting shadows as they drove across the lightly wooded landscape.

"I haven't thanked you properly, Davy. You can't have the least idea how much you being there meant to me. You were the jam on what looked like being a stodgy helping of rice pudding. Do you mind if I kiss you?"

"Mind? Damn it, I've been wondering ever since I saw you on the platform how I could get your mind off politics for a few minutes."

Her lips were as warm and responsive as they had promised to be. There were aspects of her, temperamental aspects that, until then, had reminded him a little of Julia but now, letting his fingertips trace the length of her cheek, he had a very poignant memory of his wife, lying in his arms in the winter half-light of the cottage bedroom at Stone Cross. It was odd, he thought, that she should choose that moment to say, "I know what happened to you, Davy. I was curious, and asked around when I went back to the Valley after Christmas. You've come through it with more credit than you give yourself, do you know that?" He said nothing, testing the strength of the affirmation, so she went on, "It would have embittered most men, coming on top of that pounding you had in France. You're still very much a lonely person, however, and that shows too."

"Only away from Bamfylde."

"It means that much to you?"

"Pretty well everything."

"That invitation you had last night—politics, and the power to work in a wider field—it makes no appeal at all to you?"

"Why do you ask?"

"I don't know. Maybe it was because it struck me that if it did we could do it together. It would be more fun with you around. You're a rare bucker-upper or didn't you know?"

"I seem to have lost the trick of boosting myself lately."

He told her something of the changed situation at school, of its cheerfulness under Algy Herries and its decline, in all but material ways, under Alcock. She said, "He sounds an absolute horror but you don't have to suffer him. You're young enough to make a shift, aren't you?"

"It isn't so simple. A school is a tribe. You can't switch tribes as if you were getting on and off a bus."

"You can if you're going in the wrong direction."

"There are all kind of factors. Loyalty to the boys, old and new. Loyalty to the rump of the original staff, to the school servants even. Some of them have been there since before Algy's time."

She said, smiling, "Down under all that smouldering Celtic banner-waving you're a bit of a Tory, Davy. The very nicest kind of Tory and they do exist." Then, with a sincerity that he found uplifting. "You will keep in touch? Come over whenever you can, as soon as I find permanent digs in the constituency, and write to me when you can't. I say, I'm making all the running this afternoon, aren't I?"

"I'll help you out when we've got a bigger car. Or when the ground isn't so soggy."

That made her laugh and she kissed him again, switched on and drove off down the hill. They said little until she had bought her platform ticket, and accompanied him over the bridge to the down-line. Then, as he found a seat in the little train, "Would I be welcome if I ran myself over to Bamfylde as soon as I get myself a car? I've got my eye on a third-hand sports."

"Why don't you pick up some of your separation money and buy yourself a new one?"

"You know better than to ask that. Well?"

"You know better than to ask if you'd be welcome."

The guard, slamming doors with the flourish obligatory to all official door-slammers at small stations in the shires, blew his whistle. She lifted her hand and, as the train pulled away, he had an even more vivid memory of Beth, standing where he was standing now, framed in the window of a third-class compartment, with himself where Christine stood. It was the moment prior to surrendering to that impulse on Colwyn Bay Station, nearly twelve years ago, followed by that leap on to a moving train and his madcap proposal to Beth, that had had such bitter-sweet consequences.

The comparison was so poignant that he almost cried out to her to hurry but then, as the train gathered speed, she disappeared behind a cloud of smoke.

CHAPTER FIVE

I

He was taking Lower Third history when Christopherson Major arrived. Beguiling thirteen-year-olds with Owen Tudor's dalliance with the widowed Queen Catherine, a favourite of theirs and his, for somehow, the way David told the story, the knowing impudence of the philanderer reached out to them over more than five centuries.

Christopherson Major, duty monitor of the headmaster, arrived on the crest of a ripple of laughter, David having quoted Tudor as saying, "Madame, since you can't understand a word of my spoken Welsh, I will sing everything I say, in the hope of conveying my regard for you in music." He often clowned his way through a Lower School period in this way, improvising dialogue and dialect to match it. His justification, had he been asked for one, would have been that it was the only way to capture the laggards' attention for the red meat of history later on.

The appointment of headmaster's monitors was another of Alcock's innovations. Each week a trainee prefect was employed as his errand boy and the job was popular in the Upper Fifth, for it meant, among other minor privileges, a week of sanctioned idleness and plenty of fresh air. Christopherson, however, was a studious boy, who took his duties seriously.

"The headmaster's compliments, sir. Would you please step across for a word with him?"

The laugh died, killed, no doubt, by the expression of irritation that crossed David's face. It was not unknown for members of the staff to be summoned to the presence in the middle of a period, but it was unusual. He said, "Right, Christopherson, take over here, while I'm gone, I won't be more than a jiffy, page one-o-six in the text-book, the minority of Henry VI," and dusting chalk from his gown he went

out across the quad, entering the head's house through Big
School passage.

Alcock, as he expected, was seated behind his rampart,
frowning down at a neat, taped file, the kind of file, David
thought, one might associate with an old-fashioned solicitor
or a civil servant in the Ministry of Agriculture. He knew
enough of Alcock, however, to be certain it was a file with
his name on it, possibly in private code.

"You wanted me, Headmaster?"

"Yes, please be seated. This may occupy us some little
time. You were taking the Lower Third, I believe."

"He knows damn well I was," David reflected, "since he
memorises the timetable every new term . . ." but said,
briefly, "I left Christopherson in charge. You won't want him
while I'm here, will you?"

"Er . . . *no*," murmured Alcock vaguely, and his rare
uncertainty alerted David at once. It was not often that
Alcock showed vagueness in the presence of anyone he
summoned.

"Well?"

"It's about this. I thought it only fair to ask for an explanation at once, for there may well be some unfortunate
misunderstanding. The press is notoriously inaccurate in
these matters."

He passed over a news-clipping, a single column report,
cut from a provincial paper, and dealing with Christine
Forster's adoption meeting. David was surprised to see it,
and even more surprised to notice that the introduction, set in
heavy type, concerned his own contribution to the evening's
speeches. It was headed 'SCHOOLMASTER SUPPORTS LABOUR
CANDIDATE', and below, in smaller type, '*Reference to Local
Hangings—"Martyrs to Freedom's Cause" Claim*'. A few lines
of the introduction were linked to a summarised version of
his speech on the Monmouth weavers, executed in Bilhampton Market Place, in 1685, and the closing section of the
speech itself was given verbatim. He said, carefully, "I
don't think there's any misunderstanding. This is a pretty
fair report of what I said."

"You actually appeared at the meeting, and spoke from
the platform?"

"Of course I did. It says I did. What's unusual about that?"

"It doesn't strike you, not even on reflection, as a very impulsive act on your part?"

"No, it doesn't. I know the candidate. She's related to a boy who was head prefect of Havelock's, before your time. She asked me to speak and I did. Members of the staff aren't banned from making political speeches, are they? For if they are it's the first I've heard about it. Mr. Herries once presided over a Liberal rally at Challacombe to my certain knowledge, and Mr. Carter signed the Conservative candidate's nomination papers last election. I had no idea the speech would be reported, and I'm surprised that it was, but I'm not going to apologise for it. Did you expect me to?"

"No," Alcock said, "knowing your headstrong character, I didn't, Powlett-Jones. But I would anticipate a certain reluctance on your part to appear on a public platform at a political meeting of that kind. You note that the name of the school is quoted."

David glanced at the cutting again and saw that this was true. He had no recollection of having mentioned the school to anyone save Christine and could only assume the reporter had got the information from the local secretary, who might have had his address. It still did not seem important, however, and despite his knowledge of Alcock, he remained puzzled by the man's obvious concern. "Would you like to elaborate your own views, Headmaster?"

"I need to do that?"

"I think you do. You summon me in the middle of a period, and put a newspaper cutting into my hand, implying that I have overstepped the mark in some way. I should like to know what way. We live in a democracy, and the Labour Party is at present in office. Are you suggesting school-masters don't enjoy the same political liberty as other people — doctors, clergymen and so on?"

"In a sense I am. How a schoolmaster casts his vote is, of course, his own concern. How he conducts himself in public is not. It never has been. Do you take my point?"

"No, and to make it you'll have to do better than that, Headmaster. If I had been drunk, and caused a public disturbance, or appeared before magistrates on a charge of bothering women in cinemas, you would have every justification for summoning me here, and even asking for my resignation. You could hardly do that on the strength of an innocuous speech I made at a public meeting in another county. Or in this county, for that matter." He got up. "Is that all?"

For the second time he noticed that Alcock was fidgeting, his fingers unlocking and the knuckles gleaming as his right hand closed and unclosed on an ivory paper-knife, shaped like a scimitar. Then, as though catching himself giving ground, he pushed the knife out of reach and made a 'steeple' with his hands.

"It can't be all, can it? As a matter of fact, I think it essential, Powlett-Jones, that we . . . er . . er come to some kind of understanding, here and now. I see that newspaper cutting as important. You don't. No matter, let us shelve that for the moment, and concentrate on your attitude towards me ever since I was installed. You have made it manifestly plain that you dislike me, and dislike my methods even more. I am not interested in knowing why. Within certain limits any member of the staff is free to exercise personal preferences, providing they do not affect his loyalty to a colleague. But I think even you will admit that our relationship has reached something of an impasse, that it can no longer be subjected to strain without rupture of the discipline I try and maintain here. I did not mention resignation but you did. Perhaps it *is* something you would like to think on for the remainder of the term."

David sat down again. He was red in the face but not from embarrassment. Alcock was no longer capable of embarrassing him but he could still make him almost incoherent with rage. Knowing this, he gave himself a full half-minute before saying, "You're *asking* me to resign? On account of that newspaper report?"

"I'm asking you to think about making a change. And not on account of that newspaper report. Rather on the impossibility of us arriving at, shall we say, a working compromise. Carter and Gibbs reached the same conclusion, I imagine, but they . . . er . . . acted on it."

He had himself in hand now. The rage in him cooled and in its place came a sense of release, of having suddenly seen a rift in the wall Alcock and Alcock's methods had raised between them, brick by brick, over the last few terms. He braced himself, leaning forward and staring the man down in a way that anyone but Alcock would have found embarrassing. Instead he only looked mildly astonished as David said, emphatically, "I'll be damned if you're going to bully me into resigning. And I wouldn't advise you to try on this issue. It could land you, rather than me, in a very embarrassing situation. Do I have to explain what I mean by that?"

"Not necessarily," Alcock hedged, "and I can only repeat I'm *not* asking you to resign. Only to ask yourself if a change wouldn't be the wisest course in what remains of the term. We could come to some arrangements about the usual notice."

David got up again. Suddenly, and to a degree that astonished him, he was composed, almost jaunty. Declaration of open war came as a relief.

"Well," he said, "suppose we leave it like this. Here's your clipping. Show it to whom you like. And show them the contents of that file too, providing you send me a duplicate of any allegations it contains. If it came to a show-down I could demand that. Or my solicitor could. But it need not go as far as that. I only want to make two things clear. Resignation on my part—the dignified version you're seeking—is out of the question. And I reserve the right to appear on any public platform I choose, so long as I am convinced, in my own mind, that such appearances don't reflect on the school's reputation. You can try and force me to resign, but if you do I'll fight. I'll fight every inch of the way, inside and outside Bamfylde. I've disagreed with you, yes, in all manner of things, but I've never been disloyal to you in the way you imply and I never would be. I'm far too attached to the school to act the fool in that respect. My . . . er . . . compliments, Headmaster. I'd best get back to the class now."

He went out, shutting the door carefully behind him, and was relieved, as he crossed the quad and started up the steps to the Lower Third, to hear the bell announce the end of

afternoon school. Before he reached the landing the Third
Form had erupted and Christopherson slipped out, descending the stairs quickly and pretending not to notice him. He
thought, grimly, "Is that because he has a pretty good idea
the Stoic and I have just had a God Almighty row? Or is it
because the class was out of hand before the bell?"

He turned left and cut through the Rogues Gallery to the
linen room, thence to his own quarters, glancing sideways at
a cherubic Algy Herries, beaming down from the panelling.
"I won that round on points, Algy," he said aloud, and little
Burnett-Jones, emerging from the linen room with a newly
darned pair of socks, scuttled off to tell the Second Form that
Pow-Wow was beginning to talk to himself, a certain sign of
onrushing lunacy. He was a little crestfallen when this piece
of intelligence caused no stir at all. Venn, from the lofty
peak of a third-termer, hardly looked up from a count of
grimed cigarette cards as he said, "Queen Anne's dead.
They all do that. You'll get used to it in a term or two, new
kid."

II

He had won on points, he claimed, but Howarth wasn't so
sure, and neither, it seemed, was Barnaby, usually so
sanguine.

"He'll carry it farther," Howarth said, glumly. "Don't you
see that he has to? His position here is untenable if he doesn't."

"You could say it's untenable if he does," said Barnaby.
"For one or the other of them, that is."

"You think he'll be stupid enough to lay that cutting
before the Governors?"

"A careful selection of the Governors. And not the cutting
alone, you can be sure of that. It will be a door opener and
inside will be a long-winded report embracing your stand
on that smoking incident, and your fight to save Hislop."

"If he confines himself to those issues the Governors can't
do a thing," Barnaby said, perking up a little. "Any housemaster worth his salt would fight for one of his boys, and
that's all Carter and P.J. did. No, it's the cutting that bothers
me. How many Socialists occupy seats on that board, P.J.?

Frankly, I can't see why you're so cocksure, can you, Howarth?"

"Knowing our boy, I can," Howarth said, lighting one Gold Flake from another, "but I don't expect him to unmask his batteries for our edification. Watch and wait, Barnaby!"

"I will," said Barnaby, "and I won't forget to pray while I'm at it."

*   *   *

He found the two letters on his hall table, assuming they had come by the late afternoon post, that rarely yielded anything of interest. One, from Christine, was a crackling account of her first week's canvass in the constituency, enclosing a duplicate of the cutting Alcock had just shown him. It was overscored, '*Look who is stealing my headlines! Not to say a cabinet minister's!*'

He opened the other letter, bearing the imprint of the literary agent he had chosen at random from the *Artists' and Writers' Year Book*. He read it at first without taking in the contents but then, re-reading it, he uttered a shout of glee. The agents had found a publisher for 'The Royal Tigress', Millards, a firm specialising in educational books, and were offering an advance of one hundred pounds, on a royalty of six per cent on the first five thousand copies and ten per cent thereafter. The agent enclosed the publisher's offer, and the letter quoted from a reader's report in what David regarded as flattering terms. 'A neglected period extremely well researched . . . readability one seldom finds in work of this kind . . . human insight into characters usually seen as pasteboard figures in a text-book . . . exciting blow by blow descriptions of the major battles . . . a firm grasp of military strategy, particularly that of Edward IV . . .' and so on. He sat in the embrasure of his study window, looking out over a moor touched by the first kiss of spring, savouring his personal triumph and a sense of achievement that reduced Alcock and all his works to insignificance. He had never really imagined a reputable publisher would pay good money for the book. In the far-off days when he had begun it, he saw it as a kind of private joke between himself and

Beth and later, after her death, he had resumed it as a means of keeping gloomy night-thoughts at bay. Later, when the theme and the period took hold of him, he had enjoyed writing and rewriting the battle scenes, and making fresh guesses at the principal actors in the long drama. Now, with the offer of a hundred pounds in his hands, the stack of manuscript that had occupied an undusted corner of his desk for so long had a real place in the pattern of his life and he picked up the carbon copy of the dedication page and read, '*To My Wife, Beth, who never ceased to urge me to write this book*'. He thought, "By God, I should have liked her to have shared this moment . . . but she will in a way, for young Grace will be madly excited. I'll tell her, of course, but the others . . . Howarth, Barnaby and so on, they can wait until the printed version actually appears." There was one exception, however, and he sat down and wrote a brief letter to Chad Boyer, now in his final year at Cambridge, saying nothing of his recent confrontation with Alcock but telling him about 'The Royal Tigress', and adding that he would be delighted to see him if he could get down during the vacation.

III

Knowledge that the book was in the pipeline (earliest date of publication was September) kept him cheerful for the remainder of the term. For the first time in more than eighteen months Bamfylde saw Pow-Wow Jones as the older hands among them recalled him in Algy's time, a jester who yet managed to convey to them something of the grandeur of British history, who scratched among the trivia of textbook names and treaties for something that could link dry-as-dust facts to today's headlines in the press, who was not above telling the Fifth and Sixth Forms risqué stories of Lord Melbourne, and Madame du Barry, and resorted, in Lower School periods, to a repertoire of jingles and tag-lines, in order to fix a date or an event in the memories of boys who might otherwise have made their minds a blank until the first clang of the dismissal bell. He still infiltrated current affairs into his Upper School lessons, sometimes spending an entire period discussing the League of Nations, the seven-

and-a-half-hour working day laid down under the Coal
Mines Act, or the end of the Allied occupation of Germany.
He had, that year, a particularly bright Sixth and an un-
usually quiescent Lower Fourth, so that he was able, almost
effortlessly, to lose himself in work and outdoor activities,
such as O.T.C. band-practice and the tail end of the cross-
country season. Havelock's, inspired perhaps by his own
keen interest in running, won the cross-country shield that
term for the first time in school history, and this, in its small
way, was another personal triumph. He also began to take a
desultory interest in the work of young Renshaw-Smith,
the music master who had replaced Rapper Gibbs, an aesthe-
tic-looking twenty-four-year-old, devoted to his subject but
inclined to be nervous and obviously terrified by Alcock's
occasional appearance, at a choral society or church choir
rehearsal. David did what he could to pump confidence into
the man, telling him he was just in time to prevent the virtual
extinction of musical interests in the school, a sparetime
activity that Algy had done so much to foster. David went
along to one or two choral society rehearsals himself, and
was moved, as he always was, by the sexless voices of the
juniors singing traditional songs, like 'Greensleeves' and
'Gaudeamus', always among his favourites.

Howarth and Barnaby, noticing his cheerfulness, made
characteristic comments. Howarth said, "Glad to see you
perking up again, P.J. Must be Carter's absence," and when
David denied this, saying that old Carter wasn't half bad
once you got to know him, Howarth smiled his wry smile
and added, "Well, then, it's probably the relief that accom-
panies a burst boil, old son. You've thrown down the gaunt-
let and that bounder hasn't the guts to pick it up."

"That's nearer the mark," David conceded, but he was
able to improve on this when Barnaby, marking the same
rise in spirits, quoted his favourite Horace—'The beardless
youth, his tutor being dismissed, delights in horses, dogs and
the sunny expanse of turf.'

"Not strictly applicable," David said, "but Horace can
probably tell you how I'm disposed towards the Noble
Stoic, now that I've told him to jump in the river—how about
'*Ignem gladio scrutare*'? Do I have to translate?"

"No," Barnaby said, mildly, "but I could quote back at you in the same context. 'Sometimes it is folly to poke the fire with the sword'—a proverbial phrase, I believe, don't ask me the source. If I were you, P.J., I'd let things ride for a term, and give us all a much-needed breather."

Barnaby got his wish, at least through the fag-end of the tight-rope term, and up to the time he went off, with half a dozen Sunsetters, on a walk along Hadrian's Wall. David would have liked to accompany him but it would have meant leaving Grace alone, for they had made no arrangements to go into Wales, or up to town to visit Beth's folk. He remained Bamfylde-based, therefore, spending his time riding and walking with her over the plateau.

Sometimes, when they were mounted, they pushed as far as Chetsford Water, where he told her, for the first time, of his despairing tramp through the storm the day her mother and her twin sister were killed, and how young Winterbourne, no more than fourteen then, had taken charge of him and piloted him back across the sodden moor to learn that she herself had a sporting chance.

The story touched her deeply, for she had always been close to Winterbourne, and had never ceased to acknowledge the part he had played in helping her to adjust after a year in hospital. "Spats and Sax Hoskins are the very nicest boys we've ever had at Bamfylde," she said, and he replied, smiling, "Well, let's settle for the fact that they're among the most original. It's a funny thing, but the originals are usually the easiest to get along with."

He gave her a shrewd, sidelong glance, as she kicked her pony into a trot and passed him on the down-slope to the river bottom, a healthy-looking eleven-year-old, or coming up to eleven in a week or so, with a ruddy complexion and no sign of a handicap as she sat her pony. A year or so ago she had continued to remind him poignantly of Beth, but lately he had begun to see her more as a miniature of his own sister, Megan, when she was flitting up and down the steep streets of the Valley, before the war. Living here, growing up among so many boys, she had a quality of self-confidence not given to many girls of her age, and it might stand her in good stead when she reached the proverbial awkward age.

She would never, so long as she lived, show embarrassment in the presence of the male animal, and that was something he supposed, for even his tomboyish sisters had blushed on occasion. "Somebody," he pondered, "has done a good job on Grace, and I can't really believe it was me. It took me all my time to ride out of the shock of that bloody awful day . . . Maybe she's right, and it was Winterbourne, with his painting, and Sax Hoskins, with his foxtrots, and any number of others who went out of their way to help at the time."

They got back to school about five o'clock, having left the horses at Stone Cross Farm, and walked up, and there, framed in Big School arch, was Brigadier Cooper, his personal champion on the Governing Board. He noticed at once that the old warrior looked bothered, as though planning a foray across the North-West Frontier that might cost the lives of men.

He said, briefly, "Been hanging around waiting for you since early afternoon. Like a word if you're free. Where can we go?" and when David suggested his quarters he said firmly, "No, your little lass and the butler will be there fussing with tea. It's a private word I want. How about the planty?"

"Suit yourself, Briggy," David said, and they went off across the football field, past Algy's thinking post, to the coppice marking the school's north-eastern border, now showing green where larches and the odd horse-chestnut broke the phalanx of Scots firs.

"Thought you might like to know what's going on," mumbled the Brigadier. "That chap is after your scalp and means to get it!"

"Jolly good luck to him, but somehow I don't think he will."

The brigadier's salt-and-pepper brows knitted. "Not so sure, P. J. He's a devious devil, and he's going to work in what I consider a thoroughly under-handed way. That's why I'm here, d'ye follow?"

"No," David said, "but I'd like to. You mean he's approached some of the more conservative Governors, I imagine?"

"He's got at that dry old stick, Sir Rufus, for one. And that tyke, Blunt, who still seems to have it in for you over that memorial rumpus. The hard core that never really took to Algy or to Algy's way of running the show."

"Is he still flying that damned silly kite about my right to air political opinions on a public platform?"

"No, he's played that down so far but he'll bring it forward. It's his strongest card with that bunch. Matter o' fact, I did a reccy as soon as I discovered what was afoot. Got the results here," and he fumbled in his Norfolk jacket, producing a crumpled scrap of paper on which he had written some notes under alphabetical headings. "Here it is—(a) Claims you spearhead staff opposition to everything he attempts. (b) You yourself commit acts of indiscipline."

"Such as?"

"You got up that petition about Carter's boy, the one he intended to sack. Dam' lot o' nonsense, sacking a boy for smoking in the bushes. Standard punishment for getting caught has been six of the best for time out of mind. Then there was that Hislop business—he made hay of that, implying you were encouraging gambling."

"Anything else?"

"Yes, the most serious allegation to my mind. He says your teaching methods are eccentric, that you don't stick to the syllabus, and refuse to base your teaching on previous exam papers, thus prejudicing boys sitting for school-leaving cert. For good measure, he claims you use historical doggerel that was out of date when he was a boy. What the hell did he mean by that, P.J.?"

"Aide-memoires I use in Lower School," said David, and quoted the famous 'All-Boys-Naughty-Won't-Memorise-All-Those-Horrid-Hateful-Battles-to-Bosworth', explaining to a baffled brigadier its use as a reminder of a string of fifteenth-century battles.

"But that's damned good!" exclaimed Cooper. "If someone had taught me that when I was a nipper I'd have soon had those bloody battles off pat! Fact is, I can't recall any of 'em but Hedgeley and Hexham. They stuck in the mind somehow."

"How did you get all this?" David asked, steering him back to the point, and Cooper said, winking, that 'he had put the ferret in', his usual practice when he wanted to prod rumours into the open. Alcock, it seemed, hadn't tackled a single Old Boy on the Board, and had been careful in his general approach, but had inevitably made one or two blunders, so that information of the backstairs campaign had leaked.

In spite of maintaining a casual front David was more worried than he was prepared to admit, even to himself. Championship of Hislop was one thing, and so, to an extent, was his loyalty to Carter over the smoking incident, but it was humiliating to learn that Alcock was calling his teaching to account. He saw, too, that the references to his free-ranging current affairs sessions was merely a lead-in to a direct attack on his political opinions, opinions that Tory Governors would almost surely regard as subversion of the young. He decided, therefore, to test this outright and said, "Regarding my public support of a Labour candidate, how do you feel about that personally, Briggy?"

"Bound to be frank. Don't care for it," Cooper said. "All the same, I'm not such an ass as to think we can proscribe a man's politics in his free time. Neither is Alcock, I imagine, and that's why he's played it down while the Socialists are in office. There'd be one hell of a row if Fleet Street got hold of a story you were being pressured to resign on that account. Wouldn't do any of us a dam' bit o' good, would it?"

"No," David said, "and I told him that." They stopped to retrace their steps at the point where the plantation turned a right-hand angle. "How do you regard it, then? He couldn't get me kicked out, could he? Not on this kind of evidence?"

"It's possible," Cooper said, thoughtfully, "but even if he failed you'd have trouble living it down. I've had a lot of experience of committee work, and learned enough to realise that all this is doing you real harm. What you do about it is your affair. My responsibility stops at letting you in on what's being said behind your back. You could confront the bounder, I suppose."

"That wouldn't be the slightest use. I've already confronted him, on three separate occasions."

"You might frighten him with a solicitor's letter."

"Without anything but hearsay to back it?"

"That's a point. All I know is you can't let it go on. Talk it over with one of the old hands, Howarth or Barnaby, maybe. What I'm really driving at, I imagine, is that if he can whip up a sufficient body of opinion against you he could offer his resignation unless you submitted yours."

"Would that be best for Bamfylde in the long run?"

"No, it damned well wouldn't! I told you I know more about committees than you do and here's proof of it. If he tendered his resignation on those terms they'd be obliged to ask him to withdraw it, then put the pressure on you. His seniority assures him of that. Can't go above the head of a C.O. on behalf of a sub. Throws the whole damned system out o' gear. The Old Boys would back you, of course, and so, I daresay, would some of those who voted for you, but there are the neutrals, the Any-Way-For-A-Pinters, to think of. In the end they'd come down on Alcock's side, leavin' you high and dry."

"Then it looks as if I've got to mount a counter-offensive and I think I know how to do it. Isn't that a maxim you professionals favour? The thing to do when your retreat is cut off is to advance?"

"I daresay," Cooper said, gloomily, "but damned if I can see how you'll go about it. Keep me in touch when you do, however."

"You can be sure of that. Could I have that scruffy bit of paper of yours? I'll copy it out and destroy it and I won't quote you, not even with my back against the wall."

"If I hadn't been sure of that, young feller-me-lad, I'd have kept mum and let things take their course." He stood looking down across the field at the buildings, etched in the clear evening light. "Place means a lot to me, P.J."

"More than Alcock or Powlett-Jones, I imagine."

"Yes, if I'm honest, but that's how it should be with a man's school. I spent six happy years here. Dam' place taught me everything I know. Funny thing, I often used to picture it in this light when I was sweating it out in temperatures of a hundred plus, on the far side of the world. Always cheered me up somehow."

IV

He had had an inkling of what to do while the brigadier had been listing his shortcomings, according to Alcock. Now, as twilight stole down from the moor, he sought out Molyneux, who he knew was living in school for the holidays while his lodging in the village was being decorated. He did not want Molyneux's advice but he needed his motorcycle, a heavy Brough Superior, that the French master kept in the cycle shed when he was on duty. Molyneux said he wouldn't need the machine until the following day, so David thanked him and called Algy Herries's rectory at Yatton-under-edge, the far side of the moor, catching Algy just as he was leaving to take confirmation class. "How long will that keep you, Algy?"

"No more than an hour if you're thinking of coming over. Haven't seen much of you this winter but I realise why. The weather's been foul."

"It's not that," David said, "I didn't want to involve you. But now I've no option if I'm to survive."

"You sound worried, P.J."

"I am. May I come right over?"

"Of course, I'll warn Ellie. She'll be delighted. We don't get much company until the warm weather sets in."

Algy's rectory was a large, tile-hung house, built in the era when church attendance was obligatory among a larger population, most of whom had now moved off, the young to the cities, and the middle-aged to places like Lynmouth and Ilfracombe, where the tourist pickings were good. Ellie used no more than half the house but what she called the snuggery was a very cosy room, already beginning to reek of Algy's tobacco.

He told his story simply, guessing that both Algy and Ellie already knew most of it, either from village gossip, Old Boys who had visited them and the one or two conversations he had already had with them on the subject of Alcock. He said, "I'm not asking you to take sides, Algy. That wouldn't be fair now that you're out of it. It wouldn't be fair on Alcock, either, although he isn't so squeamish by the sound of things. All I want is a straight 'Yes' or 'Nay' to a course of action I propose taking. After that I'll ask a question or two as to tactics and leave you to await results. Is that understood?"

"Are you lecturing me or asking me how to hit back, P. J. ?" but when Ellie exclaimed, "I think it's *disgraceful . . .!*" he silenced her with what was, for him a savage gesture. "Keep out of this, woman, it's a man's business," and she tightened her lips, looking quite unhappy. "Right, now let's hear what you propose doing."

"Going over to the offensive before Alcock does. I'm going to write to the brigadier in formal terms, saying it has come to my knowledge that Alcock is slandering me, and request a special meeting of the Governing Body to lay down a directive concerning how much liberty a man has or has not to engage in political activity while serving on the staff."

"Well, that would certainly stir 'em up, but it would also have a very predictable side effect as regards your future, P.J."

"In what way, Algy?"

"I really have to tell you that?"

"I came here for advice."

"Very well, I'll give you more than you bargained for. Point one, write to the Governors by all means, but not to one of them known to be predisposed in your favour. Write to Sir Rufus, the Chairman, and do it officially, through the bursar."

"But Briggy hinted that Sir Rufus was one of those Alcock had approached."

"Precisely, and made a bad error of judgment when he did it. Why? Because Sir Rufus has been a judge and is the only man on that Board trained to keep an open mind. Dry as a fossil, no doubt, but entirely free of prejudice, take it from me. Make sense?"

"Good sense, Algy. And point two?"

"The crucial one. Don't be the first to introduce that political angle. If it is raised let Alcock be the one to raise it, thereby taking upon himself the risk of involving Bamfylde in a national how-de-do. I went astray there myself during the war. Burnt my fingers defending an Old Boy who claimed exemption as a conscientious objector. Never again. Some of the mud thrown takes years to scrape off. No, no, my boy, your strategy is professional, but your tactics are amateur. Believe me, I've been dealing with Governors the better part of my working life, and if I don't know how many beans make five, nobody does."

"But surely, that's the main point at issue, isn't it? The one where I can fall back on democratic principle."

"Democratic fiddlesticks! Do I have to tell you, a crusader in the cause, that only the theory of democracy holds any attraction for the majority? And only then when it suits their book. Face the facts, man. How many headmasters or school Governors in Britain today wear a red tie? Two per cent? I doubt it, for even the Liberals don't muster a handful. The row would flare up. It would have to if you alleged political persecution. The press would get hold of it, there would be questions in Parliament, God help us all, and I daresay you'd be vindicated in the end—famous, maybe, for twenty-four hours. After that your life would be made so damned uncomfortable you'd be glad to leave, Alcock or no Alcock. There's a much craftier approach than that, my lad, and you're lucky. You have a weapon in your armoury you don't even know about and he put it there!"

"You mean his allegations of disloyalty and indiscipline?"

Herries sighed and said, as an aside to Ellie, "Bring the brown sherry, m'dear. Several terms under that fool has dulled the man's intellect," and Ellie rose and crossed to the cupboard where she kept what she still called her 'Old Boys' Decanter'. Herries spread his knees, re-addressing himself to David. "He's impugned your teaching methods, hasn't he? He's claimed they are eccentric and old-fashioned. Fair enough. So tell me, in terms of round figures, how many boys got a history pass last June?"

"Nineteen. Three distinctions."

"Out of?"

"I'm not sure, without checking. Twenty-eight or twenty-nine, maybe."

"You haven't even done your homework, P.J. But you'll have to set about it, quicksticks. In that letter to Sir Rufus you'll enclose a summarised table of pass percentages and distinctions in your subject over all the years you've taught at Bamfylde. They should be impressive, especially when set against those of preceding years. Norrington, the fellow you followed when you came in, like a dog out of the rain, averaged a dozen a year, I believe. Less in his last three years. I have a flair for remembering these things. I didn't spend all my time sitting on Spyglass Hill, listening to quad gossip." He got up and moved over to one of his leaving presents, a black-oak Bible box, converted into a desk. In less than a minute he was back again with a file entitled '*Examination Results, 1911–17*'. Opening it he did a quick cast, then beamed at David over the top of the file. "Better than I thought," he said. "Norrington's history passes averaged nine a year, over seven years. Making allowances for the smaller numbers we had in the Fifth throughout the war, that gives you a substantial margin. Around double, I'd say. Something to be said for historical jingles, eh?"

The sherry warmed his belly, and Algy's lively handling of the situation gave him a foretaste of victory. He said, "I've always thought of you as the best friend I ever had, Algy . . . you and Ellie. The best Beth ever had too, and she often said as much. It was different when you were around . . . we all missed you, but I missed you more than most, perhaps because the others were established when you got to them whereas in my case—it was as you said, a dog coming in out of the rain. And pretty sorry for himself into the bargain. I had no idea how closely you were watching us. I suppose I'd come to think of you as disengaged."

"It doesn't say a lot for your powers of deduction, boy. Do you imagine Ellie and I could spend half a lifetime building something, then never look at it again? Even from a distance?"

"I've felt damned lonely, particularly since Carter left."

"Well, I gave you a hint there but you didn't profit from it. Like everyone else you had to learn from experience."

"Don't we all?"

"Yes, I suppose we do," Herries conceded, "even in a backstairs business such as this, but there's no sense in turning up your proud Celtic nose at a short cut, is there?"

"No sense at all. Thank you, Algy, more than I can say. I'll hurry off now, for I mean to get that letter off tonight."

"Ah, you can't do that, I'm afraid. It's been a long day. A

wedding, three christenings, a funeral and a confirmation class. Frankly, I don't feel up to it."

"You don't feel up to what?"

"Do you think I'd trust you to write that letter without an edited draft? What's on the diary for tomorrow, Ellie?"

"Tomorrow is Sunday," Ellie said, primly.

"My God, so it is! Well, that's a bore. You'll just have to contain yourself until Tuesday, won't you. Afternoon post probably. And tell me all about that book of yours. Ellie was very impressed to hear it was being published at last."

"You know about 'The Royal Tigress'? But I only told Grace!"

"I have a very long telescope," Algy said. "It can range freely over three parishes, yours, mine and the one in be-tween." Somewhere, deep in the recesses of the rambling house, a small bell tinkled.

"That," said Ellie, "will be Mrs. Shawe, telling us dinner is served. Imagine ringing a bell for cold pheasant and pickles. I've always thought it silly but she will do it."

"It came to her ears," Algy said, "that for years and years and years our lives had been regulated by bells, my dear."

"Ah, but that was a real bell, Algy. Hers is an Alpine tinkle, half-heard among the edelweiss."

"I say, that's rather neat." Algy said, cocking his head like a robin, "'Half-heard among the edelweiss'. Yatton-under-Edge has reawakened the muse in you. Perhaps you can go back to composing your greeting verses thus augmenting our pitiful stipend." He turned to David. "Did I ever tell you that family secret, P.J.? Before we married Ellie earned pinmoney writing verses for birthday and anniversary cards. What did they pay you, m'dear?"

"A guinea a gross," Ellie said, "and it was very hard work, I can tell you."

"Sweated labour, I'd say. P.J. will get somebody at West-minster to look into it."

They were now, he decided, well launched on one of their time-honoured pursuits, an elaborate leg-pull that had, as its unspoken object, the disarming of an audience and a general relaxation of tension. Over the years he had watched them at it. With boys, with parents, with visiting notabilities, all

manner of people who drifted in through Big School arch
with their problems and grouses. They were very, very good
at it, so good indeed that it was impossible not to humour
them.

He got up, and Algy led the way into the austere dining-
room across the hall. Three places were laid at the Sheraton
table. Presentation silver winked from the sideboard. Above
it, hanging three degrees out of true, was an oval portrait of a
rotund little man in the frock coat and punishing cravat of
the early nineteenth century, Ellie's grandfather, he believed,
who had been a vintner with a prosperous business in Tun-
bridge Wells. The vintner looked very much at home here,
far more so than when he had sat peering down between
framed photographs of First Elevens in what was now
Alcock's monastic parlour at Bamfylde.

*   *   *

It was coming up to eleven o'clock when he set out on his
return journey over the broad shoulder of the west plateau
and down the narrow flint roads where the headlight beam
made a tunnel of the high arching hedgerows, rich with the
scent of honeysuckle and the riot of hedge flowers that grew
there. He heard Yatton Church clock strike the hour as he
crossed the Bray at the packhorse bridge and began the
gentle climb towards Stone Cross, three miles away on the
rim of a fold bathed in moonlight. He drove carefully, for
the surface was loose and the bends very sharp, and by the
time he had chugged past the church the moon was sailing
free of cloud wisps and the playing-fields and buildings were
in clear view, so that he stopped by the old, unmended
gate, straddling the machine and looking at the place from
the angle he had first seen it the day the Osborne specialist
sent him here on what he had thought of as a fool's errand.

It hadn't changed much but by moonlight, with the rearward part of the buildings in shadow, it looked smaller and
more compact. A thought came to him, the tailpiece of an
anecdote he had told the Lower Third a day or two before
the end of term, relating to Charles II's final look at England
at the end of his long flight from Worcester. Legend had it that
the king, an hour or so before joining the collier that was to

take him to France, had reined in and said to a companion, "It's worth fighting for . . ." It was too, and he felt a closer affinity with a monarch he had always admired for his common sense and humour, rare qualities in a Stuart. He said, aloud, "Well, you'll get your fight, Alcock, old sport. And it'll be a bonny one, I'm telling you!" and then restarted the machine and drove the last two hundred yards home.

PART TWO

CUT AND COME AGAIN

CHAPTER ONE

I

David began to see himself as a trial balloon for national weather, a tiny unit released to test the force of the unending series of storms and gales that had blown across the country since the long, Edwardian lull, when he was growing up in the Valleys. In an almost predictable way his personal fortunes seemed to coincide with those of the country, ever since that day he came home from school to be told his father and brothers were dead in the pit disaster. For that had been shortly before a few shots in a Balkan town had heralded the storm that engulfed everybody.

Then, again running almost parallel with what was happening in the world outside, came the death of Beth and little Joan, coinciding with the start of the long, dragging strike in the coal mines, and its climax in the General Strike of May, 1926, when the national mood had matched his own despondency. He emerged from it during the tail end of the 'twenties but soon, with the coming of Alcock, it came on to blow again, and here they were approaching crisis point, both he and the nation, in the spring of 1931, and Mac-Donald's government as beset by problems in Westminster as he was at Bamfylde.

Algy's draft letter arrived on Tuesday, as promised. By Wednesday night, a day or two before the start of summer term, he had written his own letter, and posted it to Sir Rufus Creighton, in spite of a warning that the old chap was off on yet another of his tours, this time to India, and was not expected back until June. He could afford to wait, however. His batteries were still masked and if Alcock challenged him in the meantime, so much the better.

Christine wrote twice a week, keeping him up to date with her progress in the constituency, and they met occasionally in Taunton. She was settling down thereabouts, having taken a part-time secretarial job, and gone back on her obstinate decision to leave her husband's allowance untouched. "I can use the money for things I plan to do between now and the next election," she said. "There's to be one soon enough, for Ramsay is floundering. The whole world is going broke, they say. There's even talk of a Coalition."

"Would your people stand for that?" he asked, and she said the party stalwarts would not, but it was possible Ramsay Mac, Snowden and Jimmy Thomas might. "They're proving a frightful disappointment," she admitted. "Power seems to have watered their beer. I don't mean Ramsay's grand manner, and all that rubbish they print about him kissing duchesses. It's more serious than that. The leaders aren't in touch any longer, especially with the unemployed."

"I don't see what the poor devils can do with nearly three million on the dole. This crisis is international, isn't it?"

"They could keep faith with the people who voted for them," she said, "even if it meant going into opposition again."

"What good would that do?"

"I don't know. I only know I prefer the Labour Party when it's attacking."

He sympathised with her but was more concerned with his own situation than that of a harassed Prime Minister and Chancellor of the Exchequer. The weeks drifted by, just as they had when he was nursing a tiny flame of hope that he would succeed Algy Herries. He confided, to a degree, in her, and to a greater degree in Howarth and Barnaby, but in no one else on the staff. Howarth was taciturn about the possible results of his counter-attack but Barnaby was encouraging. "You're a bonnie fighter, man," he told David, when the latter explained what he had done, and as usual he had an appropriate tag for the occasion—'*In rebus dubiis plurimi est audacia.*'

In the second week of June Sir Rufus sent a bleak reply to his letter. It contained little but a promise that he would 'take counsel with certain of the Governors' and 'consider the possibility of calling a special meeting'. He gave no hint as to whether any direct approach had been made to him by Alcock, and none as to when the meeting, if there was one, would be called, or what the terms of reference were likely to be. He did add, however, that he could rest assured the matter would be investigated and should hold himself in readiness to answer any questions put to him. David showed the letter to Howarth who grunted, "Typical bureaucratic response. So guarded and qualified it might be addressed to a blackmailer. But then, come to think of it, I suppose that's what Alcock is making us in his quaint, original way."

One of the few breaks in the rhythm of the term was Christine's visit on Sports Day, accompanied by her cousin, the one-eyed Ridgeway, home on leave from Malaya. Ridgeway found it difficult to accept his former housemaster's close friendship with someone he had been taught to regard as the family black sheep and while Christine was being shown over the kitchens, he said, half-apologetically, "She was always a bit of a Bolshie, sir, if you know what I mean." David, much amused, said, "Alas, Ridgeway, I'm a 'bit of a Bolshie' myself. That was accepted here, even in your time, but you never held it against me, did you?" to which Ridgeway replied, with terrible earnestness, "Of course not, sir, but she's a woman!"

It was no good reminding Ridgeway that even the flapper had been eligible to vote since 1928. It still seemed to him indefensible that a female relative of his should enlist under a Socialist banner, likely to shame him publicly if she ever got into Parliament, an event he considered slightly less probable than a landing on the moon. "I mean, after all, sir, politics are still a man's business, aren't they? The very idea of her standing on a platform, and spouting about the Means Test and whatnot, is a pretty bad show, taken all round. I can quite understand Uncle Willie cutting her out of his will. The pity of it is, of course, that she's not old, only a year or so older than I am. I mean, if she was a middle-aged frump it might be different."

He gave it up after that but relayed the exchange to Christine, as soon as Ridgeway was off hobnobbing with his cronies in the Old Boys' bar. It kept her amused for the rest of the day.

There was one result of her visit, however, that inclined him to agree with Ridgeway that Christine Forster was a little odd when you came to think about it. She declared herself daunted by the Spartan aspects of Bamfylde and said, "It's so frightfully austere, isn't it? Aren't there any home comforts at *all*? I mean, hasn't anyone ever heard of soft furnishings, and carpets? Or kitchen implements superseding those used in a baron's hall at the time of the Conquest?" And when he explained that the one gain of Alcock's stay among them had been an improvement in fabric, she exclaimed, "My God! What was it *before* he arrived? A Dickensian workhouse? Why does a public school have to look like a penitents' monastery as well as act like one? I never was much of a one for tradition, but I've never had anything against stainless steel, floor coverings, curtains, modern plumbing and the odd incinerator, instead of that stinking bonfire you keep burning down at the piggeries."

"The place isn't very well endowed," he argued, much on the defensive, "it needs money spending on it to bring it up to date but we don't cater for satraps, just chaps equipped to work for their living, and stand on their own two feet when they leave here."

"Well, you don't even succeed in that if my cousin's story about his glass eye is to be believed. The general picture I get of him and his type is a layabout in a wicker chair, knocking back whiskies and sodas and watching the black, browns and yellows do the hard graft. Oh, I admit that boys brought up in these cheerless barns do seem to have much more confidence than the ones in day schools, but I can't help feeling you need a few women around the place to cushion the corners. Is it true that nearly all the masters are bachelors? Or widowers like you?"

"Not always from choice," he said, thinking of Howarth, and the girl who had turned him down for a stockbroker. "You don't go into this for money, Chris. However, talking of feminine touches, come and meet Grace. She's over by the finishing tape, offering up a prayer for one of her two favourites to win the steeplechase."

They crossed behind the east drive beeches and he introduced them, noting that Grace had made an immediate impact on Christine. They chatted amiably for five minutes or so, then Grace forgot them both in the excitement of the run-in, as the leaders of the field came streaming through the gap behind the plantation, to cover the last quarter-mile of the course. Christine whispered, in an aside, "She's delightful, Davy, and does you credit! She'll break hearts in another few years."

"I doubt it," he said, glancing across at the tape, and making his almost daily comparison between the child and Beth, "but she'll be pretty, I think, in a Romneyish kind of way."

Hoskins, whose wind seemed to have thrived on all the practice he put in on the saxophone, passed the favourite Collier, within two yards of the post, and leaving Christine he crossed to the finishing post and joined Grace prancing up and down with delight as everyone crowded round the winner to congratulate him. Then, feeling a little foolish at his own display of glee, he rejoined Christine on the far side of the spectators' rope. She said, smiling, "You're really rather sweet, all of you. I'm glad I came, for at least you can rely on me going into the Tory lobby when Labour gets around to abolishing these archaic institutions. Now let's have tea, and after tea take me down to that little church you told me about, and show me where you and Beth lived when you were first married. If you don't mind, that is."

"I don't mind," he said, "and for a special reason. You and Beth are two of a kind in some ways."

He took her arm and they moved off across the forecourt. Watching them, from a discreet distance, stood Ridgeway, and with him Simmonds, an old friend of his period. Both recalled Beth Powlett-Jones and Simmonds said, "Old Pow-Wow never married again, did he?"

"No," said Ridgeway, hastily heading him off. "How about a couple of jars, Sim?" but Simmonds said, thoughtfully, "That bit of skirt he's squiring, she's not a bad-looker, is she? Know her?"

"Never seen her in my life," Ridgeway answered and if he thought of Simon called Peter, the apostle could have counted on his heartfelt sympathy.

II

He wondered whether he should show her Beth's grave but thought better of it, passing round the tower and entering the church by the west door. There was still more than two hours' life in the day but inside it was already dusk. Sniffing the faint whiff of incense, and glancing up at the Stations of the Cross, she said, "Is that new head of yours a would-be Catholic?"

"No, just 'high'. We were very 'low' in Algy's time, but Stone Cross has always been part of Bamfylde and adjusts." He ran his hand along the smooth varnish of the pew, feeling the ridges of obliterated initials carved there by three generations of boys, and it struck him then that Alcock's spring-clean could be interpreted as a kind of vandalism, symptomatic of so many changes that had occurred over the last three years. She must have sensed his disquiet for she said, quietly, "It's beginning to show, Davy. The battle with the new man. How will it end?"

"In his departure, or mine, and soon, I imagine."

"Why's that?"

He summarised the situation to date, even telling her about Alcock's clean sweep of the pew initials, and she said, after a moment, "I think you'll win, Davy."

"Why?"

"Feel there, just above that hassock," and she took his hand, guiding it to the limit of the pew-back, where his fingertips brushed against some raw indentations.

"They're already at it again. Flick your lighter."

He humoured her, producing a small flame and bending low, where he made out a freshly carved name, executed in letters about half an inch high.

It must have required a deal of patience, he thought, to chip away down there during brief intervals of prayer, but Hislop had made a fair enough job of it. He had even scooped out three full stops, one after each initial, one after the final letter. He said, chuckling, "Good old Hislop. He left his mark, after all. I suppose you could call that a sign. Not from Heaven, however."

"Was Hislop the boy you told me about, the one who was sacked for bookmaking?"

"Yes, but I'll wager he wasn't the only one to counter-attack." He moved the full length of the church, glancing at the half-seen pew-supports. Bristow, Hoskins and Collier were represented, and in the rearmost pew Winterbourne had got as far as 'B'. He drifted back to the front pew, thinking how pretty she looked, sitting there in her pink cloche hat, with the slanting light of the rose window converting the tip of a stray curl from chestnut to bronze. "You're very good for me, Chris," he said, kissing her.

"We're good for each other," she said, and then, smiling, "Now I wonder if that's ever happened before?"

"The carving?"

"No, a front pew kiss."

"They've had the occasional wedding here."

"Ah, but that's not the same. It would be done standing, there by the altar. And a chaste kiss at that." Then she added, "If the cards don't fall your way, if they back Alcock and put the pressure on you, would you make a fresh start, at another school?"

"No."

"What then?"

"I'd take that tip given me in Bilhampton and have a crack at politics."

"Could you afford to?"

"I've got a bit put by, and could use it to keep me going while I nursed a constituency. It would have to be one with real prospects."

"Not like mine, you mean?"

"You'll get promoted, as soon as they've had a chance to assess your worth. One good fight at Bilhampton and you'll be nominated for an industrial seat up North . . ." but she wasn't listening. Presently she said, "I suppose I ought to be hoping those Governors do come down on Alcock's side. That way I'd have a sporting chance."

"I don't follow. What has the Governing Board got to do with your chances?"

"You can be very thick, Davy. Put it like this. If you win then that's it, so far as I'm concerned. Oh, I daresay we'd

go on seeing one another occasionally, but it would be a case
of me trotting down here, and soon enough, wallowing in
Bamfylde you'd regard everything happening outside as
trivial. Not yet, maybe, while you're still in your thirties,
but later, when you're 'over the hill' as they say. Now look at
the other side of the coin. If Alcock wins you'll prise yourself
loose and it's possible we'd make a formidable team."

"As a pair of candidates?"

She looked at him steadily. "No, with you as candidate and
me loading for you."

He saw it as a graceful compliment. Of all her associates
only he understood how deeply she was committed and how
passionately she needed to justify herself in her chosen field.
That she was ready, eager even, to step down on his account,
and put her enthusiasm to work on his behalf, struck him
as a very positive expression of faith in him.

"You'd do that? For me?"

"Why not? One of my rare qualities is that of knowing my
own mind and having the nerve to act on it. You're very fond
of me, Davy. But I'm very much in love with you."

It didn't really astonish him. By now he was growing used
to her devastating honesty. She went on, "That doesn't
obligate you in any way, and I wouldn't have owned up to it
without the special circumstances."

"You mean Rowley's refusal to make separation final?
Because if that's so I've got a say in it now, considering what
you've just said. 'Fond' was your word and it's an understatement, Chris. There have been plenty of times since we
met . . ."

She said, gently, "Hold it, Davy! Don't say more than you
need. This came from me, and the circumstances I mentioned
have nothing to do with Rowley. It concerns you and how
you feel about me and about women in general. You were
very deeply in love with Beth. That's my impression anyway,
and there's never much wrong with my instincts. You could
make do, and put up a pretty good show of loving, but there
would always be a big slice of you that no other woman could
possess. You can protest as much as you like but it's true, and
deep down you know it."

It was all but dusk in here now but light enough to see her

eyes searching his, and she was not the kind of person who would settle for anything short of the whole truth, or the truth as she saw it.

"It wouldn't be the same and you're right about a very special relationship. But don't most couples feel that in the first years of marriage? Beth was only twenty-five when she died. I'll say this however." He took her hand, gloveless and passive, "With a person like you it would be the nearest I could ever come to starting all over again, and that's more than enough for me. Is it enough for you?"

She shrugged. "What point is there in answering that? I'm not even in a position to try."

"I'm not so sure about that. He's been abroad for years, hasn't he? If he stays over there indefinitely I daresay you could get a divorce on grounds of desertion. He might change his mind, might even want to marry again himself. So far as I know you haven't even corresponded with him, except through lawyers."

"I made enquiries, though, and it's a dead end. Knowing Rowley, it's likely to stay one. I said his family behaved well towards me but as regards divorce they'd range themselves with him. Catholics of their kind take their religion much more seriously than we do. It isn't something they put on and off like an overcoat. They wouldn't lift a finger to help, and told me so when I raised the matter a year back."

"Then to blazes with him. We owe ourselves some consideration, don't we? I'm not that stuffy."

"You mightn't be and I'm not. But, as I said in the first place, it doesn't depend on us, does it? If you still have any hope of qualifying for a headship you've more sense than to pursue that line of thought, Davy. The odd weekend is one thing. A permanent relationship, with you in the running for a post of that kind, is quite another. Besides, I might want children. Have you ever thought of that?"

He saw himself trapped in a web of conflicting loyalties and her availability, implicit in her honesty, was an entirely new factor in their relationship up to that moment. It had about it the inevitability of a Greek tragedy, with a dash of French farce thrown in for good measure. It had progressed, at a bound, from the camaraderie of their first encounters, to a stage where he was more than half in love with her and she was avowedly in love with him. Yet it promised little. They were trapped, not only by her situation but by his. It represented an equation. Rowley, plus Chris, equals stalemate; Powlett-Jones, plus Bamfylde minus Chris, equals celibacy. And there were any number of incidental factors, among them Alcock, Alcock's impact on his future, Chris's involvement with politics, and that hint of hers about children.

He gave it up. It was too much to conjure with without isolating every factor and examining them individually. He said, "Well, I'm a free agent right now, and likely to be until those damned Governors get around to sorting the muddle out. Let's get out of here, and go back to my quarters. You don't have to drive back tonight, do you? I could get you a room in Challacombe for a few days and come over every evening."

"On your home ground? Under everybody's nose? Use your head, Davy!"

"Where, then? And when?"

"Are the Governors likely to meet before you break up for the holidays?"

"I don't know. I wouldn't think they'd make a final decision. There's only a couple of weeks to go, and they don't usually meet in August."

"Well then, we'll find some neutral ground. It's time I took a holiday anyway. Until then, just hold me a little."

They sat on in the pew for another hour or so, until, carried faintly on the evening breeze, they heard the sound that had regulated his life for more than twelve years now, the far-off clang of Bamfylde's handbell, swung by the latest successor of Nipper Shawe, going his rounds as far as Algy's thinking post. Then, silently acknowledging the summons, they walked the half-mile back to school.

III

Alcock went out of his way to avoid him, or so it seemed through the fag-end of the term. Whatever Sir Rufus Creighton was about he confided in no one, yet Algy Herries, who dropped in for a chat one evening during the final week

of term, was convinced something was stirring out there.
"Don't ask me for evidence," he said, "for I couldn't produce any. I can only tell you I know those stone-faced
arbiters of our destinies and if I don't, who should? There
are probably the same three sets of plotters hard at work.
The liberals, chivvied along by Brigadier Cooper. The
conservatives, rallying to that bounder Blunt. And the un-
committed or, as Cooper would put it, the Any-Way-For-A-
Pinters. They're a majority, I'd say. They hate decisions,
and are prepared to go to extraordinary lengths to avoid
making one."

"And Sir Rufus?"

"Ah, that joker is out on his lonesome, and prefers it that
way. You mightn't believe it to look at him, but he's a slave
to the pursuit of power."

"Then it's Creighton I should concentrate on, isn't it?"

"You leave him alone," warned Algy, severely. "Believe
me, I know what's best for you. The pressure has eased,
hasn't it. Since you despatched that letter?

"Alcock and I haven't exchanged two consecutive
sentences this term, if that's what you mean."

"So much the better. We all talk too much."

"But in God's name, Algy, it ought to be possible for adults
to run a place like this without resorting to petty intrigue.
Damn it, I sometimes think I'm back at school myself, and
nursery school at that—'He was my friend before he was
your friend, so there'!"

"You should have learned, my boy, that only the rare
spirits grow in mental stature after the age of, say, five-and-a-
half. Whenever one does he qualifies as an Immortal. I'm
off now. The confounded parochial church council is meeting
at seven-thirty, and I'm in for another stint of smoothing
ruffled plumes. My advice to you is to get right away from
here for a bit. Go somewhere anonymous. Have you any
plans for the long break?"

He was obliged to lie. "Grace is spending a month with her
aunts in Kent, then another week at the seaside with cousins.
I thought I might go north, after I've paid a duty visit to the
Valley."

"Good. Well, write if you have to but meantime, put it

out of mind. I'll keep in touch with the brigadier by phone. He's our only source of news."

A day or so later the thirteen-week turmoil reached its brief climax. Homesick boys crossed the final day from their pocket calandars. Trunks came tumbling down from the platform over the covered playground. The Corps, headed by its band, marched off to entrain for a week's camp at Tidworth Pennings.

"Have a good hols, sir!"

"Can I move into the Senior dorm next term, sir?"

"Cookson's leaving sir. Who'll be Havelock's house perk, sir?"

And from the departing Cookson, "Keep me in touch, sir. I'd like to know if Havelock's hold on to that shield."

The staff scattered. Barnaby to his beloved Greece, Howarth to town for his annual spree (what did he do up there alone at the Strand Palace, David wondered?), others to the seaside. All save Molyneux who appeared, burdened with kit, to announce that he was attempting a new climb in the French Alps. "Always the chance he might fall into a very deep crevice," Howarth said, never having caught on to Ferguson's successor. "Is there any likelihood of us meeting in town, P.J.?"

"Not until early September."

"By early September," Howarth grunted, "I shall be back here, getting ready for another three months' purgatory. Enlivened, I hope, by a display of fireworks."

"That's very likely," David said, and was surprised, and even a little embarrassed, when Howarth shook his hand and said, in a rare moment of expansiveness, "Well, I don't have to tell you where my money is going, P.J. Take Herries's advice. Get clear away and forget the whole damned lot of us for a month," after which he withdrew hastily, as he invariably did after a display of human feeling.

*   *   *

They met, by appointment, at Exchange Station, Manchester, half an hour or so before the train to Windermere pulled out. She arrived by taxi from London Road Station, a breathless, carefree Christine Forster, who somehow reminded him of an overgrown schoolgirl who had given her chaperon the slip.

They had exchanged letters as regards the locality of her 'neutral ground'. He had favoured Anglesey but she said Anglesey was Welsh, and not neutral enough, and had suggested they should go to Skye, Mull, or another of the Western Isles. She had had second thoughts about this, however, reasoning that the Hebrides, at this time of year, was almost always wet, and she was badly in need of sunshine.

"It's different for you," she said, over the phone, "you're country-based. I've spent the last six months drinking tepid tea in terrace houses and my evenings in committee rooms that haven't seen soap and water since the election of 1918. I've found a place for us at Windermere."

"Are you absolutely sure you want to leave your constituency at a time like this?" he said, when he met her. "They say things are hotting up at Westminster, and there might be a snap election any moment," but she said, coolly, "Have I ever tried to teach you your business? Pipe down, Davy. Let's try a little cheerful sin for a change," and held up her left hand, displaying what looked like a new wedding ring.

He said, sharply, "Is that Rowley's? Because if so, take the damned thing off."

"It isn't Rowley's. I popped his long ago. It's the Christmas cracker variety," and she kissed him, at an awkward moment as far as an oncoming porter was concerned, for the three of them collided and the porter scattered his burdens on the platform.

It would take time, he thought, to adjust to this high-spirited girl, who seemed to find in him a source of release denied her for a long, long time, but before their first twenty-four hours together had elapsed he was attuned to her gaiety and lack of inhibition, seeing her as an unlikely amalgam of Beth, in what he thought of as their middle period, Julia Darbyshire, before he made the mistake of committing himself, and a dash of the extroverts in the Lower Fourth.

He was particularly aware of this early that first morning, when he opened his eyes and heard her humming to herself in the little kitchen of the wooden chalet they occupied on the deserted western shore of the lake, under High Dale Peak. It was a particularly isolated spot, with its own tiny beach, south of the little river Cunsey. Over on the Bowness shore the summer season was in full swing and boats were constantly coming and going, the voices of their passengers reaching them across the flat expanse of lake, like the echo of a junior football game played on the higher pitch under the planty. But nobody seemed to want to explore the south-western tip of the lake, and very few cars passed along the road behind the chalet.

She had been very clever to find it, he told her, when the taxi dropped them off, but she said it was luck mostly. A cousin of her father's had stayed here last summer when Segrave had made his fatal attempt on the water-speed record higher up the lake. She had remembered the name of the firm who hired out the chalets and a reference book had supplied her with its phone number. It was no more than a simply furnished shack, with a window looking eastwards across the water but as a hideout, she said, it had a lot to recommend it. Her father's cousin, who drove an Alvis, had taken a dislike to the place when he ran out of petrol here the day Segrave's boat had capsized, missing, as he had put it, all the fun.

It was getting dusk before they finished unpacking, and eating eggs and bacon she fried on the oil-stove, and when he proposed a walk as far as the island opposite she said, in that frank way of hers, "Is that proposal made out of regard for my modesty, Davy? I mean, waiting until the light fades?" and when he admitted that it was, she said, lightly, "Then don't bother, lad. I've waited a long time. Almost as long as you. We'll go for a walk if you need the exercise but not otherwise."

She had a way, he discovered, of sloughing off her earnestness, and her tendency to view most things from what she herself described as 'the Yorkshire common-sense angle', emerging as an altogether different personality. It was the one, he imagined, that had prompted her to dance naked on the college precincts when she was an undergraduate, a prank that reached the ears of her father and precipitated the first of many family rows. As a bedmate she was equally spirited and would have taken the initiative if he had given her the chance, for her gaiety, he discovered, was infectious. It had not been difficult to adjust to what he accepted as a final commitment, for he had learned something useful from the brief Julia Darbyshire incident.

They lay still on the rumpled bed, using the first few moments of the aftermath to assess both each other and themselves as lovers, admittedly out of practice, but then, turning to him, she raised herself on her elbow and studied him in a way that invited mutual laughter, for it was so transparently clear that each was engaged in the business of reappraisal.

"You weren't disappointed, then?"

"Did you think I might be?"

"No, not really, but as I said, it's been a long time. God knows I wanted a man often enough but I'm glad now that I obeyed my instinct to hang on and wait."

He smiled, reaching up to pull her down, saying, "I always said we're good for one another. I didn't know how good until now. It's tempting to make a virtue out of deprivation but I have. Sometimes I've come close to making a cult of the dead."

"There never was anyone else? Before or after Beth?"

"There was one, but all that Julia did, looking back, was to add a shaving or two to the chip I was carrying around."

"Tell me about Julia."

He told her the story of Julia Darbyshire, and how he had seen intense physical relief as a permanent cure for loneliness that had led to his proposal.

"Would it be so very different with me?"

"I think it would."

She looked thoughtful for a moment. Then she said, "I wouldn't commit myself, Davy, or not yet. Let's take it a step at a time. I had a special reason for asking the question."

"I can guess the reason."

"I'll wager you can't."

"It has to do with your marriage going on the rocks, and whether it was caused by inadequacy on your part. Right there?"

She sat up. "Hey! You can be sharp when you try, can't

you? I suppose that comes from listening to so many excuses, then writing those awful school reports—'Could do better'—'Doesn't concentrate'—are you going to write me one? I'd love to read it."

"If I did you'd frame it and hang it over the bed."

She eased herself back, clasping her hands behind her head, stretching out her long, graceful legs and wriggling her toes. Her long, contemplative silence implied that she was still in need of reassurance.

"Well, what's your problem? Don't hedge. I didn't hedge about Julia."

"I don't mind telling you, Davy. I went into that marriage full of girlish confidence. All my problems were solved. This was IT, and Rowley was the knight in shining armour. When things began to drift from bad to worse, I kept telling myself that it was all his fault and I still think it was, mainly. But later, after we broke up, I got to wondering whether it mightn't have been fifty-fifty. Maybe I wasn't patient enough. Or clever enough. This way, I mean, flat on my back. I don't know. It's hard to tell after all this time."

"You don't have to worry about it any more."

"But I do, if I'm to learn the truth about myself. I only know that I did try. I tried damned hard, Davy."

"Hasn't it occurred to you that neither of you was to blame? That you weren't the least bit in love with one another?"

"It's possible. I was flattered to be singled out from all those other girls, most of them much prettier, and all of them more sophisticated than I was. Maybe he needed sophistication, and felt cheated when he didn't find any. Do you suppose that was . . . what's so funny about that?"

"You are! Lying there without a stitch on, trying to make one guinea pig out of me and another out of yourself. All right, I'll humour you. Most men don't look for sophistication. They think that's their prerogative. What they like to find in a woman is generosity and you'll never run short of that. So cut the inquest on imaginary shortcomings. Ever hear what Napoleon said to his valet, Constant, after his first night with Marie Louise?"

"You mean that Austrian girl he married? The one who

could wiggle her ears, and had never been allowed to own a male animal?"

"That's her. He said, 'My friend, marry a German. They are the best of all women, sweet, gentle, fresh and innocent as roses!' In your case, for 'German' read 'Yorkshire'."

"That's nice of you but it was boorish of him. To come down rubbing his hands and discuss the bride with his valet, I mean."

"Well, he was feeling smug, and had to discuss it with someone. Constant was the only one around at that time."

She turned impulsively and her arms went round him. He sensed, somehow, that he had succeeded in dispelling some of her doubts, and it may have been this that set the tone of their relationship as lovers all the days they spent alone by the lake. And because of an overwhelming tenderness, that multiplied in him day by day, he came at length to prize her in a way that would have seemed extravagant a week ago, when he was still subconsciously comparing her to Beth. What intrigued him, what sometimes amazed him, was the range of her personality, only now fully extended, with good humour as its base, and variants all the way from a gentle withdrawal to a gaiety capable of enveloping them both in a sense of release that was balm to a man scarred by war, by a deep personal tragedy and currently holding anxiety at bay.

As the time passed it seemed to him foolish that she could have ever doubted her capacity to induce anything but restorative peace in a man, any man, that is, with his wits about him. In her arms he found an enlarged confidence in himself, and beyond this a depth of relationship in another human being that had eluded him ever since the day Beth had died.

This sense of attainment reached him from many sources. From her effervescent sense of humour, seldom absent from their most intimate moments, from a freely offered body that he came to venerate, but mostly from her ability to communicate. He had no doubts now but that he returned her love, that she could, in essentials, fill the gap left by Beth. In her arms, in her company even, Bamfylde and Bamfylde's concerns moved a great way off, a place where he had suffered and learned, but he did not believe Bamfylde alone would ever satisfy him now. It would have to go about the task with Christine as the bridge between him and personal fulfilment. Time, a wide variety of interests, physical fitness, stemming from the active life he led up there, these things and the obsessive problems of his housemastership, had healed the last of his trench scars, but his emotional re-awakening, within the embrace of this girl, went a good way beyond that. It was a process of rejuvenation, stimulating the nerves and quickening the imagination, so that what lay ahead for him seemed unimportant unless it was linked to her. He had thought himself deeply in love with Beth through that first, peacetime spring more than twelve years before, but Beth had grown on him, season by season, so that he had no clear memory of an onrush of affection such as this, a tumult of the senses that sometimes seemed too violent to last.

One afternoon, when they were lying on the bed watching the curtain of rain move across the lake, he voiced this doubt.

"It's an ideal, Davy, and something to be fought for, but face it, lad, it won't sustain us for the rest of our lives."

"Now that's a depressing thought!" he grumbled, but she went on, "It's a statement of fact, no more and no less. We'll need luck, and a lot of patience, so don't ever forget it."

"Patience, maybe, but what kind of luck, other than finding a way of getting the divorce? And that isn't the moon. Knowing our own minds is the vital factor, and I know mine as regards you. I'd be very happy to take Bamfylde plus you, but you take precedence."

"Over-simplification, Davy. Follow that through and what am I left with? Half of David Powlett-Jones, and that barn of a place on my conscience, where it would sit more heavily than Rowley. No thanks, Davy. I like you very well as you are, doing a job you enjoy."

"That's a different line from the one you took in the church less than a month ago."

"Yes it is, but I know you much better now, *really* know you. You'd never be happy or fulfilled in politics, or doing anything but what you are doing, so let's plan ahead from there."

It did not seem worth an argument. The important thing was they both had direction and this seemed enough to be going on with. He said, lazily, "That's the trouble with the Welsh."

"What is?"

"Love of discourse, especially on abstracts and imponderables. What could happen if something else happened. We run up the pulpit steps at the drop of a hat—

> Myself when young did eagerly frequent
> Doctor and Saint, and heard great argument . . .

Trust a Welshman to indulge in great argument, even when he's in bed with a girl like you."

"Even a Welshman needs a breather now and again."

He laughed and kissed her. It was easy enough to set imponderables aside with a woman like her in his arms. The future could take care of itself for a change. He was more than satisfied with the present.

CHAPTER TWO

I

The blow fell on the day of their first expedition across the lake to Bowness, indeed, to anywhere save the fells, Lodore Falls, or the village where they bought stores. Three weeks had elapsed since they had read a daily paper and there was no wireless set in the chalet. "We might," she said, "be living on Juan Fernandez. I'm sure my constituency wouldn't approve of me being in purdah this long. Why don't we hire a skiff, pull over, and find out what's going on, if you can row that far after your frightful exertions," and when he suggested that they might leave well alone until it was time to collect Grace and go home, she said, "We won't stay. Just an hour's shopping, lunch somewhere and back here for tea."

They tied up to the jetty about eleven and the first reminder that they were back in circulation was a newspaper contents bill, clamped to a billboard outside a tobacconist's shop. It announced, 'MACDONALD TO HEAD NATIONAL GOVERNMENT'.

The starkness of the statement precluded exclamation or comment. They stood quite still, backs to the kerb, mouthing the words once, twice, three times, as though neither had the courage to acknowledge what it could mean in terms of their future. Then, releasing her hand, he went in and bought a paper, re-emerging to find her standing in the same stunned position outside the shop door. He read the headlines aloud. 'MACDONALD HEADS NATIONAL GOVERNMENT', 'LABOUR PARTY SPLIT'—'PROSPECT OF OCTOBER ELECTION', and other double-column headlines, all concerned with cataclysmic occurrences that had, it seemed, been piling one upon the other during the twenty days they had spent three miles east of this same, steep street.

She said, "You know what this means, Davy?", and he replied, doubling the paper, "To everyone or to us?"

"I must go back at once. You surely see that."

The abrupt end of their idyll outraged him. "No, I don't! Or not until we've had time to digest it, to . . . plan something about what happens from here."

"How could we plan, with this hanging over us? I'm an adopted candidate. Dedicated people have put their money on me. Give me the paper."

"We could have lunch, talk things over . . . you don't even know about trains, when you can start . . ."

He was talking to himself. Already, reading as she walked, she was retracing her steps down the hill to the boat and he followed, pausing to light a cigarette when she plumped herself down in the stern of the skiff and went on reading. He said, at length, "Well, what's it to be? A private airplane? Or would a hire car do?"

She folded the paper and slipped it into her handbag. Her expression told him that he had lost her, temporarily at all events. "He's sold us all out," she said. "He and Snowden. Traitors, the pair of them! Jimmy Thomas, too, and who knows how many others?"

"But if he's going to the country . . ."

"You don't understand," she shouted at him, "this is the worst thing that could happen to us as a party, worse than being beaten at the polls ten times in a row! Ramsay Mac, the first Socialist Prime Minister. The man who stood out against everybody, when men like you were up to their necks in mud and blood. He's sold out lock, stock and barrel. Don't ask me why he did it. To keep office, I imagine, but it makes nonsense of everything we've believed since the war."

"But you always agreed you couldn't survive long as a minority government. You must have suspected something like this would happen, sooner or later."

"I thought he would resign, and try for a real majority."

"He'd never get one, with the country's finances in the state they are. You've said that too."

"It wouldn't have mattered. It was the honourable thing to do, wasn't it?"

"You don't look for scruples among politicians, Chris."

"I do. How will this look to the electorate? Leading Socialists, who can be bought and sold."

"You intend to throw in with the backbenchers?"

"Good heavens, of course I do. You've learned that much about me, haven't you? Is a National government, over-weighted with Tories, likely to do a damned thing for the unemployed? You've only glanced at that paper. There's talk of a ten per cent cut in unemployment benefits. There'll be hell to pay everywhere."

"If Ramsay and some of the others are still in office they'll block unfair economies."

"As prisoners of bankers and industrialists? Don't be naïve, Davy. And anyway, we're wasting time. I'm going to phone my Chairman. Go over to the station and find out about trains."

"You intend going back today?"

"Of course I do. With an election in the offing I can't waste an hour. I'll head for London and try and catch the paper train out of Paddington early tomorrow."

She climbed out of the skiff and moved towards a tele-phone kiosk outside the harbourmaster's, opening her bag as she went. He watched her for a moment, then went off to the station to study a timetable pasted to a hoarding in the yard. There was a London train via Kendal and Birmingham at twelve-thirty. It would give her plenty of time to cross to Paddington and catch a late evening train for Taunton, then on to Bilhampton. She could, with luck, be back in her con-stituency by breakfast time tomorrow.

She was still in the kiosk when he returned, talking earn-estly, one elbow propped on the bracket, one leg raised and resting on the ledge. She seemed smaller and remote some-how, a serious, animated girl, but removed from him, deep in her own concerns. The sudden change in their relationship made his heart ache.

She rang off at last and came out, flushed and distant. When he gave her the times of alternative trains, she said, "I'll catch that twelve-thirty. You go back, collect our things, lock up, and give the key to Witherby's clerk."

"But you haven't even got a toothbrush, woman. Besides, it'll be damned cold travelling all night down to that God-forsaken place."

"I've got a mac. How much money have you on you?"

"About three pounds." He gave it to her. He knew her well enough to know that a protest would only mean they parted with acrimony and this he was determined to avoid. "Could you bring my things on? Leave them in the left-luggage office at Taunton, then send me the ticket? There's no mad hurry in that respect. I've got a change at the digs."

"I can bring your bags to you on my way back with Grace."

Her expression softened. For the first time since she had read the poster she looked at him as a friend and not a stranger who happened to be standing around. "No, Davy. It's sweet of you, and I'm terribly sorry it had to happen like this, but you don't get yourself mixed up in this election. Not until you see how things work out at Bamfylde."

"But that's silly. Term doesn't begin for a fortnight. I'll have time on my hands once I've parked Grace."

"No, Davy. This is my show. You've got a battle on yourself, remember? Don't give them ammunition to fire at you. This election is going to be very bitter indeed. All kinds of smears are going to be laid on, all kinds of abuse thrown about, so stay clear of it until you straighten things out back there. If they make life impossible for you, and you decide to pack it in, I'd be very glad of your help. But not otherwise."

He made one last effort. "Look here, you know you can't possibly win that seat now. Everyone will be waving the Union Jack like mad in Tory-held constituencies. Is there any point in it, really? I mean, why don't we concentrate on getting Rowley off our backs and marrying as soon as possible?"

She said, slowly, "We'll marry, Davy. Some time, some place. That much I promise you, providing you don't find someone else. And if you did I wouldn't blame you. I'd always remember you with love, and a lot of respect. But in the meantime I owe it to myself to make a fight. I owe it to those people down there, who backed me against male candidates, but even more to myself. You've achieved something, but I haven't. Not a damn thing so far and here's what might be my last chance to have another go. Don't deny it me."

There was no kind of answer to that. They walked to the station, hand in hand, and when the train came in he saw her aboard, buying her an armful of papers and journals to enable her to get up to date en route. He said, as the whistle blew, "I'm beginning to hate railway platforms. You won't object to me phoning from town, will you?"

"Phone every night if you can afford it," she said. "I'll need that where I'm going."

He kissed her and held her hand after the train had begun to move. Then, releasing it, he watched her face until it was blotted out by smoke, just as it had been on most of the occasions they had met since he walked her to the station at Cardiff after that Christmas confessional in a pub.

II

The showdown, for him, came within a week of the commencement of the Michaelmas term.

The old warrior rang late at night, a few moments after he had had his talk with Christine, battling it out against frightful odds at South Mendips. The brigadier said, testily, "Been trying to raise you for nearly an hour. They said you were engaged speaking."

"So I was, Briggy. Long-distance."

"Well, it's happened. There was a special meeting of the Executive yesterday, and there's a full meeting in the library tomorrow. More than half the Board have promised to attend and they'll hear you both. One at a time of course. You first, I understand. Thought you might like to go over your brief. I'd be kicked off the Board if anyone knew I'd tipped you off!"

"I know that, Briggy. You've been a brick, all the way through. Can you give me a hint how it might go?"

"No, I can't. Might go any way. No precedent for a dam' silly confrontation like this. But if it means anything at all I'd say it was a point in your favour, them agreeing to meet in this way, I mean. Damn it, you don't carpet a headmaster every day of the week, do you, and that's what it amounts to! You'll get a fair hearing, both of you. That dry old stick, Sir Rufus, will make sure of that. It'll depend on him in the

end. The O.B.s will stand with you but there's only three of
us on the committee. God knows how the odds and sods will
react. Depends on the sort of case you put up, I imagine.
I've only got one more piece of advice and it's the same as I've
given you time and again since this blew up. Stick to the
point. Don't lambast him or his policy. Keep to the personal
issue, my boy."

"Sure. And thanks again, Briggy."

"Been a pleasure. Can't stand that fellow. Too bloody
pernickety. Best o' luck."

"Thank you."

The phone clicked and David slowly replaced his own
receiver, pouring himself a drink and carrying it to the armchair that faced the window. In the summer, and throughout
the earliest weeks of the Michaelmas term if the weather was
fine, he kept his armchair here, facing south-east across the
moor. The moon was full and silver light lay on the pastures,
silhouetting the beeches in the drive, trees still wearing their
full spread of leaves, for the earliest south-westerlies were
still a week or two away.

It was very still and empty out there. An owl hooted in
Algy's thinking post, his favourite perch because it was within
easy killing-range of vermin in the planty. He tried to mar-
shal his thoughts, but instead of rehearsing his brief found
his mind ranging over random incidents of the past, back to
the night he first sat here as Bat Ferguson's lodger, a callow,
inexperienced youth, beginning to get the feel of the place.
Towser, Ferguson's dog, now twelve by his reckoning, was
the only Havelock survivor of that time, apart from himself.
He ran his hand over the dog's head, recalling how his
barks had averted what might so easily have been a terrible
tragedy the night of the fire. Other memories stole upon
him, smoke from a bonfire that had never burned itself out.
Beth's laughter as, five months gone, she had waddled up
and down in Yum-Yum's costume; Stratton-Forbes,
earnestly discussing the root causes of bed-wetting in the
Junior dorm; Chad Boyer, making his final call, on the eve
of Beth and Joan's burial at Stone Cross, with the gift of
Bourgoyne's and Marbot's memoirs, to replace copies
David had once mentioned losing in the trenches; Carter,

offering him a partnership with no strings, Chris's one visit here last Sports Day, and her light-hearted remark, "It's the only room in the entire place that doesn't *smell* like a barracks. It's got another smell. It smells of bachelors."

He thought, "I wish to God she was here now, to hold my hand. This time tomorrow it'll be over, one way or the other, and I don't know whether to be relieved or not. If they come down on Alcock's side it's curtains for me, as far as Bamfylde is concerned. And if they don't it can only mean an indefinite period of 'passed to you, Stoic', and 'passed to you, Powlett-Jones . . .' Do I really want that? Won't it rob us all of what dignity we've got left?"

The owl hooted again and he got up to put the fireguard over the grate. Fire was an ever-present hazard here. If he stayed on he would find a way to bully the Governors into installing a fire-escape in every house, but would he ever have his way in decisions of that kind? He doubted it. He doubted it very much. He carried his whisky glass into the kitchen, washed it and went to bed.

*   *   *

It was like a playback of his vigil here more than four years ago, when he had sat waiting for his interview on the outside chance they would select him in preference to Carter, or the man who would be asked to submit a full report on him, perhaps within minutes of his own dismissal. It was a repeat performance, played to a mildly hostile house, so that he felt slightly sick and had recourse, for the second time since breakfast, to the brand of indigestion tablets Carter had always carried about. He was not too familiar with the men closeted behind that door. He could count on Briggy, of course, and his two Old Boy allies, whereas Alderman Blunt, still throwing his weight about as a Governor, would surely see this as a second chance of getting his revenge for the bust-up about the War Memorial business all that time ago. Of the others he barely knew them by sight, had never spoken to two of the latest additions. All he could count on, apart from Cooper's championship was Sir Rufus Creighton's neutrality, until the full facts were before him.

They seemed to enjoy keeping him on tenterhooks in this

dusty little lobby, one of the few school backwaters Alcock's spring-cleaning mania had by-passed. He had sat here, biting his finger-nails and sucking his indigestion tablets, for twenty minutes now, and Miss Rowlandson, the head's secretary, had still not appeared. Down in the quad the bell rang for luncheon parade and the familiar buzz and scuffle of assembly reached him, a sound inseparable from any gathering down there. Then he heard Heffling's raucous voice calling them to attention—"Paraaaaaade—shun! Leeeeeft-turn! Dissssss-miss!"—and another clatter of shoes on gravel and stone, and after that a heavy silence that lasted another five minutes. The library door opened and Miss Rowlandson bobbed out—"Mr. Powlett-Jones?" He got up stiffly, flexing his fingers, a surge of devil-may-care fatalism routing his extreme nervousness and went in, anticipating the Chairman's wordless offer of a chair.

* * *

They were ranged in their familiar horseshoe and again they reminded him of Roundhead inquisitors in that picture Carter had mentioned—'When Did You Last See Your Father?' He avoided the brigadier's eye, knowing it would be too sympathetic. Somebody coughed. Someone else rustled papers. Sir Rufus Creighton sat in the Chairman's seat, looking like a Venetian Doge in a fifteenth-century Italian painting, small, compact, infinitely old and wrinkled, but terrifyingly alert. He said, impersonally, "We have considered all your correspondence, Mr. Powlett-Jones. At two earlier meetings, and again this morning. You will agree, I think, that this is a somewhat unpleasant business for everyone. Yourself included."

"Yes, Sir Rufus. But it seemed to me I owed it to the Governors and myself to put my case last term. I had a choice of doing that or letting things drift until . . . well, until something occurred that might reflect on the school as a whole."

"What kind of occurrence did you envisage, Mr. Powlett-Jones?"

"An open quarrel, with everybody taking sides. With respect, it's not uncommon in a school crisis, sir."

"Do you wish to express your view of the headmaster's

policy as a whole? That isn't usual, of course, but it seemed to me criticism was implicit in your original letter to me. Whatever is said here will be said in confidence."

"No, Sir Rufus. That isn't my right, and I'm sorry if I implied it in my letter. I'm sure I did not intend to. I wrote on a purely personal basis."

"Regarding your alleged attempt to influence the boys politically?"

"Yes, sir. That mainly, but also a statement he made alleging disloyalty, and wilful non-co-operation on my part."

"Come now, you won't deny that you have challenged his decisions on a number of occasions?"

"Yes, I have, but I challenged them in the capacity of a housemaster. I've put forward strong views, as I think any housemaster is entitled to do, particularly as regards his own boys. Nothing more than that."

There was a moment's silence. He could sense the Warrior's approval of his answers so far. Then Blunt said, "Mr. Chairman, I'd like a word. Do I have your permission?"

"Of course."

"Right." He faced David squarely. "It doesn't do to have a headmaster and a housemaster hammering away at one another. You won't deny that, Powlett-Jones?"

"No, Alderman Blunt, I won't because I can't. But it hasn't been a case of 'hammering away at one another', as you say. We've had disagreements, as I've already admitted, but in private, with no other person present. And I've kept my own counsel about them."

"Not always. Carter told me . . ."

Sir Rufus lifted his hand and David saw it as a beautifully judged gesture. "I'm sorry, Alderman, no hearsay evidence, please. Mr. Carter is not present and not available."

"I think I know what Alderman Blunt is referring to, sir, and I don't mind it being raised. Carter asked me to plead for him when one of his boys was threatened with expulsion. I did what he asked, and several of the staff joined the appeal. Later on, when one of my boys was sent home, I naturally sought advice from Carter as to what I should do."

"On a point of order," said Brigadier Cooper. "All this is past history and irrelevant."

"I agree," Sir Rufus said, "and tried to indicate as much."
He turned to David. In his brown, freckled hand was the
breakdown of examination results Algy Herries had advised him to submit. "We've been over these figures," he said.
"Personally, I think they do you credit, Mr. Powlett-Jones."

"Thank you, sir."

"There is nothing you would like to add, then?"

"No, sir, except perhaps that the last time we had a private
talk the headmaster as good as asked me to resign."

"How do you mean, 'as good as'? Did he or didn't he?"
This from Blunt, in a tone of voice that suggested he considered himself on losing ground.

"It was a broad hint. Mr. Alcock said I 'might like to think
about it'. I told him it was out of the question."

"You still feel that way?"

"Yes, I do. I'm very attached to the school. I always have
been, from the first week I arrived here in 1918."

"Thank you, Mr. Powlett-Jones."

It was dismissal. He rose, without catching anyone's eye,
but Sir Rufus Creighton's husky voice stopped him as he
reached for the doorknob.

"No need to wait about, Mr. Powlett-Jones. We shall be
writing an official answer to your letter, of course."

He went out. The last of the indigestion tablets had left a
sour taste in his mouth. He thought, "And what the devil am
I supposed to deduce from all that, I wonder?" and although
he reminded himself of Sir Rufus's comment on the examination results, he still felt baffled and irritated. In a way the
long-awaited confrontation had been an anti-climax.

It remained so for the rest of the day, and on into the night.
No one rang and all the others somewhat pointedly he
thought, left him to himself, perhaps out of courtesy. In the
meantime, however, it was impossible to settle to anything.
He tried proof-reading the final edition of the printer's
proofs of *The Royal Tigress*, but the prose seemed turgid, the
slow build-up to the first battle at St. Albans dull and diffuse.

At eleven he tried to get through to Chris but there was no
reply. With the election looming she would almost surely be
out canvassing, or addressing a meeting in the outback of the
constituency. He said, aloud, "This won't do! Must think

things through properly," and he made a tremendous effort to project his mind into the library, where Sir Rufus and the others had presumably quizzed Alcock shortly after they had quizzed him. Did they sympathise with Alcock for having a near-mutinous housemaster on his hands? Did they wave those examination results under his nose, and tell him to stop behaving like a stuffy, overweening ass? Had the matter of his public appearance on a political platform been raised? He had no means of knowing the answer to these questions and was on the point of giving them up, and going to bed, when the door opened and Grace glided in, wearing her blue woollen dressing gown. "It's Towser, Daddy," she said, frowning with the effort of concentration, as he remembered her mother had been given to doing. "He's snoring in a funny way and I don't think he's well. Will you look at him?"

It was a relief to have one's mind switched to a practical issue, so he followed her into the kitchen, where Towser slept in a laundry basket beside the stove. "He woke me up twice," Grace said, and when he knelt beside the basket he saw at once that the grizzled old dog was in a bad way. His breath was laboured, and every few moments he tried, unsuccessfully to shift his position. He offered the dog a drink but he could not raise his head to the bowl. He said, "Towser's getting on, Grace. Only last night I reckoned his age as twelve. That's old for a dog."

"Eighty-four," she said, and knelt, stroking Towser's head. "Is he dying, do you think?"

"I don't know. He might be. All I can do is to try and get him to take a Bob Martin's and get the vet over first thing in the morning. You'd best go to bed now, my love."

"Couldn't I make tea and watch him? I don't feel a bit sleepy. Besides, I couldn't sleep with him snorting like that."

"I could shift him to the study."

"I'd sooner watch him, Daddy. Honestly. I mean, he's a very special dog, isn't he? You think so yourself."

"Yes, I do. Very well then, for a little while. It's Saturday tomorrow, and you can sleep on. Make a cup for me while you're at it. We'll have it in here."

She skipped over to the gas-stove and put the kettle on. He watched her absently, thinking how much she meant to him, and what a permanent reminder she was of Beth and her twin sister. Their relationship was very close on this account, and he wondered, fleetingly, how she would react to the prospect of a stepmother. Then, reminding himself of Christine's husband, and the complex situation they were in at the moment, he thought, "No sense in bothering about that yet. She'll be in her mid-teens before we get around to marrying, and then it won't matter so much." The kettle began to steam and she made the tea, deftly, the way she did most things. They were sipping their second cup when they heard the discreet knock on the outer door.

He glanced up at the kitchen clock and it told him it wanted a few minutes to midnight. "Who the devil can that be at this time of night? Probably Matron, about one of the boys in the sick-bay."

"There aren't any in the sick-bay," Grace said. "Vesey, the last one, went out today."

"I'll go and see. Meantime, get that pill from the medicine chest and see if Towser will take it hidden in a bit of cake."

He went out across the living-room to the landing door and opened it. Old Rigby, the head's butler, was standing there, looking like a stage butler in a bad play. Old and shuffling but very dignified.

"Excuse me, sir. Sorry to knock you up at this time of night, but I saw the study light from the forecourt and I'm puzzled, sir. It's the headmaster, and I . . . er . . . wondered if you could advise me."

"About what, Rigby?"

"Well, sir, you know he's such a regular about turning in. I've never known him stay up a minute after ten-thirty, no matter what, but he's still in his study, the door's locked, and he won't answer when I knock. I was turning in myself but saw his light under the door. It struck me he was working late and might like another of his hot lemon drinks. He has one about nine every night but he didn't ring for it tonight, and that's strange too, come to think on it. I knocked several times but he didn't answer, so I went round and tried to peep through the window but the curtains are drawn tight, sir."

"He obviously doesn't want to be disturbed, Rigby."

"That's what I thought, sir, but it struck me that . . . well, he might have been taken bad, sir. I mean, I've never known that door locked since Mr. Bull's time, sir.''

On the face of it, David decided, it was very odd. Bull had preceded Herries, and Rigby had been Bull's butler more than thirty years ago. He said, "I'll gladly come down and knock myself, Rigby, if that's what you'd like."

"I would, sir, if it's not too much trouble. I'd sleep easier if you did."

He followed Rigby down to the quad and turned in through the head's door. Light was still showing under the threshold. He knocked three times and when there was no response he called, "Headmaster? It's me, Powlett-Jones," but there was no reply. He said, "I think you must be right, Rigby. Have you got a duplicate key to this door?"

"No, sir, but I can open it. With your permission, sir."

"How?"

"The way I've opened many doors about the place in my time, sir. Mr. Bull was a rare locker-up. Sometimes he turned a key here and there, then went out the front door or quad door and closed 'em on a spring. One moment, sir." He went to his pantry, re-emerging with a square sheet of zinc that he used on his stove. Slipping the zinc under the study floor he took a button-hook from the drawer of the hallstand and inserted it in the large, old-fashioned keyhole. There was a sharp metallic sound from the other side of the door as the key fell on to the zinc. Rigby drew it out, modestly triumphant.

David said, thoughtfully, "Listen here, Rigby . . . I happen to know the headmaster has had a particularly trying day. If he's dropped off in there he'll be very embarrassed being disturbed in this way. Take yourself off, and let me deal with this. I'll explain that you were anxious about him."

"Thank you, sir," and Rigby shuffled off, gratefully it seemed to David, although he couldn't be sure. Rigby's long service at Bamfylde had brought him into close contact with so many eccentrics that he probably found nothing unusual about Alcock's frigid manner. He opened the door quietly and peeped in. The desk light was burning and Alcock was, as he had suspected, inert in his swivel chair, legs fully extended, head thrown back, mouth half-open. David coughed twice but Alcock did not stir. He moved forward and prodded his forearm and Alcock slumped sideways and would have fallen if David had not grabbed him by the hand and shoulder. The hand was chillingly cold. He realised then that the man was dead.

His first impulse was to shout for Rigby but then, as he braced himself to ease the body back in the chair, his glance fell on a sheet of paper on the desk, an unfinished letter addressed to the Chairman of the Governing Body, and beginning, "Dear Sir Rufus . . ." At the same time, his eye travelling rapidly down the few lines of closely written handwriting, his own name jumped at him, and instinct inclined him to steady Alcock with his right hand and lift the sheet of paper with his left. He acted purely on impulse, aware that, before the place erupted, it was very necessary that he should know what was written on that paper. He read, still holding Alcock firmly with his right hand, one completed paragraph and another half finished. Alcock had written,

"Touching the private conversation we had, following my full statement to the Governing Body this a.m., I can only deduce from it that a majority of the Governors, headed by yourself, see fit to regard my submissions concerning Mr. Powlett-Jones as irrelevant, and prompted by my personal dislike of him.

"I made what I consider to be a frank and full assessment of the facts, and made them entirely without prejudice. You have since explained to me your reasons for ruling the substance of that statement out of order. That, of course, is your privilege, and I bow to it. At the same time it makes my position here untenable and I hereby proffer my . . ."

He had been unable, it appeared, to write the word 'resignation'. Something, choking rage, an excess of bile, or even an interruption wholly unconnected with what he was doing, had broken the smooth flow of words and he had died here in his chair. Of what, only a medical man could determine. Awkwardly he pushed the letter into his jacket pocket and called aloud for Rigby, at the same time stooping to lift Alcock bodily from the chair.

It required considerable effort, but once the burden was adjusted he weighed surprisingly little for someone approaching six feet. Rigby appeared almost at once and David heard his sharp intake of breath. "Unconscious, sir?"

"He's dead, Rigby. He's been dead two hours, probably longer. Hold the door and switch on the landing light. Then get through to Dr. Willoughby and if he doesn't answer keep ringing."

"Yes, sir . . . at once. But . . . what was it, sir? A sudden illness or . . ." He left the sentence unfinished, but David understood what had prompted it. Rigby's unswerving loyalty to the school reached all the way back to Bull's time, when he had arrived here as a kitchen servant in the last years of Victoria's reign. He said, quietly, "It was almost certainly a heart attack, but I can't be sure." Then, "I've had more experience in this field than most people, Rigby. There's no question of it being anything but illness."

The old chap dodged in front of him and switched on the landing light, then back again to address himself to the telephone. David knew his way about the house as well as Rigby and went slowly up the curving stone staircase to the front bedroom that Algy had shared with Ellie for twenty-three years. It was not quite as Spartan as the study or parlour. Over the single cot was a reproduction of Botticelli's *Venus Rising From the Sea*, an improbable picture, he thought, to occupy pride of place in the bedroom of a man of Alcock's temperament. On the facing wall was an enlarged photograph of Alcock's educational college in Cape Town, and framed in silver on the dressing-table was a studio portrait of a jaundiced-looking woman about forty, wearing an evening gown fashionable just before the war. He noticed all this as he crossed the room and laid Alcock on the bed, straightening his limbs and closing the jaws and eyes. As he did this he had a sharp memory of trying to perform the same office for Nick Austin, who had died on the wire opposite Delville Wood. But in Nick's case it had proved impossible. He had been out there a day and a night.

He stood breathing heavily beside the bed. The folly and incongruity of the long, smouldering quarrel settled about him like a cloud of marsh gas, poisoning his nostrils and drying

out his mouth. For more than four years now they had been
at it, just as Alderman Blunt had alleged, hammer and
tongs, tit-for-tat, so that in the end they had arrived at a point
where arbitrators had to be summoned to patch up a peace
between two men charged with the education of four hundred
boys, and both behaving like the youngest of them. Alcock's
death, he supposed, in the very act of conceding defeat,
would be seen as a great stroke of luck by some, but not by
anyone who valued his self-respect. Victory, at this price,
was a kind of defeat, and as he thought this he understood
what had prompted him to slip that letter into his pocket.
Everybody concerned was likely to accept it as the token of
Alcock's surrender, Powlett-Jones's legitimate prize as a
trophy of war, and the prospect of this made him feel meaner
and shabbier than ever, so that he put off thinking about it.
He drew the spotless coverlet over Alcock's face and stole
away, meeting Rigby on the stairs.

The butler said, in a hoarse whisper, "I got him, sir. He's
coming right over."

For some reason the prospect of Willoughby arriving with
his bag reminded him of Towser, snorting his life away in his
basket, watched over by Grace. He said, "Would you do
something, Rigby? Pop up to my daughter, tell her I'm
likely to be some time, and that she's to leave the dog and go
to bed?"

"Yes, sir. Certainly, sir," but he hesitated.

"Well?"

"About Mr. Alcock, sir . . . I don't know as it's any of my
business, but he had a sort of attack halfway through last
term. It had been a very hot day, during that long dry spell,
sir. I found him gasping and a very bad colour in the parlour.
He wasn't unconscious. He could tell me where he kept his
pills, and I got him two, with a glass of water. They seemed
to have a very strong effect, sir. He was himself again almost
at once, and sharp enough to warn me to say nothing about it
to anybody. It was some kind of tropical illness, according
to him."

"Thank you, Rigby. Do you remember where those pills
are?"

"Yes, sir. He kept them in the small drawer of the sideboard. I took the liberty of getting them. Thought Dr. Willoughby might want to see them," and he handed over a small red pillbox, containing about a dozen yellow tablets the size of aspirins.

"That was very helpful of you, Rigby. Thank you again, and I'll pass them on. You can go up to bed if you want to, but if I were you I'd first help myself to a drink if Mr. Alcock kept any about the place. If not use my whisky. My daughter will show you where it is."

"Kind of you, sir," and the courteous old chap shuffled off, letting himself into the quad and closing the heavy door with exaggerated care.

David went back into the study and re-read the letter, trying to decide whether or not to replace it where he found it but then Willoughby's car lights swept round the bend of the west drive, and he heard the car pass and stop, and Willoughby's brisk steps on the gravel.

He said, opening the door to him, "Were you treating Alcock for anything, Doc? A tropical illness of some kind?" and Willoughby said he had never spoken more than a dozen sentences to him since he had come here and went quickly upstairs, with David behind him.

He made an examination, pausing to look attentively at the bluish lips. "Tropical illness, my eye," he said, "It's angina, just as I suspected the moment Rigby told me. Had a feeling about the chap the first time I met him. You do about some people. Just a few and he was one of them. He held himself in, didn't he? Kept the lid screwed down in case it blew off at the wrong moment."

"That's one way of putting it. Nobody could get close to him, but I never saw him lose his temper, not even when he was in a quiet fury, and he usually was when I had words with him."

"It fits. Did he take anything?", and when David gave him the pills he glanced at them, then pocketed them. "I'll hang on to these, P.J. There's a possibility of an inquest but it isn't likely. He's bound to have a medical record somewhere, and the bursar could look into it first thing. Will you notify his next-of-kin?"

"I haven't the faintest notion who his next-of-kin is, or

even if he has one. The bursar might help there."

"It'll keep until morning. Nothing more I can do. Bit of a shock for everyone. Lucky job you and Rigby had the sense to break in. I'll write the certificate downstairs."

David said, when Willoughby had finished his writing, "Do you notify the coroner or do we?"

"Me. He wasn't a patient but Bamfylde is. You'd better get on to the Governors tomorrow. As you were the one who found him they'll expect that." Then, with a shrewd look, "You didn't hit it off at all, did you? Not from the word go."

"Nobody hit it off. It was all a ghastly mistake, due, in a way, to that idiotic quarrel between Carter and me four years ago."

"What'll happen now, P.J.?"

"I'm damned if I know. We were both up before the Governors only this afternoon. He was alleging slackness and insubordination, so I got my oar in first. On Algy's advice, I might add. But if I had dreamed it could have led to this . . ."

"It didn't. Man's been living on borrowed time for years in my opinion. His papers should clarify that, unless he carried secrecy to the point of self-destruction, and I don't think he did. Too careful. Then there are these pills, they must have been supplied by somebody qualified. For God's sake, don't start reproaching yourself. You've no cause to at all."

"Doctors don't know the lot. How about this?"

He took out the letter and passed it to Willoughby who read it slowly, then went back to read it a second time.

"He was writing this at the time?"

"It was on the desk."

"I stick to my point. This fits too. Severe emotional strain, self-induced, and I stress that, mind. You Celts and your damned guilt-complexes! Sometimes I think guilt is a Celtic sport, a variant of masturbation. All his life that chap has been driving himself, and in the last few years he's had his foot slammed down on the accelerator. Every man needs to blow his top now and again, especially a man in authority, but he never did, you say. Probably never so much as raised his voice. Well, this is the result, and it would have happened anywhere, anywhere at all, provided his job entailed responsibility." When David made no reply he went on,

"Listen, P.J., he scared some of the others off, but not you. You hung on, another Celtic characteristic. Well, who was right about that? Carter, who packed it in, or you, who stuck it for the sake of the place as a whole?"

"Was it worth a man's life?"

"Who knows? It might be, in the long run. You've got thirty years ahead of you. He had about one, I'd say. Let things drift awhile. Let the Governors and the bursar sort it out."

He strode off, a big, bustling, hard case of a man, that nothing could rattle. David let himself out and went up to his quarters, passing through to the kitchen, his senses alerted by the silence reigning there. Towser was dead, curled in his basket and looking, somehow, as if he had died without much distress. He thought, "Funny that. Two eras closed in an hour. The Old Guard's, represented by Bat Ferguson, and Alcock's. Grace will be upset if she wasn't here when it happened, but I hope it was after Rigby sent her to bed." He sat looking down at the basket, remembering the fire of eight years before, an ordeal that was much closer to the war, but in those days he had never shirked issues the way he was inclined to shirk them now. The older a man grew the less sure he was about anything. In the end, perhaps, he came face to face with the fact that he was still looking through a crack in a door, wondering at the things he saw within. What had Alcock's fifty-odd years taught him about handling people? Or Howarth's? Or Barnaby's? They were all amateurs at the game, himself included. He wondered whether to ring Chris again but decided against it. She had enough on her plate at the moment and the new situation wouldn't do anything to aid her concentration. There seemed even less point in rousting out Howarth or Barnaby at two o'clock in the morning. Technically Howarth was senior master, and would be saddled with the job of making the announcement at morning parade. Suddenly he felt drained of energy, too confused and dispirited to devote a single thought as to where Alcock was likely to be buried, and whether or not his funeral would rank as a Bamfylde ceremony. He reeled off to bed and within minutes, against all expectation, he was asleep.

CHAPTER THREE

I

Alcock was not buried at Stone Cross, beside such classroom warriors as Judy Cordwainer and Bat Ferguson. His London lawyers had received specific instructions concerning his disposal. He was to be cremated, and his ashes conveyed to Cape Town.

He had a family after all, two sons, both living abroad, but the bursar dealt with the family and the lawyers. All David was required to do was to write a detailed report of what had occurred, sending one copy to the Governors, another to Dr. Willoughby, who took it upon himself to superintend the medical aspects, notwithstanding the fact that Alcock had never been his patient. There was no inquest. It emerged, in a matter of hours, that Alcock had been under a London heart specialist, a man of repute, according to Willoughby. "He couldn't have given the chap very good advice," Willoughby said, "or maybe he did and it was ignored. I thought you might like to know that I was right in my spot diagnosis. He left Africa for health reasons, and I suppose that accounts, to some extent, for him concealing it so successfully. They wouldn't have appointed him if it had got about he was a heart risk."

It was queer, David thought, how rapidly and completely Alcock had effaced himself. He had seemed so brooding a presence but now, in a matter of days, there was hardly a trace of him, if one excepted the new bog and his other renovations, like the donkey's breakfast floor coverings in the dormitories, and the revarnished pew-backs at Stone Cross Church. He appeared as a brief visitation. No more and no less. Algy Herries, four years absent, was a far more active ghost, and it was Algy who came to their rescue, slipping back as acting-head until the end of the term and spending four days a week at the school. He did not live in but motored home to his parish every night, so that it was not like having Algy actually restored to them but rather helping out, like Rawson, the honorary football coach, now on four months' leave from Rhodesia.

David heard nothing from the Governors concerning a replacement. They would delay it, he imagined, until the new year. There was no immediate hurry, with Algy on the doorstep, and when Brigadier Cooper rang, hinting at a renewed application, he steered him away from the subject. It was something he preferred not to think about for the time being. Willoughby had kept that letter but what use he had made of it, if any, David had no idea. He was aware of the effects of shock in the days that followed, and this in itself was strange, in view of the hundreds of deaths he had witnessed, and all the corpses he had handled between 1914 and 1917. The others, Grace included, found him very subdued, and there was the minimum of conversation on the subject in the common room. It was as though Alcock, who had divided them in life, continued to isolate them in death. Only Howarth spoke out, growling to David, as they stood watching the hearse drive off, "That's that, and I hope to God nobody asks me to comment. If there's one form of hypocrisy I can't tolerate it's sentimental regard for the dead, simply because they *are* dead. To hear some people talk at a funeral one would suppose dying was limited to the chosen few."

As it happened, however, there was a funeral at Bamfylde that same week. Towser was buried on the edge of the planty by David and Grace, just beyond the bank where the first of the trees grew. Grace marked the spot with two white stones and it was not until two days later that Coxe Minor presented himself at David's door, asking, very politely, if he might have a word with his housemaster.

Coxe was a fresh-faced thirteen-year-old, lumbering his way through Lower School. A dreamy, inoffensive little chap, no good at games or work but with a consuming passion for wild life that made him, while still in the Upper Third, Bamfylde's authority on ornithology.

Coxe was said to run a kind of birds' hospital up in the planty, a hedge-hide where he collected not merely birds but

stoats, weasels and other creatures, all reputably charmed by
his various whistles and calls. One of his owls, wounded in
some affray, had been nursed back to health in a hut down
at the piggeries and later set free. Barnaby christened him
Frankie, after St. Francis, as soon as this story got about and
the name stuck. David, inviting him inside, asked, "What's
bothering you, Coxe?" and Coxe said he was there to make
a request on behalf of himself and Davidson. Davidson, a
local farmer's son, was his special crony, also serving time in
the Upper Third.

"It's about Towser, sir. Davidson is hot stuff at carpentry
and he's made a headstone—well, head*board*. He asked me
if he should and I told him to go ahead, seeing that Grace's
dog had been about the place so long, sir. I've got it outside,
and I wondered if she could tell us where Towser is buried,
so as we could put it up, and whether it would be right to do it,
sir."

Without waiting for reassurance, he slipped outside, re-
appearing almost at once with a board about two feet by one
foot, shaped to a gothic apex, and with a smoothly planed
oblong enclosed within deeply scored lines. The lettering on
the oblong was neat and clear: *Towser Powlett-Jones, died
Sept. 30, 1931, aged about twelve. R.I.P.*

He saw it not as a tribute to Towser but as a graceful
compliment to Grace, who was popular with everyone about
the place. Each of them, apparently, thought of Towser as
Grace's dog, not his, or something inherited from the Fer-
gusons. He said, "I think that's very kind of you and Davidson, Coxe. Do thank him for me. Take the board to the planty,
and I'll send Grace along to show you exactly where to put
it." He paused, pondering a moment. "It's a pity you didn't
add something about the fire we had here. Towser saved us
all by waking me up. We always had a very special regard
for him on that account."

"You mean the Havelock fire, sir?"

"Yes, long before you came here."

Coxe considered, his head on one side. "Davidson could
add a bit if we gave him an hour or so. Would Grace like
that, sir?"

"I'm sure she would, if Davidson felt equal to it. Upper

Third's first period is history this afternoon, isn't it? Tell Davidson he needn't come in if he wants the time to work in the shop. Then I'll come up with my daughter after final period bell."

Coxe scuttled off with his headboard and David went in search of Grace who was, as he suspected, infinitely touched by the gesture.

"Frankie Coxe is a very nice boy," she said. "He wants to be a vet when he leaves."

"I'll wager a term's salary he will be, even if only half they say about him is true." Then, thoughtfully, "You don't think, in the circumstances, that it's pushing things a bit far. Marking a dog's grave, I mean, with Mr. Alcock dying here only a few days ago?"

"No, I don't. The two things aren't to do with one another, Daddy. Everybody liked old Towser and I never liked the new head."

"Why do you say that?"

She looked at him steadily, another trick inherited from her mother. "Because he wasn't nice to you," she said, simply. "You never said he wasn't but I know just the same. I'm sorry he died, but that doesn't mean I have to pretend to like him, does it?"

"No, I suppose not," he said, thinking of Howarth's comment on graveside hypocrisy. "Very well, pick me up after the final bell outside the Fifth and we'll go up and see what Davidson makes of it."

They met them at five minutes after four, waiting a hundred yards or so south of the cricket pavilion, and Grace led the way over the bank to the stones marking Towser's grave. The autumn light was already fading inside the wood hut and beyond the trees the clear sky was flooded with molten brass where the sun slipped down beyond the school buildings. Coxe displayed Davidson's additional handiwork, a single sentence, carved low on the board, '*This dog saved life when Havelock's ct. fire. He barked.*' As an epitaph, David thought, it had a smack of eighteenth-century forthrightness, and that was just the way a stolid boy like Davidson would think of it. 'He barked.' Nothing gaudy or flowery but the whole essence of Towser's spectacular feat in two words.

Coxe acted as a kind of interpreter. "Davidson's sorry about shortening the word 'caught', sir. There wasn't room, you see. Will it do, sir?" Coxe, usually a very untidy boy, had clearly smartened himself for the ceremony. With his eager eyes, his black hair neatly parted and his shiny black mackintosh turned up at the collar, he reminded David of a rook.

"It'll do splendidly," David said. "Thank you for taking so much trouble, Davidson," but Davidson blushed and stared hard at his boots.

Coxe used a trowel on the ground just beyond the line of stones and carefully inserted the board, afterwards producing a tent mallet from his mackintosh pocket to hammer it firm. Then he and Davidson heeled in the loose soil round the base and stood back. Grace said, a little tearfully, "Thank you, Coxe. Thank you, Davidson. It was *jolly* nice of you to think of it," and they all moved off in response to the clamour of the tea-bell, Coxe, Davidson and Grace moving ahead in a group.

The thought occurred to him, as he crossed the forecourt and passed under the windows of the head's house, "Funny a dog should make more impact on all three of them than a man dying of heart failure within shouting distance of where they slept," but then, partly on account of the incident, he was able to get Alcock and Alcock's reign into some kind of perspective. "I'll talk it over with Algy, then put it out of mind," he promised himself, as he turned down the flagged corridor to supervise tea.

II

The Saturday before the election he begged a loan of Molyneux's car and ran over to Bilhampton. It did not seem to matter now whether or not he involved himself in politics but Christine, drawn and exhausted after six week's non-stop campaigning, would not hear of him speaking at either of the two meetings he attended. "Your field is wide open again," she said, "and what sort of selfish bitch would I be to stand in your way a second time?" When he told her he was not disposed to play the field again, and that it was extremely unlikely, after the row preceding Alcock's death, that the Governors would short-list him for the job, she said this was no time at all for a professional man of any kind to enlist with so-called Bolshies. "It's like rolling a boulder up Snowdon," she said. "There's a kind of hysteria running loose, as if the country was waging some kind of patriotic war. The National Government is seen as a lifeboat, and whoever won't jump aboard and give thanks to God is off their rocker. One would have thought, with nearly three million on the dole, and wage cuts all round, the tide would be running for us, not them! Not on your life. You should hear the gibes I've had thrown at me, and from people living on pittances! 'You're the bastards who have landed us in the mess!' someone shouted at me on Thursday, as if the British Labour Party had engineered the Wall Street crash, back in '29. It's absolutely incredible what people will believe if it's told them often enough. There are chaps about here wearing blue rosettes and taking home thirty-five shillings a week to a tied cottage they can be evicted from at any moment. Talk about a working-class Tory being too green to burn, that's an understatement. You can dry green wood but how the hell do you light a fire with solid ivory?"

He sympathised with her but could have wished she was equipped to take things more philosophically. People were scared, he said, scared stiff of losing even that thirty-five shillings a week, and probably saw a national government as the only solution. Moreover, who could blame them, with men of MacDonald's stature, and Snowden's famed integrity, leaving the ranks? "Don't mention those names to me," she snapped, "and as for that word 'national', for heaven's sake, get it straight, Davy. It *isn't* national, it's *Tory*! How long will it be before they drop the pretence and that charlatan with it? What happened to Lloyd George when he did a deal with the Tories in 1916?"

"Lloyd George probably wishes he could back-pedal right now. So will Ramsay when things have gone off the boil."

"Do you think we'd have him back after this? The one thing that cheers me up is the prospect of him losing his seat and having to ask the Tories to find him another. Look, I can't waste any more time, Davy. I have to go over my speech for this afternoon."

It was a very different Christine Forster, he reflected, from the girl who had lain in his arms beside Windermere two short months ago. She was strong, and very dedicated, but she would need all her strength and dedication to maintain the pace for long. The afternoon meeting was thinly attended, and depressing apart from the interruption of a few hecklers, but there was serious trouble at the evening rally, with constant interruptions, a spate of abuse, and, at one time, the prospect of a general scrimmage. No warm-up speaker could make himself heard and Christine was greeted by the slow handclap and backrow jeers of "Find yourself a man and get yourself a couple of kids!" "Chuck it, love, and come and give us a cuddle!" and a few mild obscenities. It was all he could do to stop himself getting up and fighting his way over to one lout who bawled, "Yer ol' man run orf, didn't he, ducks? And buggered if I blame him!" a sally that was greeted by a gale of laughter and another scuffle in the aisle.

She was in tears when he called for her in the committee room behind the stage. The sheer weight and ruthlessness of the opposition was beginning to tell, not only upon her but on her few steadfast supporters. All her committee men looked sullen and despairing, so that David said, for their benefit as much as hers: "You've made your gesture. That's all that really matters. People will remember it when things drift from bad to worse. With a majority of over twelve thousand, and a three-cornered contest under these conditions, you can't expect to get a fair hearing. My advice is to cut out meetings and concentrate on door-to-door canvassing in the factories and working-class districts. Hold an open-air meeting beside every dole queue in the division. Then move on, speaking in every street where there's a concentration of unemployed. They won't vote Tory."

She said very little during the walk home but at the gate, where he was prepared to leave her, she said, "Come up-stairs. I'd made up my mind not to ask you in. For my sake, as well as yours, for you must have heard what that swine shouted about me being a married woman, living apart from her husband. They only need a whiff of scandal to put paid to me here, but to hell with all of them!"

He followed her up a staircase lit by a 25-watt bulb to a

front-room bedsitter in the ugly, Londonbrick villa she occupied, near the station. It was a cheerless, anonymous room,
with bagged-out furniture, bilious-green tiles in a grate
fitted with a small gas-fire, and dun-coloured curtains
screening the bed. She did her own cooking here on a primus
stove, she told him, and the smell of paraffin did battle with
the reek of lino polish and bacon fat.

He said, "Do you have to live in a place like this, Chris?
You said something about making use of Rowley's allowance."

"I do make use of it. It goes into the funds. We've hardly
any money to fight the election."

"Well," he said, "you're a game one to be sure. Keep
reminding yourself of that. It might help."

"It did once," she said, throwing her off-the-peg coat on
the bed, and filling the kettle. "It doesn't now."

"Because of a bunch of hecklers?"

"Not just them. I didn't come into this expecting miracles.
I knew that at best it would be a long, uphill fight to build a
party organisation. No, it was you, I imagine."

"*Me?*"

"Being cut off from you in this way, feeling as guilty as hell
every time I'm alone with you, because of what happened the
last time you stood up for me in public."

"But Alcock's dead. Algy is deputy head now, and Howarth will probably succeed him. Neither would dream of
trying to control what I did in my spare time."

"You're kidding yourself, Davy."

"How? I know Algy. He's a democrat and he's been teaching democracy all his life."

"It's the mood of the country. Nonconformist Socialists
are seen as revolutionaries, people who want to drag the
whole shooting match down. I know, I'm much closer to this
than you, and I *know*. And as if that wasn't enough there's the
moral aspect—a man like you, supposed to set an example,
tagging along with a married woman."

"But damn it, you aren't married in the proper sense. You
haven't set eyes on that damned Rowley for nearly three
years."

"It's still a stick to beat you with, a smear that can stop you getting what you're after, what you've set your heart on getting, being Gaffer of that place. It's a very worthwhile objective and a practical one too, for I've seen the way all those boys look at you and address you. You'll make it, but only if I let go of your coat-tails."

"But can't you see, I don't want to make it at the price of losing you? I'm in love with you. More than ever now I see you bruised and battered and still on your feet. What kind of man would that make me, to turn my back on you now?"

"A sane one, with the right priorities in view. You can do untold good at a place like Bamfylde. Not just for the boys who go there, but for all of us."

"Good God, are you suggesting we should break up on that account?"

"Yes, I am. And don't imagine it's a pretty gesture on my part. It hurts like hell, even the thought of it."

"Then don't think of it. Because I won't go along with it. Not now, not ever."

"What does that mean? We go on meeting and mating in anonymous places? We make love once every six weeks standing up in alleys, or in the back of a car on a moor? No, thank you, Davy. You deserve better than that and so do I. The fact that I was having an affair with that schoolmaster who made the famous Monmouth speech at my adoption meeting wouldn't only ruin you, it would ruin my candidature. We're up a dead end, Davy."

Something warned him to stop arguing with her now, with her so tired and dispirited, with the echo of that heckler's gibe ringing in her ears. It was wiser to sheer away and wait for the feverish atmosphere to spend itself, to wait patiently, if that was possible, for some kind of break that would offer hope. Away in the back of his mind was the thought that perhaps this baptism of fire would prove too much for her, that she would emerge so ignominiously from the polls that she would swing away from politics, and if she did that they could soon find a way to get married and put both Rowley and politics out of mind. To his way of thinking, there was not much prospect of him being encouraged to take up the fight again. Even Howarth had as good as conceded that, when he and Barnaby had been speculating idly about Alcock's successor. The best he could hope for was another stopgap man, and a chance to persuade the Governors, over a long period of time, that he was something more than a born trouble-maker, who had quarrelled with Alderman Blunt, Carter and his headmaster in rapid succession. That might take a decade and by then he would be in his mid-forties, and as set in his ways as old Judy Cordwainer.

She made tea and they sipped it in silence. He noticed the colour had gone from her cheeks and the sparkle from her eyes. For the first time he understood why she persisted in regarding her nose as a feature that spoiled her looks. The heat and turmoil of the meeting had made it glow in the light of the Woolworth's shade. She had lost weight, too, a surprising amount of weight, in a few weeks. He had reason to know that her breasts were round and full but tonight she looked flat-chested. Only her elegant legs reminded him of the Chris Forster of Windermere, and earlier.

He said, earnestly, "Listen, Chris, you've got to ease up a little. What's an election, anyway? There'll be other, luckier elections, with the tide of events on your side. It won't help to tax yourself this way. You look as if you haven't had a square meal since we parted in August."

A flicker of her independence showed.

"I look anaemic? I'm losing my sex-appeal?"

He said, taking her cup, "Who lives here? Who is your landlady?"

"Dora Beavis," she said, "a widow with three cats called Shadrach, Meshach and Abednego. She's a strict Methodist. However, we're in luck tonight. She and her blasted cats have gone to Langport to stay with a sister."

"I've got to drive back tonight. I'm on duty tomorrow, and Molyneux wants his car. But I'm staying here until the small hours. I'll make sure I get away well before daylight."

She made no protest. The temperature of the dismal room was rising a little, now that the curtains were drawn, and the gas-fire had been singing for half an hour. He turned off the overhead light and the outlines of the cheerless place were softened. "Go to bed," he said, "God knows, you look as if you need some sleep," and she replied, "That's gallant of you, after a hundred-mile drive, and the prospect of another in slashing rain." Then, forlornly, "I need you right now more than sleep, Davy."

He took her at her word. There was not much room in the narrow bed but in one another's arms they found at least a temporary solution to their problems. She might be tired out, he thought, but she still had reserves of vitality and enfolded him with desperate eagerness, too impatient and too much in need of solace to give a thought to contraceptives.

She said, before she drifted into sleep, "That would just about put the tin lid on it, wouldn't it? A candidate, separated from her husband, and several months gone." But there was a trace of laughter in her voice.

III

She must have been as tired as she looked. About five o'clock, long before it was light, he relit the gas-fire, slipping a shilling into the meter and glancing over his shoulder to see if the click had disturbed her. It had not, so he dressed quickly in the feeble orange glow, determined to let her sleep on until one or other of her supporters roused her. She looked more or less herself again, with colour in her cheeks. Deep sleep had brought a total relaxation of her face so that he was able to see her less as a woman than one of his first-termers, relieved by sleep of the strain of keeping up appearances during the day. He thought of himself as having loved Beth to the limit of his experience but it had never quite reached the pitch of intensity he felt for her at this particular moment. He and Beth had achieved what he thought of as a supremely successful partnership, but Beth had never stood in such terrible need of his protection, had never once appeared to him so defenceless and spent. In the last few years Chris had taken any amount of hard knocks, and the passage between her awakening at university, and last night's rowdiness in a small-town drill hall, was marking her spirit, now masked in sleep that would sustain her for another day or so. After that, he would say, it would be touch and go, depending upon how she fared at the polls. He was sure of one thing. She was not capable of absorbing humiliation on a grossly wounding scale.

He had seen himself, up to that time, as a committed radical,

but he understood now that he was really no more than a
dilettante. Bamfylde had replaced his hunger for social
justice, quickening in him since his schooldays in the Valley.
He was much tougher, too, and far more resilient. Trench
warfare had seen to that long before he had come of age. It
was something she would have to work out for herself, win or
lose. Nobody could help her much, except maybe by the odd
word of encouragement at the right time and place. He took
one of her leaflets from the bamboo plant-table in the window and wrote, in the glow of the fire, "You needed sleep.
Good luck and God bless. I love you very much, so bear this
in mind, no matter what happens on Thursday. God knows,
dearest, love is what it's all about really. If it isn't, does it
matter who runs the show? One other thing—you look
younger, prettier, and more desirable than ever at this
moment. Davy."

He put the leaflet, written side up, on the chair where she
had thrown her clothes and tiptoed out, groping his way down
the steep stairs to the front door and striking a match to help
him grapple with its fastenings. The doorknob felt greasy
under his hand and the narrow hall smelled unpleasantly of
cats.

IV

The furore of the Governors' meeting, followed by Alcock's
death, and Chris's dilemma, had banished all thought of his
book from his mind. Perhaps he was beginning to see it, in
retrospect, as a mere time-consuming enterprise over the
ups and downs, mostly downs, of the last few years. A means
of escaping, for an hour or so, first from the pressures of grief,
then Alcock's nagging presence. At all events he had forgotten it completely, so that he stared at Barnaby uncom-
prehendingly when, soon after noon that same Sunday, he
saw him waving a newspaper as he passed under the front
of Nicolson's on his way to confer with Heffling, head prefect, about the prep roster for the ensuing week. Barnaby
shouted, "*Hi*, there! You're being very modest, aren't you?
I knew we had a literary presence about the place, but I was
under the impression he was a cub, not a lion!"

"What the hell are you waffling about?" he called back,

but then he saw that the newspaper in Barnaby's hand was yesterday's *Times* open at the book page. The Sunday papers would not get here until late afternoon, so that they had formed a habit of saving Saturday's papers to combat ennui between Saturday night and Monday morning.

He said, excitedly, "There's a review of my book in there?"

"There is, my dear chap, and a regular corker! It's either a first-class book, or you've struck uncommonly lucky with a critic." Then, bleakly, "Are you telling me you didn't look for it yesterday?"

"I was travelling," David said. "Would you lend me that paper, Barnaby? You can have it back."

"I don't want it back. You can mutilate it as far as I'm concerned. Everyone else has read it, but you can't expect anyone but me or Howarth to glance at the book reviews on the way to the sports pages. Take it, and congratulations, and I mean that, P.J."

"Thanks very much, Barnaby. Will ... er ... has Howarth seen it?"

"Probably not. He was off duty yesterday and over at Algy's. And the old bird doesn't usually surface until Sunday afternoons if he can help it. Were you supposed to be taking lunch today?"

"Yes, I'm duty wallah."

"I'll take it for you. We can't expect bona fide authors to sit watching boys stuff themselves with boiled cabbage and beetroot on occasions like this."

David thanked him and set off across the playing field to Algy's thinking post where, in the two winter terms, the roller was parked under its tarpaulin. There were a few boys about but just then the lunch-bell rang and within minutes the field was empty. He sat on the shaft of the roller and read the review from start to finish. Then he went back and read it again, letting his eye rove up and down the column in search of phrases that pleased him most, those in which the reviewer, who signed himself 'John Ellicott', had used to emphasise an overall theme that here was someone who could make an absorbing narrative out of the confused canvas of fifteenth-century England.

Ellicott made his first point (or perhaps his literary editor

made it for him) with the headlines: "FRESH SPARKLE ON
DULLED SURFACES—HIGHLY READABLE ACCOUNT OF WARS OF
THE ROSES", and on the same theme—

> Amateurs interested in English history, in the middle
> decades of the fifteenth century, approach it with the cer-
> tain knowledge that they will soon lose their way in a welter
> of warring dynasties. Until now, that is, for an unknown
> biographer (this is his first published book) has shown that
> patience plus enthusiasm can crop something very palat-
> able from these pastures. The book is *The Royal Tigress*, a
> study in depth of Margaret of Anjou and her period, and
> the author is David Powlett-Jones, a West Country
> schoolmaster, a man with an obvious passion for the
> bloody struggle of York and Lancaster from first St.
> Albans to Bosworth Field . . .

Here followed a summary of the narrative that was more than
a busy journalist's rehash of the publisher's blurb.

> It requires more than a detailed knowledge of the period
> to convert shadowy figures like the saintly Henry VI, his
> vitriolic French wife, the Duke of York, Warwick the King-
> maker and others into the flesh-and-blood portraits Mr.
> Powlett-Jones has drawn for us. He has brought to this
> thinly chronicled period a searchlight that reveals some
> of the motives and methods of power-hungry men, of the
> kind frequently encountered in later centuries. It is this
> that makes the book unique. As well as being as exciting as
> a well-constructed thriller, it is a warning to all men in
> high positions who allow personal ambition and pride to
> dominate their lives. Most of them, as we know, came to a
> very sticky end and Tudor England was the richer for their
> demise. But, apart from being a cautionary tale, this book
> is a romance set in the twilight of feudalism. The author is,
> I suspect, a romantic, who began writing *The Royal Tigress*
> biased in favour of Lancaster. He ended a dedicated York-
> ist. Edward IV, that genial, womanising giant, is seen here
> as the first modern sovereign of England, and his brother,
> the much-maligned Richard of Gloucester, as its last war-
> rior king. Between them, the one consciously, the other un-
> consciously, they prepared the way for modern England.

In addition are portraits of many colourful characters; Margaret herself, indomitable, cruel and always unlucky; Tiptoft, the sadistic scholar, who said to his executioner 'Behead me with three strokes, in honour of the Trinity'; the Kingmaker, playing for high stakes all his life and dying like a gladiator at Barnet and many others. Mr. Powlett-Jones has also taken the trouble to make a study of the military strategy and tactics of the period, supplying us with comprehensive maps of the campaigns. Altogether an extremely readable book and one that can be recommended to student and layman.

Nobody, he thought, could be anything but flattered by Mr. Ellicott's review, and he wondered if he could hope for equally encouraging notices from other papers. It occurred to him then that here, if he was looking for it, was an alternative livelihood. A modest one, perhaps (the agent had warned him he would be very lucky to make four hundred a year from historical biography), but a living on a par with the one he was getting now, and this might mean he could abandon teaching if he felt inclined. It occurred to him also that it was strange he had not yet received advance copies of the book, and thought it possible that the parcel had arrived and was unclaimed in the parcels room.

The mere prospect of touching the book, of feeling it under his hand, sent him down the field at a trot to seek out Heffling, head prefect, and ask for the key of the parcels room. Heffling said, at once, "Sorry about yours, sir . . . it came Friday afternoon and was on Saturday's list, but you were away, so I asked Taylor to leave it at Havelock's. It must have slipped his memory, sir."

"Come along with me and get it, Heffling, for this is a magic moment I must share with somebody. Unless I'm mistaken it's my author's copies, copies of the book I've published on the Wars of the Roses," and Heffling, taken slightly aback, said, "You've actually written a book, sir? A real book?" and David laughed and said, "Real enough in that it represents quarts of midnight oil. I began it before you arrived here in the winter of '25."

It was the books right enough, six of them, clean, crisp and emitting that singular bookish smell everyone here associated with the start of the new school year, when all classes were issued with new exercise books. It was a fatter, heavier book than David had imagined, and the maps and illustrations had reproduced extremely well. Heffling turned the leaves reverently, almost as though he was handling the Book of Kells.

"Gosh, sir," he said, at length, "this'll put Bamfylde on the map, won't it? I mean, the chaps will be tickled to death. Even chaps who think history is a bit of a bore."

It slipped out, a virtual confession that Heffling spent most of David's periods planning the tactics of the next game with Blundell's or Queen's School, Taunton, but Ellicott's review had worked wonders on his goodwill. He said, "Look here, Heffling, you were the first in on this, apart from Mr. Barnaby, who had to remind me I'd written the book at all. Would you like that copy as a keepsake?"

"Me, sir? I'd like that very much, sir!" and then, shyly, "Would you . . . could you *autograph* it, sir?"

"Delighted. Never had the honour before. Here . . ." and he took out his fountain pen and wrote on the flyleaf, "*For George Heffling, presented by the author on the day of publication,*" and signed his name with a flourish. "It isn't strictly true. Official publication day is tomorrow, but what's in a day? Hand me those others. I'm going to autograph copies for Mr. Howarth and Mr. Barnaby.

He left Heffling clutching his windfall and carried the books up to his quarters, wishing Grace was around to share his triumph, but she was pony riding on the moor and lunching at Ma Midden's. He signed copies for Barnaby and Howarth, and a third for his mother, who would never read it but would take it up and down the street. Then, just as he was going to seek Howarth, Chris rang, calling from 'The Mitre', the Bilhampton pub.

"Davy? I'm so glad I caught you. I've only got a minute before they pick me up for the motorcade. Motorcade! One Morris, one Austin Seven, and two tradesmen's vans. I just wanted to say thank you . . . thank you for everything, Davy darling, but especially the note you left. I feel much better, honestly. I don't know how I would have coped last night if you hadn't been there. But when I woke up and found you gone, then read your note and had a cup of tea and a serious talk with myself, things seemed different. I'll show these baskets what I'm made of yet!"

It sent his spirits soaring even higher to hear her talk that way. "All you needed was a good sleep."

"Ah," she said, chuckling, "but I wouldn't have had that if it hadn't been for you. They always say it's the best soporific in the world, don't they?"

"No hangover?"

"None. I love you, remember?"

"Good. Then here's something that might send your mercury up another point, as it has mine," and he told her about the review in *The Times*, and the early copies of *The Royal Tigress*.

Her enthusiasm crackled over the line as she said, "But that's wonderful! And to think I never asked about it."

"Don't let that bother you. I'd completely forgotten it myself. Hi, you read all the papers. Will you keep an eye open for other reviews?"

"I'll do better. There are papers right here on the hotel table," and he heard her slam out of the booth and a moment later her voice saying, "I won't have time to read them but I've got the *Chronicle* here, and some others . . . hold on," and he listened, grinning, to a prolonged rustling, ending in a shout, "There's one here! In the *Empire News*, of all papers . . . 'When Knights Were Bold!' What an awful heading! . . . But it's nice. The man seems quite taken by it, says it reads like a thriller."

"That's what Father Times says."

"You'll be famous by tomorrow!"

"Nonsense!" he laughed, "but I must say I'm bowled over by them reviewing it at all. After all, I'm not a professional historian."

"Of course you're a pro if you teach history, then go on to sell it between hard covers. Will you make a lot of money?"

"The publisher says around four hundred if it sells out. A bit more on a reprint."

"This will send your stock soaring at Bamfylde, won't it?"

"I don't quite know, they've never had an author before. But there's another aspect of it, Chris. If I go on to write other books, and I'm sure I could, couldn't I think about doing it full-time? Who gives a damn whether an author is married, single or living in sin?"

She said, in an incisive voice, "Cut that out, Davy! Write as much as you like. Make as much money as you can, and jolly good luck to you. But stay with what you're doing. I know you far better than you know yourself, and you wouldn't enjoy doing anything else, no matter how successful you were. They're paging me now, darling. I can't stay, except to say thank you over and over again, and how terribly pleased I am for you. Goodbye, darling, darling Davy."

She rang off and he sat there with one hand holding the receiver, the other resting on the small pile of books, considering the unequivocality of her advice, and wondering how she could be so sure of his vocation when she was not in the least sure of her own. She had predecessors in this field. Both Beth and Julia Darbyshire had given him the same advice, and usually, when the ride was smooth, he found himself in agreement with them. But four years under Alcock had gone some way towards undermining his confidence. Now he was not at all sure. It would depend, he supposed, on how Bamfylde lurched into the new year, when the Governors met again to fill the vacuum. Until then there seemed no profit in seeking a hard decision. It was a time, surely, to drift along with the tide.

He went over to the bookcase and pulled out a copy of *Who's Who*, thumbing through the flimsy leaves until he located 'Ellicott, John Ernest; historian and author...' with a long list of books to his credit. He even recognised the title of one that he had read and enjoyed. "So much for chaps who write books," he said aloud. "I didn't even remember the author's name," and for some reason this made him chuckle. He put two copies of the book in his bookcase between Oman and Macaulay, picked up those destined for Barnaby and Howarth, and went down the stairs whistling. "Queer that," he thought, as he crossed the empty quad on his way to relieve Barnaby. "I often used to whistle my way down these steps in Algy's day, but I stopped doing it when Alcock took over. Maybe it's the end of the tunnel."

CHAPTER FOUR

I

He had no difficulty in recognising the pattern. Ever since he climbed the winding road from Bamfylde Bridge Halt for the very first time, it had forever reasserted itself, a personal within a national cycle, so that he could always see Bamfylde and the outside world as reflections of one another, hope countering disappointment, slump following boom, pain giving way to pleasure, failure to modest triumph.

The term, after such a gloomy start, was settling down to a minor boom, with Bamfylde back on course under Algy's caretaker administration, with the surprising success of the book and the queer, quirkish satisfaction that it brought when he realised staff and boys took pride in his achievement. And after that, in mid-October, Chris's amazing rally in South Mendips, where she too made headlines, with her unexpectedly high turnout against impossible odds, the Liberal pushed into third place, and a total of eleven thousand, four hundred and two votes.

There had never been the slightest hope of victory. All over the country Labour strongholds were falling, as the electorate opted for business as usual (whatever that meant) and the economies of the 'National' government were approved by all who were not directly savaged by them. The Government was back with four hundred and ninety-nine seats, Labour losing a total of two hundred and thirteen, including those of thirty-four ex-ministers. Socialism was in retreat everywhere and yet, in South Mendips, that had returned a Tory by mammoth majorities ever since the earliest days of extended suffrage, a slip of a girl beat the Liberal by over a thousand votes and cut the overall Tory majority by fifteen hundred.

He phoned the day after the election to congratulate her, finding that she was naïvely proud of her achievement. "It's almost as good as being elected," she told him excitedly, and added that she had had a telegram of congratulations from Transport House, together with a promise that they would set about finding her a constituency where her chances of getting elected would be appreciably improved.

"Will you accept, after so much groundwork right where you are?" and she said she would think about it, for that, after all, was politics.

After that the term slipped by, with nothing much to distinguish it from any other term this time of year. The weather worsened. Flurries of sleet slashed down from the moor, and all the lanes following the river valleys became shin-deep in red porridge, making it impossible for leaders to maintain average times during the runs. David still went out with them, arriving back in the quad in the winter twilight wet through and plastered from head to foot with Exmoor mud. The area between the rugby posts became a quagmire, scrums slithering across in a mad, splashing frolic whenever the weaker side lost anchorage in the mire. Sometimes you could hardly follow a game through the curtain of mud and every other pass was fumbled as the three-quarters dropped the soggy ball. Then the frost came, with every hedgerow hawthorn bush transformed into a chandelier and a cloud of breath rising over the house warm-up runs like vapour over cattle, and everyone blowing on his hands and jostling for seats nearest to the defective hot-water pipes, that gurgled like a gourmand's belly, giving the professional time-wasters any amount of excuses to practise their craft.

Coxe, inspirer of Towser's headboard, found a half-frozen blackbird up in the planty and restored to it the power of flight. The sick-room was full, the matron irritably busy. Skelton, notable cricketer, left at very short notice to take a job in Christchurch, New Zealand, embarrassing himself and everybody else by piping his eye at a farewell supper in Nicolson's. Barnaby sympathised. "Poor chap's been here since he was nine. As a Sunsetter, it's the only home he's ever known. Must be damned frightening being uprooted by a telegram, and sent halfway across the world to muddle along among strangers." Barnaby was more discerning, David thought, than most people would have you believe.

Heffling, poor wight, broke a wrist when tackled by the visiting full back on frozen ground far out on the touchline, and had to be driven to hospital over treacherous roads by Molyneux—the small change of a term, but the big pay-off was on its way so far as David was concerned. In the last week of term, while David was superintending the unblocking of a frozen drain in the forecourt, he saw Sir Rufus Creighton drive up in his Daimler and give him a distant nod, descending a moment later to make his way into the head's house without a backward glance.

He thought, "That old brown nut still has it in for me, despite his qualified support the day Alcock died—probably regards me as responsible for it, the way I did myself when it happened," but then Algy bobbed out, pink-cheeked and excited, saying, "Leave that infernal drain, P.J.! Let the outside staff see to it. Chairman wants a word with you. I'll get Rigby to bring in coffee at break-time and rejoin you then."

"Hi, wait! What's this in aid of?" he demanded, but Algy was giving nothing away. "Not my pigeon," he said, "I'm only the caretaker here, old son!" and skipped away, moving, David thought, more like a first-termer trying to keep the blood-circulating than a parson in his seventies.

*　　*　　*

Sir Rufus was seated in what Algy called 'The Privileged Culprit's Chair', at angles to the study desk. It was a chair covered with petit-point, used by parents, members of the staff being consulted, and seniors being lectured by the head. Junior or Middle School defaulters were never asked to sit in here. "They wouldn't know what to do with their hands and feet," Algy had once told him. "They much prefer to face the music standing." The old judge still looked like Buddha, his smooth brown flesh stretched tightly over his skull, his mottled hands tidily folded, as in prayer or meditation. The mark of his years in the East lurked in posture and sunken eyes. He said, quietly, "Take a seat, Powlett-Jones. Behind the desk, please." Then, surprisingly, "Do you smoke?"

"Yes, Sir Rufus."

"Try one of these? Burmese. I indulge once a day, after

dinner. One now would give me heartburn. I have them sent, you know, in boxes of one hundred. All the way from Rangoon."

David accepted one of his cheroots and found it very strong. Sir Rufus, who seemed in no hurry, waited for it to draw. "Well?"

"It's . . . er . . . very good, Sir Rufus."

"I think so. Never could be bothered with whiffs. If you like to smoke then smoke the leaf, as God intended. Don't poison yourself with chemical products, hashed up in Nottingham or Bristol." He paused, looking down at his brown, wrinkled hands, splashed with age spots. Then, raising his head, "When Herries retired a few years ago you had hopes of succeeding him, I recall?"

"No real hope, sir."

"But you applied."

"I was talked into it."

"Indeed? By whom? By Herries?"

"Not really. By Brigadier Cooper for one, by Mr. Howarth for another. But I realise now that I applied against my better judgment."

"You wouldn't back yourself to take over here?"

It took him getting on for a minute to absorb the shock. Then he said, carefully, "It isn't that, sir. But I see, looking back, that my original application was a brash gesture on my part. I had only been teaching for nine years, and needed a great deal more experience."

"I see. And now?"

He smiled. "Well, I've had four years' more experience. And I'm that much older and wiser."

The little man pondered a moment. Then, with the greatest deliberation, he drew a folded sheet of paper from his inside pocket and spread it out on his knees. With a sense of shock David recognised it as Alcock's unfinished letter. Sir Rufus said, "Dr. Willoughby passed it to me. It was correct of you to give it to him. Some men, I think, would have hesitated to do that in the circumstances."

"I was tempted myself, sir."

"Ah, I daresay. However, it tells us a good deal, I think."

"Sir?"

"I don't see why I shouldn't be as frank with you as you have been with me. I consider we made a haphazard choice as regards Mr. Alcock. We shirked the issue. We owed it to everyone to take more time to probe a little deeper. Do you blame yourself for his death in any way?"

"A little. I was clearly a contributory factor."

"That's nonsense, Powlett-Jones, and I believe Dr. Willoughby told you so at the time."

"Yes, he did."

"Well, then, oblige me by putting it out of mind. Alcock was a very sick man and deliberately concealed the fact. The point is, how would you feel about taking over as deputy here? Until the next full meeting of the Board in March?"

"Deputy? You mean, take Mr. Herries's place for the time being?"

"Not exactly. To deputise with confirmation in mind. As a near-certainty, I should add."

It had come. After all this time. Right out of the blue, on a frosty December morning, getting on for fourteen years since he had first sat in this room, and shared Algy's sorrow over the slaughter of the 1913 Fifteen. He was lost for words. His hands shook a little, reminding him again of that first interview, half a lifetime ago it seemed. Before Beth. Before Chris. Before Alcock and the dragging weight of Alcock's corpse in his arms. He stammered, at last, "I . . . I'd like that more than anything in the world, Sir Rufus. It's extremely kind of you to make the offer."

"It isn't an offer in that sense. I can't make it official. You realise that, I hope?"

"Naturally, sir."

"It would have to have the full approval of the Governing Body. But . . ." he came as near to smiling as was possible with that taut, brown skin—"I have a feeling that could be managed. With tact and gentle persuasion. I'll go farther and risk getting myself into a scrape. In your place, Powlett-Jones, I would take it as read. Take over from today and see the term out. I'll accept full responsibility for that. But first, are there any conditions on your part?"

"Conditions?"

"Preferences, then?"

He suddenly realised there was one. "I'd like to go on teaching, sir, other obligations permitting. The Upper School at least. And perhaps one period a week in Middle and Lower Schools. I would confine myself to current affairs."

"That could be arranged. We should have to get a junior for history, of course. Anything else?"

"I . . . er . . . don't know exactly how to put this, sir, or not without seeming presumptuous. I'm sure you must be aware of my political outlook. I wouldn't preach it in class. I never have, or only in the very broadest sense, despite anything you might have heard to the contrary. But I do have to feel free as regards my deep personal convictions. I said nothing about them at the time because they seemed to me irrelevant, but there was friction concerning them between Mr. Alcock and myself, especially after I appeared on a Socialist platform a hundred miles from here."

Sir Rufus placed his finger-tips together. "I know about that. I wouldn't be much of a Chairman if I didn't, would I? But we're looking for someone who cares more deeply for the school than any segment or faction in the world outside. I have it in mind that is true of you. Isn't that so?"

"Yes, it is."

"I also happen to know how you came by those convictions, Powlett-Jones, and they seem relevant to me. In fact, I tell myself that had I been reared in a Welsh valley, and seen my father and brothers sacrificed to industrial greed, then I would have gone through life as a militant radical. More militant than you, probably. It's mostly a matter of milieu, and mine happened to be different. Cushioned . . . very conformist. But a judge learns to evaluate each factor objectively. Speaking personally, all I would require is a pledge that you don't embarrass us on home ground. What you do well beyond that, in the exercising of your democratic privilege, is entirely your own concern. You're a free-born Englishman—I beg your pardon, Welshman. Many good Welshmen have sacrificed their lives for the liberty of conscience you demand. Who am I to deny it?" He paused, as though to give David time to digest this, but went on; "I'm more than twice your age, Powlett-Jones. I'm older even than Herries, and I've seen a great deal in my time.

Tyrannies overthrown, new ones set up. The ebb and flow of reforms and repressions in many parts of the world. I have few real convictions left, but I can think of one. This country, although it still has a great deal to learn, is the flower of the flock as regards the theory and practice of maintaining a free society. Its party politics, to me, are a charade. They have a part to play in the democratic process but they remain a charade. This is going to be a stormy decade, and will almost certainly end in a drawing together of all shades of political opinion, here in Britain at least. At a time like this we need flexibility, particularly if our work takes us among growing boys, with their way to make in the world. I think you're flexible enough. More flexible than most. There's the bell. I believe Herries promised us some coffee."

"Rigby is brewing it now, sir."

"Good. Then I think I'll break my rule and smoke one of those cheroots of mine," and he took out his worn leather cigar-case, snipped the end with a cutter and lit up, blowing a thin stream of smoke towards Alcock's freshly distempered ceiling. "This is a pleasant room," he said. "I've always thought so. But its original atmosphere needs replacing, wouldn't you say?"

"Yes, Sir Rufus, and I have plans for it."

Algy bustled in after a perfunctory knock, carrying the coffee tray. On his heels came Rigby, with a bottle of Old Boys' sherry, miraculously restored to the cellarette in the parlour. "Had a notion we should want to drink a toast," he said. "Pour it, Rigby, there's a good chap. Do you remember that toast we drank in the parlour to your twins, P.J.? My word, that was a turn-up for the Bamfylde book! Won't happen again in my lifetime."

With a kind of wonder David watched him hand round the coffee while Rigby, ceremonious as a small-town mayor, filled the sherry glasses.

II

There was a price, of course. He was under no illusions regarding that, and was called upon to pay the first instalment only a week or two later, when, on Christmas Eve, he met Chris by appointment outside Piccadilly Underground, and took her to dinner at a restaurant Howarth had introduced to him years ago, a quiet place off Leicester Square, renowned for its cuisine.

It had been a hectic eight days, with the school breaking up, the Sunsetters' Christmas to be arranged, Grace to convey to Elmer's End (it was Grannie Marwood's 'turn' that year), and all manner of plans sketched out pending his return to school the day after Boxing Day, for he wanted plenty of time to work on his blueprints.

It was a notable end-of-term, one of the liveliest he remembered, as he stood on the steps of the head's house in the forecourt, and watched the school bone-shaker take its final load down to the station at the tail of a procession of private cars, driven by parents who had called to collect their sons. Trunks and hand luggage were trundled out, roped and labelled, the turmoil beginning before it was light, with any number of mufflered boys coming and going, shouting their usual farewell quips.

"Have a good hols, sir!"

"Don't forget matron's present, sir!" Matron was getting married, late in life, and the boys had collected for a leaving present she was unable to accept in person.

"I'm going to miss Grace like nobody's business, sir!"—this from Sax Hoskins, who was also leaving them, and finally Heffling, shaking hands with his left because of his plastered wrist, "I've persuaded the pater to let me stay on until July, sir. Wrote the day I heard what had happened. I had to bluff. He thinks I'm dead set on having another go at the Cambridge but it's the cricket really, sir."

It was touching, he thought, how they had all seemed to come alive again and that within an hour of the news leaking that he would be taking over, and he wondered, a little anxiously, if he would be able to justify their ebullience and goodwill, or whether, once they had adapted to his headship, they would begin to keep their distance, as they always had with Alcock. Well, that was up to him, he supposed, and it might be a good idea to regard the term ahead as a honeymoon period. He had his own innovations in mind and not all of them would be popular. Besides, it was well known that he was not yet officially appointed, so they had every right to regard him as a caretaker's caretaker, standing in for Algy, whom many would not recall as the resident occupier of the house at his back.

Grace came down, looking very pretty, he thought, in her Red Riding Hood cape, trimmed with fur. She seemed to have shot from childhood to full girlhood in a term and was growing more like Beth every day. Her limp was almost unnoticeable now, unless you studied her walk from a distance. Sax swore that she could out-foxtrot any of his holiday partners, whereas Winterbourne, who had offered to collect her, and bring her back from Elmer's End on January 14th, the day of reassembly, was enthusiastic concerning her ability to capture a mood of the moor with her brush. "Especially in spring," he told David one night, when they were glancing through her sketches. "You see, she's a spring painter. There's absolute honesty in every sketch she makes between March and June, but after that . . . I don't know . . . she loses the trick. They might be anyone's watercolours."

There was significance here, he supposed. Grace had always seemed a springtime person, ever since he had lifted her from the taxi that brought her back from that Kentish convalescent home five years ago. For him, as for Winterbourne, Hoskins, and even for young Coxe, the embryo vet, she carried the promise of the primrose and the daffodil whenever she moved among all these boisterous young ruffians, indeed, she introduced a little extra fragrance into the place at all seasons of the year, and although he knew it was time she became a weekly boarder over at Challacombe, he still delayed making the change. One of the things he had looked forward to most was a crumpet tea with Grace, when winter dusk was closing in on the moor. He made a rapid check of her exact age as she ran down the steps, carrying a book of patterns she had been inspecting, prior to replacing Alcock's neutral curtains. Eleven years, eight months, from the day he dashed up these same steps in response to Stratton-Forbes' annunciation of her arrival, down at the long-jump pit. She looked older. Around thirteen, he would say, but then, she had always seemed mentally and physically mature after that tight-rope walk between life and death when she was a mite of five.

She said, in between his farewells of boys, "Never mind them a minute, Daddy. This is most important. Rigby is going to order the curtains for us when he goes into Challacombe tomorrow. Which do you prefer? I've pinned back the two I like best, the rose pink and the primrose yellow."

"Primrose yellow," he said without hesitation. "It's you, Grace."

She ran up the steps again and he resumed his farewells. It was going to take a lot of getting used to, this ordering and rearranging of what he never ceased to think of as Algy Herries's house. The last car sped away, its tyres scattering gravel. A few Sunsetters (they always looked forlorn at this moment of term) emerged from Big School arch with a ball for a puntabout, and he spared them a sympathetic thought, boys with parents at the ends of the earth, thinking of them no doubt at this time of year. Then he remembered that Barnaby, who was spending Christmas at school, had promised to take them all into Challacombe to see a gangster picture at the Capitol Cinema this afternoon, and bent his mind to his own affairs. They promised to keep him pretty well occupied until he left for town on the twenty-third.

*   *   *

She looked her usual, pert self as she emerged from the Regent Street exit at six o'clock sharp on Christmas Eve. She had bought herself a pair of Russian calf boots and they looked very fetching on her long, pretty legs. She had matched them with a Cossack-type hat, perched at an angle, so that he thought, "She looks more like a well-heeled Tory's wife than the only Socialist candidate to emerge with credit from that shambles", and told her so, as soon as she had kissed him.

"Thank you, sir. Very civil of you, sir! I've never actually kissed a headmaster before, although I had my bottom pinched by one in Yorkshire. 'The Octopus' we used to call him at Chapel. You look pretty spry yourself, Davy darling. Where do we celebrate? I'm going to drink half a bottle of champagne tonight, I promise you!"

They walked along Coventry Street to Leicester Square and all the way she held his arm, her touch giving their relationship a permanence it had not had on earlier occasions. Her conversation was sustained but brittle, a shade too chirpy, he thought, and this was confirmed two hours later, when the cadaverous waiter, who had been hovering about them all evening, bustled away to attend to a stage party in the far corner of the room.

"You've got something to tell me yourself," he said. "You've been saving it for the right moment," and suddenly she looked disconcerted and said, staring hard at her glass, "Yes, I have, but I should have known one can't keep guilty secrets from old Pow-Wow. It's a plan, at least, you could think of it as that. It might help. I don't know. It'll depend on you, I suppose. Like everything else in the end."

He said, dismally, "Let's hear it. At least we've wined and dined."

"It's two things, really, one hinging on the other. One is an offer I've had—no, not of a good constituency, but an exchange, under a Labour Party Educational Trust, the Jesmond Foundation. I've been selected as the likeliest young hopeful to take advantage of a year at Montreal University. They have very advanced syllabuses over there—far wider in scope than most of ours. I'm told I could get a Canadian degree in a year. Not that that means much in academic terms, but from the practical viewpoint it could do me a lot of good, and give me the edge on most candidates. Providing I emerged with credit."

The prospect of not seeing her for a year dismayed him. In the months ahead he was going to need her as much as she had needed him before the election.

"How do *you* feel about it? Honestly. No hedging."

"I should enjoy it, if I could separate it from you, Davy."

"But we can't separate it, can we?"

"It might be wise to try. At least for a year."

"Say exactly what's in your mind."

"You know what's in my mind. What's been in my mind concerning you for long enough. The plain truth is, Davy, you simply can't risk an affaire with me. I believe you know that but won't face it. Not that I blame you. I have enough trouble doing it myself."

"Hasn't it occurred to you that you might be exaggerating the risks?"

"No. It hasn't and it won't. Listen here, Davy. I'll draw a picture for you. We go on seeing one another—not as close friends, that's quite another thing, but as lovers. Okay, we're careful. We keep a sharp lookout. We only meet in out-of-the-way places. That's a dreary enough prospect, but we'd cope, I daresay, until the unlucky moment. Don't say it mightn't come because it would. Hundreds of boys pass through your hands. Sooner or later we'd run into one and he'd talk. 'Hi, Porky, what do you know? I ran into old Pow-Wow with that cousin of Ridgeway's. He's doing okay. They were staying as man and wife at the same hotel!' The snippet is relayed and sooner or later a parent comes to hear of it. She passes it on, and it gets expanded a little. 'But I *know* her! A married girl, with a husband somewhere, the one who turned her back on her family to stand as a Socialist. Of course, Powlett-Jones is that way himself, isn't he?' From there it's anybody's guess. All I know is that it would damage you, might even bring you down, seeing that all Bamfylde parents are Tories. Do you want me to let my imagination run ahead?"

"No," he said, "there's something in what you say. I'd be a fool to deny it."

"Well, then . . ."

"That's the rub, Chris, the 'Well, then . . .?' What are you really saying? That now I'm acting head of Bamfylde, with every prospect of it being made official, we should stop seeing one another? Break it off? Finish?"

She said, tracing a pattern in breadcrumbs, "I'm saying we should give this break we've both had a fair chance. For a year at any rate. You won't miss me nearly as much as you think you will. You'll be fully stretched in that job."

"And you?"

"I'll get by."

"And a year from now?"

"All kinds of things can happen in a year. A year ago we hadn't even met."

"You said something about a plan."

"A sort of plan. It's sheer coincidence this offer leads to Canada. Rowley was still in Canada the last time I heard."

"Where does that take us? Assuming he's still there, and assuming you get to see him and talk to him?"

"I don't know, Davy. How could I know? It's getting on for three years since I set eyes on him."

"*I* know, Chris. You could sue him after seven. That's four years from now, and God knows how long after that the divorce comes along. I'll be forty and you'll be over thirty. You once mentioned children."

"Don't make it harder, Davy."

"Is that possible?"

"Yes, it is possible. You've got what you've always wanted and worked for, and I'm making progress. How many can say as much in their mid-thirties and late twenties?"

"It isn't enough. Not for me."

"It'll have to be, Davy. At least for the time being. Deep down you know that."

The sparkle had gone from the evening. Across the restaurant the stage party was erupting. Jokes and laughter emerged from it and the place was filling with customers, most of them oiled with Christmas cheer. Gloominess invaded him, making objective thought and discussion all but impossible. First Beth, then Alcock and now this. And away behind that a serious-eyed boy coming home with his satchel, to be told at a street corner that his father and two brothers had died underground. And after that the trenches. Three unspeakable years of trudging to and fro across a desolate swamp, three years of seeing friends torn and mutilated. When the hell did life settle and lie on an even keel? When could a man hope to enjoy the fruits of personal fulfilment, of the kind he had glimpsed so briefly, in the early days of his marriage? He said beckoning the waiter, "What choice do I have? What choice do I ever have?" and she said, "How about me, Davy?"

"You're making the decision."

"No, I'm not, circumstances are. All I'm doing is facing them. Or trying to, and you aren't helping much. It isn't like you. I always took you for a fighter."

"I'm bloody well sick of fighting. Sick to death of it. Some way this has to be resolved. If it isn't we'll drift apart." He remembered Howarth, husked and emotionally sterile at

fifty, showing him that photograph of Amy Crispin, the day
he received her legacy. Well he could level with Howarth at
around forty. He, too, would have photographs tucked away
in a drawer, one of Beth, one of her. Three, if you counted
Julia Darbyshire.

"I'll write," she said, "often, and telling you everything.
It's the best of a bad job."

"Yes, it is," he said, "but you've got more guts than I have.
Or maybe less need."

"Need? No, Davy, we're even on that score. God knows,
there have been times lately when I would have risked everything to spend one night in your arms. That night before the
election was only one of them."

"It's more than that with me. That way a man can manage.
Howarth has, and Barnaby has or seems to. Even I did for a
long time after Beth. It's sharing, unloading, talking things
out with someone who matters, understands. I'm supposed
to do all that on paper from here on. Indefinitely."

"Not indefinitely, Davy. Only until you've had a sporting
chance to concentrate on something you love. You think of
me as important and so I am, but not so important as that."

They left it there. She was staying in the flat of a university
friend at Cricklewood. There was no question of them going
there, and none of taking her home to the Marwoods, at
Elmer's End. They could book in somewhere, but he did not
fancy Grace waking on Christmas morning and asking where
he was. She walked him down to Charing Cross, saying she
could get a bus or tube any old time. In forty-eight hours he
would be on his way back to Bamfylde and she, he supposed,
would be making ready for the Canadian adventure. At the
barrier he kissed her, noticing that her cheeks were wet and
that she had difficulty in speaking. Compassion, of the kind
he had felt for her after that rowdy meeting, returned to
him.

"It's still a case of hanging on, of waiting for the next spin
of the wheel. I can't say any more just now. Will you be
going back to Bilhampton before you take off?"

"If I do I'll ring. I'll ring, anyway, wherever I am. I can
cope when you're at a distance."

He left her then, sensing that she preferred it, but knowing that she was watching him move along the platform to catch yet another train. Bamfylde, like Paris, he had once told her, was worth a mass. But was it, now that he had it under his hand?

* * *

He was able, to his own surprise, to keep thoughts of her at a safe distance during the next few weeks. Bamfylde engulfed him like a long, rumbling avalanche, a clamorous torrent of letters, decisions, long- and short-term plans, the least of which was that perennial bugbear of the schoolmaster, the timetable.

Throughout the early part of January he worked alone, spending long hours in Algy's old study. When he could escape he set out on tours that took him into every nook and cranny of the great sprawling place, noting down its deficiencies, conjuring with changes, adjustments and adaptations, and getting an inspiration now and again from all he saw and remembered.

One came when he turned out the contents of Alcock's study cupboard and came across the cane he had inherited from Algy. He tossed it aside, with a pile of other rubbish. There would be no question of him beating mischief out of Bamfeldians. He made up his mind as to that long ago. Neither Algy nor Alcock, to do them justice, had been floggers, in the old tradition of headmasters and towards the end of his long reign Algy had all but discarded corporal punishment, but the right to beat Junior and Middle School boys was still reserved by senior prefects. Alcock had preferred outright expulsion for what he regarded as major crimes, and subtle humiliations for minor infringements.

David, over the years, had given a good deal of thought to the maintenance of discipline, accepting the fact that it wasn't something to which spot decisions could be applied. Every boy varied as did every offence to some extent. What he aimed at—an ideal, he supposed—was the maximum use of the average boy's response to fair play, to seeing authority's point of view, accepting reproof and apologising with good grace. But every now and again one ran across a boy totally unresponsive to this approach. Then, if one ruled out corporal punishment, what did one do? How did one safe-guard the system?

He came up with an experimental idea, one that seemed worth exploring. The institution of a forum of peers, based on where the culprit was lodged. Several such committees might be set up, with jurors voted in, term by term, by boys themselves, sitting under the chairmanship of the current house prefect. As to penalties, here again he opposed the principle of boy beating boy, any boy. In a majority of cases it didn't matter a jot but if the boy at the receiving end was sensitive, or the prefect at the distributing end a bully, it could do untold harm. The whole thing was too fallible and in its place there would have to be a range of sanctions, all the way from the withdrawal of privileges to a vote of censure, expressing disapproval of the majority. It was an idea that Barnaby, with his easy access to the wisdom of the Ancients, might find workable and he made a note of it in his memoranda book.

Scores of random thoughts were finding their way into what Grace was already calling The-Book-From-Which-There's-No-Rubbing-Out. A resolve to tap Old Boys' funds for a gymnasium to replace the old covered playground. An additional classroom block, abutting Big School, that would, in itself, greatly simplify the timetable. Concrete litter disposal units designed to put an end to those stinking bonfires Westacott was always building down by the piggeries. Revival of the Choral Society, that had languished under Alcock. Upgrading of the Owl Society into a Sixth Form Club. Studies, if they could be squeezed in somewhere, for the Upper Fifth. A thorough turnout and restocking of the library. And, with Algy's help, revival of the annual Gilbert and Sullivan opera, an event that had never failed to fill a vacuum in the Michaelmas term, when the days were at their shortest and the evenings not wholly devoted to prep.

Prep was another aspect of the system he hoped to revise. He had unpleasant memories of homework in his Grammar School days, of sitting hunched in the fireless parlour with a mountain of work to get through, and organised periods of evening prep such as existed in the routine of most boarding schools, had been an improvement on this. It had its faults, however, especially in summer term. It might be an improvement to introduce a period-length spell of early morning prep, between April and July, and possibly through the first weeks of the Michaelmas term. Thus evening prep would be shortened, and boys freed for communal activities, not necessarily aligned with sport.

There were, he soon discovered, whole new vistas to be explored, and much would depend on available funds, no doubt. He had no more than a working knowledge of the school's finances, and a talk with Redcliffe, the bursar, proved depressing.

"We've always run on a tight budget," Redcliffe said. "So tight that I confess I was frightened when I took over from Mr. Shawn, early last year. The fees are too low, if you want my opinion, Headmaster."

It would take time, he thought, to adjust to this form of address. Somehow he was unable to rid himself of the notion that his leg was being pulled. He said, "There's no need to call me 'Headmaster' when we're alone, Redcliffe. I know Alcock insisted on it but I don't. Will you pass that around? It's embarrassing to have to tell everyone separately."

Redcliffe, a young, eager man, looked flustered but said, with a smile, "Er . . . what exactly do we call you, sir?"

"Well, it can hardly be what every boy from the Second Form up calls me behind my back and the Old Boys to my face, Pow-Wow, that is. How about taking a tip from Barnaby and Howarth? They've settled for P.J. and it looks to me as if you and I have got a lot of conspiratorial work ahead of us. Do you think the majority of parents would stand for a hoist in fees?"

"Yes, I do," Redcliffe said, unequivocally. "It would be a matter for the Governors and would need the approval of the Ministry, of course, but there wouldn't be much difficulty. I could prepare a case for you."

"You do that," David said, "and we'll try it on the dog later in the term. Let me have a look at the waiting-list."

The waiting-list was even more depressing, the lowest, according to Redcliffe's summary, since 1921. The graph had risen steadily up to a peak in 1929, the second year of Alcock's administration, but then, just as Howarth had predicted, Bamfylde had begun to feel the pinch of the Depression. There had been a slow falling off in 1930, and a steep plunge in 1931. This would have to be considered in relation to any proposed increase in fees.

Already he had learned the trick of dividing his problems into categories of the kind that encouraged the enlistment of one confidant, selected in advance. Thus, major changes such as those he was now discussing with Redcliffe, demanded the shrewdness and experience of Howarth, but what he thought of as climatic changes, like a new approach to discipline, demanded the more flexible approach of a mind like Barnaby's. He soon made a friend of the newly appointed music master, Renshaw-Smith, whom he tackled about the revitalisation of the Choral Society.

Renshaw-Smith, a young man with a narrow face, thinning hair and a sharp, predatory nose, always put him in mind of a fledgling sparrow-hawk, but although shy and inclined to be self-effacing, he responded to encouragement. When David told him of his intentions he said, eagerly, "That's good news, Headmaster. We've some very promising trebles and at least two good tenors. I was wondering, would you think it too ambitious to start training a choir for the Devon Musical Festival, in April? At my last school we won high placings, although of course, we had girls there, Melbourne House being co-ed. I really would like to try."

"Try by all means," David told him. "You'll have the whole of the Lent term to bring them on. Who is your best tenor, by the way?"

"Dobson, without a doubt, and keen to improve."

"Really? I would have said he was the hairy outdoor type but I'll tell you why I asked. I'm hoping to revive the annual Gilbert and Sullivan. We were famous for them in Mr. Herries's time. Would Gilbert and Sullivan be too lowbrow for you?"

Renshaw-Smith looked shocked. "No, indeed, Headmaster. Sullivan wrote some excellent light music, and I know about the Bamfylde operas. I've seen the photographs and old scores. Mr. Gibbs gave them to me."

"Would you enjoy getting some kind of orchestra together for a production next December? It's a chore, I warn you. We hold the auditions in summer, and rehearse every night throughout Michaelmas term."

"I should enjoy it. I found time hang rather heavily last term. You see, Melbourne House was close to Bristol, and I had most of my evenings free. I miss the opportunity of getting to a concert now and again and this place . . . well, it is something of a wilderness, isn't it?"

"It's seemed that way lately," David said, "but it never did in Herries's time. We made our own entertainment and a lot of it was very stimulating. I'm going to do my damndest to start everything up again, but I should have to rely on your help, Renshaw-Smith."

"Oh, but you can," Renshaw-Smith said, seeming to peck with excitement, and David left him, wondering if he knew the boys referred to him as 'Pecker' and had done, since the day of his arrival.

He went next to Howarth to discuss finance in relation to building plans. "I don't intend to tinker, like the Stoic. I've always believed in Rothschild's dictum—'Buy on a falling market'. With a shrinking waiting-list we need to offer something extra, and get plans for an extension into the new prospectus. God knows, that old one needs rewriting. It always reminds one of a spa holiday guide, about the time of Victoria's Jubilee."

"And we thought of the Noble Stoic as a new broom," Howarth said, wryly. "Well, I'm with you by and large. You recall I foresaw this shortage of cash reacting on us, but don't talk to me about retrenchment. I never did trust that word. It's usually a sluggard's euphemism for parsimony and cowardice. Still, it all comes down to cash in the end, and how the devil do you hope to raise the ten thousand or more that a new classroom block and gymnasium will cost you?"

"From the Old Boys. There's a couple of thousand in the kitty. It's been accumulating and I'm planning a big appeal next Whitsun, when I can corner more than a hundred O.B.s at their annual meeting."

"You honestly believe you can squeeze eight thousand pounds out of Old Boys? Good God, man, half of them are still looking for jobs, or living on their parents' fat. Boyer, for instance, he's still on his uppers, isn't he?"

Boyer was, or more or less. He had come down with a good enough degree two years ago but had since had to make do with starveling appointments in private schools. He wrote, from time to time, but he had not revisited the school and David had the impression he would find it difficult to scrape together the rail fare from the far north. He said, "I'll get the money somehow but it would help if you took over as O.B. secretary. I've been doing it for six years now, and no complaints, but I don't see how I can combine it with the headship. After all, Howarth, who was it pushed me into this job in the first place?"

"Me," said Howarth, with one of his frosty smiles, "but my sponsorship went off at half-cock. I don't mind admitting I had nothing whatever to do with this latest turn-up. That was all Algy's doing, or Algy's and Doc Willoughby's."

"Willoughby got at Sir Rufus?"

"How do you think our respected Chairman came by that bit of evidence you pocketed from Alcock's desk, the night he died? Willoughby took it to Algy and they hatched the plot between them. They asked Sir Rufus over to dinner, filled him with old port, and set him to work on the waverers. But for God's sake don't let them know I told you and don't thank Willoughby yourself. He's like me that way. Feels a damned fool if he's caught out doing a good turn."

They began to fit together, all the pieces of the jigsaw that had been assembling from the moment of Alcock's death, but it seemed unlikely now that he would ever know just how the final picture emerged as a likeness of himself. Howarth was right, however, it would never do to probe too deeply. All the same, the information made him glow a little. It meant that he had the full trust of at least two dedicated Bamfeldians apart from Howarth's steady patronage.

He said, "I always knew you approved, Howarth, but how does old Barnaby feel about it? After all, he's senior to me, and was piqued when I pipped him as housemaster," but Howarth said, "Barnaby's purring, so leave him be. He's happy enough. A house is as much as he cares to handle. Besides, he's like me. Too idle to envy you your job. It wouldn't surprise me if, in a year or so, we didn't start wishing to God that you'd run out of steam."

"Will you take over that Old Boys' job *pro tem*?"

"Just long enough to tide you over. Then one of the younger chaps can have it, and I'll put my feet up until I retire. Only another four years, thank God."

"I can't imagine this place without your crustiness to give it savour. What will you do then, Howarth?"

"Go abroad and die in the sun," Howarth said. "I often ask myself why the devil a sane man, with money in the bank, should spend eight months of the year with his coat collar up and his toes to a gas-fire."

* * *

He shelved his forum idea for the time being. It needed more thought, and he was not yet ready to take either Barnaby or Howarth into his confidence. Instinct told him that he would need to win over some of the younger masters, especially Scott, a stern disciplinarian, who had come to them from a prestigious school to replace Carter on the science side and take his place as Outram's housemaster. Scott was forty-eight, and a cut above their usual replacements. He was here, it was said, because of his chest, that played him up in the damp Thames valley, and a somewhat prickly little man. The best approach to him, David thought, would be a juicy carrot in the form of an improved laboratory, and science was low on his list of priorities just now.

There was one other thing, however, concerning which he consulted nobody. The night before the new term began he checked through his records and traced Hislop's home number, for Hislop, penalised for straightforwardness over the loss of his ill-gotten gains as school bookmaker, was still on his conscience.

The shrewish voice of Mrs. Hislop answered the phone and he was glad it was her and not Hislop's father. He said, "Mrs. Hislop? It's Powlett-Jones, calling from Bamfylde. You remember me, I hope?"

"I remember you, Mr. Powlett-Jones. I remember everything about that disgraceful business."

"It's about your boy I'm ringing. It may sound presumptuous on my part, but is there any chance of him wanting to return here? He's still only sixteen plus, isn't he? Of course, if you've got him in elsewhere he'll probably be better off where he is, but I'm acting headmaster and I'd like to have him back, if he wants to come."

He heard her sharp intake of breath and waited, letting the prospect of a fresh start for Hislop make its impact. Then she said, "You mean that? You . . . *want* him back?"

"Yes, I do, Mrs. Hislop. You may remember I thought he had been very unfairly dealt with by Mr. Alcock but I could put that right now, providing he undertook to work, and toe the line generally. I always did believe in him."

"Thank you," she said, and then, after a long pause, "He's with a private tutor. He seems keen to study for a short-service commission in the Air Force. That awful business changed him. I don't mean for the worse, maybe the opposite, but well . . . he's never been quite the boy he was when it happened."

"Would you like to discuss it with him? He could go into the Lower Fifth, and I'd keep a sharp eye on him until he settled down. I know he was happy here."

"I don't need to discuss it with him," she said, "although of course I will. I know he would like to come back, particularly under you. He came to understand precisely how you were placed, and that things were very difficult for you at the time."

"'Difficult' is an understatement, Mrs. Hislop. I came close to getting sacked myself more than once. Can I take it that he'll come then?"

"Yes. When exactly?"

"Right away if you can arrange it. It doesn't matter if he's a week or so late starting term. Bring him over yourself if you like, and we'll have tea."

"I'd like that. A week, you say? Sunday? That's the best day for me, on account of the business."

"Sunday will be fine. I'll look forward to it."

"Right." And then, with a little difficulty, "I very much appreciate this, Mr. Powlett-Jones, and I know Rex will. Mr. Hislop will stand on his dignity but leave him to me. Goodbye for now."

"Goodbye, Mrs. Hislop."

He rang off, reflecting that one did not always take the
privileges of power into consideration, but they were there, as
he was beginning to discover. He thought, "I daresay eyebrows will be raised when Hislop shows up but to hell with
that. His reinstatement will make Chris chuckle but she at
least will approve."

And within hours the shut-down Bamfylde dynamo went
into action, with cars and attache-case-carrying railway
arrivals, moving up both drives to converge on the grey
buildings that sat so incongruously on the ridge, palisaded
with leafless trees, moated by seeping fields where veils
of mist deadened every sound, converting Bamfylde into a
battleship alone in a vast, grey-green sea.

For him there had never been a first day of term like this.
It was not merely an occasion for another new boys' tea but
an entirely new beginning, with himself feeling rather like
Keithley, smallest of the new arrivals, who drifted in at dusk,
clutching his overnight case and a plaid rug, and looking as
if, given the least excuse, he would drop everything on the
study floor and flee across the moor. He said, calling to Grace,
"Look after Keithley, Grace, while I check the last batch in.
He's come a long way, haven't you, Keithley?"

"Y-yes, sir . . . from Manchester. Change at Bristol," he
added, a little pompously.

"By George, that's a long journey for a chap your size! And
you made it in one. Bravo! Don't be scared, you're going to
like it here, they all do after a day or two, and my daughter
will show you the ropes once you've had tea and a warm-up
by the fire. He'll be going into Nicolson's, Grace."

"Well, that's a shame," she said. "We've only got three
new ones this term, hardly enough for the cake, but Keithley
could come, couldn't he?"

"My dear girl, they'll all have to come, not just the Havelock new boys. We can't have the head showing house
favourites."

"Havelock's will always be my favourite," she said, but
added, doubtless for Keithley's benefit, "Nicolson's is second-
best."

He left her then, ministering to the encumbered Keithley,
and went out through the quad door to take the first start-of-

term callover by lamplight, for the school's generator batteries were not yet fully charged.

Standing there, on the plinth of the Founder's statue,
where Keithley and his peers would soon be making their
bow, he gripped the clipboard tighter than necessary, aware
of an underswell of emotion and hoping it passed unnoticed
by the very few senior boys who would recall Algy Herries
standing here, on the first evening of every new term. It was
a memorable moment, one to be put under glass, alongside
many others—the Kassava brothers, huddled under that
dormer window three storeys up; the first overtures of peace
between Carter and himself, in the library passage; Algy's
white head emerging from the window under the arcade, to
demand, of little Daffy Jones, who had won the house match
that first spring afternoon, when Ludendorff was still attacking on the Western Front. These memories and many, many
others, standing like pennants on a hard-fought battlefield
and somehow adjusting to the rhythm of the roll-call, so
that he seemed to be checking not merely on the present
but also the past. It made him feel much older than thirty-
five.

PART THREE

ISLAND IN A TORRENT

CHAPTER ONE

I

David Powlett-Jones had always thought of himself as a political animal, and perhaps he was, up to the moment Sir Rufus Creighton offered him the acting headship. After that a streak of parochialism, that had been broadening within him ever since he had been absorbed into Bamfylde, began to spread until the men he had once jested about, stick-in-the-muds like Judy Cordwainer and Rapper Gibbs, became in a sense his prototypes. The overall effect upon him was curious. His personality both narrowed and deepened.

He did not see himself as inward-looking but was honest enough, in reflective moments beside Algy's thinking post, or sitting within earshot of the muted clamour of the quad to, acknowledge a definite shift in the centre of gravity. What happened here under his nose began to assume an importance that someone in close touch with the world outside would have mistaken for extreme insularity.

For a time he resisted it, telling himself that Bamfylde was not really the crossroads of human affairs, that casting round for some means to alleviate little Keithley's homesickness ought not to take precedence over, say, the state of the economy, or the Japanese invasion of Manchuria, but in the end, after a term or two, he had to admit that it did, and soon abandoned any attempt to keep abreast of national and international affairs. Running Bamfylde was a full-time job, even when the parent ship of state was on course. When it looked like foundering, as lately, it was comforting to address himself to the problems at hand and turn his back on the world beyond school bounds.

It was a conscious withdrawal, for the plight of Bamfylde, and the frightful disarray of the world outside, were inseparably linked. His acting headship began at a time when politicians had abandoned all serious attempts to solve the unemployment problem, when processions of sullen men trudged south to the capital to voice their grievances, when America, for so long a country said to be capable of achieving anything, was reeling under the blows dealt by the Wall Street crash of October, 1929, when bizarre adventurers like Ivar Kreuger, Swedish match king, were bankrupting governments, when the optimism of the 'twenties had spent itself and the League of Nations, hope of liberals the world over, was being scuttled by Japan.

These events, remote as most of them were, redounded on Bamfylde, destroying confidence in traditional values and inducing a general shortage of cash. Warned well in advance by the prescient Howarth, David had expected school numbers to fall but the steepness of the drop surprised and dismayed him.

In 1928, shortly after Algy had retired, they had mustered three hundred and ninety-one. By the spring of 1932 they were down to under three hundred, with a greatly reduced waiting list. Parents, having a hard struggle to make ends meet, tended to encourage boys to leave at seventeen, or even sixteen, instead of letting them progress to the Sixth and move on to university. There were noticeably fewer majors and minors on the roll, for often a father whose eldest son had done well at Bamfylde left younger sons at their local grammar schools. The modest increase in fees was paid but the belt-tightening it produced could be seen in the waiting-list. Indeed, the only marginal advantage gained from the slump was the comparative ease in finding trained servants, or masters with academic qualifications that would have gained them more important appointments in better times.

For all this, he turned away from Baldwin's policy of retrenchment, and was aided and abetted by Algy Herries, to whom he went, in the Easter break of his first year.

It was not the first time he had sought Algy's advice. Often, during that first tight-rope term, he lured Algy into his quarters on the excuse of a glass of Old Boys' sherry, and put some problem to him, knowing he could rely on an opinion free of prejudice. He did not invariably follow the advice given but he was always influenced by it. In the case of an appeal to expand he was gratified to discover Algy's views coincided exactly with his own.

"I have always thought," the old man said, revolving sherry glass between forefinger and thumb, "that that chap Danton was the most positive windbag to emerge from the French Revolution. What was it he said, when things were at low ebb, and Brunswick and the emigrés were after his scalp?"

"'The kings of Europe advance against us . . .!'" David prompted, but Algy exclaimed, "Don't tell me! I remember exactly. '. . . We throw at their feet, as gauge of battle, the head of a king!' Rather splendid, wasn't it? Reprehensible, of course, but what a gesture! What a pity his career was cut short by that frightful prig Robespierre."

"I didn't get you here to philosophise on the French Revolution, Algy, but to confirm my opinion that this is a time to attack rather than run for cover. If you agree then I'd be delighted to hear you say so. It's all I need."

"You don't need it all, P.J., for I'm no more than your longstop now and well you know it. You ask me back here out of sentiment, but don't think I fail to appreciate it."

"That's not true, Algy, but let it pass. I've discussed it with Howarth and Barnaby, and they both take a more cautious view. Howarth has been grousing about lack of classroom space for years, but now that our numbers have dropped, and we've got more elbow room, he counsels patience. As for Barnaby, he'll never make an important decision if he can avoid it. The Ancients have taught him to keep an open mind about everything. But you're different. In many ways you're still younger than any of us. All I really need to know is why you favour attacking instead of waiting for better times."

"When you've been sitting in that hot seat as long as I sat in it," Algy said, "you'll learn that the time is never ripe for advance on any one front, let alone all of 'em. Someone will always be around to shout 'Whoa!' to tell you to stay looking instead of leaping. If you pay the least heed to 'em you'll fossilise at fifty. See here, we look at the place now and what do we find? Numbers down, waiting-list shortening, head-wagging all round. Very well, but aren't they very sound

reasons for a special effort, and the right sort of advertising?
Education in the public sector is improving and expanding
all the time. We've got to give a parent something extra to
tempt him to invest in us. I've always believed that although,
as far as the fabric is concerned, I'm the wrong chap to be
lecturing you. Alcock did more for the buildings in four years
than I did in twenty-four, but I was here at a time when
fabric didn't count for much. That's all behind us now.
Parents think their little darlings are entitled to as much
comfort in term as they get in the holidays, at 'Green Gables'
and 'Windy Nook'. Can't have 'em warming their bottoms
against the hot-water pipes, and giving themselves constipa-
tion, or finishing off Saturday's joint with shepherd's pie
and bubble and squeak until Wednesday. They judge a
school on its fabric and its menus. Why, if that cold fish
Alcock hadn't seen to those latrines you would have had the
County Sanitary Inspector breathing down your neck by
now. Just go right ahead with your improvements, and use
every trick in the book to raise the wherewithal. Get the
Governors to sanction a big overdraft if necessary and,
talking of Governors, I'll let you into a secret. I'm taking
Blunt's place on the Board at the start of summer term."

It was excellent news and David greeted it with a schoolboy whoop. "Going on the Board? But that's marvellous!
And here I've been biting my nails and wondering who
would replace that old blockhead."

"Hush now," Algy said, holding out his glass for a refill,
"the distinguished Alderman is hardly cold in his grave,"
but David said, "He was stone cold before he reached it.
He blocked everything and in the end even Carter admitted
we'd made a damned bad bargain enlisting him after the war.
But with you in there, wheedling and cajoling . . ."

"Cajole I often do, but wheedle never. There's a difference,
P.J. Always leave the options open on dignity. Well, now, to
sum up, I take it you'll go for a gym, new science lab and
three new classrooms. That demands a one-storey new wing,
at right angles to Big School. The gymnasium? Simple
matter of roofing over the space between present stables and
fives court. Even I got as far as drawing up plans for that. But
what about the concert hall?"

"Concert hall? Good Lord, suppose we could afford one, where would it go?"

"Cheapest way would be to make the new wing a two-storey block, with the hall on the ground floor and a flight of steps giving access to the labs and classrooms from the quad. Cost you half as much again, but you'd have a real focal point for entertainments. I won't tell you how sick I became of playing Gilbert and Sullivan to audiences soggy on the smell of boiled greens and pig-swill bins. And while you're at it you might as well give the kitchen a face-lift, Never did care to show mothers over *that*. Once had a big hotelier here who peeped in when I wasn't looking. We never saw him again. They tell me he kept all his sons at a secondary school until they were fifteen, then sent 'em to learn the trade in Switzerland."

"But, hold on, Algy," David protested, "where the devil are we to find money for renovations on that scale? I set our target on a modest ten thousand."

"Change it to twenty. Make a splash. We'll tap new sources that way. With Marie Stopes' contraceptive campaign catching on we can't rely on more than a hard core from the Old Boys in the future. When I started here the average family was five. Now it's two and a bit. Money shortage isn't the only acid eating into the waiting-list."

It was good to have such enthusiasm behind him and David launched his initial personal appeal at the year's Whitsuntide reunion.

It was a great occasion. So many familiar faces were there, ranged in rows in the library, and their presence assured him as to a general feeling of goodwill. At least a dozen covenants were forthcoming on the spot, a particularly generous one from the red-headed Letherett, one-time crony of Boyer in his wilder days, who had struck oil, so he said, in a large advertising business, inherited from an uncle who had died of drink. "Took a fancy to me, Pow-Wow," Letherett told him later. "My family is very straitlaced, and dropped him when he took to lifting his elbow too much, and buying fur coats for his typists. But I went to work for him, and used to get him home and put him to bed, and pass the typists off as my private harem. He changed his will in my favour a week before he snuffed it. Said I was the only relative he had who wasn't a snivelling Puritan and therefore the only one who could hope to succeed in advertising, lair of the accomplished liar. Put me down for £100 a year over seven years."

There were several equally refreshing encounters. The Gosse brothers, Archy and Starchy, were doing well in the paper-making business, David, accepting a covenant from Starchy, reminded him of the occasion when sitting on Algy's Mount Olympus, he had heard himself described as a Bolshie.

"You still are, according to whispers reaching me, Pow-Wow," Starchy told him, "but so what? This place needed a bit of fresh air after the war. Makes you think, doesn't it? I came here in 1916, when I was still wearing short pants, and look at me now. Not only shorter of wind, but pretty thin on top!"

Not all the re-encounters were breezy, however, and one in particular left him with a feeling that life was still very much a matter of pot-luck. After they had all gone, and plans were being drawn up for a rebuilding scheme, provisionally costed at sixteen thousands pounds, Boyer showed up, wan and a little threadbare, so that David did not have to ask how he was riding out the slump in the north. Over a beer in the living-room Chad confessed the real reason why he had not attended the annual reunion. "It wouldn't do much for my morale to admit to chaps like Letherett that I couldn't stand a round at the bar, Pow-Wow. The fact is, I earn well under two hundred a year at a private school in the north. The head and his missis are very kind but the place has to be run on a shoe-string, with the general shortage of cash up there. It's no good advising me to look for something better. I do, every time I nip around to the reading-room at the public library. It never struck me that jobs would be this hard to come by if I had a degree, but there are chaps with better degrees than mine who are on the skids. You need family money to tide you over something of this size and I never had any. Both my parents are dead and neither left me small change."

"What's this place of yours like, exactly?" David enquired, remembering the original Boyer, chockful of humour and boisterous high spirits. "It seems to have got you down more than somewhat and it isn't just shortage of cash, is it?"

"No, it's the general atmosphere of the area—defeated and played out. I don't mind cities all that much but cities are places to work in and half the population seems to be on the dole. We've got a little Scots skivvy up there, pretty kid from the Highlands, mad keen to get an education. She sneaks up to my room whenever she can, not only for the obvious reasons but to cram. I don't see much of her, mind. Her working day is around fourteen hours. She gets her keep and about ten bob a week. Talk about sweated labour, but cases like that are common in all the industrial areas today."

He glanced out of the window across the moor, now touched by the advance of spring. "I was very happy up here, Pow-Wow. They really look like proving the happiest days of my life." And then, with a touch of shyness that reminded David of the time he had called on him the night of Beth's funeral, with the gift of books to replace those lost in the trenches, "I almost forgot the O.B. Appeal. It's only a token, of course, but Bouncer Acton was always fond of the widow's mite parable."

The envelope contained a new pound note and he was far too moved to protest. The poignancy of the gift nudged his memory, so that he said, suddenly, "Look here, Chad, how would you like to come back? To take my place as history master? We couldn't pay a lot but we could improve on what you're getting, and at least we'd put some Bamfylde beef on you. I can't guarantee, of course, as to how they might feel about taking an Old Boy on the staff, but I know Algy would approve. He was a kid here and came back as head. I've been looking about for someone I really fancy and if you'll give me a term to sort things out . . ."

He stopped there, as moved as he had been by any incident over the last few years, for Boyer whipped out a handkerchief and gave his nose a long fog-horn blast, of the kind he had often used to infuriate Howarth in class. He said, "It's possible? Working here under you, Pow-Wow?"

"The only thing I see against it is it might encourage other O.B.s down on their luck to apply, and that might cause embarrassment in some quarters. However, leave that to me, and I'll write you in time to give a term's notice. The time will come, I hope, when the Ministry of Education will have to do something drastic about some of these bloody little private schools dotted about the country."

He was delighted to see the familiar grin split Boyer's face, who said, "I may as well confess now. I wrote after a job at Carter's school last term, and would have landed it, if another O.B. hadn't jumped the queue. Needless to say, the chap who beat me to it was ex-Outram's."

"I don't blame Carter for that. We say we don't show favouritism but we do, all of us, and why not? Your epileptic fit was my first introduction to Bamfylde."

* * *

About a week later Nun Stratton-Forbes drove up in a black Austin Seven, a vehicle he managed to leave in the sidelong manner of a portly undertaker making an unobtrusive exit from a Rolls-Royce hearse. He looked like an undertaker, too, in black jacket, Homberg hat and owlish glasses, still fighting a losing battle with his squint. He made a businesslike entry, and after solemnly shaking hands told David he was in charge of the classics section of an old and reputable correspondence college. "It has a bearing on why I'm here, sir," he said. Alone among the Old Boys, Nun never addressed boy or master by nickname. "My work brings me into touch with a variety of educational establishments and I have a suggestion you might like to consider. It relates to that leaflet you sent through the post. I've given it some thought, sir, and I can't help feeling the appeal might be canalised by the introduction of a more specific scheme, promising a far better yield."

"Nun," David said, chuckling, "you always did make ten words do the work of two and you haven't changed a bit. What the devil are you driving at?"

"Geographical selection, sir."

He unzipped his brief-case and produced a sheaf of tabulated cards. "I did a trial scheme, sir. You see, Old Boys will be scattered all over the world and perhaps we have the addresses of several hundred of them."

"Just under a thousand, I believe."

"Well, then, of that total at least two dozen must be both centrally placed and attached to the school. My idea, worked out in detail here, is to enrol those O.B.s as agents, each giving an undertaking to make personal contact with all the Old Boys in his immediate area. Most of them will be known to them and within travelling distance. People ordinarily throw postal appeals in the wastepaper basket, but no one dismisses the direct solicitation of an old friend. You could even work out a quota for each area. I'm based on North London and I'll be responsible for my district. I think I could undertake to raise three hundred, sir, either in covenants or direct subscriptions." He looked at David mildly. "Does the scheme recommend itself to you?"

"Nun," said David, respectfully, "you are Bamfylde's Carnot, organiser of victory. It's a brilliant idea. I could have sat here a month without producing anything half so good. Would you lend me those cards for a day or so?"

"Oh, you may keep them, sir. I prepared them with that in mind. And now, if you will excuse me, I must pay my respects to Mr. Barnaby. He would be hurt to learn I had been here and left without giving him a progress report."

"Barnaby will be delighted to see you, Nun. He regards you as his raison d'être for remaining in the profession," and Nun quietly withdrew.

"Extraordinary chap," David said aloud, as Grace wandered in, sketch-book tucked under her arm, and asked, "Who, Daddy?"

"Nun Stratton-Forbes, whose first notable feat here was to present himself at the long-jump pit and announce your arrival. He's just made me a gift of the product of the tidiest mind we've ever had at Bamfylde. What have you got there today?"

She opened her sketch book and showed him a water-colour of a scene looking north-east from the corner of the planty, painted, it would seem, in the course of a cricket match, for in the distance were strategically-placed blobs, representing two elevens and the umpire. It was very good, he thought, impressionistic but sufficiently defined to catch a fleeting moment of the Bamfylde scene on a May evening. "Do you ever title your pictures, Gracie?" he asked, and she said she called this one 'Close of Play', one of a series she had done on the school year.

"I'd like to have them some day," he said. "They say more than a photograph. I'll tell you what, if this represents summer do one for the other three seasons and we'll get them framed and mounted and hang them in the study."

"Oh, I should have to talk to Spats about it," she said. "He's the only one who would know whether they were worth framing." Spats, of course, was Winterbourne, who now paid them monthly visits. It struck David, for the first time, that it was Grace, rather than Bamfylde, that prompted his twelve or more drives to and from London throughout the year. He said, teasing her, "Has Winterbourne always been hot favourite, Grace?"

"Not really," she replied, seriously, "but he's always in the first two. Sax is the other."

"Ah," he said, "you didn't have to tell me that. How about also-rans?"

"I should need pencil and paper for that," she said, and, giving him a shrewd glance, "Daddy . . . do I . . . I mean, is it absolutely a 'must' for me to start as a weekly boarder at Challacombe Convent School, in September?"

"I'm afraid it is," he said. "Frankly, I'd much sooner you stayed here, for you're a real help to me these days, with the name of every Old Boy back to 1925 in your head, but we can't have you as the only girl in a school of three hundred boys. At twelve it's bad enough, for you've already got more courtiers than Gloriana. At sixteen the competition would be frightful. After all, it isn't as if you were a plain, puddingy miss, is it?"

She drifted over to the convex mirror above the fireplace and studied her distorted reflection. "I look like one in this," she said, "and if it meant staying here, instead of spending Monday to Friday away, I wouldn't care if I *was* plain and puddingy."

"You wouldn't have any courtiers then. Go and give Rigby a hand with the lunch."

She went out and he stood thinking, one hand on the mantel-shelf, the other still holding Nun's card-index. She was as much a part of the place, he thought, as Algy and himself, as integrated into the structure and texture of Bamfylde as Big School, the horse-roller and the planty, and the process had begun that autumn evening nearly six years ago, when he had lifted her from the taxi bringing her home from that convalescent home. He saw her now as his special bonus, something tossed him by the fate that had deprived him, in a moment of time, of Beth and her sister, Joan. She had come to represent all that part of his life between the plummeting descent of Beth's beret, from Colwyn Bay's pier, to the evening he stood on the plinth of the Founder's statue, taking his first roll-call as head. It would be a wrench to part with her, even for five days a week, eight months of the year, and if there had been a way of avoiding it he would have done it gladly, but there wasn't. She had to begin mixing with other girls, so that she began to think as a woman, and how was this possible so long as she remained here?

The bell clanged in the quad, the jangle reminding him of a parting shot of Algy's, when they had been discussing plans for the new buildings. "We'll have to crown that new wing with a bell tower," he had said. "We must be the only school of our size in the country that continues to regulate our comings and goings by that discordant clamour," and when David had reminded him of the special status of school bell-ringer, acknowledged by all as long ago as Nipper Shawe's day, he said, "We'll hold on to that. Imagine the status conferred on the chap who pulls the rope! We might even invest him with a ceremonial collarette, on the style of the Orange Order. Make a note of it, P.J., jot it down now, for these things count," and he had.

II

The old terminal pattern reasserted itself, the memorable incident surfacing among the flotsam of the school year, so that he could always look back on a specific period and say to himself; 'That was the time of poor old Lackaknacker Briggs' abduction . . .' or, 'That was about the time we had trouble with Crispin', and so on down the seasons, down the terms, down the years.

The two highlights of his first full year centred on misfits, similar in many ways. And yet, in retrospect, the one was quite ridiculous and the other something that could have ended in tragedy, but for luck, and the lessons he had learned since his first day here.

Briggs was the first celebrity, a boy whose unfortunate nickname, 'Lackaknacker', dated from the day it was broadcast that he had had a malformed testicle removed as a child. Anyone but Briggs would have filed this away as top secret, for what could be more certain than that it would earn him instant notoriety? It was nothing serious, it seemed, no more than a trifling piece of surgery, performed upon his undistinguished anatomy years before he ever set foot at Bamfylde, but the moment news leaked it found its way into school legend, so that Briggs was dubbed 'Lackaknacker', or alternatively, 'One Stroke', and the wags got busy on rhymes concerning his affliction, the most popular being a chant that ran:

> *Mr. Briggs is much improved*
> *Since he had a sphere removed.*
> *Shorn of passion, shorn of fire,*
> *He now sings alto in the choir.*

Most boys would have found the situation intolerable but somehow Briggs adjusted to it. Very easily, David would have said, for Briggs was an accomplished adjuster. You never found him out of humour and rarely out of mischief. Similarly, you never challenged him without hearing an excuse of marked originality. His excuses were, in fact, among the most original David had ever heard, and were offered with an air of innocence that exonerated him from any failing, save guilelessness. Briggs had the frank, slightly bemused expression of a cherub seen in a Renaissance painting, with blue, trusting eyes, heavy pendulous cheeks, a small, rosebud mouth, and no chin at all. A dullard at work, he was equally indifferent to games. Never once had he been known to catch a ball, or arrive anything but last in a heat over any distance, so that time would have hung heavily on his hands had he not possessed an inventiveness that led him into all manner of bizarre adventures during his rough passage through Lower School. The first, and possibly the most spectacular of these, was his alleged kidnapping that led to his acquisition of yet another reputation, that of Bamfylde's Baron von Munchausen, with a capacity for romantic lies that stunned the imagination. The story of Lackaknacker's abduction emerged at the time, of course, but the truth behind it had to be pieced together over the years, so that David, with an academic interest in such things, never got confirmation until Briggs himself admitted the facts as a returning Old Boy.

It all began with a raid upon Man Chilcott's orchard. Most of the farmers in the vicinity of the school had adjusted to the presence of some three hundred young savages, settled in their midst, but Chilcott, a particularly sour smallholder, never had, and for years maintained a running feud with boys who, for the sheer hell of it, would descend on his hen-roost and orchard.

It seemed that Lackaknacker was engaged in one of these forays when it happened—at least, that was his story when, tired and heel-blistered, he reappeared at school early one October morning, with a lurid tale to account for his overnight absence. He found Bamfylde alerted, despite the darkness of the hour before the dawn, for he had been missed at call-over, search-parties had been out and his parents had been notified by telephone that he would probably appear as a runaway on the milk train.

David saw that he was fed (he ate breakfast like a ravenous castaway), showered and sent to bed, after which he conferred with Barnaby, Briggs' housemaster, as to what should be done about him. Barnaby had already questioned him and rejected his bizarre explanation but confessed himself worried about the boy and inclined to lay the blame on that piece of surgery, carried out when Briggs was at kindergarten.

"Damn it all, P.J." he said, "it can't be good for the chap's morale to have them chanting that obscene doggerel at him. You know how fiendishly cruel the juniors can be, and they've made hay over Briggs's missing equipment. I knew about it, of course. I've already warned Gosling, the house prefect, to report anyone ragging him on the subject, but it's turning the boy into a loner and we all know loners go one of two ways. Either they mope around, until they fall by the way-side, or they set about proving themselves by spectacular acts of brigandage. Briggs seems to have chosen the latter course."

Barnaby went on to relay Briggs' story of his truancy. He admitted frankly that he had gone to Chilcott's orchard to steal apples but had not, he said, had the chance to pocket any, not even windfalls. He was merely surveying the field of operations from inside Chilcott's hedge, when he heard the approach of a car and had dived for cover behind the gate-post. It had been touch and go after that. Somebody (he couldn't say who because he was crouched behind the gate-post) had opened the padlocked gate and entered the orchard and Briggs, seizing his sole chance of escape, had doubled through the gate but not, he claimed, to regain the road to Stone Cross. A blanket, 'smelling of linseed, sir', had been thrown over his head, he had been trussed with a coil of rope, 'smelling of creosote, sir', bundled into the back of a car and driven away at high speed.

He could give no details of the ride—'I think I must have blacked-out, sir . . .'—but when the car stopped he managed to wriggle free of bonds and escape into the market square. The town turned out to be Norton Dip, some twenty miles north-east of Bamfylde, and it was dark, so he at once set out to walk back to school. "I didn't catch a local train, sir, although I had the money for the fare. I thought I should get clear of those chaps, so I walked as far as Crosshayes, where I hid near the station until the slow goods came in. I got a lift there in the guard's van as far as Bamfylde Bridge Halt. Walrus Tapscott can back me up about that, sir, for he saw me. I told him I'd been lost on a run. Then . . . well . . . I just walked up, sir, and here I am."

"You don't believe a single word of this rigmarole, do you?' David enquired, but Barnaby said he was obliged to believe part of it, for he had checked with Tapscott at the station, and Briggs had indeed descended from the Crosshayes goods train at about five a.m. that morning. "He's also got marks on his wrists that could be caused by ropes," he added. "Otherwise he's in good shape."

"Then even if you believe some of it, it's a matter for the police, isn't it?"

"No," Barnaby said, "it isn't, but not for obvious reasons, the bad publicity we should get over a thing like this. I believe it's about half the truth, that is to say, I believe he did motor to Norton Dip, and return the way he claims, but don't ask me why, or how much he's hiding, or for what reason. All I can say is Algy's 'little man' tells me we should let well alone, P. J."

It was interesting, David reflected, how all of the old hands here borrowed from Algy's repertoire. Algy declared that he made his spot decisions according to the dictates of his 'little man', an inspired agent residing just below the navel and David recalled him consulting this infallible informant when they had been faced with Winterbourne's disappearance. He said, "Very well, Barnaby, I'll go along with Algy's little man. After all, you're his housemaster, and what you say about the ragging makes sense to me. But I'd better see the boy, hadn't I?"

"Rather you didn't," Barnaby said, "he might be encouraged to elaborate to a point where we should be obliged to investigate. Besides, between you and me I've a grudging respect for Briggs, dating from the day I caught him smoking, and he excused himself on the grounds that they were asthmatical cigarettes, recommended to him by his father. They were, too, for I checked on that. They smelled like incense when I burned the packet. Wouldn't surprise me if Briggs didn't go into Fleet Street when he leaves here. First-class recruit for somebody like Rothermere or Beaverbrook, for whenever there's no hard news he invents some."

They left it at that, and it was years later when, propping up a bar at an Old Boys' annual dinner in London, an adult Lackaknacker told him the truth, amid shouts of laughter from former cronies. Finding no cover on the open road when he emerged from the orchard, he had dived into the back of Chilcott's Morris and crouched there, undiscovered, while Chilcott drove into Norton Dip and parked outside the Woolsack. He had then made his way back in approximately the way described. Briggs, as it happened, did not gravitate to Fleet Street but he did the next best thing, becoming a Public Relations officer for a big concern selling detergents. "A post calculated to give the utmost scope to his undoubted powers of imagination," commented Barnaby, when the story was relayed to him.

The Crispin story was equally sensational but had some alarming undertones. Crispin, a Sunsetter, and no relation to the Amy Crispin of Howarth's long buried romance, was an exceptionally shy boy, who never seemed to make any friends but was tolerated as a hanger-on by other coteries all the way up to the Lower Fourth. Sensitive, withdrawn and intelligent, he arrived in Middle School before he was fourteen, but then, one bitterly cold day in early December, his frail roof fell on him in the form of a charge of shoplifting in the village shop.

Old Mark Trescott appeared with the felon in tow towards teabell, presenting evidence of the theft, one bar of Mackintosh's toffee, value twopence, and the shopkeeper was threatening to prosecute. "Tidden offen I ketch one red-'anded, as I did this jackdaw," he told David, while Crispin stood staring down at the carpet, and when David begged him not to go to these lengths over a bar of toffee, he growled, "Ah, tiz easy for you to talk, Headmaster, you don't have to make a livin' up there. Tuppence iz tuppence in my book."

David had been at Bamfylde long enough to know the real source of Trescott's resentment. Until the new tuckshop had opened in 1924, his confectionery counter had been one of his main sources of income, but latterly his takings had dwindled. Here was a splendid opportunity to drive what he would see as a straightforward peasant bargain. "I'll tell 'ee what," he went on, a shade too eagerly, "I won't press charges if you drop the hint to the bursar's missus to give over stockin' Mackintosh's. I don't want to zeem 'ardfaced, but toffee was my best line bevore she took it on."

"You really think I could persuade her to do that, Trescott?"

"Why not? Youm the Ade up yer, bain 'ee?"

"Well," David said, eyeing Crispin, "let me propose a slightly different bargain. I won't report you to the police at Challacombe for trying to blackmail me, providing you accept the price of the goods here and now. How's that?"

Crispin looked up quickly, perhaps not wanting to miss

Trescott's outraged expression as he roared, "Tiz bluff an' you know it! I got a witness to 'im pinching that toffee but you abben got one to this bit of a tork we'm 'aving."

"Indeed I have. Crispin's a witness, aren't you, Crispin? And how do you know he didn't mean to pay, before you scared him half to death by pouncing on him? Good God, man—a twopenny bar of toffee—you'd be laughed out of court in three minutes. He's got a good character here and I'd say so."

There was a silence. Out in the quad the tea-bell rang. It always seemed to, David thought, at moments of crisis. Finally Trescott said, "You know and he knows, he 'ad no bliddy intention o' paying." Then, "You'll give 'im a damn good thrashing, I hope?"

"He'll get precisely what he deserves, Mr. Trescott, and thank you for bringing the matter to my attention."

With a long, resentful look at Crispin, Trescott withdrew, and David waited until he heard the door in Big School passage slam before saying, "Why, Crispin? You don't get much pocket-money but twopence—it's absolutely ridiculous! You see that now, I suppose?" but Crispin resumed his study of the carpet.

"You've stolen small things before? From Trescott's, from the tuckshop, the lockers?"

That found its mark. His head came up. "*No*, sir. *Never!*"

"Then there *must* be a reason, possibly a good one and I'd like to hear it. I've got to hear it, Crispin."

He said, carefully, "You wouldn't understand, sir."

"I might."

"Nobody would."

"You leave that to me, Crispin. Sit down and think it over. We've got all evening if necessary, but you don't leave here until I know, understand?"

About a minute passed. "I suppose it was because of Towers, sir."

"Towers was with you? He suggested you took it?"

"Good Lord, no, sir!" He sounded even more outraged than Trescott. "Towers wouldn't do a thing like that!"

"Then how does Towers come into it?"

"He doesn't, sir, he doesn't know a thing about it. I meant to give it to him, that's all."

"Sit down, Crispin, and let's get this straight. You say Towers doesn't come into it, yet you admit stealing it for him? You hadn't the price of it on you?"

"Yes, I had, sir."

"You had? Do you often give Towers things?"

"Every Wednesday."

"Why every Wednesday?"

"Wednesday's pocket-money day, sir."

"Towers is a close friend of yours?"

"No, sir."

"But you'd like him to be?"

He didn't answer this. Neither did he accept the invitation to sit down. David said, "When you buy him things, how does he react?"

Crispin took his time. Finally he said, doggedly, "He doesn't want me. He's got chaps like Coxe and Nesbitt. I bought him a pot of Mrs. Redcliffe's baked beans last Wednesday but he sent it back."

It was one of the most complex cases he had ever handled and he thought longingly of Algy's vast store of experience. There was little to go on here save instinct, but instinct told him to tread with excessive caution.

"Listen, Crispin. I'm guessing and you aren't helping very much. Whatever's said here won't get around, it'll be between you and me, understand? I don't intend punishing you, either. What I said to Trescott was said to get rid of him. You're in bad trouble, sure enough, but it's not on account of that bar of toffee. Your people are a long way off. India, isn't it?"

"Yes, sir."

"When did you last see them?"

"I saw my mother last year, sir, just before she went out. I haven't seen my father in three years."

"Well, then, meantime I'm your father. That's how it has to be with most Sunsetters. Not perfect, but a lot better than nothing. Now tell me if I've got this right. You want Towers to accept you on the same terms as he accepts Coxe and Nesbitt, but he won't, so you buy him things. But that isn't working, so you go to the village and steal a bar of toffee from Trescott's counter. Can I assume you had already spent all your pocket money on that jar of beans?"

"No, sir, the beans were only fourpence. I had twopence left over."

"Then why the devil didn't you pay Trescott for the toffee?"

"Something Towers said, sir."

"What did he say?"

"He said you don't buy friends with beans or cream horns. Me and Towers—well—it just wouldn't work, sir."

"But after that you deliberately stole the toffee for him."

Crispin's lip quivered and his teeth clamped over his lip. "I'm sorry, Crispin, but if I'm to help I've got to know to understand. Maybe you find it difficult to explain, but try, boy, for God's sake, try!"

"It was *doing* something, sir."

"Doing something? You mean, *proving* something?"

"In a way, sir."

"To yourself or to Towers?"

"To both of us. If Trescott hadn't seen me I was going to tell Towers I'd pinched it."

"But you told me Towers wouldn't do a thing like that himself. Wouldn't he be even more inclined to turn you down when he knew you were a thief?"

"Yes, but it wouldn't have mattered, would it? I mean, he'd have thought about it, wouldn't he? You see . . . I can't *do* anything, sir. Towers knows it and everybody knows it. I'm no good at anything. I never have been."

The terrible poignancy of it assailed him. On one side Towers, a popular boy, strutting round with any number of friends to choose from, a boy with a father owning a big sports business in the Midlands, who drove up here in an Alvis and took his son and his son's cronies out for the day. And on the other side of the wire, looking in, Crispin; friendless, rejected and aware, every minute of the day, of his own inadequacy. There was no ready solution. It would need, he would say, a good deal of sober reflection, a careful weighing of every factor. He said, "Well, that's all for now, Crispin, and I'm glad you brought yourself to tell me. Go and have your tea and don't say anything about this to anyone, not even Towers. And don't worry about Trescott either. He won't do a thing, do you hear?"

"Yes, sir."

He went out, dragging his feet, and through the window giving on the quad David watched him, noting that he did not go through the arch towards Big Hall but across the quad towards the one-storey buildings that comprised the tuck-house, armoury, stables and coke-hole. He thought, "Let him mull it over tea-less if he wants to, he won't have an appetite to speak of," and rang for Rigby to order tea in his study, wishing that it was Friday, when Grace would be home. It was a problem he might, conceivably, have discussed with her. A twelve-year-old might be likely to approach it with more detachment than an adult.

He was crossing the quad an hour later when he saw Manners, a Sixth Former, emerge from the northern arch at a run. Seeing David, he changed direction rapidly, doubled round the Founder's statue and rushed up, gasping, "Better come, sir . . . that kid Crispin . . . down in the coke-hole, blue in the face . . .!", and spun round, rushing back through the arch with David at his heels.

They jumped the three steps into the coke-hole together. The low-powered naked bulb did not do much to light up the windowless interior but what light there was touched Crispin's right hand, flung out towards the squat boiler, as though to ward off the reek that filled the cellar. He was lumped on a coke-container and a glance showed him that Manners had cause for alarm. Crispin's face was purple, and his teeth were bared in a kind of snarl. David gathered him up and ran back up the steps where a long gust of the north-easterly wind caught them, strong enough to make him reel. He shouted, "After me, Manners . . . into the Third Form . . ." and ran past the entrance of Outram's, turning right at the foot of the slate steps that led up to what had once been Julia Darbyshire's quarters. The Third Form fire was dead and it was cold in here, with the sash cord of an open window rotating in the draught. He laid Crispin flat on the desk, tore away collar and tie, and began massaging his chest, throwing all his weight into the exercise as Manners said, distractedly, "Is he ... is he *dead*, sir? He's my fag. I was looking for him, going to clout him ... one of the kids said he'd seen him go into the coke-hole after tea ..."

"He would have been dead in another ten minutes ... get matron here ... tell her one of the boys is sick but don't tell anyone else. Wait around until he's in sick-bay and report back to me."

"I'm taking prep, sir."

"Find a stand-in."

"Yes, sir."

He ran off but before he had reached the far end of the room Crispin vomited, turning face downwards, gripping the edge of the desk and retching violently. David continued to work on his back. He knew little or nothing about artificial respiration, but applied his strength as common sense dictated and it appeared to work. Crispin, having emptied his stomach, drew several long, shuddering breaths and sat up as Ma Kruger sailed in demanding to know what had happened. He told her briefly that Crispin had gone into the coke-hole to warm himself and had been overcome by the fumes. "That place is out of bounds from now on," he said. "It's a marvel something like this didn't happen long ago. Put him straight into sick bay. Is there anyone else there?"

"No, Headmaster. The last 'flu case went out yesterday. Can he walk?"

"I can walk," Crispin said, thickly, and proved it by sliding off the desk and steadying himself on the nearest blackboard peg.

"You had a close shave, Crispin. He's had nothing to eat since lunch, Matron. Get him some soup, if he can keep it down, but get him to bed first."

"I know my job," said Mrs. Gorman, tartly, and he remembered, too late, that Ma Kruger could be very touchy if her methods were called into question.

* * *

He said nothing of his suspicions to Manners when the senior reported. In his own mind there was little doubt but that Crispin had gone there deliberately, seeking not warmth but oblivion, and the nearness of their escape made him catch his breath. He thought, "I didn't handle it right, I should have offered the kid tea and gone to work on him straightaway—anything but let him mooch off like that, with his packload of misery . . ." but Manners helped without knowing it, saying, "He's a frightful weed, sir, one of the worst we've ever had. He does everything you tell him but no more, if you follow me, sir. He's just the kind who would sit there like a kipper and wait to get cooked." He paused and it crossed David's mind that Manners might be wondering if his own approach to Crispin had not contributed to his fag's wretchedness. A moment later this was confirmed as he added, "I . . . er . . . I did try talking to him straight, sir. Early in the term I told him to pull his socks up and try harder at games. Would you like me to have another go at him, sir?"

"No," David said, definitely, "just try putting yourself in his place once in a while. He's cut off from his people, and hasn't the knack of making friends. Not everybody has, you know."

It was no use telling Manners to hold his tongue about the incident. It would be all over the school by now, and even if it wasn't it would leak as soon as he put the coke-hole out of bounds.

He went over to the library and browsed about looking for a book that might help to make Crispin out of himself. He found a copy of Williamson's *Tarka the Otter*, slipped it in his pocket and went up the slate staircase to matron's room. Crispin, she said, in her quaint hospital phrase, was 'comfortable'. The vomiting had probably prevented unpleasant after-effects, although he might have a bad headache for a day or so. He had taken soup, and kept it down, and later a cup of tea and a purgative. Ma Kruger was a great believer in purgatives and, crafty as some of her patients were, few found means to avoid swallowing them.

He said, "I'll pop in and have a word with him. He wanted a book," and left her to her darning, going through into the sick bay built the year after the fire.

Crispin was sitting up in bed looking at nothing. He said, as soon as David pulled a chair up, "I meant it to happen, sir. They say if you sit there long enough you pass out."

"Never mind all that, Crispin. It's time you and I put all our cards on the table. We've got to scrape a hole for you somewhere, and if you don't feel like co-operating try and see it from my point of view. What sort of headmaster would I be if I let boys get so depressed that they did what you did to-day? And don't kid yourself that your case is an isolated one. I've been at Bamfylde fourteen years, and there's always a few who can't settle in. You don't sing, I suppose?"

"No, sir." Mercifully he seemed to find the question amusing. "I sound like a stick on railings, so Mr. Renshaw-Smith says."

"And there's no one game you like more than another?"

"Not really, sir."

"You're not bad at English subjects. Maths aside, you've always had pretty good reports."

"That doesn't get you far at a place like this, sir."

"No, it doesn't." He thought hard. "There must be something you can do that nobody else can. There always is, Crispin. The key to getting by at a place like Bamfylde is to find that something, and build on it. It doesn't matter a jot what it is, so long as you're better at it than the next chap. Can you think of anything? Anything at all?"

"I play the handbells, sir."

"Handbells?"

"I've got a set, sir. My uncle left them to me when he died. He used to go around playing them at charity concerts, and . . . well . . . I got interested, so he taught me. They aren't as easy as they look, sir."

"I'll wager they aren't. Where are they now?"

"In my box in the Sunsetters' store, sir."

"You've never had them out since you came here?"

"No, sir. It seemed . . . well . . . a bit cissy, sir."

"Cissy my foot! It's a very old English craft, and very few people can play them as they should be played. You can ring out recognisable tunes?"

"Oh, yes, sir. I can do all the carols."

"The carols? Well, that's promising. We've got a carol service the night after the opera and that could be a star turn. Have you got the nerve to stand up on the stage in Big Hall and play, in front of the whole school?"

"I'd need to practise, sir. It's a long time since I had them out."

"Then I'll tell you what you do. You bring them over to my house after prep tomorrow night. Only my daughter and I will be there and you can practise all you like. Then we'll make sure you get star billing at the carol service, a surprise item on the programme that not even Mr. Renshaw-Smith knows about in advance. Will you do that?"

"Are you sure they won't laugh, sir?"

"At carols? Expertly played on old English handbells? You can take it from me they wouldn't. Everyone will be pestering you for a go at them, you see if I'm not right. How do you feel now?"

"Still muzzy, sir."

"Then get some sleep. Matron says you'll have nothing worse than a headache in the morning. You needn't come in. Take it easy over the weekend. Good night, then."

"Good night, sir."

He went out, feeling a good deal more hopeful than he went in and thinking, "A purgative can't do him much harm but a big hand up on that stage will do him untold good."

He went down and out into the quad, standing a moment with the wind whipping his gown and sniffing the air for snow. It was time it fell, having been threatening for two days now. From the direction of Big Hall he could hear a solo—Frobisher, playing the Grand Inquisitor in Algy's revival of *The Gondoliers*, and singing 'There Lived a King', one of Beth's favourites. A soft burst of laughter came from the lighted windows of the Outram senior dorm, then Vinnicombe's bellow at a skylarker making the most of the few minutes before lights out. He thought, "God knows, we get problems, but taken all round we seem to cope with 'em better than the politicians."

He hunched his gown and turned in through Big Hall arch to look in on rehearsals.

III

The thought returned to him often during the last fortnight of term. An island in the torrent; a small bastion of refuge, where some kind of order still prevailed, where most

things worked fairly well, where there was fellowship of a
kind missing since Algy's day, a time when the outside world
had seemed to steady before shooting off course again. Now,
as Yeats might have said, 'all was changed, changed utterly'
out there beyond school bounds. The old doctrine of Free
Trade, bulwark of the Empire for so long, discarded,
alienating Philip Snowden, the one man of genius left in the
Cabinet. Hunger-marchers proliferating. De Valera, arch-
enemy of the old-style British, of which Bamfylde, like it or
not, remained a symbol, triumphing at the Irish polls.
World conferences that resolved nothing. Mosleyites confronting the militant Left on streets where, only a few years
ago, a General Strike had been staged without a casualty.
And it was worse still overseas. France, her President shot
down, was in turmoil. The Japanese were making nonsense
of The League of Nations covenant. And all about them
was a confusion of tongues, a bankruptcy of policies. But at
Bamfylde, in that final month of 1932, things were more
hopeful. Algy's *Gondoliers* played to thunderous applause,
and Crispin, darting up and down his trestle table in Big
Hall, won the status symbol of Bamfylde with his handbell
rendering of 'Silent Night' and 'The Holly and the Ivy', for
thereafter he was known as 'Ringer' and with a nickname
integration was achieved.

Watching his performance David felt he had earned the
right to a little smugness, for Ringer Crispin was only one of
many manifestations of the new reign. Aside from the Gilbert
and Sullivan revival, Renshaw-Smith's Choral Society was
thriving, spurred on by a Certificate of Merit gained in the
Devon Music Festival and his changes in discipline had
produced no explosion. After the oppressive atmosphere of
the Alcock era, there was a geniality in the common room
that had not been evident in the 'twenties, when Carter kept
tempers on edge most of the time. Hislop settled in effortlessly,
a different Hislop to the bull-necked extrovert who had shouted the odds on the sports field. He had developed a flair
for maths somewhere in exile and, even more surprisingly,
a taste for authority, so that Gibbons, Havelock's new housemaster, appointed him house-prefect the day he reached
the Sixth. David, watching him take parade one morning,

wondered how he would act if he stumbled on a pontoon
school in the old smokers' hideout behind the stacked trunks
in the covered playground. Or what he would do if he caught
one of his cronies studying the formbook. Howarth and
Barnaby seemed to have entered into a tacit conspiracy to
give him the kind of loyalty they had given Algy, and sometimes he saw the three of them as the new Magi, ageing
harmoniously in the wilderness. Grace, her stillness seasoned
by a developing sense of humour, was a great help to him
during weekends and holidays, and even parents accepted
her as his semi-official chatelaine, whereas Old Boys
of recent vintage never thought of her as anyone but his
deputy.

Thus, one way and another, the gap left in his life by Chris
closed to some extent. He missed her, of course, but not as
keenly as he would have thought. Mostly he was so busy, too
busy indeed, to heed his publisher's plea that he begin work
on another historical biography.

Financially he was better off than he had ever hoped to be,
with a salary of six-fifty a year, free living expenses and about
three hundred a year from royalties on *The Royal Tigress*.
Chris told him his book was on display in Montreal book-
shops, and that there were two copies in the University
library. She wrote, on the average, once a week, chatty,
mildly affectionate letters that seemed unrelated to the woman
he had held in his arms in the seedy bedsitter at Bilhampton.
She had detached herself, somehow, not only from him but
from the British scene, so that sometimes he wondered if she
would ever settle here again or, if she did, would see him as
someone too pedestrian for her taste.

The centre of what he thought of as his political gravity
was shifting and he was inclined, on the whole, to lower his
sights and put his faith in tradition, in ripeness, habit and
continuity. Even old Howarth commented on the change
when David championed Britain at a gin-party discussion in
Nicolson's on Howarth's fifty-sixth birthday.

"I can give you twenty years, P.J.," he said, jovially, "and
Barnaby can give you fifteen, but at heart you're less of a
radical than either one of us, notwithstanding that reputation you once had as a firebrand. You should watch it, lad,

before the Bamfylde fungus gets a fatal hold on you."

But then, he told himself, he had excuses for feeling paternal these days. Chad Boyer appeared the first day of the Christmas holidays, seeking temporary quarters, and when David asked him what he meant by 'temporary' he looked, as Algy Herries would have said, 'felon-shy', and added, half-apologetically, "Well, the fact is I've just taken a three-year lease on your old cottage, over at Stone Cross, P. J. A bachelor room is out, I'm afraid. You see, there's Alison."

"Alison who?"

Boyer grinned. "My wife, Pow-Wow."

"Great God, you're not thinking of getting married?"

"I am married," Chad answered, grinning. "Alison and I are on our honeymoon, as from last Tuesday. We were married in a Manchester Register Office, and she's outside now, awaiting the abbot's permission to cross the monastic threshold. Shall I fetch her in?"

"Well, for God's sake," David said, quite taken aback, "you'll have to, won't you? You can't expect the girl to bivouac on Exmoor in December," and he ran to the window to peep out at a still, rather keyed up figure, hunched in the passenger seat of Boyer's ancient Austin Seven. She had flaming red hair, a small, pinched face, and a very definite air of uncertainty, so that he called, "Grace! Go out and fetch Mrs. Boyer in while I give this room a tidy."

It was very difficult to surprise Grace, even at twelve-and-a half. She threw aside her apron and ran out into the forecourt, where they watched her trying to coax Alison Boyer out of sanctuary. Boyer said, "It's that Scots girl I mentioned at Easter, Pow-Wow, the one who was a domestic at the school, and came to me for coaching. I suppose you think I'm crazy on my salary."

"That depends," David said, remembering his own spot proposal on Colwyn Bay railway platform, in 1919. "How did it develop, exactly?"

"We were both lonely and very much down in the dumps, and . . . well, we kind of grew together. She's a real brick, and a tonic when she forgets to be shy. She's got the Celtic awe for all seats of learning. Oh, I daresay you'll think me an absolute idiot for saddling myself with a wife at this stage, but there it is and I don't regret it. I asked her to marry me the day I got your letter saying you'd wangled it."

He moved around the room, glancing at all the familiar pictures and pieces of furniture brought over from Havelock's. "It's like a dream, Pow-Wow. I mean, you being Gaffer here, and me on the staff. Sometimes I pinch myself and wonder if I'll wake up in that bloody awful attic I occupied in that prep school, or find myself back in the Havelock dorm, with Dobson and Ridgeway snoring away on either side of me." Then, seriously, "They say you're making a rare go of it, Pow-Wow. Would you say you were?"

"Feeling my way, Chad. It's trickier than it looked from the outside. I'm even beginning to appreciate some of Alcock's points of view, particularly as regards parents."

"But not us, I hope?"

"No, Chad, not you. The O.B.s have been marvellous, and so have Howarth and Barnaby. They're beginning to call us the New Magi now, the heirs of Judy, Bouncer and old Rapper Gibbs."

Grace came in with Alison, who looked even smaller and more uncertain in the open. She gravitated to Boyer at once and David noticed, with approbation, that she obviously adored him. Her red head finished level with his broad shoulders, and a gleam of sunshine, touching her hair, made it glow like a fire in a draught. She had cornflower-blue eyes, a small chin as resolute as Beth's and the kind of handknitted jumper that Beth had worn when she was dressing on a nurse's salary. He thought, "It's odd he should be bringing her to that old cottage of ours. Like watching yourself in a mirror of time . . . hard to believe Beth made her bow to Algy and Ellie in this room, thirteen years ago . . ." but then he remembered his manners and said, "I should be used to Chad surprising me, Mrs. Boyer. Congratulations, and I hope you'll be very happy here. Chad was, but it's going to take us a little time to get used to him at the distributing end of authority. He was a holy terror here in his salad days."

"Och, Chad'll do fine," she said, with almost staggering directness. "It was time he moved on. It was only a wee school. Nothing like this."

Her unexpected forthrightness made an immediate impression on him so that he thought, "She's just what he needed, come to think of it. Someone to rally on, someone who matters to him," and when Grace accepted Alison's offer to give a hand with the lunch, he said, in response to Boyer's interrogative glance. "You've got more sense than you think, Chad. I always had a morbid fear you'd turn up one day with one of those mincing little blondes, all promise and no performance. My mother would approve of Alison instantly, and so would Beth. They both had a preference for down-to-earthers."

CHAPTER TWO

I

Chris wrote early in the new year, when he was beginning to wonder how soon it would be before he heard her pleasant Yorkshire brogue over the phone, asking when and where they could meet. But she wasn't coming home, after all, or not for some considerable time. She had been selected for what she described as a 'McKenzie-Solomon Travelling Scholarship (financed by a couple of reformed robber barons, buying their way into heaven with an educational trust fund)' and would be working in Western Europe for six months, a trip that would take in shortened courses at Strasbourg, Rome and Munich Universities. And after that, on the strength of the travelling scholarship, she was committed to lecture her way across the States, all the way from the eastern seaboard to the Pacific.

She wrote, with a touch of her old breathlessness,

I was lucky to be selected but I was slow to accept. It meant not seeing you for almost another year, and even that isn't certain for, at this stage, I'm not sure how many cities the U.S.A. tour takes in. However, if I am to play fair with the people who sponsored me I owe it to them to be available for a candidature in early '34. I see the date of the next General Election as '35 but I may get pushed forward at a by-election much earlier. I've decided to resign the South Mendips candidature. Not even Keir Hardie could win that seat from the Tories, but that's enough about me. I treasure every scrap of Bamfylde news you send and am sure (despite your becoming modesty on paper) that you are proving a whale of a success as headmaster of that hallowed establishment! My love always, Davy dear . . . and I miss you so, and will go on missing you . . . your male gentleness and your sanity.

Where did you get them both? Not in the trenches and not, I think, in the Valleys, where folk are exciting and amusing but intolerant. It follows that it must have been at Bamfylde, and that's funny when you think of it. I always saw those places as bastions of prejudice . . .

He accepted the letter, despite its breezy reassurances, as virtual disengagement, a gentle placing of their association on a platonic plane, and although this saddened him it was not unexpected. Like him, she was finding fulfilment and their inclinations no longer pursued parallel courses, but divergent ones, likely to carry them farther and farther apart as each of them spread their wings. He was sure now that she would never willingly exchange politics or even an academic life, for the role of a Martha, here in the wilderness. While he might have adapted, she never would. Always she would see herself as a walk-on player, meriting a leading role. Perhaps the only things they had ever had in common were physical hunger and a deep, personal loneliness.

He folded the letter, feeling that he needed time to reflect on an answer, and went into the Sixth to take his period on current affairs, beginning half-heartedly, his mind still on her implied renunciation but, as always, warming to his theme, and the rallying questions of Hislop and others, who enjoyed these occasions as much as he did.

The letter spurred him to make yet another decision, to enrol a commercial tutor and start courses in shorthand, book-keeping and typing as soon as the new classrooms were ready. It had been put forward by several parents and at least one Governor a year ago, when he first took Alcock's place, but it had made no special appeal to him then. Bamfylde had produced several merchant princelings over the years, but few of them entered commerce at the clerical level, despite the usual poppycock talked by fathers about the importance of starting at the bottom. Businessmen's sons, he noted, invariably began their business life several rungs up, but now times were changing rapidly. More and more Old Boys came to him, or wrote to him, with tales of long spells of unemployment, and the inadequacy of a formal education in the scramble for jobs on an open market. It was time, he thought, to give seniors approaching school-leaving age a head-start, by introducing them to the kind of jobs they might have to use as footholds in the free-for-all of competitive business.

There was, however, another and strictly personal reason for introducing a commercial course, and it was Christine's letter that brought it into the open. Grace would be thirteen in May, and could expect about four more years at school. Nothing would please him more than to have her back here permanently. With the prospect of her acquiring secretarial skills at Bamfylde he could hope to reduce those four years to two. Bamfylde needed a woman's touch at the centre of affairs, and she was already half-qualified for the job. She knew hundreds of Bamfeldians by name and almost as many parents. Algy said she was tarred with the Bamfylde brush but in softer hues—"Shades of sweet pea, wouldn't you say, P.J.?"

The builders moved in during a dry spell in January and everyone had to adapt to the uproar and vast array of bricks, wheelbarrows and cement mixers about the place. When the foundations of the new wing were dug, and the first line of bricks had been laid, Stratton-Forbes wrote suggesting they should place a school muster-roll in a cavity, and this was done at an informal public ceremony. Even David, however, who thought himself attuned to Bamfylde's eccentricities, was surprised by the orgy of commemorative inscribing that followed. Half the boys in the school scratched their names in wet concrete, some of the bolder ones defacing the pier supporting the stone where the memorial plaque would be fixed. He took no counter action but mentioned the outcrop at assembly one morning, referring to that particular section of the foundations as the wailing wall, and advising vandals to beat their heads against it in moments of stress. It was a successful joke, of the kind he was beginning to fashion nowadays, and a matter for secret pride when he discovered that the facing side of the new block was permanently dubbed The Wailing Wall.

He gave Chad and Alison Boyer an unusual wedding present that spring, undertaking to pay for the installation of an indoor privy at the cottage. "Beth and I abominated that feature of the place," he told them, when they were moving in. "It's no joke to wade across that yard in dressing gown and slippers in a north-easterly. I've given Grover instructions to take in a small section of the landing and connect it with the kitchen wastepipe." When Boyer said, chuckling, "It's lucky we aren't displaying our gifts at a wedding breakfast, Pow-Wow," he said, "Ah, you may laugh now but Alison will live to thank me for it."

The term slipped by and it was Easter before he knew it. The sodden moor to the west came to life again and the Sunsetters began their traditional task of preparing the cricket pitch. Then, suddenly, it was full summer again, with extra half-day holidays reintroduced for the important cricket matches, and the inter-house drill competition, and Certificate 'A' examination, conducted by a spruce young captain sent from the War Office.

He was still disinclined to take an active interest in the Corps, apart from keeping a fatherly eye on the band, now capable of playing Sousa's marches, 'Soldiers of the Queen', and many another martial tune, but still saddled with the derisory title of the Orpheans. The School Forum made progress, and another innovation, a housemasters' fortnightly conference was successful, although Howarth was cynical about it. "No more than a cast-iron excuse to skip a period and sit around guzzling coffee, P.J.," he said, but Algy approved. He was over here a good deal nowadays, sometimes to the shameful neglect of his parish, and was already recruiting for next term's *Pirates of Penzance*, but warned that, when the nights drew in, David would have to take over production. "My eyesight isn't what it was," he said, "and it would be undignified to finish my time here upside down in a bog."

"No more than a case of the moor claiming its own," David told him. "How many years have you been up here now?"

"Forty, counting my five-year stint under Wesker," Algy said. "Half my lifetime, and I count the other half wasted. Look at me, my boy, well beyond the allotted span and I could still head the Second Form round the buildings, given a modest start!"

"I believe you could," David said. Then, diffidently,

"How am I making out, Algy? For my private ear alone?" and Algy replied, cheerfully, "Fair to middling. What are your own conclusions?"

"Rather on the lines of a hospital report, 'as well as can be expected', but I still find authority over the senior staff a bit embarrassing. Can't help feeling, sometimes, that it's a bit of a liberty to give orders to chaps like Howarth, who were learning their trade when I was learning to read."

"The point is you don't, P. J. One of your rare qualifications—and I flatter myself I spotted it a week after you came here—is that you have the knack of gentle persuasion. Men like Howarth respond to it, even when they have reservations about your policies."

"They aren't my policies at all, they're extensions of yours, Algy."

"Perhaps, but where do you suppose I got mine? Invented 'em? Of course I didn't. Something rubs off from everything you read, observe and tinker with. The job's really no more than a lifelong process of subconscious distillation of other men's successes and failures. Point is, most chaps in our line of business let their arteries harden at thirty-five and become their own worst enemies on that account. Self-doubt never did anyone any harm, so long as it's offset by the gambling spirit. And by all accounts you've got your share of that. Your prefects don't beat any more, I hear."

"No, they don't and never will under me. That was something I always thought you'd sit on, Algy."

"Never had the nerve. I was lazier, too. But I approve, none the less. You seem to be bringing on a decent lot of seniors, but don't be surprised if you come across the odd rotten apple. You lay odds with yourself that you know how to spot them from afar but every now and again you come a mucker, particularly as regards the selection of prefects."

"What do you do then, Algy? Demote him on the spot?"

"Never. Bad for the system."

"Why?"

"Gives the old lags in Middle School the notion they can unseat any perk providing they go the right way about it. No, you tail him, everywhere he goes, until he gets nervous and keeps looking over his shoulder. That tames 'em. They either pull their socks up or leave a term or two ahead of schedule."

"You see, I still have to consult the oracle at least once a week."

"I should think so. I was the despot here nearly twenty-four years, and you're coming up to your second. Be reasonable, old son. If you lived two lifetimes you'd still be carried away in a box without knowing the half of it."

II

Sports Day, Whitsuntide Reunion and Opening Day.

Carter, suave and successful-looking, arrived for Sports Day, telling David he now had over two hundred boys and was, in his jubilant phrase, 'fairly coining it, old man'. David did not envy him. His approach was too much like merchandising, as Howarth was quick to comment on over a gin and tonic that night, when dusk had fallen, and the last parental car had swept off down the drive.

"Man might as well be churning out those bloody little gnomes for suburban lily-ponds," he growled. "A place of that kind isn't a school, it's an assembly belt, with the staff stationed at stipulated intervals, screwing up nuts and applying the odd touch of solder."

Many others appeared that same day, some of them faces that David had not seen in years, and a few he had never seen at all. One comparatively new friend was Mrs. Hislop, whom he had first met when she restored her son to them in his first term as head. A Northerner, she found it difficult to express gratitude but managed it somehow. "That man Alcock did the boy a good turn," she said. "Pulled him up short and don't think I didn't know he needed a jolt. But you did him an even better turn by letting him come back again. My guess is you're going to be proud of him before he's finished."

"In a way I already am," he told her, "but for Heaven's sake don't tell him I said so."

At Whitsuntide there was a swarm of visitors, among them Stoker Monk who, now that he was at liberty to smoke himself to death, had taken up rowing and renounced the weed. Twitted on this account, as he and David contributed their quota to the sustained uproar in the Old Boys' bar, he justified his eccentric behaviour. "After that first pipeful in the Third, when I wasn't sick but everybody else was, I had a reputation to maintain," he said, "but now, who gives a damn whether I smoke or not?"

Archer the Third elbowed his way forward, back for the first time since leaving in 1924, and reminded David of the occasion when he got lost during a run-in and the whole field had to be turned out to search for him. Archer, now a captain in the Royal Engineers, had seen action on the North-West Frontier. "They recommended me for a decoration for completing a bridge under sniper fire," he said, "but I'd swop that experience any day for the two hours I sat under that hedge, waiting for you to show up. Never so pleased to see anyone in my natural, Pow-Wow."

It made him feel, as the day wore on, he was now a sizeable thread in the Bamfylde pattern of legend. Skidmore drove up, confirming every prophecy made about him by appearing in a dog collar, just as they had feared when he spent so long at his prayers, but unlikely, David concluded, to qualify for martyrdom. He had charge of a big Methodist church in what he called 'the Yorkshire Bible belt', a place where 'the presentation of a good *Messiah* every year is the key to the kingdom of heaven'. It amazed David to hear Skidmore talk like that and he put it down to a general broadening of the mind among Methodists since the recent amalgamation of rival factions, a subject upon which Skidmore had some interesting comments. "If we can do it after all this time, then any denomination can," he declared. "Wouldn't that be something? An amalgamation of all the Christian churches in Britain?"

"I'm afraid it's a pipedream, Preacher," David said, but Skidmore said he wasn't so sure. "If things get rough enough it could happen," he said. "I think I'll live to see it."

"I hope you do," he said, and turned to greet the younger of the Kassava brothers, Jimmy, the eleven-year-old who had clung to the ledge until his brother had knocked him out so that he could be lowered into the quad like a sack of flour. Kassava was now a lieutenant in the Indian Army and his brother, he told David, was walking the wards in Manchester Infirmary and had plans to practise in Delhi. It

made David glow a little to hear all these titbits but it also
made him aware of his age, as though he had come to Bamfylde as a toddler instead of an old-young crock of twenty-one.
Time, they said, speeded up after one's thirtieth birthday,
and it seemed to be true in his case, for here he was, at thirty-
seven, feeling as superannuated as Algy. Then something
reminded him that others were growing older. Blades
buttonholed him, in order to introduce his fiancée, a shy,
extremely pretty brunette, with a pleasant smile and a low-
pitched voice. Blades had gone into publishing and talked
enthusiastically of David's best-selling account of the Wars of
the Roses, tucking his publishing card into David's breast-
pocket—"In case you don't get the best terms with your
people when you come up with something new," he said.
"They say we don't poach authors, but that's a polite fiction."
Talking to them David recalled a comment by Julia Darbyshire, after she had shown him Blades' parody of Herrick,
written in her honour—"He'll make some lucky girl a
wonderful husband one day . . ." and it looked as if Julia
might be right, for the girl gazed at Blades all the time he was
talking, glance steady and lips slightly parted, as though
she could hardly wait to get him to bed. He wondered then
whether Blades had told her about his brush with the Second
Form mistress and decided he had not. She was the kind of
girl who wouldn't want to know, and Blades was sharp
enough to realise this.

He drifted off then, to take Alison Boyer into tea, for Alison
was quite overwhelmed by all this parading and gossiping,
and all the smartly dressed women strolling about. She said,
in an urgent aside, "They're awfu' fine, some of them. I hope
my outfit didnae let Chad down."

"Don't ever worry about letting Chad down, Alison. One
of the most sensible things he ever did, and in his youth he
didn't do so many, was to marry you. How are your evening
classes coming along?"

The evening classes were those devoted by Boyer to Alison
and Chad had told him she tackled them with fanatical zeal.
"She's even approached Barnaby about elementary Latin,"
he said. "I thought that was going over the top a bit. Damn
it all, why does she need Latin?"

"To draw level with you and keep your end up with all the other masters' wives."

"But good God, Pow-Wow, no master's wife here knows a word of Latin."

"That's so, and acquiring some would give her the edge on them and you the edge on their husbands. The Scots are a very competitive lot, Chad. How do you suppose they managed to populate Canada single-handed, give or take a handful of English fur-trappers and remittance men?"

Opening Day was a more ceremonious occasion, with Lady Hopgood pulling the tapes on a sheet of tarpaulin screening the inscription plaque of the new wing, and any number of county dignitaries standing around to contribute a dutiful round of applause. The new block looked horribly raw against the grey stone and weathered red-brick of Big School but Algy, commenting on this in a breezy speech, said the sleet that came over the moor between October and March would soon take the gloss from it. By Christmas, he assured them, the block would have learned to lurch into the wind, like all the other buildings on the plateau.

The new hall was all but finished then and work began on the classrooms above. The O.B. Fund had topped the ten thousand mark, and the Governing Body were successful in getting an overdraft at the bank, so foundations were dug for the gymnasium and sports room that were to replace the covered playground, the fives court and library block. If the money ran to it there was provision in the plans for a dozen new studies but if subscriptions slowed down Fifth Form studies would have to wait on better times. David, contemplating the overdraft, extracted some comfort from the fact that the drop in numbers had levelled off and next term's figures promised an increase of about a dozen, with the waiting-list still fluctuating around a hundred mark. "We'll break even at about three-fifty," the bursar told him, but Barnaby came up with a very ambitious idea, although it was one that would have to wait upon a sizeable legacy or endowment. "The great thing nowadays," he said, "is to catch 'em young. What we ought to aim at, P.J., is our own prep department, catering for upwards of thirty nine-to-ten-year-olds, and a bright young graduate to run it. That way

we should soon climb to four hundred again and be absolutely safe. Think about it. The country won't always be
wallowing in this slough of despond. Even Wall Street is
picking up a bit, I hear, in spite of that chap Roosevelt, who
seems to have scared the bankers half out of their wits."

David did think about it but deferred it until they had a
slice of luck, of the kind they had in 1912, when a wealthy and
eccentric father, having lost his only son in an overseas
drowning accident, died a widower, leaving twelve thousand
pounds to Bamfylde solely because the school had been mentioned in his son's last letter home, written the day he died.

Then, with building progressing rapidly, the summer term
slipped away, and everybody went home, and he and Grace
toured the Western Isles as far as Skye, then came south
again, where he left her to spend the last fortnight of the
holidays with her grandparents at Elmer's End.

He had a big backlog of work before the new school year
opened in mid-September, and was glad of Boyer's help,
spending a good deal of his time in the cottage, where Beth's
rowan tree and wild Devonshire garden were thriving.

It was after contemplating them, on his way back to school
one warm September evening, that he turned aside at the
lychgate and went down the path to the Bamfylde preserve,
on the excuse of satisfying himself that the sexton was mowing
the grass.

He had no morbid feelings about being here, in the secluded
spot under the yew where Beth and Joan had lain since that
unforgettable summer of 1925. Over the years his memories
of them had merged into the school, riding the western skyline. Their dust was as much a part of it as that of Judy
Cordwainer and Bat Ferguson close by, and of his own
flesh and blood too, he thought, as he stood with the evening
sun warming his back and looking across the huddle of Ma
Midden's farm and Chad's cottage to the higher slope of the
moor. Blackbirds sang here and all but the Bamfylde head-
stones, or the few raised to newly dead villagers, leaned in
one direction or another. Gray could have written another
elegy here, he thought, and then doubted it as, beyond the
low hedge, he saw a sports car rush past, hurrying towards
the farm. A stray Old Boy, no doubt, anxious to assure him-

self that Ma Midden still made the tastiest pasties in Devon.

He went into the church and sat down to collect his thoughts. He often came here these days, ostensibly to work something out but actually to escape the clamour of school and yet remain within call. It was odd, he had told himself more than once, that a man born and raised a Welsh Baptist should seek and find peace here in what his mother would have dismissed as a Popish church, and he was recalling Preacher Skidmore's remark on the prospects of a sectless Britain, when he heard steps echo on the slate slabs outside the west door, then the door open, and a familiar voice said, "Had an idea I'd find you here. Boyer said you were on your way back but I didn't pass anyone." He stood up, dumb with amazement. "Yes, it's me! The perennial bad penny, home from the sea."

It took him ten seconds to convince himself that Chris was standing there, leaning against the oak door and smiling across at him. Chris Forster, sunburned, relaxed, and far more sure of herself than the girl he remembered even in their carefree Windermere days.

"Why the blazes didn't you ring or write? Why didn't you let me know you were home? I'd quite made up my mind you had gone for good. Damn it, you haven't sent so much as a postcard in weeks!"

She said, quietly, "Stop being a bear and come over here and kiss me. It wouldn't be the first time in this church, would it?"

He dived round the end of the pew and threw his arms round her and they stood there for several minutes saying nothing. Behind the swift rush of affection he was aware of a number of inconsequential things; the sunburned V on her neck; the fact that she wore her hair in the fashionable long bob; an unfamiliar perfume, that reminded him vaguely of sandalwood; a persistent blackbird, whistling a repetitive theme in the big yew clump beyond the belfry tower, things that somehow compounded Beth rather than her. She said, gently. "I'm not home for long, Davy. It's very much of a flying visit and I'll explain why. But first I've a surprise for you outside in the car. It's all right, don't scowl! It's male, but it isn't a husband."

They went out into the evening sunshine and up the path to the road where a little sports car was parked, the kind of silver grey toy some of the wilder spirits drove when returning to school a term or two after they had left. It was empty and he said, "You mean *that*? The car?" and she laughed, calling, "Ulrich? You don't have to hide! Where are you?"

A dark, rather sallow boy of about ten sidled into view, returning from the direction of the farm, hidden by the bend in the road. He was a continental. David could see that at a glance and this was established not so much by his clothes, grey knickerbockers and pork-pie hat, with a little feather tucked into the band, but by his bobbing little bow in David's direction. He was a spindly, undernourished little chap, with large, melancholy eyes that at once sought Christine's, apprehensively he would say.

She said, briskly, "This is Herr Powlett-Jones, Ulrich, headmaster of the school. Don't be shy. He's a very kind man. Come over and shake hands."

Ulrich approached gingerly, hand fully extended continental fashion, and when David shook and released it, he stepped smartly back, made another little bow and came smartly to attention.

"Ulrich," she said, "has just lost his father and his mother died a year ago. In a way I've adopted him, haven't I, Ulrich?"

The boy's defenceless eyes sought hers again, so that David thought, "He's in a rare pickle of one sort or another, and she's fishing him out of it," and Ulrich at once confirmed this, saying "Always you have been most kind, Fraulein Forster."

"We'll go back to school now, Ulrich, for I have to make arrangements for you," and the child climbed obediently into the back seat, where he folded his arms and sat very erect, looking as expressionless as a page on ceremonial duty.

Chris said, as David squeezed in beside her, "His name is Meyer. I'll explain about him later. He's been fed. I introduced him to Rigby, who kindly took him down to the kitchen and while he was eating I looked for you but couldn't find you. Then a groundsman said you were down at Boyer's cottage so we both came looking."

She was like Grace in that way. She never forgot anything he told her about the school and was well aware Chad Boyer had been one of his favourites and had recently joined the staff. She was a fast and expert driver. In a flash they were shooting up the east drive and skidding to a halt on the fore-court gravel.

"Would it be asking too much to let Ulrich stay here with you until term begins, Davy?"

"That's no problem," he said. "I'll tell Rigby to bed him down in the sanatorium. The boys return on Thursday and when they do he can go in Nicolson's until you collect him." He turned to the child, now standing to attention. "You don't have to be correct here, Ulrich, and certainly not in the holidays. Go with this gentleman, and he'll show you where you can sleep," and as the door closed behind child and butler, "You're a great one for springing things on me. You haven't really adopted him, have you?"

"Not officially," she said, "but I intend to, providing it can be arranged."

"Well, it can't," he said. "I've had occasion to go into these things, and as our law stands someone in your situation wouldn't be allowed to adopt a boy. Maybe Canadian law is different. Has he any relatives in the States?"

"No, Davy. None."

"How long do you want to board him?"

She said, looking at him steadily, "Permanently, Davy. If it could be arranged. I'm getting him registered as an official refugee and in time, if all goes as I hope, he'll take up British nationality, but I don't want him regarded as a charity boy. I'll pay his fees."

"*You* will? Two-fifty a year?"

"Well, not me exactly, an organisation set up for cases like Ulrich by the Jewish Rescue Committee in the States. I'm not worried about that part of it, it's more or less fixed. The point is, I want him to have affection . . . help . . . someone to turn to. He's been through a dreadful time. His father was kicked to death in front of his eyes in July. I almost witnessed it myself. Those bloody Brown Shirts, out on the rampage."

"His father was anti-Nazi?"

"His father wasn't anti anything. He was a harmless little

jeweller and his shop was picketed in an anti-Jewish demonstration they staged. You must have read about what's going on in Germany since that foul little bastard took over but maybe it hasn't registered over here. Well, it's real enough there, a daily occurrence. There are scores of Ulrichs in Bavaria alone. I should like to have scooped them all up but I had enough trouble getting one out."

He looked at her with wonder. "Just how *did* you get him out?"

"Kept him hidden in my hotel for a fortnight, then passed him off as my nephew. The point is, it's all happened at a very awkward time for me. I'd have taken him back to the States and given him time to settle a bit, but I'm due to begin this lecture tour on Monday week, and I couldn't have got him a passage at such short notice. The only thing I could think of was to bring him here."

"Tell me about it. But first of all, have you eaten?"

"No, but any old thing will do. I've got to leave in an hour or so. I'm due in London by morning and I sail the day after, from Southampton."

He rang for Rigby and cold supper for two was brought in. She ate at speed, as though racing the clock, and he began to notice she did most things like this. Between gulps she told him how she came to be involved with Ulrich Meyer, towards the end of her three months' stay in Munich. "I'd heard about what was taking place over there but like you, like everyone else outside Germany, it didn't make an impact. I mean, one regarded it as a wave of street riots but it isn't like that at all. It's the end of the world for anyone opposed to Hitler, and for neutrals too. It's like living in Czarist Russia during a Cossack pogrom. Everyone's looking over their shoulder. They've set up camps for Communists, Socialists and Social Democrats, and for any Catholic or Lutheran who speaks out. Gangs of louts range the streets, knocking on people's doors and smashing windows. Before this happened to Herr Meyer, he had '*Juden*' scrawled across his shop windows and men posted outside to turn customers away."

"You mean just in Munich and other Bavarian cities?"

"No, all over. Ever since the Reichstag fire in February.

People outside have got to wake up, Davy. I'm going to start campaigning during my lecture tour but it needs far more than that."

"You mean it's likely to last? That there won't be a counter-revolution of some kind?"

"There might, but even that would mean civil war in the streets, and tyranny of one sort or another. Democracy is finished over there, so long as Hitler and his thugs are around. You can depend on that."

It made him acutely aware of his isolation, a political isolation that he would have found shaming a few years ago. He read the newspapers, and occasionally listened to radio bulletins on the library four-valve set, or one of the homemade radio sets built by radio enthusiasts, of which there were a dozen or so in Bamfylde. But strife and persecution on the scale she was describing, and of which Ulrich Meyer was living proof, had not emerged from news bulletins, only the political instability one had come to accept as the post-war norm in Germany, France and Italy.

He said, "You're right, of course. Down here we're cut off," but she countered, sharply. "*No*, Davy! *Not* just down here. Everywhere on this side of the Channel. I've heard Germans talk openly of '*Der Tag*' again, the way they did before the 1914 war. It's no better in Italy. Fascists there kidnap political opponents, sometimes murder them, and dose others with pints of castor oil. Sooner or later everybody's got to face up to what's happening, and when I get a constituency I'm going to make sure they do."

"That won't win you many friends in the Labour party. They're all for disarmament, aren't they?"

"I can't help about that. I've seen what's happening and they haven't. Ulrich is going to be a *cause célèbre* before I'm done with him."

"And in the meantime I'm in *loco parentis*?"

"I can't think of anyone better suited for the job, can you?" She smiled, got up and came round the table to kiss him. "That's all about my obligations. How are you coping with yours, Davy? How is it working out?"

"Algy Herries tells me fair to middling," he said, "but I'll say one thing. Standing in for three-hundred-odd parents eight months of the year is an ageing process. Look at the hair above my ears."

"There would have been a lot more grey if you hadn't taken the bit between your teeth, Davy. You were a born worrier when I met you, muddling along under that man Alcock. Thank God somebody on that Board had the sense to push you forward. It'll be the saving of this place and the making of you. You already look fruitier than the old Davy."

"I wish I could say the same for you. When are you going to stop driving yourself, Chris?"

She gave him one of her half-humorous and speculative looks. "When I've dropped anchor, like you. When I can see where I'm heading. In that respect you're lucky, Davy. I'll keep in touch and you must write regularly, too, and tell me every last thing about that poor little beggar upstairs. Could I go up and say goodbye to him?"

"Surely. It's left at the top of the stairs, and the door facing at the end of the corridor."

She went out and he rang for Rigby to clear away, moving over to the windows where the last glimmer of light glowed in the far west. It was very quiet and still out there, as though the place was conserving its energies for the tumult of the approaching term.

III

Grace was due back the next day but in the meantime he took 'Stilts' Rhodes into his confidence, sensing that the Sunsetters, above all, would have to be briefed about the arrival of Ulrich Meyer in their midst. They had no continentals at the school and the fact that the boy spoke near-perfect English was a help. But those clothes, and that little bow, would mark him down from the first day of term, and he would have to rely on Stilts to weight circumstances in Meyer's favour.

Stilts was an immensely tall, long-legged Fifth Former, whose father was a railway superintendent in Lahore, an easy-going chap and a brilliant cricketer, who had captained the Bamfylde Eleven through the summer. He was head boy of the Sunsetters and although David did not credit him with much imagination, he relied upon Boyer to press the message home.

Stilts said, aghast, "A Jerry, sir? We've never had one of those, have we?"

"No, we haven't but if things continue to happen, like the circumstances that brought the poor kid here, we're likely to get a steady trickle in a year or so. The point is, I don't want him ragged, not even gently. You've got to behave to him 'correctly', as he understands that word. He's bright but he's had a pretty rough deal for a kid his age. His father was booted to death in front of him only a few weeks ago, and he's a refugee."

Stilts was visibly shocked. "*Booted*, sir? You mean mobbed —lynched?"

"That's exactly what I mean. He's a Jew, and they're attacking Jews on the streets all over Germany. He was smuggled out by a friend of mine."

"A kid his age? Good Lord, sir, they wouldn't have man-handled him, would they?"

"My information from an eye witness is that there's nothing they won't do. You probably read about how they set fire to the Reichstag and charged a half-wit with the crime."

"You mean I should . . . well . . . spread it around, sir? What happened, I mean?"

"Yes, but discreetly. It's the best way of getting him sympathy."

"Well, I'll do what I can, sir. He'll be going in with the Sunsetters, won't he?"

"As soon as term starts. Meantime I'll have to coach him a bit. I daresay he'll regard this place as another kind of bear-garden if I don't. Can I rely on your help, Stilts?"

"Well, yes, sir, under the circumstances . . . I mean, it's a bit much, isn't it? Kicking a chap's pater to death. But I suppose it's the kind of thing you can expect from them, isn't it?"

"I wouldn't have expected it. I fought the Germans for three years, and although I came across the odd brute, most of them seemed pretty decent fellows. I remember upsetting the Fifth when I first came here, telling them how two Jerry prisoners carried me across open ground under a barrage on the Somme, and how front-line infantrymen soon stopped calling them Huns. Some of the chaps thought it pretty odd of me to put in a good word for them. Now, I imagine, I shall have to do it again. The point to remember is it's only a section of Germans who go along with that kind of thing. I hope to God some of the better people sit on Hitler before he gets a real grip on the country."

"Oh, that chap won't last long, sir," Rhodes said, cheerfully, "I mean, he's nuts, isn't he, sir? He looks nuts and he acts nuts. Not like Mussolini."

"You admire Mussolini?"

"No, not exactly, sir, but I was reading in the Sunday paper during the hols that he's smartened the Eyeties up a bit—new roads and suchlike."

"Well, don't believe all you read. My information from the same witness is that he murders his opponents and doses others with pints of castor oil."

It did not seem to shock Stilts as much as the booting. "Is that so, sir? Well, you never can tell what they'll get up to over there," and David thought his attitude was probably reflected by almost every boy at Bamfylde, including the dozen or so coloured boys, and the odd Colonial on the muster roll It made him reflect upon Chris's warning that, on this side of the Channel, everyone tended to lower a safety curtain.

He had a long talk with Ulrich that same day and took him to tea with the Boyers. Alison warmed towards him and he responded to her in the way he had to Chris. "Wouldn't it be a good idea to let him stay here for a term or so?" she asked, but David said no, it would only delay integration. The best way to drop him gently into the deep end.

"It won't be the deep end once the word gets around," Chad said. "If someone had shot his old man it mightn't have made much difference. But kicking, that's different. The chaps won't go for that."

The chaps didn't. Within two days of reassembly Meyer became an object of respectful curiosity. Nobody chivvied him, nobody jeered at his outlandish clothes, or his formal manners. He was an extraordinarily bright little boy. Barnaby and Howarth said he was up to Lower Fifth standard, and Renshaw-Smith discovered that he had a rare appreciation of classical music and was a promising pianist. "It only goes to show," Howarth grumbled, "that there's something bloody wrong with our system of education. Here's a child of eleven who is already at home with Goethe, and we have louts in the Sixth who make nothing at all of Goldsmith and Tennyson. I don't know, maybe we're all on a wrong tack, P.J."

"I wouldn't say that," David said, "there's nothing wrong with Continental academic standards but the boy's presence here proves they've got a hell of a lot to learn about the art of government. I know which slant Algy Herries would favour."

"Question of priority," said Barnaby, and came up with the inevitable tag from his favourite Tacitus—'*reipublicae forma laudari facilius quam evenire . . .*' translating it, in response to Howarth's bleak stare, as "It is easier for a form of government to be praised than brought about; if brought about it cannot be made lasting."

"I prefer Burke," grunted Howarth. "More down to earth. 'Among a people generally corrupt liberty cannot long exist.'"

David left them spouting at one another and went about his business, but Ulrich Meyer proved a springboard for some lively current affairs discussions with the Sixth that term, particularly as regards recent events in Germany. The trial of Van der Lubbe, for the Reichstag fire, followed by the threatened withdrawal of Germany from The League, were two sizeable straws in the wind and Meyer's presence among them gave both items an immediacy they would not otherwise have had. Hislop was particularly aggressive, declaring that Germany, left to herself, would soon prove the menace she was twenty years before, and 'ought to be sat on, pronto!' The mild-mannered Christopherson II took the pacifist line, declaring that a new armaments race was the most certain way of bringing about a second World War. Where did David stand, he asked, looking for support from such a well-known opponent of militarism but David, who always tried to be absolutely frank with the Sixth, had to admit that he did not know.

"The fact is," he said, "any sane man should prefer civilised discussion to war, as a means of settling international disputes, but what do you do against brute force? Meyer's father was a pacifist. It didn't stop the louts picketing his shop, kicking him to death and running off scot-free."

"There's provision in The League of Nations Charter for the application of economic sanctions," protested Christopherson, but Hislop came back with, "Nobody seems all that anxious to stop trading with Japan since its invasion of Manchuria."

Christopherson, one of the few seniors with strong religious convictions, held to his point, aware that he was in a minority of one. "If a nation professes Christianity, oughtn't it to practise Christian virtues in politics, sir?" but before David could think of an answer Mainwaring growled, "Christian virtues, my eye! If anyone started shoving my Governor around he'd wake up in hospital if he woke up at all!" and everyone laughed as the bell rang, and the familiar hum of dismissal rose from surrounding classrooms. They hustled out, most of them, for a quick puntabout until lunch bell, but Nixon, a boy who had travelled the Continent during his holidays, remained and seemed, David thought, troubled.

"Well, Nixon?"

"Excuse me, sir . . . something I didn't like to mention in front of the others—I mean—seeing we had a kid like Meyer here. Have you read *The Road Back*, sequel to *All Quiet on the Western Front*?"

"No, I haven't, Nixon. Does it have a bearing on what we've been discussing?"

"In a way it does, sir. It's concerned with what the Jerry front-line troops found when they went home after the war. The whole country had been sewn up by the war profiteers while they were away at the Front."

"That wasn't peculiar to Germany. Every country had its own crop of profiteers who made a pot of money while others slogged it out in the mud."

"Yes I know, sir. But I met a one-legged ex-service chap in St. Moritz when I was there in the Easter hols and he said the German Jews had sat up and begged for what they were getting. What I mean is, maybe it's a case of six of one and half a dozen of the other? Hitler recruits from ex-service chaps, doesn't he? I daresay a lot of them have got it in for the Jews. Mightn't that be a reason why a screw-ball like Hitler gets so much support?"

He was glad Nixon had asked that question. It gave him a chance to get the situation into a better focus. He said, "The fact is, Nixon, the two things don't match up. Jew-baiting has been a time-honoured sport on the part of despots for centuries, a means of diverting attention from failures on the part of the government. The Tsars went in for it, so did the Spaniards. And Henry V—a chap I never could stand—kicked the Jews out of England at one time. It was Cromwell who had the sense to invite them back. I daresay there were Jewish war profiteers in Germany, but profiteering isn't a Jewish prerogative by any means, so don't fall for that one, however convincing that one-legged Jerry sounded. The Jews are singled out because they're easily recognisable."

"Yes, sir. Thank you. You didn't mind me mentioning it?"

"I'm very glad you did," David said, "but gladder still you had the sense to raise it in private. Baiting sects on account of race, religion or colour is wrong on any account, wouldn't you say?"

"Yes, I suppose it is, sir," and Nixon pottered off, still only half-convinced, so that David reflected both he and Bamfylde owed Christine Forster a debt for dumping Ulrich Meyer in their midst. The funny little chap was already serving as a catalyst.

He went through Big School door into his quarters and saw, on the hall table, a pile of letters that had arrived with the midday post. One from Chris was among them. She was keeping her promise to write once a week and this one was was post-marked Cincinnati. She was well-launched on her tour, it seemed, and he was looking forward to the pleasure of reading her latest news when he heard an apologetic cough at his elbow. Little Meyer was standing there, as usual at attention. He was holding an unsealed letter, addressed to 'Fraulein Forster', but with nothing else on the envelope. He said, "Well, Meyer? What can I do for you today?" and Meyer said, "Sir I have made my report to Miss Forster. I would be happy if you would address this letter for me. After approving it, of course."

"You mean you want me to look it over for grammar, Meyer?"

The child did not blink. "No, sir. The grammar is correct. I took great pains with the composition. But you will want to approve what I write."

"Censor your letter? I don't want to do that. We don't censor boys' letters home. Why should I have to read yours in particular?"

"Sir?"

He realised that Meyer was confused and said, "Come inside, I'll try and explain," and they went into the living-room where lunch was laid. "Sit down, Meyer, and listen. It was polite of you to invite me to read it and I will, of course, if you really wish it. But don't get the idea it's standard practice here. Most of the boys would be angry if they thought masters read their private mail, and rightly so. Letters to parents and friends are personal, private things, and everyone is entitled to personal privacy as a right, do you follow me?"

"Yes, sir . . . but it is unusual, is it not? I mean, that would qualify as an English custom?"

"Well, you could put it that way. Now then, do you really want me to read it before I address it? Or would you honestly prefer that I didn't?"

Meyer seemed to give the matter considerable thought. Finally he said, extending his hand, "I wish to observe all your customs, sir. If I am to become an Englishman that is important, is it not?"

"I think it is, Meyer," and improbably he thought of Beth and how, in these circumstances, she might have reached out and hugged the child, as someone in desperate need of love. He experienced the same impulse, almost as though it was relayed to him, but all he said was, "Here's a letter from Miss Forster with her last address on the back. Copy it down, seal it and put your letter in the post-box."

"Yes, sir. Thank you, sir," and Meyer clicked his heels and gave his formal little bow.

He was relieved, a fortnight or so later, that Meyer had decided to observe English customs. Chris wrote saying

You might be interested to learn Ulrich sees you as a combination of Luther and Frederick the Great, with a dash of Moses thrown in. It's quite obvious he's settling there, as I knew he would with you to keep an eye on him, so I want to say thank you again, Davy, for making the effort, when you obviously have so much on your plate.

I'm two-thirds through this tour now and it looks as though I shall be home in the spring. There's talk of me being put forward for Ben Cathcart's constituency, in Openshawe South, when he retires and this is far better than I hoped. It has a Labour majority of over eight thousand, so, given ordinary luck, I couldn't fail to get elected. I won't catch you on the hop, again, Davy. We'll meet somewhere as soon as I get back, and if it's term-time you'll have to drop everything and come.

It was good to think of her impending return after all this time but he was resigned now to her marriage to politics. With a seat like Openshawe South in the offing she was already as good as elected, and once in Parliament she would be lost to him. He filed her letter with all the others and locked the file away. It seemed to him a symbolic gesture.

CHAPTER THREE

I

The terminal-season rhythm caught him up again, so smoothly and compellingly that he often forgot he was now its arbiter here, with the power to vary the tempo and volume, to throw away the book if he felt like it, and replace it with a new one—but he did nothing so drastic. Most of the changes and adjustments he introduced were marginal, infiltrating themselves into the system within a matter of weeks or days, so that visiting Old Boys of Algy's vintage were rarely prompted to make disparaging comparisons, the privilege of all Old Boys everywhere. His life was a calendar within a calendar, so regulated that he could even predict the weather in advance. Mid-December, for instance, with Chad Boyer back in his former role as the pirate king in *The Pirates of Penzance*, a sequence of tingling, frosty days, when the ruts in west drive were coated with ice and Chivenor, head prefect, crossed the lighted quad at lock-up 'clothed in his breath' as Tennyson might have seen him, save that Chivenor carried a large bunch of keys instead of Excalibur. The Christmas lull, with light snow turning to slush, and the lowest boughs of the east drive beeches dripping down his neck as he walked, heavily mufflered down to Chad's cottage for tea and muffins by a familiar hearth.

A new term, slowed by January mire, with a stream of cars arriving in slashing rain, disgorging cargoes of boys for the tight-rope term. Howarth's winter cough, booming a warning that his old enemy bronchitis would lay him low before March. The new buildings deserted by the builders' men, who could do nothing in this kind of weather, leaving the half-finished gymnasium raw and skeletal against a grey winter sky.

Then February, with everybody's tempers edgy, Moly-neux and Howarth bickering over trivial issues and young

Dennison, who had followed Irvine as geography master, resigning command of the Corps on account of cartilage trouble—few of these things actually impinged on him but the Corps vacuum did, and he made what seemed to those who remembered his earlier prejudices, a revolutionary decision, taking command himself and appearing in the quad for the first time in a brand new khaki outfit, with three pips on his shoulder.

"I feel a very bogus captain," he told Barnaby, when the latter ironically saluted him. "I would have wagered ten pounds to a penny you'd never see me in this rig again. But, hang it all, the Corps is there, and no one else seems to have a clue about how to run it. Besides, I'm only half a pacifist nowadays."

"I daresay the drill book is a bit above your head these days, P.J.," Barnaby said. "You won't have them kneeling to receive cavalry, I hope?" But the drill book hadn't changed all that much. They were still using Lewis guns, of the type David had lugged up the line in 1917, still forming fours, still singing the same old songs on route marches, choruses that had brought tears to his eyes on Armistice Day, in 1918, but now seemed as harmlessly nostalgic as carols.

One or two of the Old Boys pulled his leg about his conversion. One (it was Starchy Gosse, now a stockbroker) raising his hat and giving a cheer as he watched Captain Powlett-Jones dismissing his troops on the playing field after the drill competition.

"Permit me to recant too, Pow-Wow," he said, after following David to his quarters for the obligatory glass of Old Boys' sherry. "I once regarded you as the envoy of Lenin and Trotsky. You probably don't know how close you came to getting stuck with 'Bolshie' instead of the cosy 'Pow-Wow'!"

"I knew all right," David told him. "I overheard you or your brother discussing me while sitting on Algy's Mount Olympus, so let me tell you something in return. I'm still Bolshie as regards the fun and games chaps like you play in Threadneedle Street. If we'd guillotined the whole damned crowd of you in Trafalgar Square, maybe I wouldn't be doing this now."

Gosse took the gibe in good part, as they all did whenever

they came back here, poking around and indulging in their orgies of reminiscence. His approach to them was that of an equal, with no obligation to counsel and patronise, now that they were out in the world.

March, with weeks of cold, drying winds, hardening the pitches, so that Nicolson's was able to confound the form book by winning the rugby shield, beating Havelock's, the hot favourites, by fourteen points. But March, for him, was a sad month, too, his sister Gwynneth wiring to say his mother had died in her sleep on Good Friday, a week before he was due to pay one of his bi-annual visits.

He and Grace travelled to Wales for the funeral, and Grace waited in the crowded little kitchen while he went into the front parlour to take a final look at her, surrounded by armfuls of daffodils and narcissi. She looked not merely peaceful but girlish, so that he caught his breath, wondering how so much sorrow, and so many years of unremitting toil, could leave so small a mark on her features. For her, for him too, at that moment, time stood still and he was looking at the same woman who had gone about her chores that sum-mer evening he sat stunned in the kitchen, choking on the high tea she set before him only hours after they had told her that she had lost a husband and two sons in the pit explosion down the Valley. For sheer grit and stamina there had never been anybody like her, not even in the trenches. She had the kind of faith that made molehills of mountains of trouble, enabling her to absorb any shock, any disaster, any dis-appointment, with the dignity one associated with eighth-century saints.

He stood there aware of a sense of loss but no grief, for they told him she had given no sign of pain, or even discomfort, on retiring to bed the night she died. She had even spent the morning giving the parlour a spring-clean, as though she had a premonition it was likely to be seen by strangers within the week. All the wreaths and sprays surrounding the coffin trailed the usual black-edged cards, with assurances that struck him as a little smug, even though he was accustomed to the conventions of death in the Valley. 'Safe in the arms of Jesus', 'Gathered to her eternal rest' and 'In the certain hope of a glorious resurrection'. He wondered if the neighbours

who had penned them had possessed her kind of faith, a
deep-rooted assurance in the natural order of things, an
unassailable belief that a Blessed Redeemer would forgive
her sins, if she had any, and reunite her with the stocky little
man buried a few miles from here, far below the surface of
the mountain. It was a faith that had sustained her through
every trial and hazard, something intensely personal that
had very little to do with the chants, prayers and affirma-
tions proclaimed in the Elim Chapel down the hill. No one
he had ever met had possessed such a faith, fused as it was
with a sense of duty, and an obligation towards everyone
her life had touched, a faith impervious to grief and penury,
the faith of a child, buttressed by loving parents against every
eventuality, even death itself. A faith like that was worth a
million in the bank, and half a dozen Bamfyldes. Yet, in a
sense, he had been able to borrow a little of it over the years.
The spark it had lit in him as a child had never been entirely
extinguished, as he had once believed, by the crashing bom-
bardments of the Somme, and the long, dragging ordeal of
Passchendaele. It had survived, to be blown upon by Algy
and others on the moor, by the fortitude of kids like Briarley,
whose father had been killed in action in the last days of the
war, when he was still a new boy, and of Winterbourne, by
Beth's love, by the patience of young Grace, by the friendship and encouragement of men like Howarth and Barnaby,
but, above all, by a sense of contributing that had grown
upon him like another skin, a little every year, a fraction
every term.

He squeezed the small, cold hand and went back into the
kitchen where Ewart, his brother-in-law, was sitting smoking
half a Woodbine. Ewart said, "There's four years left on the
lease yer, Davyboy. You wouldn't have no objections to me
and Gwyn moving in, and taking it over, would you now?
It's three shillings a week under the rent we pay for our
rabbit-hutch, and me being on short-time . . ."

"Whatever bits and pieces she left are Gwyn's and Megan's,
Ewart. That was always understood. Aren't things any
better up here?" and Ewart said a little but not all that much.
The Valley had never recovered from the strife and shutdowns
of 1925 and 1926.

"Why don't you think about moving south? There's no future here and you're still in your prime."

"What else could I do, boyo? Been underground since I was fourteen, I have."

"How much do you earn in a good week?"

"Three-five," Ewart told him, "and I'm one of the lucky ones."

He thought, "We pay our groundsmen four pounds a week and they have accommodation thrown in. Old Westacott is due to retire in September, and that means everybody will move up one. I wonder if I could wangle Ewart the handyman's job? Or if he'd accept it, with me being head. I'll have a word with Gwyn after the funeral."

As he had half-expected, his sister had reservations. "Suppose I should talk him into it," she said, "would it be right? A headmaster, with a sister married to the odd-job man? What I mean is, wouldn't it make you look a little bit silly, Davy? Because if it did Mam wouldn't have heard of us going. You know that, boyo."

"Mam was old-fashioned that way. I tried to talk her into coming down when I first got the job but she wouldn't and I daresay that was the real reason. However, times have changed. I've got Old Boys with degrees taking jobs as counter-jumpers and clerks, and in one way it's a good thing. If things improved in the mines you could always move back. Why don't you think it over?"

"I'll do that," she said, "and thanks anyway, Davy," and she kissed him.

II

Chris rang as he had feared, in the first week of the new term, when it was impossible to snatch a weekend and meet her in London on her way up north, where she was due to be interviewed by the selection committee of the Openshawe South Division. Her candidature was regarded as a near-certainty, for she was on a short-list of two, opposed by another academic. "Male, of course," she said, "but wet. He's written a book on political economy. I tried to read it. It was like eating my way through four helpings of Bamfylde suet pudding."

"How old is he?" David wanted to know, and she said thirty-two or three. "He's a prominent pacifist, so at least our approaches offer alternatives. His father was a friend of Bertrand Russell, who served time during the war as a conscientious objector."

"Seems grass-rooted," David said, "you'd better watch him."

"Come, you don't really believe that, Davy. Not after what happened to Ulrich's father."

"I don't know what I believe any more. Sometimes I think the Sixth Formers have a clearer picture of what's happening than I have. Politically speaking I'm a museum-piece nowadays. Listen, hustler, it's hopeless for me to think of getting up there this weekend. Assuming you get chosen, when is your adoption meeting likely to be?"

"Second week in May, but how can you attend that? You know what happened last time."

He could chuckle at that. "It's not the same," he said, "these days I call the tune and they'd have the devil's own job to unseat me now. Algy and Howarth say I'd see 'em all off. How about the Saturday after next, in Manchester?"

"Please, *sir*," she said, and then, "I still love you very much, Davy."

"I'm delighted to hear it. But will it survive a wildly ac-claimed maiden speech in the House?"

"It would survive me becoming the first Prime Minister in petticoats and you know it. You're just fishing for compliments."

He rang off, feeling braced. There was no positive future in their association but it was good to feel they still enjoyed the easy comradeship of the past, after such a long separation.

*   *   *

He had not expected her to meet him at the barrier, assuming she would be too busy, but she was there, peering anxiously at the stream of passengers from the West Country train, and he realised at once that something was amiss. She looked as bleak and tense as the night he had escorted her home to her lodgings, after that rowdy meeting, in the autumn of 1931, and bore no resemblance to his assessment of the eager girl he had talked to on the phone ten days before. He said, at once, "What's happened, Chris? That long-haired chap hasn't pipped you, has he?" and she said, "I could have faced up to it if he had, but you can't call a unanimous vote in his favour a pipping, can you?"

"The same old story? A woman can't win a Labour seat?"

"No, a very new story. They're incapable of facing facts and that's a tragedy, not just for me but for the party, and the country, too, in the long run. Where can we go? I need a drink."

"I booked the night at the Queen's and shall have to sign in. We can get a drink and a meal there. I'll get a taxi."

"It isn't worth it," she said, "it's just down the approach to Piccadilly," and she walked silently beside him down the setts to the hotel lobby, waiting while he signed in and sent the man up with his key and bag. He ordered two double whiskies and noticed she downed hers like a toper.

"Was it so very bad?"

"It's the end of everything for me. For some years, at least."

"But why, for God's sake? There'll be other vacancies, and there are rumours of an election next year."

"You don't get the message. I made a declaration. Some people would see it as tempting Providence, but I can't work any other way, and neither could you if you were in my shoes. The Labour Party is traditionally pacifist. I don't have to remind you of that, do I?"

"No, you don't, but hang it, Chris, even Baldwin is playing it in low keys these days. What the hell did you say to them to set them against you en masse?"

"I told the truth, as I saw it. They asked me my views on disarmament, and I told them it would be sheer madness in view of what's happening in Germany and Italy. Good God, they read the papers, don't they? They must know Jews are being forced to sweep the streets, that their property is being confiscated, that even the toddlers in Germany are being drilled, that anyone who questions Hitler and his Brown Shirts is dragged from his bed in the middle of the night and never seen again. I told them children in schools were being taught to inform on their parents, that the declared policy of Hitler is to build the biggest military machine in history. I told them Socialists were being murdered in Italy, and that newspapers were being sold on the streets of Berlin with cartoons showing Jews eating Christian children. I was there a mere three months but I saw some of these things, and what I didn't see was confirmed by people who had. I told them about Ulrich. Do you know what the Chairman said in reply? The only way to stop it was by Christian example— that disarmament on our part would be a gesture everyone else would follow! How's that for wishful thinking?"

"You don't have to convince me," he said, "I admitted I was confused but I've since had several talks with Meyer. As a matter of fact, I got him to come and talk to the Sixth. It set them thinking, I can tell you. The point is, where do you go from here? Newspaper articles, or a report to Transport House that the party should rethink its policy?"

She made a gesture of impatience. "What good would that do? I'm not the only one who understands what's happening, but how do you set about persuading a caucus to reverse its thinking? For that matter, how do you alert the right wing, never mind the left?"

"I suppose the same way you convince anybody of anything. By simply pegging away."

She said, thoughtfully, "There's more to it than that, Davy. The ability to use Ulrich to make your point for you, at a place as hidebound as Bamfylde, gives you the advantage on all of us. As a matter of fact, since they rejected me in favour of that self-opinionated little whippersnapper, I've been doing some rethinking myself. It's time I did. You can get punch-drunk on blue books and pamphlets and I'm beginning to suffer from a hangover."

"What does that add up to?"

She smiled. "Dear Davy . . . I can't tell you here. How well do you know the country about here?"

"Hardly at all. It's flat and built up, isn't it?"

"No, it isn't. It's only flat on the Cheshire side. We'll go to Dovedale, the best walking country in England. I was there last weekend, with a chum of mine from University days."

"I shall have to catch an early Sunday train back. It's slow and will take me eight hours. Howarth is standing in for me and he's not too well."

"I'll get you back in time."

He followed her out to catch a bus to Openshawe, where her bumble-bee car was garaged and an hour later, meeting little but cycling and hiking parties on the road, they were deep in the Dales, and he saw that he had underestimated Derbyshire, despite doing 'Peveril of the Peak' with the Middle Fourth, when Howarth was off sick last winter. The hills, shimmering in May sunshine, were crowned with masses of rock, and the slopes down to the Dove were clothed with older, more civilised woods than the straggling thickets on the banks of the Bray, Barle and Exe. They had tea in a pub and she led him down to the floor of the valley. Her spirits lifted when they saw the word 'Chatsworth' on a signpost and he reminded her that Mary Queen of Scots, had spent part of her nineteen years' imprisonment up here. She said, "Another poor devil trapped in men's politics. Was she really guilty of all those plots, Davy?"

"As guilty as hell," he said, "She was party to a plot to assassinate Elizabeth by exploding gunpowder under the bed. But it never stopped her being a great favourite in the Junior School. She's got a romantic aura. I can always guarantee attention when I'm telling the Third about the last scene at Fotheringay. Especially that bit about the red wig coming off and exposing her as a grizzled old hag."

She laughed and he was glad to note a rise of her mercury. "You really do go for the gory details, Davy. But who are you to sneer at the romantics?"

"Oh, I don't. I make 'em work overtime for me. Until I get to the Fifth, that is," and suddenly she stopped in her stride, swung him round and kissed him on the mouth.

"You're wonderful medicine for me, Davy."

They were moving along a down-curving track, about some two hundred feet above the river. Oak, beech, thorn and chestnut grew in profusion, and although this was clearly a popular hikers' path they had met none over the last mile. She said, "In here, Davy . . ." and steered him off the track into a tiny glade, carpeted with the skeletons of last year's leaves and sown with bluebells and wood anemones. "We've waited long enough, Davy. Too long for our good. I'm sure of you, absolutely sure and, just for the record, there never was anyone else in Canada or the States."

"You don't have to justify yourself to me."

"I do. No one else means a damn to me."

Until then, until the moment she stopped, he had been aware on her part of something that had not been there in the serene days when they had been lovers on the shore of Windermere, or even that occasion he had been able to bring a measure of peace to her after that rowdy meeting at Bilhampton. But now, screened by the thickets, she seemed to reflect and as his arms went round her she said, mildly, "Here, Davy? Now?" and the way she said it gave him pause. He lowered his head and kissed the swell of her breast above the neck of her blouse.

"That's for you to say, Chris. At Bilhampton you needed me. I'm not so sure now, in spite of what happened back there. You've grown a lot since then. You'll shake it off with or without me."

"I daresay. But I'll always need you. Not just when I've taken a tumble. I had a special reason for bringing you out here. If it had been simpler we could have stayed in town. I'll try and explain, but kiss me first. As though you meant it."

He kissed her mouth and felt her tremble. She said, "It's enough, you see. You've only got to touch me, Davy," but then to his astonishment, she moved apart from him and taking lipstick and mirror from her handbag set about restoring her make-up.

He had a picture gallery then of the three women he had held in his arms, performing this same office, and in a way it emphasised their differences. Beth did it absentmindedly, as part of a daily routine. Julia Darbyshire did it painstakingly, as though the face she meant to show to the world was her sole capital, but Christine was different again. She applied lipstick, powder puff and comb with swift, impatient flourishes, the way she tackled most things, following through an impromptu plan but with half an eye on the clock. He said, "I wouldn't bother with the war paint. We're not going home yet, are we?"

"That could depend," she said, "on all manner of things."

"Such as?"

"Your tolerance to, start with."

"Take that for granted. Especially as you cheered me up by saying there was no one else in the picture."

"Not that kind of tolerance, Davy."

"Well?"

"I've always thought of you as my husband, my real husband, that is. If I hadn't I wouldn't have gone to bed with you, not even that night in Bilhampton when I was in the depths of misery. I'm not really promiscuous, although I suppose some people would say I was. I thought I loved Rowley. But I've known I loved you, from the second time we met and I went to confessional in that Newport pub. No, I mean something more important. I'm free, Davy. Or will be, in August."

She could not have said anything more calculated to astonish him. "Free? Rowley's agreed to let you divorce him?"

"Well, not exactly." Her smile was a little crooked, revealing a tinge of malice that was uncharacteristic of her. "I cornered him and forced him to let me go. On pain of being divorced the hard way. Now I suppose you'll want the entire sordid story."

"Don't you think I'm entitled to it?"

She considered. "Yes, you are. You've been very patient. A damned sight more than most men would have been!"

"You're saying we can get married? That you'd settle for Bamfylde?"

"I wouldn't marry you any other way, Davy. That would be treachery."

"Well, then," he said, catching up her hands, "to hell with how you got rid of him. I don't give a damn if you beat it out of him with a club," but she said, "Wait, Davy—you might as well hear it now. It isn't something I'm proud of. There was a lot to be desired in Rowley, but I never did doubt the sincerity of his religious convictions and I left more scars on him than he's left on me."

"Serve him damn well right."

"I can't look at it that way. I wish I could but I can't."

"What happened?"

"I got word of him through a mutual friend and dropped a hint that I'd be delighted to see him again. As an old friend. For a chat, say. He came over one day last summer all smiles and dear-old-girlish. After a pat and a pinch he implied he was all in favour of a form of reconciliation."

"How do you mean, a 'form of reconciliation'?"

"Rowley's kind. I was to remain his official wife, eager and available when he was randy, busy or between mistresses. He was to have a long leash. Say a couple of miles at full stretch. I saw my opening then and pretended to go along with the idea. I even let him get to the point where he was convinced the next time he'd make it all the way back. That wasn't difficult. Bright as he is, he's got a colossal male ego, and wrote off my reservations as a Nonconformist hangover on account of his other sleeping partners. It meant using my body as a bait but it worked like a charm."

"And after that?"

"I had him watched by the seediest little private detective you ever read about, if you read that kind of fiction. His work was a lot better than his appearance. He came up with cast-iron evidence in ten days and all I had to do then was threaten. Rowley holds an important position out there, and the Scots Presbyterian influence is strong in his university. He had no alternative but to cave in and supply evidence for a divorce over here. The decree absolute comes through on August 1st. There's no prospect of complications, or not unless he's been watching us with a telescope this afternoon and that I doubt. He never was one for country delights."

It did not seem more than a defensive statement on her part but he knew she would not view it that way. She would be more likely to regard it as moral blackmail, and at the time it had probably disgusted her. He said, "You can't expect me to feel sorry for him. Plenty of women would have taken him for a lot more than a straight divorce, and you never spent a penny of his money on yourself. Put it out of mind. Look on it as a case of tit for tat." Then, with some difficulty, "In the preliminary skirmishes, didn't you feel anything of the very strong affection you once had for him?"

"Simply as a man? Yes, I did. You were a long way off, and I never did kid myself that celibacy is my strong suit. In that sense it was lucky it was Rowley, and not some other red-blooded male. But what came over to me again, this time in added measure, was his absolute bloody selfishness. Rowley is more than ordinarily selfish, anyway, but measured against someone like you he isn't much more than an animal. At least, that's how it seemed to me. I like to be wanted as a person, not as an instrument. That's important to me, Davy."

"It's important to most women, so don't be too generous with the haloes. If it wasn't I would have said to hell with it and gone off on the rampage now and again, and I daresay you'll discover I can run Rowley pretty close for selfishness sometimes. At least, as far as my job's concerned. Are you absolutely sure you want to take me on? A husband pushing forty is one thing. Motherhood to a horde of growing boys is another."

"I'll cope, somehow. Providing you've got more patience in reserve. In any case, it's you who are taking the risk, Davy. Maybe you should take time off to think about it."

"I've had all the time I need. Meantime I'm starving so why don't we celebrate? Do you think we could get a dinner at that place where we left the car?"

"If we can find our way back to it before dark."

He pulled her up and they went back up the long, winding path to the saddle of the two rock-strewn hills they had crossed an hour ago. In that brief interval or so it seemed to him, they had found a row of signposts pointing the way into a new era.

III

Not since the long, hot summer of 1919 had a term passed in such a succession of fleeting, sunlit days. His mood, in the span between early May and late July, was at one with the period just prior to his earlier marriage. There had been other smoothly running terms but always, at one or another stage of them, something sour or explosive had occurred, a flare-up with Carter, a confrontation with Alcock or even a let-down reminding him yet again that it was all too easy to grow too complacent about one's ability to judge character. But this term, with Bamfylde under his hand, it was all plain sailing and even the highlights were amusing.

There was Hislop's momentary reversion to his original
form, when he hit a spectacular six that soared over the
western boundary, ricocheted from the bonnet of a Governor's
Daimler, and plopped through the open window of an adjoining car, where old Bouncer, back on a visit, was enjoying
an afternoon nap. A dozen witnesses stepped forward to
swear that Bouncer, leaping from his car, threatened the
batsman with his statutory four penal marks for an act of
lese-majestie.

There was the sudden appearance of Molyneux's outlandish Australian uncle, who looked exactly like a Colonial
gent masquerading as Bernard Shaw, a man so unfamiliar
with the taboos of English schools as to appear in the Upper
Fifth one morning and address Molyneux by his carefully
concealed Christian name, Aloysius, a gaffe that stunned the
French master and bid fair to undermine his class discipline
for all time. And soon after that there was the overnight visit
of Sax Hoskins and his Rhythmateers, touring the West
Country resorts, who descended on Bamfylde one Sunday
afternoon and gave what Sax called a 'Bamfylde Benefit
Session', an honour bestowed upon them in Grace's
honour.

Sax had always been popular. Unquenchable high spirits,
a rumbustious sense of humour and, above all, an uncanny
mastery of many so-called musical instruments, dating from
his Second Form variations of 'Alexander's Ragtime Band'
on a mouth organ, had won him an enduring place in Bamfylde legend. His reappearance, at the head of a professional
dance orchestra was a triumph and he played for two hours
by Big Hall clock, the only man among his sweating Rhythmateers impervious to the heat, recorded as reaching the
high eighties that night.

David had anticipated some difficulty with Grace concerning the prospect of a stepmother. Not much, perhaps, for
she had always been an exceptionally biddable child, but their
relationship was close and it would not have been surprising
if she had viewed Christine with a certain amount of resentment. He told her of his plans the night he returned from
Manchester, and was relieved when she took it calmly.
Not as a matter of course, exactly, but more like an intelli-

gent adult than an adolescent. She said, after he had outlined the history of his long, frustrating friendship with Christine, "Poor old Daddy! It sounds frightfully complicated. I knew you were keen on her, of course, and one time, two years ago it was, I made sure you'd marry her and was scared, even though she seemed nice that time she came here. But then, when you stopped talking about her, I made up my mind you'd stay single, especially now you're head."

"I'd come to the same conclusion myself," he said. "This came out of the blue. I didn't even know there was any hope for her getting a divorce, and even if there was there was always her determination to get into Parliament. She would, too, if she kept at it. She's that kind of person."

"Won't she ever try again?"

"I don't know. That'll be up to her."

"And what do you think about that?"

He was fortunate, he reflected, to be able to discuss the situation so frankly with a fourteen-year-old. Her objectivity had to do with her long isolation here among so many thrustful males, he supposed. Their resilience, their tendency to treat every new day as a fresh start, had rubbed off on her over the years. He said, "She might try for a local candidature, and I wouldn't stop her. This is Tory and Liberal country, and Labour are keen to get a foot in the door. I imagine it all depends on how she settles in here. She hasn't much confidence in herself as a headmaster's wife. It'll be up to you and me to try and give her some."

"You once had an idea of training me for the job, didn't you?"

"Yes, and in a way I still have. You could help a lot, Tuppence. The commercial courses start in September, when the builders' men move out, and after school-leaving certificate you can take typing and shorthand. Then you can take Miss Rowlandson's place when she retires as secretary. Would that appeal to you?"

She told him it would and that she wanted, in addition, to improve her French and learn German. Her French was already good and she seemed to have a flair for languages. "Oughtn't I to meet her again soon?" she added, "I mean, *before* you get married? We shall have to have a good chinwag about you," and he laughed, telling her that this was obligatory, if only to warn Chris of his likes and dislikes.

The meeting, when it came on Sports Day, was an unqualified success, adapting to the amiable pattern of the term. He had not realised how much he must have talked to Chris about Grace, or how observant Chris was when it came to assessing people. It was fun to watch Grace showing her round and familiarising her with every odd corner of the place, as though Chris had been a conscientious mother, hoping to send her son here in the autumn. And afterwards they gave him the slip and set out on a walk across Middlemoor, returning dusty and hungry, having achieved some kind of conspiratorial affinity while removed from the world of men and boys. It was only later, shortly before Chris set off north to pay a duty visit to her family in Yorkshire, that she indicated the level of intimacy they had achieved.

"She's an extraordinary little body, Davy. I don't think I've ever met anyone quite like her. Or not anyone under forty. Beth must have been a singular person. I mean, I'd expect any child of yours to be bright, and fairly easy to get along with, but she's more than that. She's . . . well . . . a born go-between. Now I'd say that's rare in a person her age. The really satisfying thing, however, is that she seems to have made up her mind that I'm the best of a bad job."

It was characteristic of her, he thought, to put it like that and he said, laughing, "Don't give me or Beth special credit for Grace. The boys have done that for her. I've always thought of Grace as a woman, even when she was six."

She had left her car up north for an overhaul, so he saw her off at yet another railway station, a familiar one this time, so that the parting was less urgent. When she had gone he walked home along a road cordoned by summer foliage, and rich with the scent of honeysuckle. At the playing field gate he paused, listening to the distant *snack* of the ball at the nets and the odd isolated shout that carried all this way in the evening lull, acknowledging both sounds as part of Bamfylde's summer pattern and welcome on that account.

Standing there, looking over his shoulder at the stark outline of the buildings silhouetted against a lemon, coral-streaked sky, he found it difficult to think of himself as a bridegroom-in-waiting, on a par with the callow young man who had passed this way on summer evenings in 1919. So difficult, indeed, that he could chuckle at the prospect, thinking, "It's impossible to think of oneself as young in this job . . . almost everyone around is so much younger . . . easier to see oneself as an up-and-coming Judy Cordwainer . . . I'm thirty-seven, sound of wind and limb, certainly in the right job, but there have been times over the past few years when I've felt as old as Jehovah in one of His Why-don't-I-give-it-all-up moods . . . ?" And then, unaccountably, he suddenly recalled that ridiculous incident in the train on their honeymoon trip to the Isle of Wight, when Beth had been so embarrassed by the onset of a period and he laughed, standing there by himself, for a thing like that wouldn't be likely to bother many couples nowadays.

As always, his reverie was terminated by the bell, ringing out over the plateau as Norman Minor, seventh in a long and distinguished line of bell-ringers he recalled, made his ritual circuit of the buildings, calling boys to prep like monks to prayer. He never had got round to replacing the handbell with a fixed one and now that he came to think about it he decided it could wait. The longer he stayed here the less he was inclined to disturb the old routine, even though, in a matter of thirty months, he had introduced a variety of new ones. It was a hangover of Algy's philosophy, he supposed—"Concentrate on essentials, expand all you like, but don't pull up anything by the roots before making absolutely certain it's dead."

He extinguished his cigarette carefully, for there were fire hazards in this kind of weather, then went along under a forest of six-foot cow-parsley stalks to the cloverleaf exit of the east drive. By the time he reached the forecourt the prep hush was on the school and he welcomed it. Four weeks wasn't long, for all the jobs he had in hand.

PART FOUR

PLENITUDE

CHAPTER ONE

I

Years later, when twenty-three new names had been added to the memorial outside, when he could look back on the period between his second marriage and the weeks preceding the summer of Dunkirk, he thought of the interval as his time of plenitude, strangely at odds with everything that was piling up outside. That, however, was an ultimate verdict, after he and Chris had met and survived a crisis that was new to him but morbidly familiar to her. So that, whereas he viewed it as no more than another sizeable hump in the rhythm of the years, she saw it as something infinitely more threatening and hazardous than he would have admitted at the time, shrugging it off as her playing-in period, the equivalent of a sensitive new boy's first school year.

It was at one with much that was happening in the world outside, where there seemed no prospect of harmony, where trouble flared in one capital or another, and her worst fears of the early 'thirties were justified, but her own inward struggle had no link with world turbulence, or the looming threat of war. It was a deeply personal challenge, fought without benefit of his armour, his sense of dedication, and there were times, many times, when she envied him his anchorage here in this small, close-knit community. His roots were well down and manifold. Hers, such as they were throughout that testing time, were pitifully shallow, save only the one, strong fibre of her love for him and what this place seemed to have made of him over the years.

*   *   *

It was a more sophisticated honeymoon than the sedate fortnight at Shanklin with Beth, in 1919. They took turns to drive her silver bumble bee all the way from Calais to Brittany, then down through the château country of the Loire,

of which he had written in his single literary foray but had
never visited. They enjoyed perfect weather, staying at old
inns and eating alfresco meals beside the dusty high-roads.
She found him an entertaining guide, for as they moved
south to Gascony, then south-east to Carcassonne and Marseilles, and finally north to the battlefields of his youth, loose
ends of his undisciplined reading would return to him,
prompted by some place-name like Poitiers, or the sign-
board of an inn calling to mind some jack-booted, blustering
character from the past, who had made his outcry and
departed, forgotten by all but historical magpies.

In St. Emilion, for instance, he told her the story of Madame
Bouquey, who had hidden the fugitive Girondins in her
courtyard well, and paid for the impulse on the scaffold in
Bordeaux. Near Chalons, his excitement describing the final
rally of the Imperial Army in 1814 made her laugh aloud,
but who could help sharing his enthusiasm? Farther north,
when they drove through the miraculously restored pastures
and red-brick villages of the 1915–18 battlefields, he again
surprised her, for she had looked for a sombre approach to
this tormented ground, where his generation had died, but
found instead detachment, so that she said, "I made sure
you'd sheer away from this part of France, Davy. I would
have, in your place. What happened here, not so long ago,
must have scarred every man who survived it."

"Yes, it did that," he replied, thoughtfully, "but I had to
come back nevertheless. Perhaps just to satisfy myself how
completely Bamfylde had exorcised the past. Maybe the
equivalent happened with some of the others who came out
of it with a whole skin. What I mean is, a man had to start
fresh or cut his throat and, taken all round, I've been lucky."

"Tell me."

"I had a job I could lose myself in before the guns had
stopped firing. I had Algy as counsellor and friend. I had
Beth for more than six years, then Grace, and now I've got
you. A fair deal all round, wouldn't you say?"

She wondered if it was, and whether it was the job, or a
generous measure of domestic peace that had played the
major part in his rehabilitation and thought, on balance, it
was the former. For although she saw him as two men, the

thruster with an *idée fixe*, for which he was prepared to sacrifice anything, and an amiable lover, respecting mental privacy and claiming his own as the price of that indulgence, it seemed to her that Bamfylde was never far from his thoughts. Or only in moments of rarefied intimacy, when he seemed to her very young and ardent for a man who, as he was fond of reminding her, was 'pushing forty'.

And here there was another aspect of him that surprised her. He had learned something very valuable from that girl Beth, whatever kind of person she had been, the trick of blending positive virility with an innate respect for a woman's body, so that she could never quite decide whether he approached her as conqueror or pilgrim.

He was surprisingly frank about his first marriage. He told her of Beth's eagerness to conceive a child as soon as they were married, and her recurrent disappointments at her failure to produce a son in the time left to them, and it made her wonder whether she, too, was likely to fail in this respect, for time was running on and she would be thirty next birthday. She said nothing of this to him, however. Although children were important to her, she had an idea they were not a vital factor to him. After all, he had so many substitute sons, with more coming all the time, and it was his passing reference to September's recruits that made her aware of this and vaguely uneasy regarding her ability to adjust to Bamfylde as effortlessly as he promised. It sparked off her very first doubt regarding the irrevocability of marriage to a school rather than a man.

They were on their homeward stretch, driving west from Newhaven across open stretches of the New Forest. He said, as they took the road to Ringwood, and pulled in to picnic at a spot overlooking a bramble-sown pasture, "It was just about here they ran that fool Monmouth to earth. He'd come a fair way from Sedgemoor, and what courage he had had run out of the toes of his boots."

"How was he caught?"

"He was collared by a couple of militiamen hiding in a ditch, with a few dried peas in his pocket. The real tragedy of that uprising was that Monmouth valued his head above his dignity."

"You can't hold that against him. Don't we all when it comes to the crunch?"

"His men didn't. They had everything to lose and damn all to gain, but at least they didn't crawl on their bellies, begging for mercy," and then he chuckled, saying, "There's a coincidence. John Churchill won that battle for James, and we've got a John Churchill coming next term. Youngest we've ever enrolled."

"How old is he?"

"Nine. We generally refuse 'em until they're eleven, but Churchill's people are abroad and he'll go in with the Sunsetters. Timid kid he seemed to me. Hope he doesn't find it too terrifying."

His casual tone irritated her a little. "Of *course* he'll find it terrifying! Who the devil wouldn't, at nine? I don't know what their mothers can be dreaming of to let them go at that age. Thirteen is the absolute minimum to my way of thinking."

He still seemed unconcerned. "Sometimes it's not a question of choice. All the Sunsetters' parents are abroad, some of them in places where there's no school. What do you do with kids in those circumstances?"

"Anything but isolate them from their families and plonk them down among a lot of young toughs."

"You'd be surprised how quickly they adapt. Better than some of those who come to us half-spoiled at around fourteen."

"They have to or go under, don't they?"

He gave her an amused, sidelong glance. "Well, that's part of your new job. To mother 'em a bit."

She said, experiencing her second identifiable qualm, "What gives you the idea I'm qualified for that? Herries's wife had years and years of experience."

He took her hand, alerted more by her expression than her tone. "You aren't getting cold feet already are you?"

"I don't know. Sometimes I'm scared for you more than myself."

"Don't be. I'll cope. A lot better with you around than on my own. You'll find it easier than nursing a constituency. A lot more rewarding too."

"Davy."

"Well?"

"I'll need time. And I'll need watching."

"You've got time. And I'll be watching." He seemed as though he was about to add something to this but checked himself, pretending to be busy spreading the rug and opening the sandwich lunch they had brought.

"You were going to say something else."

"Yes, I was. But it'll sound pompous. God forbid I should take that line with you, Chris."

"You say what you had in mind."

"Well, just this. I realise you've mortgaged your political prospects by marrying me. It was a spot decision on your part, brought about by hurt pride and the attitude of those idiots up in Manchester. I should be grateful to them, I suppose, but that's no reason why you shouldn't have second thoughts about it. You probably have already."

"About marrying you? *No*, Davy. Definitely not."

"I didn't mean that exactly. I meant about a candidacy somewhere fairly handy. Get this straight. I wouldn't stand in your way and I want you to remember that. And as for the school Governors, well, they couldn't either, for I'm beyond their reach now, so long as I'm up to my job." He faced her. "If you feel you have to try again and get back in the swim then for God's sake tell me, Chris. Don't bottle it up because you think it'll make things hellishly difficult for me. It won't, or not to any great extent, and even if it did I'd go along with you all the way."

His tolerance touched her deeply, the more so because she knew it cost him something to go as far as this and make so light of any complications that might result from her re-entry into the political arena. She caught his hand where it rested on the door of the car, pulled him down and kissed him.

"Thank you, Davy. That's you talking but this is my problem. I'll tackle it if I have to but I'm not going to anticipate it on my honeymoon. I love you very much and I'm sure you love me. So why don't we give me a term or two's trial?"

They left it there for the time being. The exchange had helped, if only in stiffening her resolution to do her damnedest to justify his faith in her.

II

There was more mothering to be done than either he or she had anticipated. Chance, plus a short waiting-list and an exceptionally high number of July leavers, had combined to lower the average age of the Second Formers by nearly two years and Churchill was not the only nine-year-old among the Sunsetters. There were two others, and several ten-year-olds not really up to the standard of the Second Form, so that David was obliged to improvise and split the lowest unit of the school into two unequal halves, the Second Form proper, comprising about a score of boys, and what amounted to a First Form approaching a dozen.

It was a great nuisance for it meant extensive revision of the timetable and a good deal of shuttling to and fro in the Lower School, but it was better than seeing their numbers drop, as they might well have done had he adhered to the earlier age limit.

He was so busy during those first hectic days that he had little opportunity to devote much of his time to Chris and was relieved when she admitted, without being asked, that Bamfylde was more terrifying at a distance than it was in close up. It seemed to him then that she was settling in very well, especially as she went on to say that the chief factor in her absorption was the unexpected warmth shown her by most of the staff, and all the senior boys, especially those who qualified as his secret favourites. It told him that she had been prepared for a certain amount of resentment on the part of the senior men, like Barnaby and Howarth, but it was soon evident to her that they both wished him well, and enjoyed the exceptional freedom he extended to housemasters. She got on very well with Alison, Boyer's Scots wife, and with many of the Old Boys, a proportion of whom seemed to share Boyer's almost mystical friendship with Davy. She took a great liking to Brigadier Cooper after he whispered, on being introduced to her, "Just what we were looking for, that husband of yours, m'dear. Been tellin' 'em so ever since we began casting round for someone to replace Herries. Difficult chap to follow, but P.J.'ll manage it, given time. Especially with a nice gel like you about the place."

"I think Briggy is an old duck," she told Davy later. "Has he always been a fan of yours?"

"I struck lucky with his boy my first term here. It works that way sometimes."

She derived a certain amount of amusement from learning her way around and discovering where to tread softly and where to take a chance. "It's a bit like the Habsburg Court," she said one day, "a frighteningly complex system of protocol, checks, counter-checks and balances, with all kinds of silent pressures and intrigues going on, and you hovering over the safety-valve watching for explosions. Really, you men are the most colossal frauds! For centuries you've been accusing women of gossip and backstairs politics, and we're absolute amateurs at the game compared with you!"

"It doesn't get you down, then? That aspect of it?"

"Not a bit. As a matter of fact, it makes me feel superior." And he had laughed and gone blithely about his business, unaware that there were other aspects of Bamfylde that were not so easily dismissed.

One was the obvious lack of flexibility about the system, despite the humanising effect David had obviously had on the school. Tradition, she supposed, was all very well at a remove, but the experience of the last few years, especially on the other side of the Atlantic, pulled against her ability to take the rigidity of the school calendar seriously, especially when it seemed to her to push education into second place. The high spots of each term were as fixed as the stars, beginning in October with the first of eight runs, and the play-offs of Senior and Junior house matches. Then there was the opera and ceremonial Middlemoor run, the Choral Society's concert, the drill competition, Sports Day, the War Office Certificate 'A' exam and interminable games of cricket. The new school year began with Speech Day and the Armistice Service and by then they were into the cross-country and rugby seasons again, and inside this framework of special occasions were countless minor rituals, so that she sometimes wondered what the parents were getting for their money in the way of down-to-earth education, for sport and red-letter days invariably took precedence over instruction. She raised this subject with David one night and found that he could be very touchy when the rituals of the school were questioned.

"I've been trying to explain for years that education isn't a matter of text-books and blackboards," he said. "At least, it isn't in schools of this kind. That was an article of faith with Algy."

She took a calculated risk then, saying, "But you're head now, Davy, and Algy, dear old chap that he is, stands for the past. The boys here are going out into a highly competitive world, aren't they?"

"Damn it," he said, irritably for him, "you're talking just like Carter before the Stoic outstepped his limits and he came over to our side. Of course they have to be taught something, and of course they have to be coached through the Cambridge Senior or some qualifying exam, but that isn't *why* they're here. Go and read *Tom Brown* and see what the old Squire had to say about it."

She was tempted to reply that Squire Brown had lived in the days of privileged classes and virtually no taxation, but she was not sure enough of her ground to risk a first quarrel. All the same, his extreme sensitivity bothered her, inasmuch as it threw her back upon herself and made her uneasily aware that she had no real place in his life in term-time. And term-time, she reflected, consumed two-thirds of the year. Clearly he was now a fervid convert to tradition and equally clearly she was not and never would be. From then on the open cheque he had handed her regarding her freedom to apply to Transport House for a candidature was prominent in her mind, so much so that twice she sat down and began a letter reminding the party of her existence and availability. She threw both letters in the wastepaper basket. Instinct warned her that, notwithstanding his pledge on the last day of their honeymoon, endless problems might result from taking up the challenge again. Instead, she looked around for some means of integrating more closely into the world of school and making some kind of attempt to justify her existence other than as a kind of camp-follower.

She found it, oddly enough, through Howarth, whom she had come to like and respect as a man at war with humbug. Howarth gave her her first tenuous foothold by privately seeking her advice on Bradshawe, yet another of those unfortunates pulled apart by divided loyalties after his parents (surely, in this instance, the world's prize idiots!) sent him a stream of letters explaining their individual views on the rights and the wrongs of their divorce.

Bradshawe, an intelligent fifteen-year-old, was making heavy weather of the issue, or so Howarth told her. From a cheerful extrovert of a few months ago, he had become morose and solitary, and his work, according to a consensus of opinion in the common room had gone to pot. "Tell me, Mrs. P.J., as an expensively educated woman, how would you tackle it from my stand-point? Those fools are imposing unnecessary stress on the boy. As his housemaster I feel I'm falling down on the job and that really rattles me."

"What makes you think I'm qualified to advise someone who has been at the job as long as you?" she protested, but he growled, "Oh, don't give me mock modesty! You're much nearer Bradshawe's age than I am and must have ideas, so let's have 'em! You can rely on me to throw 'em back at you if they're too academic."

"Well," she said, doubtfully, "you could try writing to each parent, pointing out the damage their letters are doing."

"I tried that at the beginning of term and all that happened was *I* got a blow-by-blow description of the fracas. Puerile nonsense it was, too—wretched woman can't even spell, and she finished her bleat with a split infinitive."

She laughed, deciding that, in this kind of situation, Howarth could be funny. "I'll tell you what might work," he went on. "I'll brief you on the case and you have a straight talk with the boy."

"Good heavens, how could I do that?"

"The same way as I'll have to if you don't," he said, "and passing the buck to P.J. won't work either. Too magisterial. Not him, of course, but his mantle of office. No, I'm serious. You'd be doing me a favour and, after all, it's a job that comes within the province of a head's wife. Ellie Herries got landed with it often."

She said, obstinately, "I won't do it without Davy's approval," and he said, with one of his rusty chuckles, "Leave

P.J. to me. Told him a good many home truths in his time. Ask him if you don't believe me."

The upshot was that she made her debut as counsellor within forty-eight hours, trapping Bradshawe in her parlour when the treacherous Howarth sent him over with a note, with strict instructions to wait for an answer. The note read, 'Since you didn't see fit to invite me to the wedding I didn't buy you a wedding present. Here is a hot-plate for hot potatoes. Respectfully, Ian Howarth.' Below was a postcript, 'Fragile. Handle with care!'

She had the greatest difficulty in keeping a straight face as she said, "Er . . . do sit down, Bradshawe. I won't keep you a minute," and watched him out of the corner of her eye as she went across to the bureau and wrote, 'No hot-plate, thank you. I'm sitting on one, thanks to you', and sealed it.

She said, as he rose, "Hold on a minute, Bradshawe, we haven't met before, have we?" and he mumbled that they had not.

"I'm just making tea. Will you stay and have some?"

He looked at her suspiciously, she thought, but he could hardly refuse so he sat down again, stuffing the note in his pocket. She called through to Rigby, "Make it tea for two, please, Rigby," and then, deciding on the direct approach, "I had a chat with Mr. Howarth yesterday. He tells me you've had a wretched term so far. Would you care to talk about it, to someone right outside? It would be confidential. I wouldn't dream of passing it on to the headmaster or Mr. Howarth, if you preferred not." And when he said nothing, "You see, I've had personal experience of this divorce muddle myself. Nobody has to tell me how awful it can be."

He looked at her with a touch of wonder, a nice-looking boy, with serious grey eyes and a friendly mouth. Tall and well-made for his age and possessing, she would say, exceptionally good manners.

"Did Mr. Howarth tell you he had written to my people, ma'am?"

"Yes. But it didn't help, did it?"

Rigby padded in with the tray, set it down and went out again. She turned her back on him to pour and he said, "My mother keeps saying she put it off until I was old enough to understand. That if she had had her way they would have split up years ago. I . . . well, I don't really believe that. I mean, in a way it shifts the blame on me, doesn't it?"

"How does it?"

"Well, things must have been getting worse all the time. They quarrelled, of course, but everyone's people have a bust up now and again, don't they?"

"If they're human they do. What's your Christian name, Bradshawe?"

He looked surprised. "Nick . . . Nicholas, ma'am."

"Well, look here, Nick, it's time you faced up to something. As your mother implies, you're quite old enough. People drift apart for all kinds of reasons, but a divorce in the family isn't the end of the world. It used to be but it isn't now. I dare say more than a dozen boys here have parents who have got themselves divorced and married again, and nobody a penny the wiser. The thing is, everybody is an individual, and has his own life to lead. You can sometimes help but not all that much. Do your sympathies lie in one direction or the other?"

"Not really. I gather my father has been running around with his secretary but mother . . . well, in a way she asked for it. I mean, ever since I can remember she's filled the house with people, all kinds of people. Painters, writers and so on — drips most of them, and father was all for a quiet life."

"I see. Are you an only child?"

"I've got a brother older than me. He was here several years ago. He's married now."

"Have you discussed it with him?"

"He doesn't want to know. He says the governor is in his second childhood, and the mater isn't through her first yet, and all one can do is write 'em off. How can a chap do that? I mean, after all they are one's people."

"It's not bad advice for all that. Providing it's done kindly. Would it be so very difficult?"

He looked confused and she realised she would have to be more explicit. "Before this happened, did you get along with them? Both of them?"

"More or less. I didn't see much of the governor and, as I say, mother was always surrounded by long hairs. They left me pretty much to myself."

"Then what is it that's upset you so much?"

He said, with a baffled frown, "Well, it's being a sort of referee. I mean, a chap doesn't want to know all the grisly details, does he? They've split up and that's that. I'm sorry, but I can't do anything about it."

"Do you answer their letters point by point?"

"I try to."

"Well, here's my advice for what it's worth, Nick. Stop trying. Keep in touch, the way you used to, a letter every week to each of them but full of school gossip that they'll find frightfully boring. Don't comment on a thing they say, and if you see another appeal to the ref coming up throw that letter in the wastepaper basket without reading it. My guess is they'll soon leave you alone to get on with your own life. Does that make sense?"

Surprisingly, and rewardingly, he smiled. He had, she thought, a very wise smile for a lad of fifteen. "Yes, it does. It makes a hell . . . a real lot of sense." He stood up, carefully replacing his cup on the tray. "I'd better get back with this note. Mr. Howarth said he was waiting for it," but he didn't go and finally went on, "Er . . . was that note about me, ma'am?"

She said, with a smile, "Yes, it was, Nick. As a matter of fact, Mr. Howarth insisted I had a chat with you. He seemed to think I could do it better than he could, or the head could, but I'll tell you this. They're both very much on your side, and so am I after what you've told me. Will you give what I suggested a try for the rest of the term?"

"Yes, I will. And thank you, ma'am . . . I just had to spill it to someone. That's the trouble with a place like this . . . I mean . . . regarding things outside . . . a chap tends to go round in circles."

He held out his hand and she shook it, thinking as he left, "That's about right. That *is* the trouble with a place like this and not only for the Bradshawes." She was aware, however, of having made her first real contribution and it gave her a lift until she reflected that she had only been able to make it by chance. Very few boys would have been as frank and explicit as Bradshawe about a personal problem. To run a place like this had seemed a more or less straightforward job

from a distance, a matter of training and educating boys
within a system of do's and don'ts, but it wasn't like that at
all, not when you saw it from the inside. It was a task of fearful complexity, where it was so easy to lose one's way and
flounder. All manner of unlooked for situations arose day
by day and each demanded a personalised approach. In a
way—and she grudged the admission—Davy was right.
Education, of the kind outsiders associated with schools, was
a relatively unimportant part of boarding-school life. The
human side of it, the sheer effort needed to keep a place as un-
wieldly as this on a level keel, required infinite imagination,
endless patience and heaven knows what else besides. The
case of Nick Bradshawe, for instance, was no more than the
tip of one iceberg, and here she was, preening herself for
having smoothed it off, so to speak. Yet people like Davy and
Howarth and all the other old stagers were expected to do
what she had done off the cuff and still get boys through the
examinations the outside world demanded of them.

* * *

The Bradshawe incident did have a side-effect, and that
despite the fact that she did not discuss it with him. It made
her aware of the true breadth of the demands made upon
conscientious schoolmasters like Davy or Howarth, but it
also increased the sense of her own inadequacy, so that it was
fortunate that, within a month or so, her thoughts were
switched by the near-certainty of a pregnancy, a circumstance
that somehow surprised her, so much so that she kept her
own counsel about it until the helter-skelter of the end of
term was behind them and she had him more or less to herself.

The opportunity occurred on the last night of the old year,
a few hours after she had received confirmation from Doc
Willoughby. They had both attended a Sunsetters' party and
after that a mild celebration with Howarth, Barnaby, Boyer
and Alison, and he dropped off to sleep at once while she lay
awake, listening to the storm getting up over the moor and
marshalling its forces for an onrush on the school. Presently
it struck and a dislodged slate from the roof went crashing

down into the forecourt, landing with a noise loud enough to wake him.

"What was that?"

"A slate. You'd best get someone to look at that roof before term begins."

"Yes, I will," he mumbled sleepily but she said, "Don't go to sleep again, Davy. I saw Doc Willoughby this afternoon, while you were in town getting the party supplies."

He was wide awake now and sat up, switching on the bedside light. "You're okay? Nothing wrong?"

"Nothing to get worked up about. I'm pregnant," and his reaction to the bald statement was so dramatic that it reminded her of situations she had seen in so many bad films and plays, and had dismissed as improbable until now.

"Good God! This is a hell of a time to tell me. In the middle of the night, when we've accounted for half a bottle apiece!"

"I wasn't sure myself until teatime, and I could hardly tell you in front of the Sunsetters or a bachelor staff, could I?"

He laughed then and hugged her, holding her in a way that told her he was delighted but was attempting to play down his initial sense of shock.

"You're glad about it, aren't you?"

"Of course I am," he said. "Aren't you?"

"I'm not absolutely sure yet. Yes, I think so . . . but . . ."

"But what?"

"I would have liked a little more time to play myself in."

He rubbed his eyes. "Rubbish! You're doing fine . . ." but then, as an afterthought, "This will put paid to any prospect of a candidature. Does that bother you?"

"No. I've put that out of mind, Davy."

"You didn't have to. I told you . . ."

"I know you told me, but it wouldn't work. This will, maybe."

"What do you mean, Chris?"

She kissed his cheek. "Dear Davy. You're so bright in some ways and so dim in others. No, not dim exactly, but the tiniest bit prejudiced. That's Bamfylde's fault, I suppose. You can't live and work in a place like this without taking it for granted that everyone else sees the place through your eyes."

"What are you getting at?"

"That a child of my own will give me real purpose in your life. I really haven't got one yet, you know."

He thought about this for a moment. She granted him that. He was always willing to take time to see someone else's view, a rare trait in schoolmasters in her experience. Finally he said, "I went through a longish period of uncertainty when I came here, Chris. Several times, during those long-drawn-out rows with Carter and Alcock I almost threw in the towel, but I'm damned glad I didn't. It's even more difficult for you, I imagine, without a defined role, and I'm only absolutely sure of one thing. You'll find one, with your brain and guts. I'd back all I have on that."

"You already have," she said, and then, "Go back to sleep now. We'll get around to making plans in the morning. We're not pushed for time. It isn't until the end of summer term."

The storm built up, prowling round the buildings like a sullen enemy looking for a chink in the defences, but it didn't bother her. She felt reassured somehow, and more hopeful of the immediate future than she had been since the Bradshawe incident.

III

The feeling grew on her isolating her from the place as a whole and even, to an extent, from him, so that she persuaded herself she was beginning to get things in proportion at last. It would be fun to have a child, especially his child, and the prospect released her into a more tranquil world, an intensively private one where she was content with her role as a bystander, a touchline supporter of Bamfylde's day-to-day being.

Her health remained good and the slight embarrassment she experienced moving among so many males with a swelling figure was a small price to pay for the mounting confidence she felt in herself. The winter tailed off, with its frosts and gales, and spring came, a dry, windy, sunny spell, lasting through April and May. But then, like a vicious kick from behind, her new-found peace was shattered in an hour and she was lost again, this time out of sight and sound of a guide.

It struck without even a token warning, a sudden spell of dizziness, and a single spasm of pain, as she was climbing the stairs to the first landing to see how the decorators were getting on with the little room overlooking the quad that had been selected as a nursery. She caught the iron rail of the banister and stood there, waiting for the spell to pass before moving up the last few stairs into the bedroom and finally she reached it with a sense of panic mounting in her as she hauled herself over the threshold and fell sideways across the bed.

The second spasm made her cry out and old Rigby heard her from the stairwell, calling up anxiously, "Is that you, ma'am . . . ?" and when she was unable to answer she had a terrible certainty that she would die here alone before anyone was aware of what was happening. Mercifully he called again, "Ma'am? Did you call?" and she knew then that Rigby was her sole chance of summoning help and shouted, "Rigby! Up here . . . !" and the old chap came at a trot, peering round the edge of the bedroom door and blinking at the sight of her sprawled sideways across the bed.

"The doctor . . . quickly . . . then the head, but phone first!"

He had his wits about him, senile as he appeared to most people, and was gone in a flash as the waves of pain crashed down on her submerging everything save a sense of maddening frustration that she was going to lose the baby within the hour. Then, unaccountably, the room seemed half-full of people, among them Davy and the matron, and her sense of time and place evaporated so that she was adrift on an ocean of pain and wretchedness, with only occasional glimpses of land in the form of Davy's anxious face and the fumbling hands of the matron as they wrestled with her clothes and tried to ease her into bed.

Willoughby must have arrived soon afterwards but there was little he could do but ease the pain to some extent and then, quite suddenly, she was aware that some hours must have passed for the sun patterns on the west-facing wall had lengthened telling her that it was evening. She heard Willoughby say, "Take it easy, now . . . it's all over," and she wanted to ask if there was any chance that a seven-months-old child could live but could not frame the question for her mind was still confused and her strength utterly spent.

It was nearly twelve hours later that she came to grips with it, opening her eyes to find the room empty save for the matron, who was standing by the tall window, her back to the bed, looking out on dawn creeping over the eastern edge of the moor. She looked cool and very clinical in her uniform, so cool that Chris found herself hating the woman's detachment. She said, "It was stillborn, wasn't it?" and the woman gave a slight start and turned back to the bed, saying, "I'm afraid so, Mrs. Powlett-Jones. A boy. I *am* sorry . . ." but stopped, looking troubled and embarrassed.

"Where's my husband?"

"He's asleep, I think. He was here until an hour or so ago. Doctor made him go and take a nap. Shall I fetch him?"

"No."

She didn't want him fetched and she didn't want his sympathy or anyone else's sympathy. Anything anyone said to her now would sound banal and would stoke the rage and bitterness that glowed in her like a furnace.

"Could you eat something? Some soup, perhaps?"

"Later. What time is it?"

"Getting on for six. At least let me get you some tea."

"Very well."

She did not want the tea but she did want to get rid of the woman, if only for a few minutes. The sense of doom and failure enfolded her like a huge, soggy blanket and she turned her face from the wan light, lying still until matron came rustling in with the tea.

"Did Dr. Willoughby give any reason?"

"He said it might be one of many . . . maybe a fall, or some heavy exertion . . ."

She wanted to hurl the teapot at the woman's head. She had had no fall, had done nothing out of the ordinary beyond climbing a few extra stairs. But it was her second dead child and she remembered she had told Willoughby of the first.

Davy came in, saying little but sitting by the bed and holding her hand. What was there to say, anyway? Then Willoughby tried the medical guff 'Chance in a thousand . . . no reason at all why she couldn't bear a live child . . . happened sometimes quite inexplicably . . . touched off by an incident too insignificant to be recalled . . .' She wished them all to the devil, along with the scores of boys who erupted in the quad at stipulated intervals during the day, their assemblies and dispersals regulated by that damned bell.

A day or so later Davy tried a new tack. They would go away on a long Continental tour the day term ended. Down the Rhine, maybe, to Switzerland and then Italy if she fancied. Her responses were mechanical and he did not press her, sensing that the depression was too deep to be charmed away by reassurances and promised treats.

In another day or two she was allowed up but had no wish to go downstairs and still took her meals in the bedroom. They brought her books but she could never summon enough concentration to get beyond the first paragraph or two. All day the sun shone strongly through the southern window and in the evening, when Davy came up to take supper with her, the room was flooded with the pink reflection of sunset on the rim of the moor. On the third day she had been out of bed, he said suddenly, "You've got to snap out of it, Chris. Not for my sake but your own. God knows, I realise how keen you were to have that child and why, but this isn't *you*. You're a fighter and you've got to come to terms with it sooner or later. Willoughby swears there's absolutely no reason at all why you shouldn't have a child and I never once heard him use soft talk on a patient."

"How long did it take you to 'snap out of it'?"

"Me? Well, it's not the same for a man . . . I realise that."

"I'm not talking about losing the baby. I'm talking about the time you lost Beth."

She caught him off guard and he looked away. "A hell of a long time. But this place helped."

"It can't help me, Davy."

"It can if you'd let it."

She changed the subject. She could never make him understand her affections were centred wholly upon him, owing nothing to this great pile of brick and stone and timber that had succeeded, God alone knew how, in steering him through a succession of crises.

"Where's Grace? Why hasn't she been to see me?"

"She's still in France, brushing up for the exams."

She remembered then. Grace had gone off to spend a month with a pen-friend in Caen, with the object of improving her chances of getting a distinction in French, her best subject. She was glad the kid was out of it, glad too that she did not have to parry someone else's sympathy. The bell went again and he said, "That'll be the end of prep. There's a prefects' meeting in the Sixth and I promised I'd look in. I'll only be an hour. Will you go to bed now or would you like matron up for company?"

"No. Do what you have to Davy. I'll be all right."

He went out with a troubled face and she heard him descending to the hall and the quad door opening and closing. The harsh clang of the heavy door decided her, symbolising what Bamfylde had become, a prison where every inmate, save only her, had become acclimatised to its routines and strictures. She knew then what she must do and went about her preparations with feverish haste, cramming a change of clothes into a night bag, checking the money in her handbag and detaching her car key from the ring on the mantelshelf. She opened the door and slipped on to the landing, listening for sounds from below. There were none. All the boys had gone into Big Hall for supper and the forecourt, overlooked by the landing window, was empty in the fading light of the sun's last rays. She hesitated a moment longer, wondering whether to leave a note but decided against it. A note would mean immediate pursuit and in any case what was there to explain that he hadn't already guessed. Prisoners didn't leave notes when they went over the wall to look for better luck on the outside.

She went down the stairs holding firmly to the iron rail, out of the front door and then round by the shrubbery path that led to the ramshackle car- and cycle-shelter. Nobody heard her go for the incline of the west drive was enough to coast down to the road without starting the engine. A minute later and she was turning right at Stone Cross and speeding between the huge clumps of rhododendrons in the direction of Bamfylde Halt.

IV

It was by the merest chance Molyneux saw her. He was driving back from the village, after his customary two pints at the Fleur de Lys, when he saw the glint of the car as it coasted out of the drive and disappeared round the curve of the bank between the two exits. He recognised the beat of the engine and paid no particular attention to the incident until, an hour or so later, he happened to encounter David crossing the quad and say, "Glad to see the Missis is perking up, P.J.," a remark sufficiently puzzling for David to stop short and ask if he had been in to visit her while he was at the prefects' meeting. Molyneux said he hadn't but assumed, after seeing her drive off in the direction of Stone Cross, that she was up and about again.

"You *saw* her drive off? *Tonight?* Are you absolutely sure, Molyneux?"

"Well, it was her little roadster. About an hour ago. Caught a glimpse of it just as I was turning in the west drive."

"It couldn't have been her. She hasn't come downstairs yet. Somebody must be joy-riding."

"One of the boys?"

"Who else? No one on the staff would have borrowed the car without asking. I'd better check," and before Molyneux could reply he hurried off to the rear to the car-shelter behind the kitchen to confirm the fact that the car was gone.

Even then he had no inkling that it was Chris who had driven it off but it was just possible someone might have required transport in a hurry and, unable to locate him, had gone up to the bedroom to ask for the keys. He went into the head's house at a run and, hurrying upstairs, experienced an unpleasant qualm when he found the room empty and two of the drawers wide open. The nightdress and dressing gown she had been wearing were on the turned-back bed and he called, "Chris? Are you there, Chris?" but then he noticed her handbag was missing from the dressing table and the near-certainty that she had gone hit him like a blow between the eyes.

He ran downstairs to the kitchen where old Rigby was having one of his stoveside naps.

"Did you see my wife go out, Rigby?"

The old fellow rubbed his eyes. "Out? No sir. She's upstairs, isn't she?"

"No, she isn't. Has anyone been in while I've been with the prefects?"

"No, sir. No one."

Driven by instinct he ran back through the arch to the car-shelter and stood beside Molyneux's still-warm machine, trying to check the panic rising in him. Women who had recently given birth sometimes behaved very oddly and Chris had been frighteningly depressed since the loss of the baby. He felt the night breeze strike him cold under his arms and shivered. Where the hell could she have gone and why? He took several deep breaths and forced his mind to think logically. Stone Cross direction, Molyneux had said, and about an hour since, for he had only been absent about ninety minutes. Stone Cross probably meant the road to the Halt but she couldn't take a train anywhere at this hour and, in any case, she had the car. A tiny gleam of hope pricked him. There was less than half a gallon in the tank. He knew that because he had used the car earlier in the day to get her tablets from Doc Willoughby's dispensary. The car averaged, on these gradients, no more than thirty-two miles to the gallon, usually less, and she couldn't get petrol until morning and even then no nearer than Cooper's ramshackle garage in Steepcote, ten miles or so on the road to Dulverton; providing she was heading for Dulverton and those open drawers indicated she had taken some luggage. Perhaps this in itself was reassuring. At least it indicated that she hadn't rushed off into the night in response to some half-crazed impulse.

He dashed back to Rigby, his profound agitation causing him to catch the old chap by the lapel of his old-fashioned tail-coat, a relic of pre-Herries butling. "Listen, Rigby. Find Mr. Howarth. Tell him I've got to dash over to Dulverton and I'll phone him inside two hours. Tell him to wait up in my study and that it's very urgent." And then, making a snap decision to half-confide in the old servant, "Mrs. Powlett-Jones seems to have overestimated her own strength. She took it into her head to go for a drive and I'm going after her. In the Dulverton direction. If I don't ring back after midnight ask Mr. Howarth to contact the doctor, do you understand?"

"Well . . . yes, sir. Certainly, sir."

The man looked more bemused than he had at the time of Alcock's fatal heart attack but there was no time to waste in further speculation. He ran back through the arch and wheeled out Molyneux's heavy machine. It started at the first kick and in less than a minute he was roaring down the drive and heading for Bamfylde Halt.

Rage as well as concern stirred in him. To go out like that without a word to anyone, at ten o'clock at night, was an utterly irresponsible action, providing she was in full possession of her faculties and he could not believe that depression had brought her that low. He took his profound irritation and anxiety out on the motorcycle, slowing it round the wide bends between the rhododendron clumps and screeching to a halt in the station approach. There was a gleam of yellow light on the platform. That would be Walrus Tapscott, stationmaster and signalman waiting for one of the two goods trains through here each week night. He called over the picket fence, "Tapscott! It's me, Powlett-Jones! How long have you been on duty?"

"Since around nine, sir."

"Did you see any cars pass either way."

"Yes, sir. Just the one."

"What sort of car? Small or large?"

"I dunno, sir. I on'y got a glimpse as I was coming down the signal-box steps. Smallish, I'd say. It went by at a pretty good lick. Any trouble up at skuel, sir?"

"There might be. I'm finding out. Which way was it going?"

"Took the Dulverton road at the fork. Saw the tail light."

"Thank you."

"Anything I can do, sir?"

"No."

He was off again, roaring over the gritty surface to the fork and setting the machine at the one-in-six gradient that led over the shoulder of the moor. Ten miles of twisting by-road would bring him to the eastern edge of Middlemoor, looking down into the heavily wooded valley of the Barle and as he went his mind conjured with a variety of destinations beyond Dulverton or the nearest probable filling-station. It might be Taunton, or even London, if her strength held out that long. It might be the north. More likely it was anywhere chance took her, for he had nothing but instinct to help him follow a trail. In the heavy silence of the moorland night the motorcycle seemed to make a prodigious noise. A barn owl swooped out of a spinney and flew diagonally across his vision, causing him to swerve so violently that he almost went into a speed wobble. After that he took a partial grip on himself, slowing down and peering about him in the darkness.

It was lighter when he emerged on to the open moor. A few stars were glimmering over Tarr Steps to his left and somewhere over on the right, in a fold of the plateau, they shone on a patch of water. He thought, savagely, "God damn my luck with women . . . first Beth, then Julia Darbyshire, now this . . . It's all so bloody disorganised . . . they all do the first thing that comes into their heads and jib at making a plan and sticking to it . . . they all get carried away by their emotions . . ." and in his misery he even found himself blaming Beth for not acting quickly enough to avoid that damned lorry on Quarry Hill. It was only when he caught himself thinking, "She could have slammed into reverse and shot off the road . . ." that he checked the onrush of hysteria and forced himself to review the wisdom of this blind pursuit into the night, thinking, "I'm just as bad . . . I should have seen Willoughby . . . consulted someone . . . anything but lose myself chasing a will-of-a-wisp."

*   *   *

He saw the reflection of his headlight beam with the tail of his eye as he shot past a wide open gateway on the very crest of the moor. Just a dullish flash but enough to bring him to a halt, abandon the machine in the hedge and run back twenty yards or so. The car was there, blocking the opening. The lights were switched off and it seemed to have been parked very carelessly on a hummock of dried mud.

He approached it with his heart in his mouth and saw,

with a great surge of relief, that she was slumped in the nearside seat. She did not move when he went round the bonnet but when he reached through the open window and touched her shoulder she stirred and moaned before shaking herself and then sitting bolt upright, one hand raised as though to ward off a blow.

"Are you all right?"

She stared at him as though he had been a passing moorman. There was just enough starlight to see the bafflement in her eyes and the tight compression of the mouth. He went round the bonnet again and got into the driver's seat. Her hand, surprisingly, was warm. She said, slowly, "Where is this? What's happened?"

"You tell me."

Relief put an edge on his tongue. He had to make an effort to check an outburst of recrimination.

"I drove off by myself."

"Yes. You'd still be driving if the tank wasn't dry."

"It isn't dry." She sounded maddeningly rational. "I saw there wasn't enough to get me much farther so I pulled in."

"Why, Chris? For God's sake, why?"

She did not answer but half-relaxed again. "You must have known I'd be scared out of my wits. I only caught up with you by sheer luck. You don't even seem to know where you were heading."

"It didn't matter."

He had no answer to this, even though it went some way to explain her state of mind. Presently he said, "Do you feel all right? I mean, you got this far . . . we're only a mile or so short of Dulverton."

She said, "Odd how far you can get without trying. I had no idea where I was going . . . how far I'd come. First I wanted to break out and then all I wanted to do was sleep. Sleep and never wake up."

Compassion and concern returned to him with a rush. "That's no way to talk, Chris! People are concerned for you. Not just me but Willoughby . . . everybody. If only you'd tried to explain . . . Turn up that window. I'll back out and drive back. She might just make it."

"No, wait, Davy!" Then, "How did *you* get here?"

"Following my nose on Molyneux's motorbike. It's up there in the hedge. I can get someone to pick it up in the morning."

"Before we start back . . . we've got to talk. It might as well be now. I'm not ill, not physically ill, that is. It's quiet out here. Away from that bell."

It gave him a hint, broad enough to encourage him to humour her.

"It was pressing down on you?"

"Unbearably."

"There's a reason for it. After a pregnancy—even a normal one—women get all kinds of fancies, or so Willoughby told me a day or so ago."

"He told me, too. But there's more to it than that."

"You aren't happy—quite apart from the baby?"

"It's nothing to do with you, Davy. You must believe that."

"I'd like to, but how can I?"

"You must. I haven't stopped loving you."

"Then what? Try and tell me, no matter how crazy it sounds."

"I feel so bloody useless."

"Useless? *You!* But that *is* crazy! I thought you were settling in. Slowly, maybe, but a bit more every month. Then, when you were expecting the kid . . ."

"That led us both astray, gave a wrong impression."

"About what, exactly?"

"About me being someone, doing something useful, having a purpose back there."

"Isn't being my wife purpose enough?"

"No, Davy. Being anyone's wife wouldn't be. That's the way I'm made and I can't do anything about it."

"All right. The minute you're fit we'll go all out to get you a constituency. If it's so important . . ."

"I don't think that's the answer. I did once but I don't any longer."

"Then what? What kind of role would help?"

"If I knew that we'd be home in bed, Davy."

He thought, distractedly, "There's a way out of this mess somewhere, if I could find it. It's been half-suggesting itself for a year or more but it's so damned elusive neither of us can find it." He said, "At least you must know what isn't the answer. To cave in, to do the first damn silly thing that suggests itself, like coming out here on your own without letting any of us know how hard-driven you were. We've always been able to talk, or I thought so."

"Not really, Davy. Bamfylde's a big place. Most times I can't hear you and you don't seem to hear me."

He acted on impulse then as though he was faced with something more tangible than deep, personal despair. He reached over and swung her round roughly and shouted at her as though he was dealing with a case of hysterics. "That just isn't so! You know damned well it isn't so! You aren't making any allowances at all for your physical condition, for the fact that you've had your hopes dashed about the baby. You *were* settling in, and everything would have been plain sailing if the baby had lived."

She said, calmly, "Does it matter—the root cause of it? The fact is I made a hash of this, just as I did with Rowley, and the candidature, and two marriages, and everything else I've attempted."

"That's your view. It isn't mine and it isn't anyone else's and the sooner you get that into your head the better. I'll tell you something else. My Mam came home from the pithead after they told her she'd lost her man and two of her sons, and within five minutes of taking her coat off she was getting my tea and washing sheets in the copper. She wasn't all that singular. I daresay half the women in the terrace were doing the same—adjusting—facing up to what couldn't be altered. Hardly one of them could write or read English, or do more than scribble their names on a clothing club card, but you've had an expensive education. What's it worth if you crack up like this under a few bad deals? Will you think about that?"

She began to cry, quietly at first but then, both hands grasping one of his, unrestrainedly, so that her body shook and they sat there for what seemed a long time, with silence and emptiness all about them save for her dry, gasping sobs and the long sigh of the breeze. She was quiet at last and freed his hand, fumbling in the glove pocket for her handbag and dabbing her eyes with a crumpled handkerchief. She said, at length, "Take me home, Davy. Don't say anything more. Just drive on home."

He reversed out of the gate and switched on the lights. The beam seemed to probe a limitless expanse of the moor and away down by the tarn a nightjar screeched. He saw by the luminous dial that the petrol needle was not quite settled at empty. It was mostly downhill and there might be just enough to see them home. They did not exchange a single word until the car coughed at the summit of the west drive and ran over the flat to the forecourt, where the engine petered out. He saw it as a kind of sign, a pledge that his luck would turn and hers with it maybe. The study light was on. She said, "Is anyone else out looking for me?"

"No. I told Rigby to tell Howarth. That'll be Howarth in the study now."

"We can trust Howarth," she said, and scrambling out went swiftly in and up the stairs.

* * *

Howarth was sitting slumped in the swivel chair. The air in the room was thick with stale tobacco smoke and when David entered he hoisted himself up, then relaxed again.

"Well?"

"She's back. She had some damned silly idea about running away. I found her up on the moor, near Dulverton."

"She's all right?"

"As far as I can tell. Did you phone the Doc?"

"No. Had an idea you'd bring her in. Get Willoughby over here at this hour and everyone in the damned place would hear of it."

"Thanks, Howarth."

He went over to the decanter and poured two stiff whiskies. "Where do I go from here? Can you tell me? Can Willoughby . . . anyone?"

"We might. Between us that is. But if you'll take my advice you'll bring Barnaby in on it."

"Barnaby?"

"It was his idea, wasn't it?"

"What are you driving at?"

Howarth shot his legs out and savoured his drink. He

looked particularly thoughtful and thought always made him look disagreeable. "That prep class notion he had. The Second Form is hopelessly unwieldy. That woman we have can't cope with it. Too rule-of-thumb. Needs imagination. Christine might provide it. She seems to have a surfeit that needs siphoning off. Maybe you could solve two problems at a stroke."

He sat down, gaping at Howarth. The path out of the slough suddenly became clear, a tricky one, certainly, but at least some kind of promise to higher, safer ground. "You mean separate the under-elevens and put Chris in charge? Take her on the staff?"

"Why not. She's a graduate. She ought to be able to cope with a dozen youngsters that age. Give her something constructive to do. Keep her mind off her own fancied inadequacies."

He said, "That's a brilliant idea, Howarth. When did you think of it?"

"I've been sitting here twiddling my thumbs for three hours. Look at that ashtray."

The ashtray, a large one, was full of butts. The air in the study was like that of a taproom. David crossed and opened a window on the forecourt. When he turned Howarth was crushing out yet another Gold Flake and heaving himself up. "Give you another tip. Sleep on it before you put it to her and when you do have all the answers to her protests pat. Don't go off at half-cock again." He looked at David humorously. "You're inclined to do that, P.J. It's the Welshman in you, I imagine. Too damned impetuous, the Welsh! Good night to you." He went out, closing the door softly. In all the years they had worked together David had never known him bang a door or make any noise that could be avoided.

CHAPTER TWO

I

So often it had happened that way, a sudden closing in of baleful factors that threatened to overwhelm him and then a single fissure that offered an escape route and, once exploited, presented a variety of alternative new courses. Within a day of his putting the proposal to her the means to achieve it without a great deal of fuss and improvisation came to hand in the form of a legacy; providing sufficient cash to expand Howarth's idea in a way that made it practical.

Until then he had not seen it as much more than a marginal involvement on the part of Chris, who could devote a couple of hours a day to the smaller, younger half of the swollen Second Form. But with the money, and the accommodation resulting from the new wing, he began to see the development as the founding of a bona fide preparatory department that could be expanded term by term, giving her all the scope she needed. He went about it with enthusiasm and when the builder's estimate for a junior dormitory was in hand he put the scheme to her in detail, expecting and getting some reservations on her part regarding her fitness for responsibility of the kind demanded.

"I don't know, Davy. You need special training for a job of that kind. I've had absolutely no experience with kids, or teaching of any kind, save that one term just after I left University. I don't think I could even keep order if it came to the point. Taking an odd class is one thing. Running a whole new department is quite another."

"I'd back you and so would Howarth, Barnaby and Briggy. They think you'd be ideal for the job. Give it a try, anyway. For all our sakes."

"Especially mine," and she smiled, wryly. "Well, that's the general idea, isn't it?"

"Up on the moor you wanted a role. Here's a real one and you'll get paid for it. Not all that much, for we can't afford it, but something."

"Won't you have to put it to the Governors?"

"Ultimately, but I don't expect any trouble there. I've got two trump cards. That legacy and your degree. Well?"

"I'll give it a go, Davy. I'll try. I'll try like hell."

"That's all I want to hear."

*   *   *

They soon had a nickname for it. The boys called it the Cradle and soon the term became general, even among the staff. The Cradle. Eight scruffy little first-termers and two more seasoned recruits, including John Churchill, the ten-year-old whose presence she had questioned at Ringwood on the last day of their honeymoon. From the first hour of the first day it was a resounding success so that within a week she came to accept the fact that she had a gift for teaching, an instinctive knowledge of how to estimate their potentialities, apply the spur to the embryo timewasters and nurture confidence in what Barnaby called 'the premature transplants'. Some of the enthusiasms of her own childhood and adolescence returned to her, so that she found herself rereading books and responding to them in a way she had all but forgotten. And at the same time she developed a fierce pride in obvious results, in seeing the timid take heart and the would-be jesters put firmly in their place. Young Churchill (whom she never ceased to regard as the rangefinder for the Cradle) took her fancy from the start, a sensitive, eager boy with a good memory, who had lost much of his initial shyness after a resounding success as Yum-Yum in last year's *Mikado*. The rest, for the most part, were a guileless, merry-hearted lot and it was tremendous fun breaking them in, as Howarth put it, on *Poems of Action*, *The Water-Babies* and *Huckleberry Finn*. She liked her English classes best but they were quick to respond to elementary maths and the garishly illustrated *Le Livre Rouge* that she chose to give them their first lessons in French. Sometimes their high spirits were a little overwhelming.

"Please, miss, can we move on to the Sheperdson-Grangerford feud? I read it last night before lights out and it's spiffing . . ."

"Please, miss, what's the French for 'it doesn't matter'? Ford says it's 'Sanfairyann' but it isn't is it?"

"Miss, can I change places with Grisewood? He's a frowster and won't have the window open."

They all called her 'Miss' and when she asked Davy about this he said to let it pass. 'Mrs. Powlett-Jones' was too much of a mouthful and 'Ma'am' would make her feel like Queen Vic coming up to her Second Jubilee.

It was better therapy than any of them guessed and right through the tail-end of the summer term, the succeeding term and into the new year, she was aware of having got a grip on the situation, so that the memory of that humiliating surrender to what had seemed a conspiracy of events to wreck his life and hers receded into the subconscious. Both of them were happy to leave it there. It was a time of new experiences and a drastic reappraisal of her entire expectations up here on the plateau. But she realised he would be unlikely to see it as anything so dramatic. It was just one more tiresome problem solved, lost in the familiar pattern of humps, dips and level stretches of the school year although, every now and again, something occurred to make a period memorable in terms of Bamfylde history, Bamfylde lore, Bamfylde's ever-expanding gallery of oddities.

To her they were all oddities, but even by his standards there seemed to be a plague of them in 1935. Sometimes a new entry would yield a crop of faceless boys, who merged into the background like a stage chorus. At other times a clutch of singular personalities would emerge by the end of a full year. Nineteen-thirty-five was a vintage year.

Hookham, for instance. Thirteen when he arrived, and too old for the Cradle, he was sent instead to the Second Form, ruled by Miss Nixon, spinster daughter of Prebendary Nixon, and known by the boys as 'Bo', herself quite a character.

Venn, in the long line of Bamfylde's official jesters, invented the name within days of Miss Nixon's arrival, the nickname emerging painlessly from a discussion in the Upper Fifth on her somewhat overbearing presence. Almost as tall as Frobisher, the lankiest boy on the roll, she was also broad-shouldered, bell-toothed and possessed of a furious energy that had her charges panting in her wake. Venn made a hobby of cataloguing staff idiosyncrasies and was currently regarded as Bamfylde's best mimic, so that idiosyncrasies were his stock in trade.

"The kind of woman one associates with the garrisons of beleaguered towns in the Indian Mutiny," he drawled. "True daughter of the regiment, don't you know? I see her as the unmarried elder sister of that nifty little brunette in the picture in Big School, 'The Relief of Arcot', where the nifty one is drawing attention to the approach of the pipes. However, seeing that even she could have landed a sex-starved subaltern in India, I think of Miss Nixon as someone more regal. How about a warrior queen, driving one of those chariots fitted with revolving meat slicers?"

"Boadicea," prompted Dodge, who was Venn's feed, and Venn said, "Right! Scattering arms, legs and helmets in all directions!" and Miss Nixon had been safely christened.

It was to Bo Nixon that David went, in puzzled mood, one November day, with a grubby note written on graph paper, seeking more precise information concerning little Hookham, but he was obliged to pretend to an absorbed interest in the skyline when Miss Nixon declared his evidence the clumsiest forgery she had seen in twenty years in the profession!

"Oh, I wouldn't say that," said David, gently pulling her leg, "I've seen worse, and you have to admit it's highly original. Let me read it again," and he took the note and read its contents aloud, savouring every laborious down-stroke; "*Dere Headmaster, Please send Hookham home at wunce. I need him here. This is urjent. (Signed) Mrs. Hookham.*" And below, the inevitable postscript, "*Put the trane fare on the bill. L.H.*"

"You don't regard it as anything but an insolent joke, I hope, Headmaster? I know just how I should deal with it. Its perpetrator wouldn't sit comfortably for a week," but she added, as though not yet absolutely sure of her ground with an officer newly risen from the ranks, "Naturally, it's not my province to advise. It was addressed through the post to you."

"That's so," David said, "but to be frank I don't recall Hookham, save as a scared little beggar without a word to say for himself, and that's why I'm here, to get information. You've had him several weeks now, although I do seem to recall he arrived a week or so late."

Miss Nixon glanced at her register. "On October 1st. I'll tell him to report to you at once, Headmaster," and looked quite baffled when David said, hastily, "No, Miss Nixon! I don't want him reporting to me. That'll scare the living daylights out of him, and if he has any sense—and I'd say he had a good deal—he'll simply deny all knowledge of it."

"How could he do that? It's in his handwriting, if you call it handwriting."

"Well, that's one to us, but what's he like? To teach and handle?"

She said, knitting her brow, "You can judge his work standard from that ridiculous letter. As to handling him, there's no pertness or impudence as I recall. He's just a sack at the back of the class. As a matter of fact . . ." but she stopped, looking a little baffled.

"Well?"

"I was only going to add that, if it hadn't been Hookham's handwriting, I would have looked elsewhere for the authorship. A joke played on you and him by one of the others, possibly someone in the Third or Fourth."

"Thank you, Miss Nixon. You've been very helpful," and he sauntered away, with an uncomfortable impression that he had made an unwise choice as regards the Prebendary's daughter. Although undeniably a character, she was entirely without humour and therefore not the best Bamfylde material.

He was surprised when Chris affirmed that Miss Nixon was the right person in the right place at the right time.

"Is that based on what the women's magazines call feminine intuition?"

"I don't have intuitions here. I learned to discard them after a week. When I give you advice about anyone in this crazy place it's based on logic. I seem to be the only one capable of applying any up here."

"You're saying Bo Nixon is the right person to cope with thirteen-year-olds?"

"She fulfils a necessary function just now. Think back a bit.

Before you set up the Cradle all the beginners looked for their
mothering in the Second Form, right?"

"Right. Ma Fender, Mrs. Parminter that is, was said to
press them to her bosom, and Mrs. Arscott was pretty soft
with them."

"Well, now we've got some kind of prep department they
arrive in the Second fully fledged, so they can do with a dose
of Miss Nixon. But what's behind all this?"

He showed her the note, expecting her to laugh but she
didn't. She said, seriously, "This poor little wretch is clearly
an exception. He must have been desperate to go to these
lengths. Has anything like this ever happened before?"

"Not to my recollection. I told Miss Nixon this took the
Bamfylde biscuit for originality."

"Then do Hookham a favour. Let me deal with it."

"You really think that the kid is going to the wall? I mean,
Miss Nixon's right in a way. We could regard it as an elaborate legpull."

"It isn't a legpull and could lead to a lot of unpleasantness."
Without waiting for his assent she took the note and marched
out, leaving him almost as baffled as Bo Nixon, but then,
thinking it over, he remembered the rare tact she had shown
in Bradshawe's case, and it occurred to him that she was
already overhauling him at a breathtaking rate, overhauling
them all, in fact. Hookham, he decided, was in safe hands.

*   *   *

She had observed the solitary paths taken by the loners.
Always they followed the same spare time route between
bells, when there were no compulsory games. Loners
mooched off on a parallel line to the hedge dividing the
main playing field from the Juniors' pitch, drifting towards
the swimming bath, then turning off into the planty, where
their heedless steps brought them to Towser's grave beyond
the first of the trees.

Hookham took this route, book in hand, and she followed
him, coming on him seated on a beech log, out of sight and
sound of his private purgatory. She said, casually, "Hallo,
old chap. What are you reading?" and he offered her the
book, a battered library edition of *Treasure Island*.

"One of my standbys," she said. "The Cradle is halfway through it this term, reading it aloud. But you'll be done with all that, I suppose."

He was trying, she thought, to categorise her, to find her niche in his long, long catalogue of tormentors, and was finding it very difficult. It was therefore time to press her advantage and she said, turning the pages, "How far have you got?"

"I finished it," he said, guardedly, "and *Kidnapped* was out, so I didn't hand it in but started all over again." Then, very carefully, "Is that against the rules, miss?"

"Oh, no," she said, cheerfully, "quite the opposite. Mr. Howarth is a great believer in second readings. Who is your favourite character, Hookham?" and he replied, without a moment's hesitation, "Ben Gunn, miss."

"Oh? Why exactly?"

"Because he managed, I suppose."

"You mean he managed to survive on his own all that time?"

"He was the hero really. *They* wouldn't have managed without him."

Her opinion of Hookham shot up. She saw his line of reasoning at once, and it underlined not so much his originality but his remarkable powers of deduction. He would see himself as the maroon. Scoffed at, put upon, mocked and belittled, when justice, had justice been done to Ben Gunn and himself, proclaimed that their wits were so much sharper than those of Dr. Livesey and Captain Smollett.

She said, "You know, I think you're absolutely right, Hookham. They *couldn't* have managed without him. I'll tell my boys that this afternoon. Happy reading."

His startled gaze followed her all the way down the path to the planty's edge and it might have surprised him had he been in a position to notice that her eyes were bright with tears, but it all worked out satisfactorily and that within hours of the encounter. Hookham was demoted to the Cradle where his age and erudition gave him certain advantages and Chris was not slow to exploit them, going to work the second day Hookham had arrived among them, by announcing, during the reading hour, "Hookham has the advantage of us. He's read *Treasure Island* twice. He's an expert on it, aren't you, Hookham? That's why I'm going to ask him to judge the maps. Has every pair finished their map?"

Eager hands shot up and the maps were gathered in, blotched and grossly distorted variations of Stevenson's map, in the front of the standard edition. The Cradlers had been divided into pairs and told to assume the role of Jim Hawkins and make a treasure chart of their own devising.

Purposely she did not so much as glance at them but handed them all to Hookham, telling him to leave class and stay out until first bell in order to select the winner and runner-up. It was difficult to keep them quiet while he was absent and when the bell rang excitement erupted in squeals of glee and a great deal of bobbing up and down. Then, conscious of making an entrance, Hookham re-appeared. "This one, miss. It's easily the best," and he handed her a brownish roll of cartridge paper that had about it a definite stamp of authenticity. "Good. Help me unroll it, Hookham. You hold that end. Yes, this is very good indeed! It looks as though it might have come straight from Billy Bones's chest. Which pair did it?"

Gosse and Meadowes, both blushing, raised their hands.

"Well, come out and tell us about it. How did you make the paper and writing look so old, Gosse?"

Gosse expanded under her approbation. "We boiled it, Miss."

"*Boiled it?* In what?"

"In tea, miss."

The Cradlers received this news with gasps of delight.

"That was really Meadowes' idea, miss."

"Good for you, Meadowes!" and Meadowes hung his head.

"And which of you did the drawing and invented the clues?"

"I did, miss. I borrowed Whatmore's fountain pen because of its green ink and crossed nib. It came out all spidery and faded-looking."

She pinned the map to the blackboard. "Twenty out of twenty for that, Gosse. And some of these others aren't bad at all. Dismiss now. I'm going to show the winning chart to the head. Wait a minute, Hookham. Off to tea, you others."

They scuttled out, with the usual desk-banging and competitive scuffling, while Hookham remained, looking at the floor. She said, "Thank you for helping, Hookham. It wouldn't have done for me to judge them."

His head came up. "Why not, miss? You're the teacher and give the marks."

"Yes, I know, but you see, I invented the exercise, and you noticed how they all accepted your decision. Would you like to be class monitor?"

"What does a monitor have to do, miss?"

"Oh, all kinds of things. Give out test papers, collect up books, clean the blackboard and even take charge if I have to pop out. You see, you're the biggest and the oldest now, and they'll take it from you. They'd skylark with any of the younger ones."

He said, doggedly, "I'll be monitor, miss." And then, warily, "How long will I stay in the Cradle, miss?"

"Just a term or two. Until you get the hang of things. You're beginning to settle, aren't you?"

"I'll get used to it, I reckon."

He said it as though addressing himself and she had a conviction that he had made the same affirmation many times over the last few weeks. He had surfaced, certainly, but she had an idea he would sink again if she let go too soon.

"Hookham?"

"Yes, miss?"

"What's your initial 'R' stand for?"

He looked surprised, "Roy, miss."

"I'll tell you something, Roy, something I wouldn't want the others to know. A secret between us. I'm fairly new here as well and getting used to it, a bit at a time."

"But how can you be? I mean, Dixon Major told us all you were the head's . . ."

"It doesn't matter who I am, I'm new. New at this job and new at the school, so don't think I don't understand how hard it is. Put it this way. To play me in they made *me* a monitor. Monitor of the Cradle."

Surprisingly, and to her great relief, he grinned. Davy was right about him. He really was an original, and the grin encouraged her to gamble again. She opened her handbag and extracted his grubby little note. "The head said I was to give you this. He's read it but he thinks you ought to stick it out a while longer, and so do I."

He took the note wordlessly and stuffed it in his pocket. Then, as a clamour rose from the quad, he said, "That's tea parade. May I go now, miss?"

"Yes, of course, but be here before first bell tomorrow. We're doing nature study and there's a lot to give out."

He nodded and hurried out and a moment later she heard the duty prefect's command, "Para*aade* . . . *shun*! Dis*miss*!" and the prolonged scrape of boots as the four contingents turned left and fell out. She took a closer look at Gosse's map, deciphering three blurred crosses, marking the treasure. The crosses were not scratched in green but in red, almost certainly in blood. Meadowes' blood, probably, for Gosse would see him as the obvious donor. She thought, "Davy's always said adults learn more than they teach in a place like this and, by God, he's so right!"

II

Despite his admitted experience, despite his sly Celtic trick of winning most people round to his point of view in the end, she did not wholly trust him with the Hookhams. It was very different, however, in the Middle and Upper Schools, where she would sometimes watch him at work.

He was, she decided, uniquely tailored for the job and once they were through the Upper Third, and beginning to notice such things, a majority of boys acknowledged this as freely as she did. This was particularly true in the Sixth, where he was able to step outside his tutorial role and move among them as a kind of group leader, appointed by popular ballot. She realised this one October afternoon when all the Cradlers were down on the lower pitch, practising for the Sevens Competition, and he invited her to attend a current affairs period on the dominant issue of the day, Mussolini's defiance of The League of Nations and invasion of Abyssinia.

Ordinarily, she said, she should have stood in the punishing wind on the touchline, pretending to take a professional

interest in Lower School frolics in the mud, but she could
never arouse more than a casual interest in their interminable
games, and had, indeed, questioned the emphasis placed on
them.

Up to a point he shared her view but added, on this occasion, "You'll find they grow on you. They did on me, after a
year or so, but, strictly for your ear alone, I can still take 'em
or leave 'em. Cross-country running excepted, that is, for
that offers a change of scene. If you're at a loose end this
afternoon, why don't you sit in on a Sixth Form current
affairs? We often have the occasional visitor."

The Sixth subjected her to the half-amused appraisal that
Beth and Phyl Irvine had received at their first Saturday
dance, and he didn't fail to notice it, thinking, "It's good to
have a pretty woman about the place again. Sweetens the
atmosphere somehow," but took good care to ignore her
during the discussion until Venn, with a brisk show of
gallantry, turned to her and said, "What do you think?" and
she looked apprehensively at Davy and then quickly away, for
he was grinning. She said, "Coxe made a good point just
now. Sanctions won't stop Mussolini. He'll be in Addis
Ababa by the new year."

"But Coxe said we should have gone to war over it."

"It wouldn't have come to war. Bluff would have done the
trick. We should have sent the fleet to Suez, and the whole
thing would have fizzled out. As it is, who knows where it
could lead?"

They were impressed, every last one of them, and Coxe,
finding his minority views supported, was encouraged to
prompt. "Could you say where, ma'am? To another World
War?"

"It might. Mussolini isn't the only braggart on the rampage. There are plenty of others throwing their weight about
in Berlin and Tokyo. How can they be anything but encouraged by the way he's getting away with it?"

After that she was embroiled and they went at it, cut and
thrust, until the bell rang. It was not until after lock-up, when
they were having their final cup of tea by the fire, that she
glanced across at him and remembered how effortlessly he
had chaired that lively discussion and how, in the end, every

boy in the room turned to him, not to her, for the summing-up.
She said, "It was very stimulating. But I won't come again if
you don't mind."

"Why not? I thought you made out a pretty good case for
military sanctions."

"So did I but they didn't think so. They were just being
polite. Now if you told them the moon was made of blue
cheese, they'd accept it as gospel, and that's victory, Davy.
You're coming down the straight now, whether you realise
it or not," but he said, seriously, "It's a damned long straight."

"Then, deep down, you're as scared as I am, especially
since Mussolini got away with it. You're scared for boys like
Venn and Coxe. And even for some of the younger ones. If it
ever did come to the crunch, how would you regard them
having to go through what you went through?"

He was a long time answering. It was something he had
thought about very deeply. That much was obvious by his
concentrated expression and the deliberation of his answer.
He said, finally, "I'd feel like you, that I'd been right all
along. Oh, not about politics, or the way things have drifted
from bad to worse since Versailles. I'm not pretending to have
foreseen that, or anything like it. All along the line you've been
the only Socialist prophet of doom I've met, and every day's
newspaper headline keeps reminding me of the fact. I'm
talking about something different, more general, if you like."

"Could anything be more 'general' than another World
War?"

"For me it could. Our approach to it, if and when it came.
Looking back, that's what I've been working on ever since I
settled in here, and saw things through adolescent eyes. But
it's late for amateur metaphysics, love."

He was getting up but she stopped him. "Tell me, Davy.
It's important."

He said, "I remember a story Algy told us to illustrate the
same point years ago. The night of his farewell supper, it was,
and it made a terrific impact on everyone at the time. They
gave him a cheer for it. Loudest cheer I ever heard in Big
Hall and won't hear a better, not if I'm here in my dotage."

He told her the story of Petherick, O.B.E. and 'Chuff'
Rodgers, killed at First Ypres, of the train ride they shared

with Algy over to Barcombe, the baby who was sick, and how Chuff had mopped up mother and baby with his hand-kerchief. It had always stayed in his mind so that gradually, over the years, it had become a kind of slide rule he applied to the potential of every boy he taught. There were the Pethericks, who went on to become presidents of insurance companies, who had their names in the Honours Lists, and there were the Chuffs, a majority he liked to think, although sometimes he wasn't sure.

"It's a good story," she said, "and very relevant. But shocking to my way of thinking."

"Why?"

"What you're really saying is that you accept the fact that the Chuffs will be sacrificed and the Pethericks, who stay put, will make a pile, grow fat and die in their beds."

"That's the way it usually goes."

"But it's too awful to contemplate, Davy. We ought to try and change it."

"You saw how difficult it is to change The only consolation is that it seems to work and if I don't know who should? I came here absolutely convinced that every Chuff in the world had gone west, but they hadn't They seed themselves somehow. I've got a good many of them here at this moment, nearly twenty years after they blew half-time out there."

"But that's what I mean, Davy, you're accepting it passively and that's as wrongheaded as that ostrich attitude that drove me out of politics."

"Not really. Neither is Howarth, Barnaby or any of the others who believe in what they're about. My job, yours too now, is to encourage the Chuffs and slap down the embryo insurance presidents, while grabbing their parents' money with both hands. The more we can swing our way the better our chance of survival, if it ever does come to another show-down."

III

There had been a time when his personal fortunes had seemed to run a parallel course with the roller-coaster ride of the world outside, a world where quarrelsome tribes con-

tinued to collide with one another all the way from Manchuria to Madrid. But things were different now. All about
him, if the newspapers and radio bulletins were to be believed, was conflict and disarray, but here on the plateau it
was sometimes difficult for a man, busy from rising-bell to
lockup, to think of himself as involved in the ferment beyond
bounds, and this despite the fact that he shared bed and
board with a woman who was half-convinced they were all
riding an express to perdition.

His own objectivity stemmed from several sources. His
splendid health was one, and her presence was another, for
sometimes immersed like him in the come-day-go-day trivia
of successive terms, she too could join him in looking at the
outside world through the wrong end of a telescope. Her
restored confidence and her new tendency to value the
smaller bonuses of life, governed her moods so that for weeks
together she could join him in forgetting what was going on
outside.

She was made aware of this, and even acknowledged it
with a private chuckle, when George V died a day or so after
the Lent term began in 1936, and the boys put on their black
ties and marched to Stone Cross Church for the memorial
service. Everyone had liked harmless old George, whom they
saw as a country squire, and everyone was sorry for Mary,
but there was nothing personal about their regrets. Somewhere, two hundred miles to the east, a seventy-year-old
stranger had died but that was less immediate than the Corps'
attempt to play 'The Dead March from Saul' over the last
two hundred yards of the journey to Stone Cross.

Now and again, of course, she was jolted out of her com-
placency and so, to a degree, were David and a few of the
Seniors. As the months spent themselves in a succession of
regularised assemblies and dispersals, in sports fixtures,
Choral Society concerts, examinations, O.T.C. field days
and the climatic event of the Christmas term, with Algy
Herries as yet another Ko-Ko ("Seventy-five, by the Lord
Harry, and still capable of warbling 'Tit-Willow' to Kati-
sha!") the malaise of the world across the Channel would
cross boundaries, and the Owl Society would debate the
Popular Front in France, Mussolini's rape of Ethiopia,

Hitler's re-occupation of the Rhineland and purges in Moscow. But as soon as the bell rang the inner rhythm of the place would reassert itself, and it would require something as immediate as the abdication of Edward VIII to turn Bamfylde eyes outward. But even then not for long. When a school had spent four months rehearsing *The Mikado*, even someone like Mrs. Simpson has to wait her turn.

Occasionally something would occur on the plateau that would make them aware that there was still abysses to be crossed on frail rope-bridges and usually they would cross in convoy, as in the case of young Driscoe's miry flirtation with death, in December.

Driscoe II was the youngest brother of the Driscoe who sang treble in the 1919 *Mikado*, when he was the third little maid from school, partnering Beth and Phyl Irvine. At the London dinner in January he reminded David that his kid brother would be arriving at Bamfylde in the summer term, and added, "Kid's a bit of a weed. As the youngest of five he's been spoiled to hell, particularly by the old lady, but he's okay upstairs. Might even pass an exam or two, and that's something I never did, did I, Pow-Wow?"

"You had compensating distinctions as far as I was concerned," David told him, and reminded him of his appearance on stage before an audience of four hundred beside an obviously pregnant Yum-Yum, but when Driscoe said, "Will you keep a special eye on the kid, Pow-Wow? Mater's orders, I'm afraid," he added, drily, "Hang it, I'm paid to keep an eye on all of them, but you can tell your mother I shall regard him as special if it's likely to stop her worrying."

But Driscoe II was seen to be something of a special case when he presented himself the following April, a morose little boy, light as a feather, with glasses, a slight stutter and exceptionally knobbly knees. It was those knees, singular enough to earn Driscoe II a lot of ragging, that encouraged David to put him straight into the Upper Third. Upper Third boys had discarded short pants and the boy's entrance exam paper justified a flying start. Moreover, it did not look as if Driscoe was likely to distinguish himself outside a classroom.

One could not always prejudge these things, however.

Driscoe, II, far too frail for rugby, showed unexpected promise as a cross-country runner, astonishing Outram's shield-holding team by averaging nine points in the first three runs of the season. Nine wasn't many, set against the impressive total of Outram's long-striding house-captain, Parker, but it was reckoned good for a shortsighted, knock-kneed first-termer, and Parker, a fanatic in this field, selected the boy as his fag, partly with the object of encouraging him when he was doing odd jobs about the study.

The result was predictable. Driscoe became fired with a desire to develop his unlikely talent to a pitch where the splendid Parker, an all-round sportsman, and in line for the house prefect-ship, regarded him as an asset to the house. When the run-in started from the crest of Middlemoor, the final run of the term, the new boy went off like a fugitive slave a few yards ahead of the bloodhounds.

He had no luck. At a gap in the hedge, dividing Man Dixon's sheep pasture from the marshy river bottom, he fell flat on his face and lost his glasses. Groping for them in inches of Exmoor mud he was trodden flat by a succession of runners determined to keep up with the leaders, and in a momentary lull between his involuntary prostration he decided to continue without them and return to recover them before first bell in the morning.

It was a reckless decision. Badly winded, and quite unfamiliar with the route, he ran far wide of the track, reaching the soggy floor of the valley at a point where the river bank was approached by a broad area of marsh, screened by a fringe of last year's sedge and partitioned off from firmer ground by a fence of two-by-four palings.

Any country-bred boy would have realised that a crossing here was impassable and that there was a very good reason for fencing out here on the open moor, but Driscoe had lived the whole of his life in Golders Green, and even his summer holidays had been spent with a doting aunt in Worthing. He made nothing of the flimsy barrier, scrambled over and plunged waist-deep into a slough as thick as black treacle.

He had time to yell and somebody heard him.

Gosse, maker of treasure maps, was passing the gap higher up the slope, moving at a deliberately leisurely pace, with

the object of evading the whippers-in at the next belt of
timber and making for Ma Midden's farm, where he could
exchange a sixpence (carefully wrapped in his handkerchief) for two hot pasties, one for him, one for his crony,
Meadowes.

Gosse, his curiosity aroused, changed direction, descended
the steep field and stopped short at the barrier, appalled
by what he saw on the far side. It was no more than half of
Driscoe, who looked like the stump of a small tree hammered
into soft ground.

Gosse was not only resourceful, he was also quick-thinking.
Out of the corner of his eye he noted two things. One was his
henchman Meadowes, who had followed his angled descent
but stopped higher up the slope, puzzled; the other, a few
yards to the right, was the remains of what had once been a
wire fence, no more than a rotted post enmeshed in rusty
wire. Above the frantic howls of Driscoe he put his hands to
his mouth and shouted, "He's stuck! He'll never make it!
Find the whippers-in—tell 'em a new kid is drowning in Man
Dixon's bottom. Run like hell . . .!" and as Meadowes
scudded off across the great, slab-sided field, Gosse made his
own dispositions, slopping through mud on his side of the
fence and dragging the isolated stake from its bed.

The wire was rusted and tangled, but it was a matter of
seconds to unravel some ten feet of it and loop the free end
round his shoulder. Then, wading as far as the fence, he
threw the billet to Driscoe and was immensely relieved when
he saw flailing hands grasp it either side of the staple, and a
mud-spattered face stare up at him with an expression of
baffled hostility—"Just as though I'd flipping well pushed
him there," as he told an enthralled audience in the Outram
dormitory that night.

The wire tautened and the strain paid out another three or
four feet, so that Gosse, his shoulder wedged against the
nearest upright of the fence, was able to get some kind of
purchase and even attempt to twist the loose end round the
lower horizontal. He did not ask himself how long he could
hold on there but as long as the fence stood the strain, the
billet held by Driscoe did not crumble, and the wire did not
part, there was a prospect of supporting Driscoe until some-

one with more muscle and more practical apparatus arrived on the scene. In the meantime Gosse gritted his teeth and closed his eyes. He did not want to see Driscoe disappear under the mud, or watch his final struggles through the wide gap in the planks. It was enough to know he was still there, chest deep in the black, filthy stuff, and would sink no deeper so long as the wire remained taut.

*   *   *

Gosse did not see the combined approach of Coxe, Venn and Davidson, who arrived in a bunch, their whistling breath indicating that they had run a downhill mile in approximately the time it would take the best of them to complete the 880-yard circuit of Lower Side pitch. They crowded him even closer to the fence, Coxe taking the strain and Davidson, himself a moorman, straddling the fence and lowering himself on to the far side. Then, with what Gosse thought of as great cunning, making a bridge of his body by taking a grip of the lower horizontal and calling to Driscoe to grab his ankles. Venn, unable to find more wire, replaced Coxe as anchor, and Coxe, taking his cue from Davidson, scaled the fence farther along, noticing as he crossed it a section of loose planks. It took him only a moment to prise one loose and squirm along the inside of the fence to the spot where his friend Davidson was lying face downward in the mud. Driscoe was no farther down and had even contrived to flounder a few inches nearer the fence in order to improve his grip on Davidson's shins but it seemed that he had not entirely lost his head for he still held the wire between his teeth.

They huddled there, all five of them, in an ungainly group, a tableau that, viewed from a distance, looked like a clumsy exercise in gymnastics. Driscoe was hardly more than a black bubble on the surface. Davidson was only visible above the thighs. Venn was now flattened against the near side of the fence, with Gosse still trying to loop the fag-end of the wire to the cross-piece. There was progress of a sort, however, for Davidson, turning his head to spit out mud, saw Coxe's plank and shouted, "Under my knees, Frankie! Hard under my bloody knees! Quick, for Christ's sake . . ." so that Coxe, kneeling, plunged the board deep into the slime, aiming

to burrow under Davidson's thighs. Despite ample lubrica-
tion, the passage of the rough timber made him wince but he
found that it strengthened his purchase so long as Coxe
remained kneeling on his end of the board. Beyond that,
however, there was little they could do and glancing sideways Coxe saw that Driscoe could not hold on indefinitely.
Then Venn called from the other side of the fence. "They're
coming, Frankie. Pow-Wow and Man Dixon. They've got
ropes!" and Davidson, ordinarily a very taciturn boy, made
the only joke of the operation, grunting, "Shout up to them!
Tell 'em not to hurry, will you?"

IV

His instinctive front-line reactions were not as immediate as
they had been, at the time of the Havelock fire. The war was a
long time ago now, and although he thought of himself as
very fit for a man turned forty, the habit of contemplation
slowed him down when it came to making snap decisions.

He had been at the tail of the field, shepherding the few
Second Formers running the course over the crest of the
pasture and down into the valley, but once he saw the last of
them wade the ford, and disappear into the spinney, he
stopped to have a word with Man Dixon, remembering him
not as he saw him now, a stolid, thickset moorman, but as the
day-boy who, in 1925, had been credited with killing old
Bat Ferguson with a buzzsaw rendering of the French
adjective *vert*. He reminded him of the incident now and
Dixon, as master of the family holding, could afford to grin.
"Arr," he mused, never having lost his upland burr, "and
there was a particle o' truth in it, Pow-Wow. I never could
get my tongue round his ole French words, and I reckon
he would ha' knocked me across the class if he hadn't seized
up on the spot." He spoke philosophically and man to man, as
though, at the ripe old age of twenty-three, he was David's
contemporary. "Things are looking up downalong, I hear,"
he added.

All the local farmers, even those who had attended Bamfylde as day-boys, referred to school as 'downalong', just as
they qualified for the majestic title of 'Man' when they be-

came farmers in their own right. David confirmed that things were indeed looking up, that they now had more than three hundred and fifty on the roll, and a waiting-list of a hundred and seventeen. "Well," Dixon said, unsentimentally, "that'll be your doing, Pow-Wow. We never did take to that foreigner they brought in," and at that point three rearguard whippers-in came over the crest, Venn, Coxe and the local boy, Davidson, loping abreast and in no particular hurry, for they were all First Fifteen rugby colours and lukewarm concerning other sporting activities.

Then, plunging up the reverse slope, and sobbing for breath, Meadowes appeared, gasping out his news, and David's first impulse was to dash off down the steep slope but Dixon grabbed him, shouting, "Wait on! It's all but a mile. The youngsters'll make it in half the time. Wait, 'till I fetch tackle ... had a heifer in that mire only last week ...!" and he went off at a heavy run to his outbuildings farther along the crest, and David turned to speed the seniors on their way but they were already a hundred yards down the slope, heading for the spot indicated by Meadowes' stabbing finger.

He said, making a tremendous effort to control himself, "How bad is it, Meadowes? How deep is he in?" and Meadowes, as blown as he had ever seen a boy, wheezed, "Deep, sir ... Up to his waist" and was sick, bowing his head and sagging at the knees.

For a man weighing fourteen stone, Dixon was very quick on his feet. Almost at once he reappeared, pounding along the crest carrying a coil of rope and what looked like a leather harness. "Leave the kid here," he shouted, without checking his stride, "but look where you're going—bog patches right along that bottom," and went ponderously down the great, angled slope, and through a belt of brushwood that brought them to the river north of the ford.

He thought, as he ran, "Dear God, don't let it happen. Not *now*, not *this* way! A kid of thirteen, drowned in a bog ... it'll be the end of everything ..." and then he remembered that Coxe and Davidson would be there by now, and that both were tough and resolute, although he wasn't so sure about the jester, Venn.

They came on the group suddenly, at a spot where the cattle had churned the floor of the valley into a sticky, glue-like porridge, not unlike the crater-landscape of Passchendaele. They were still holding on, and his instinct for authority, trimmed and tested over the years, reasserted itself as he took in the situation at a glance. Coxe called, from the far side of the fence, "Throw us the rope over, sir! Davidson's got a good hold on the fence . . .!" and Man Dixon grunted, "Tiz harness, boy . . . Get it under his armpits somehow," but by then David was across the fence and crawling along to the point where Davidson was still lying prone, with the unrecognisable Driscoe clinging to his shins, both of them half-enmeshed in what looked like a coil of rusty wire.

They were only just in time. Despite Coxe's efforts, his success in reaching Driscoe's left arm, and his tremendous efforts to drag him closer to the palings, the boy was weakening and his fingers were slipping the length of Davidson's legs. He had also lost his end of the wire and with it the feeble anchorage it had provided. By wading in beyond his knees, however, David got a firm grip on Driscoe's right arm and his presence enabled Coxe to enlarge his hold on the left, so that between them they managed somehow to slip the leather harness over his shoulders. Floundering there, dragged forward into the mire, the task proved fiendishly difficult and even when it was accomplished they had no room to pay it out so that Driscoe could be dragged clear by sheer weight of muscle. But then, as though he had materialised out of the slime, another mud-spattered Junior appeared and David recognised Gosse, who piped, "*Leave it*, sir! Hold him, and I'll take it . . .!" and somehow he did, without rising upright, and the rope tightened almost at once as Venn began to haul.

They came clear in a flurry of mud, Coxe, Gosse, himself and Driscoe, whose legs, plucked from the slough, made a sound like a cork being drawn from a bottle. Even then, with Davidson lying prone between bog and palings, they would have got no farther forward had not Venn shown initiative by ripping away the bottom section of the barrier so that they could scramble through en masse, a jumble of arms, legs, wire, rope and splintered fencing.

Man Dixon took charge of them at that stage, lifting Driscoe in his arms and trudging back along the river to the point where a gravelled path climbed to his yard. The rest followed at a distance, with Davidson, the last to emerge, spluttering and coughing in the rear.

It was with a sense of wonder that he heard Driscoe speak, sitting with his head between his knees on Dixon's bagged-out sofa in the big farm kitchen . . . "Lost my glasses . . . went off the path . . ." but then he too was sick, obligingly on Dixon's hearthstones, clear of the sheepskin rug spread there. One of Dixon's Welsh collies drifted in, sniffing curiously at the vomit and Dixon, cuffing the dog, called over his shoulder, "Fetch a cloth an' bucket, Mother, and clean him up. We could all do with a wash, I reckon."

* * *

He remembered little of the shuffle home, with Driscoe carried pick-a-back by Coxe, and little Gosse, who had lost both shoes, picking his way fastidiously over the stretch of flint road beyond Stone Cross. Venn told him how they had managed until he and Dixon had arrived but it was not until later, when they had all had a shower, and Driscoe had been dosed and put to bed in the sanatorium, that he remembered to send for Coxe, senior of the trio, and get a detailed story.

Coxe said, "I did what I could, sir, but it wasn't much. Davidson took the brunt of it. I had to wedge one of those planks under his legs and it took the skin off his knees. There were old nails sticking in it. I think matron's bandaging him right now."

David said, "Go up and wait for him, Frankie. Then come down again, with Venn. You can skip prep, all three of you. And send someone else for those infants, Gosse was one . . . who was the other?"

"Meadowes, sir. Gosse was the one who saw him first. He's a plucky kid, and had his wits about him. He threw Driscoe the wire, but that was before we got there. He would have gone under but for that. I'll find Davidson, sir," and he left.

He sat at the desk stirring his tea, a desk occupied by a succession of Bamfylde headmasters, all of them including Alcock, now gazing down at heedless newcomers in the

Rogues' Gallery in Remove passage. He felt drained, used up and disconsolate, thinking, "My God, but it was a near thing. We should have been finished if it hadn't been for that bunch and that's a fact. I'd best write to Mrs. Driscoe tonight, for the kid will, as soon as he perks up," and then, following a perfunctory rap on the door, Miss Nixon appeared, holding an envelope that she laid on the desk. "Driscoe's glasses, Headmaster. He seemed anxious about them and Parker went out to look for them with a flashlight. They aren't broken, and I've cleaned them as best I can."

"Thank you, Miss Nixon," he said, absently, "and thank Parker for me, will you? Driscoe will be all right after a good sleep, or so matron says. He was sick and got the filthy stuff off his chest minutes after we pulled him out."

She withdrew quietly, disapprovingly he suspected, and he let his tea go cold. Presently there was a more subdued knock and all five of them sidled in, Davidson walking stiffly under his bandages, then Coxe, then Venn, miraculously transformed after his tussle with the mud, and finally the two Second Formers, Gosse and Meadowes. He said, "Find a seat somewhere. Nothing official," and they disposed themselves, only the dandy Venn at ease.

"That was a terrific show," he said, "and I wanted to thank you all in private before I do it in public. I imagine Mrs. Driscoe will write to you later. I'm not making any bones about what happened down there. But for you chaps Driscoe would be dead. And buried. You all appreciate that, I suppose?"

They said nothing and each of them studiously avoided his eye. "It's odd," he thought, "it's always so damned difficult to find the right words to compliment the English," but he went on, "I'll write an account of it exactly as it happened, and print it in this term's register. All I really wanted to say, beyond that, is don't play it down for fear of putting on side. I've a reason for saying that. I'd like to think we've all learned something about playing fast and loose with the moor in winter."

Gosse piped up then, so unexpectedly that Meadowes hiccoughed with embarrassment. "It wasn't Driscoe's fault, sir. He's as blind as a bat without his specs."

"I daresay. So the moral seems to be, no specs no movement. And that goes for anyone overtaken by dusk on any of the runs. Stay put and holler. Good night, and thanks again."

They got up and filed out but he sat on brooding. Presently Chris came in, carrying the whisky decanter and soda siphon.

"You need a drink, Davy."

"I need a bottle," he said. "Neat. I've just had them all in and thanked them. You've heard the full story I imagine?"

"Matron told me. You put up a pretty good show yourself, Davy."

"I didn't," he said grimly, "and I've been sitting here coming to terms with the fact that I'm slowing down. If it had been left to me, or even to me and Dickie Dixon, that poor kid would be as dead as Carver Doone. All we did was to speed it up a bit. They'd have coped."

"You're forty plus," she said. "Most men your age wouldn't have gone on the run at all, so don't sit there blaming yourself for an unforeseeable accident."

"It wasn't unforeseeable. Or shouldn't have been. I've been over that Middlemoor course every year since December, 1918, and I knew there were patches of dangerous bog in that river bottom. I should have talked Dixon into fencing all the level ground and putting up a damned great notice."

"Most boys will climb fences, and all boys will ignore notices. Besides, you appear to have forgotten something."

"What?"

"Your indirect contribution."

"Come again?"

"Those five boys. Just tell me something, how long is their aggregate stay here?"

He began to discern her line of reasoning. "I could work it out. Venn is just entering his fifth year. Coxe and Davidson are old stagers. They were here one term with the Stoic. The two Cradlers can only sport a year between them, they both arrived last spring. That's a total of sixteen years, give or take a term or two."

"During which time they've all been taught and trained by you."

"Me among others."

"No, Davy. Not as regards what they did this afternoon. That's your doing."

She got up, removed the tea tray and set the drink in its place but then, noting his frown, took his face between her palms and kissed his mouth in that assertive way of hers. "It's true," she said, "think about it. They all seem to me to qualify as handkerchief donors, and that's your doing. Not one of them was here when Algy Herries told that story."

His arm slipped round her. At times like this, when he was feeling vulnerable, he was immensely grateful for her and as always, when aware of a need of her, his senses stirred, demanding close physical contact. He said, "By God, I was lucky to talk you into coming here, and even more right to persevere when you wanted to pack it in. I couldn't cope alone any more."

"You've had to most of the time. Let's make an early night of it. Leave all that bumf on your desk. I'll get supper now and when it's lights out for them it'll be lights out for us."

"That's two hours or more. I'm not sure I can wait that long."

"You'll have to," she said, "for I'm hanged if I want last-minute interruptions by the duty prefect. It's happened more than once."

She switched off the desk lamp and they went through into the parlour where a bright log fire burned in the everlasting down-draught. Supper was laid. It looked very cosy in here. His overall grasp of the job returned to him a little soggily but definitely, like Driscoe emerging from the bog, and with it a buoyancy that stemmed, he supposed, from a sense of reprieve. He said, taking in the trim lines of her figure as she stooped to throw another log on the fire, "I wish it was holiday time. I wouldn't bother with supper or bed," but she was equal to him.

"There's always old Rigby, and even if he's asleep beside the kitchen stove, there are the Sunsetters. We haven't that much dignity to squander, sir."

CHAPTER THREE

I

In his relaxed moods he could still think of himself as ruling an island in a stream, protected to some extent, from lethal flotsam that coasted by on either side, touching shore here and there, probing, fussing, worrying, but finally moving on round the bend in the river. But latterly lodgments were made, and unexpected pressures exerted, so that a certain amount of erosion was evident, fissures showing in his defences. Whenever this happened he was troubled, for they always appeared at places where he thought himself buttressed against adversity. Such a case was Christopherson's, in the spring of '37.

There had been a time when Bamfylde's remoteness made nonsense of faraway commotions but latterly, as the decade sped along, there had been dramatic improvements in communications. In the early 'twenties their newspapers had arrived almost a day late, while only the odd crackpot thought of wireless as anything more than an amusing toy. Today newspapers were delivered in bulk, and were distributed to classrooms before first period bell. There were also half a dozen wireless sets on the premises, some of them complicated-looking pieces of apparatus, and their stream of bulletins kept everyone informed of what was happening elsewhere. It made a difference, as his encounter with Christopherson II proved.

Christopherson, thought to be enjoying his first year up at Oxford, appeared on a motorbike in the middle of the Easter holidays and said, over a glass of Old Boys' sherry, "Glad I caught you, Pow-Wow. Had a feeling you might have taken Mrs. Powlett-Jones away for Easter. Should've rung, of course, but there wasn't time. I'm hellishly pressed as it is," and when David enquired where he was going, he replied, "You'll probably think I want my head examined. I know

my people do, and so does my tutor, but there it is, a chap has
to make his own decisions as regards fundamentals. I made
mine in the new year. I'm off to Spain."

If it had been someone like Hislop, or a natural belligerent
like, say, Paddy McNaughton, or Ruby Bickford, he might
have been surprised, but not dumbfounded. He remembered
Christopherson II as the most convinced pacifist they had
ever had in the Sixth, a boy who supported Canon Dick
Sheppard's Peace Pledge Union, and God alone knew how
many other pressure groups. Chris would remember him
that way too, as the boy who took the unpopular pacifist
line at that current affairs discussion a year or so back, when
he insisted that confrontation with Mussolini would mean
another World War and that this was unthinkable. Yet here
he was, appearing out of the blue on an old Douglas motorcycle, announcing that he was about to embroil himself in
the bloodiest civil war of the century.

"You're going as an ambulance driver, Chris?"

"No, Pow-Wow, to fight. To hell with turning the other
cheek."

"Then I don't wonder your people think you're crazy,
quite apart from the fact that Spain is Spain's business,
whatever we may think of the rights and wrongs of what's
going on there. You've only just started at Oxford and from
all I hear likely to do well up there. What the devil do you
imagine you can achieve singlehanded in Spain?" but before Christopherson could reply Christine came in, with an
armful of daffodils and narcissi cut from the forecourt beds,
and said, sharply, "Are you on your way to Spain?" and
Christopherson, leaping up so quickly that he spilled his
sherry, replied, smiling, "I always did think you were quick
on the uptake, Mrs. P.J. I'm travelling overland to Bilbao,
providing that old crank of mine outside stays the course. If it
doesn't, I'll flog it and push on by train!" and she said,
fervently, "Good for you. You won't get his blessing but you
can count on mine. Give him another sherry, Davy. He's
spilled most of that being polite."

He took Christopherson's glass and moved over to the
decanter, frowning at his reflection in the sideboard mirror
and thinking, "She's already guessed his motives but I'm

hanged if I can. That International Brigade everyone's yammering about will be full of starry-eyed amateurs like him, and the professional Communists will take full advantage of them if I know 'em!" He refilled the glass and came back to where the pair of them were talking in the window bay, saying, "You can't wonder I take a dim view of it. You were a pacifist when you left here, just over a year ago. Would it be too much to ask how pacifism fits in with what's going on over there?"

"He's asked for his card back and got it," Christine said, "and I think he's done the right thing. I wish to God more of Dick Sheppard's converts had his moral courage," but Christopherson said, "Don't rub the salt in, Mrs. P.J. He had his basinful on the Western Front and I can understand his point of view." He turned back to David. "You don't think anything can be solved by war, do you, Pow-Wow? Or that was my impression after I got into Upper School."

"Then it was a wrongheaded one. I'm all for standing up to those bastards, and she'll tell you the same, but this is a local quarrel. Spain is still living in Philip II's time, and you won't be long finding that out. If you feel so strongly about it you would have done better to enlist in your college O.T.C. That way you'd be preparing yourself for the real showdown if and when it comes."

" 'If' is the operative word, Pow-Wow. Do you believe we'll ever have one?"

"Oddly enough, he does," Christine said, "he believes we'll wake up with the Fire Brigade on the doorstep and we've had any number of arguments about it. But I'm on your side. With Chamberlain and his set in Number Ten you'll be old to fight by the time our people realise what's happening. So good luck to you, and anyone else who takes a crack at Franco. Even P.J. will drink to that, won't you, Davy?"

He drank to it, but without enthusiasm. It was all very well for people like her and Christopherson, who saw everything in black and white, but you couldn't read history and teach history for thirty years without coming to a conclusion that almost every cause, from the Punic Wars onward, came in a shade of grey.

They gave him lunch and watched him chug away down

the east drive on his elderly Douglas, trailing a cloud of blue exhaust, and signalling his departure with a series of sharp explosions, that reminded David unpleasantly of a machine gun sweeping a traverse. They never saw him again. Before Christmas news came that he had been killed at Teruel and that night, sitting alone in his study, he realised how Algy Herries must have felt when an early casualty list of the First World War had included Monson, killed at Château Thierry, in August, 1914. There was a difference, however. Christopherson, gallant idiot that he was, did not qualify for a place on the memorial outside. He died in what most people would think of as a foreign cause, and at a time when politicians were mouthing the newly fashionable phrase, Non-Intervention. But that did not make his death easier to bear. Not for him, who had always seen Christopherson as a warm, wise and lovable boy, and not for Christine, who wept when he showed her the letter from Christopherson's parents.

II

That was the very beginning as he saw it, the first major breach in his island defences, but thereafter, right through that year, the strength of the current increased to a point where it was impossible to stand off, in the manner of his early days as head, and leave the brawlers to get on with it. The war in Spain divided everybody, scoring a demarcation line not only through Westminster and Fleet Street, but through the Owl Society, solemnly debating the issue on an Exmoor plateau.

"Does Guernica mean battleships are out of date, sir?"

"The *News Chronicle* says Franco is relying on Moors, Eyeties and Germans!"

"*The Times* says the Reds are shooting nuns. Is it propaganda, sir?"

Questions fired at him not only by the Sixth and the Fifth, but the Fourth, so that he had to give them all a warning regarding the confusing references to the protagonists, variously styled Loyalists, Nationalists, Communists, Falangists, Reds, Fascists and even Liberators, according to the individual prejudices of correspondents and editors.

And, as if this was not enough, there was the occasional maverick like Hotchkiss, who subscribed, if you please, to the Left Book Club, and pressed Koestler's *Spanish Testament* upon him, declaring it made everything crystal clear. He obliged Hotchkiss on this occasion, and was shocked by Koestler's revelations, but the book did not rid him of a sour belief that Spain was a country full of gloomy bigots and that the Moorish streak in the Spaniard seemed to put a premium on acts of savagery.

Neither was Spain the only battleground. Some of the sharper ones had their eye on Paris, Berlin, Rome, Vienna, and even Manchuria.

"Sir, is there any chance of *us* forming a Popular Front, like the French?"

"What about the Anschluss, sir? Is it true all the Austrian Jews are jumping out of windows?"

"Does Japan's new invasion mean the Chinese Government and the Reds will join up, sir?"

He envied Chris, who seemed to have some kind of answers to these questions. For himself, it was getting a little above him, particularly as he had so much on his plate that summer.

He was still building, still encroaching bit by bit on their elbow room up here, and yet another Old Boy's legacy, enabling a sizeable reduction in the bank overdraft, encouraged him to push on after completion of the new wing that now comprised concert hall, classrooms, a new laboratory, seven studies, a gymnasium and a sports locker-room.

The familiar silhouette of the huddle of buildings, seen against the backdrop of a sunset, began to change, the looming bulk of the hall and classroom block rose only a few yards north of the last east drive beech, and what had been the old covered playground, once seen as a dip in the rooftop line, now straggled as far as the fives court on the northern boundary. The new buildings were, as Algy had predicted, mellowing rapidly, but there was still, in his mind at least, need for expansion since they were now aiming at a target figure of four hundred plus. The Cradlers were still without adequate quarters of their own but that, he decided, was less imperative than the provision of a real library, replacing what he regarded as a jumble of tattered books, mostly of the kind one might come across in an under-endowed convalescent home.

He put up a scheme to the Governors and they approved it at a single session. He had very little trouble with the Governors these days. Old Sir Rufus, still looking like a shrivelled walnut, continued to preside, and Briggy Cooper never missed a meeting. Between them they could always swing the waverers into line, so that he thought, "Next year will be my twentieth anniversary up here. I'll make myself a birthday present of that library," and the work was put in hand, the builder giving his completion date as August of next year.

Then, dramatically, other matters engaged his attention. Christine came to him with the news that she was pregnant again and seemed cheerful and resolute about it, saying she intended to spoil herself throughout the spring, and would take no chances at all while on a course of tablets prescribed by the Bristol gynaecologist Willoughby had called in. She had no intention, however, of surrendering the Cradlers, now averaging twenty-five a term.

"They take very little out of me," she told him. "In fact, they'll keep me from worrying. This is the brightest bunch I've ever had, and I actually find myself looking forward to Monday, which is more than you can say of others. Yourself, included, on occasion."

But suddenly he found he had almost more than he could handle. Howarth went sick again, this time with pneumonia, necessitating a longish spell in hospital, and in his prolonged absence he was lumbered with Upper School English, and obliged to hand over his few Lower School periods to Boyer.

He did not mind the extra chore, despite the considerable pressures it exerted on his time. It was a pleasure, sometimes, to scamp the correspondence, letting Grace answer letters, guided by a pencil scrawl at the foot of the page, and spend an hour or two with his old favourites, Swift, George Eliot, Gray, Cowper, John Donne and even the war poets Owen and Sassoon, whom he had neglected lately.

He tried the Upper Fifth with Shaw's *Man of Destiny*, and found that they enjoyed it immensely, and this encouraged

him to try *John Bull's Other Island*, when he heard himself re-
counting the story of Paddy McNaughton and his rusty
revolver. He was still inclined to be a drifter in class and the
boys knew it, and took shameless advantage of it, but that
didn't bother him overmuch. He had never seen any specific
subject as watertight, so that his English had often spilled
over into history, geography and even divinity, and sometimes, when the bell went, he would again remind himself
he had learned more than he had imparted.

There was a price to be paid for this diversion, however,
and it arrived on his desk one morning in the Lent term, in
the form of an almost illegible letter from Howarth, asking
him to drive over to the Challacombe Hospital, where he
was convalescing. He went at once and was shocked, on
being shown into a private ward, to note that Howarth was
still a very sick man. He had lost a great deal of weight, and
under his heavy woollen dressing gown he looked as shrivelled
as Sir Rufus. He said, the moment they were alone, "You
might as well have it straight, P.J. I'm finished. They can
make as many cooing noises as they like, but it's a fact. I
thought it only fair to tell you before the Easter break, so that
you can start looking round for someone." Then, with some
difficulty, "That isn't the real reason I got you here. I'm
asking a favour, and I daresay you'll regard it as a big one
when you hear it."

"You don't have to ask me to keep the job open, I'd do that
in any case. I can cope. Grace does most of my correspondence, and Boyer has taken over my odd periods. As a matter
of fact, I'm enjoying your work with the Fifth and Sixth,"
but Howarth made one of his irritable gestures. "I'm not
talking about the job. I'm talking about dying, man."

"Dying?"

"That's what I said, so don't let any damned quack fob
you off with anything different."

"But, good God, you're more or less over it, aren't you?
A summer in the south, the kind of sun-soak you always
promised yourself and never took . . ."

"I left it too late." He looked at David very carefully, as
though he had been an enterprising boy in Middle School,
who had just presented him with an outrageous excuse for a

scamped essay. "I finally got the truth out of them. I have about six months. Cancer, here," and he tapped his chest.

It was not particularly surprising. For a year or so Howarth's booming cough had been as much a part of Bamfylde's background as the iron notes of the bell. Howarth had even made jokes about it calling it his forerunner. "Not the John the Baptist variety. Hairy John promised eternal life, didn't he? Mine tells me they'll soon be burning a pile of rubbish somewhere."

It might be rooted, David supposed, in Howarth's lifelong addiction to tobacco, and he said feebly, "If you cut out cigarettes . . ." but at this Howarth snarled, "Don't give me that, P.J.! I've already given 'em up, or they think I have. But if I had done it when it meant anything I should have been carted away from that barn frothing at the mouth years ago. Tobacco is an absentminded habit with most people. It never was so with me. It was a source of enormous comfort to know that, the minute that bloody bell went, I could light up, and there it is. Some take to drink, and some can't get by without women. I liked my gin, yes, but it was never important to me. Neither was I ever in your category, with my eyes on the stars. You're fortunate to be committed to a job and I hope you've sense enough to realise it."

"What was the favour, Howarth?"

"An eccentric one and you'll have to bend rules to grant it. I'm not scared of dying but I'm scared to hell of dying here, among the sick, sorry and senile. I want to die where I belong, within scent and earshot of familiar smells and sounds. If I discharge myself, can I come back to my own quarters? I've plenty of money to pay for a day and night nurse later on and I wouldn't be a bother. You and Barnaby would be handy for a chat, and all the latest scandal. Is that asking too much? Because if it is, say so and be damned to you."

"I daresay it can be arranged, so long as you don't tell anyone else what you've just told me. If that got out we should all be in trouble."

Howarth relaxed and said, "I'm much obliged to you, P.J.," and then, with a twitch of a smile, "Wouldn't be the first rule we've bent, eh?"

He left him feeling absolutely desolate. Ever since that

first exchange of conversation in the common room twenty years ago, he had leaned heavily on Howarth, more so since he had taken Alcock's place. The man's enormous experience, and his deep love of Bamfylde that he was always at such pains to conceal, had proved rallying points time and again over the years. If it had been difficult to picture Bamfylde without Algy it was impossible to imagine it without Howarth. He never had believed that story of his about scuttling off to the Riviera the moment he was pensioned. "You can't love bricks and mortar," had been one of Howarth's favourite maxims but he had belied it every time a fresh crisis blew up, and here he was begging to be allowed to die on the premises. He drove back to Bamfylde very slowly, coming to terms not only with the fact but with his decisions to confide in nobody, not even Chris.

III

Howarth installed himself in his old quarters, just before the summer term opened and seemed to rally, shuffling out and about on sunny days, and sometimes making his way as far as the nets, where he would sit on the roller, his rimless glasses flashing in the sun, as he drew carefully on a forbidden cigarette, holding it under his hand, like a Fourth Former in one or other of the smokers' hideouts about the place. David and Chris spent a good deal of time with him, and so did Barnaby, who probably guessed the truth, but he must have fooled most of the others, for every now and again the bursar, or one of the junior staff, would refer to his impending return to work with phrases like, "When Howarth is fit . . ." or "Just until Howarth is back on the job."

But then, in the latest flare-up over the Sudetenland dispute, and the sordid scuttling to and from Bad Godesberg, Berchtesgaden and finally Munich, even Howarth was all but forgotten; and the writing on the wall became so stark and clear that sometimes, reading the latest headlines, he felt physically sick, as though he had eaten an indigestible meal. Possibly he had. It was not pleasant to see the sons and daughters of the men who had stormed Vimy Ridge squealing with glee over the human sacrifice of Czechoslovakia.

He was very glad then that Chris was so obsessed with her child that her approach to politics was muted, although, every now and again, she would curse Chamberlain as a fool and a coward. Like him, she winced at Chamberlain's brief triumph, when he arrived back from Munich, to be received with hysterical cheers as he waved his absurd bit of paper.

"It's the most terrifying spectacle I've ever seen," she told David, when they watched a news-reel on a rare visit to the cinema. "Nobody sane could believe in it and I don't think any informed person does. They'll be evacuating children and digging air-raid shelters in a week or so, and I hope to God somebody somewhere profits by the time that idiot is supposed to have bought us. But I wouldn't bet on it, would you?"

No, he told her, he would not, and with the onset of the new school year a sombre mood settled on him, not improved by a surprise visit from Carter, with an even more surprising proposition in his brief case.

Carter, it seemed, was someone else who wasn't taken in, and was making his dispositions well in advance. "If it does come to a show-down they'll evacuate my beat on the coast," he said. "We'll qualify as bona fide evacuees, and I want to get in on the ground floor. I don't want them sending me and the left-overs to some Godforsaken place up north, where I've no local contacts. You have plenty of room here now. Could you accommodate, say, an extra fifty under fourteen, if you had to? It would let you out too. They're bound to regard you as a host school. The Luftwaffe isn't likely to bomb Middlemoor, is it?"

The scheme had a good deal to recommend it. Carter's venture had prospered, and he could pay a good rent. It would also mean that at least some of his youngsters would automatically qualify as Bamfeldians as soon as they passed their fourteenth birthday, so he gave Carter a promise that he would put the proposition before the Governors and ring back within a fortnight.

He carried out the first half of his promise and, as he had fully expected, the Governors approved. But then, like balanced buffets to the left and right of his head, two other events put everything else out of mind. In the second week of a new term Chris was rushed off to the nursing home, and he had barely settled her in, horribly anxious but outwardly bearing up, when Howarth died, a week or so short of the six months given him by the specialist in the spring.

* * *

They sent for him early in the morning and he found Howarth conscious and very restless. His blanched face was a parody of the man he remembered. It looked like the face of someone in the final stage of starvation, but the breakfast bell seemed to alert him, as though that same sound, repeated down three decades, at precisely the same hour of the day, was still able to recall him to duty. He opened his eyes, gestured feebly to the nurse, then fixed his gaze on David. The male nurse got up and left, obviously in response to some previous instruction and Howarth whispered, as the door closed. "This is it, P.J. Wanted to see you . . . know you were still around . . ." and he moved his left hand in a way that impelled David to take it. They sat there for a minute or so, listening to the clamour of boys hurrying down the long stone passage to Big Hall and breakfast. Then, after the hall door had banged on a prolonged bumping of forms and rattle of crockery, he said, "Curtain . . . what kind of day?"

David got up and pulled the curtain of the window facing south-east across ploughland and the blur of copses screening Bamfylde Bridge Halt.

"Very clear," he said. "No rain about. Can you see it from where you are?"

Howarth nodded briefly and said, "Wife all right?"

"Any minute now," but Howarth seemed not to be listening. With his free hand he made an attempt to reach under the pillow, finally succeeding in exposing a stiff folded document that David recognised as his will. In response to Howarth's nod he opened it out. It was a very simple will. Everything Howarth possessed had been left to the school. There was a brief codicil, dated two days before, naming Chris as the beneficiary of two hundred pounds, and meeting David's questioning glance, Howarth said, with a grimace that might have been one of his wry smiles, "Not for her really. For that boy . . . if you get one."

"I'm going out there this afternoon. This is very good of you, Howarth. Chris will be touched," and Howarth, husbanding each syllable, said, "Never . . . touched . . . anyone . . . Never . . . wanted . . . to . . ." Then, framing the words clearly, "Bureau. Top drawer," and David knew what he sought. He crossed to the bureau and opened the drawer. The portrait of Amy Crispin still lay on top of a pile of neatly laundered shirts and he took it out, holding it so that Howarth could see it. Perhaps a minute passed before he said, just audibly, "Wish I'd been able to believe. Leave it when you go."

He put the photograph on the cluttered night table and tried to think of something comforting to say, something that Howarth would not find embarrassing. It was not easy. All his life Howarth had been trying to increase the thickness of the shell that encased his emotions. He took his hand again and said, carefully, "Can you hear me? Don't talk, just nod," and Howarth nodded, so obediently that the gesture seemed grossly out of character. "You've done a thundering good job here. That's something to believe in. I won't ever forget you. Neither will any of the old stagers, or any of the boys you taught. As for me, I'd like to say thank you, from the bottom of my heart. But for you I wouldn't be here. Since I am, I'd like you to know nothing is going to shake me loose now, Howarth. Did you get that?"

Howarth nodded twice and closed his eyes, lying so still that David thought he had slipped away, but he hadn't. Presently he began to cough, and half sat up, his eyes blazing with fury, so that for a moment he looked his old self as he spluttered, "*Bloody* cough—fetch him . . ." and David called the nurse, who sidled in and picked up a beaker half-full of barley water.

He left then, his thoughts in a whirl, and it was not until he reached the sanctuary of his study that he realised he was still holding Howarth's will. He glanced at it again, realising that Bamfylde was richer by something like eleven thousand pounds.

*   *   *

The nursing home matron rang soon after lunch and he almost choked on the words identifying himself. She said, coolly, "No panic, Mr. Powlett-Jones. Dr. Willoughby thought you'd like to know it's started. He seems very pleased with her. Will you be coming over?"

"Now?"

"Whenever it's convenient."

He wanted to shout, "Of course I'll come! Get back to her, you idiot!" but then he remembered Willoughby and the specialist would be with her, for the Bristol man had promised to make a special trip down that day and had phoned mid-morning to say she was in excellent shape. He said, hoarsely, "I'll come within the hour," and she said, impersonally, "Good . . . good . . ." and rang off.

He stood there holding the receiver, his mouth parched and dry, his knees trembling so violently that he had to brace them against the door of the cupboard supports of the desk. The bell rang for the first period. "It would," he thought, savagely, "it always does somehow . . ." but then he got hold of himself and went in search of Barnaby, catching him crossing the quad on his way to the Sixth.

"Chris is having her baby," he said, breathlessly, "Can you take the Sixth for Howarth?" and as he said it he realised that, like everybody else, he was assuming Howarth would be back on the job in a day or so. Barnaby said, gently, "Don't worry about a thing, P.J. I've got a free period myself mid-afternoon. You're driving over now?"

"Right away. Thanks, Barnaby. Have you looked in on Howarth today?"

"No, the night nurse told me he was having a bad spell . . ."

"He won't last the day but keep it to yourself. Sorry to put so much on you. I'll ring if I'm delayed." He left Barnaby looking very startled and went round to the cycle sheds where Bamfylde's few cars were parked. Chris's silvery bumble bee stood there under a tarpaulin and his mind, conjuring with possibilities as it always did when he was seeking escape from unpleasant thoughts, toyed with the idea of pulling down the ratty old sheds and building a garage block here. In the years ahead, he supposed, almost every adult at Bamfylde would own a car or motorcycle, and they wouldn't want them kept under tarpaulins.

He headed west into a golden afternoon, thinking of Chris, of all the high hopes she had pinned on this moment, and of poor old Howarth, gasping his life away in those bachelor quarters, off Nicolson's landing. It would take him a long time to get accustomed to life up here without Howarth. Algy had gone, but Algy was still available when he was needed. With Howarth gone he and Barnaby would be the only survivors of the First World War rump, and it would seem lonely, just the two of them. Staff were not much different from boys in that way. They came, stayed a little longer than the average boy, and then left, either by way of Bat Ferguson and Judy Cordwainer, or by way of Carter and Irvine. The same thing had happened with two of the three women in his life, Beth and Julia Darbyshire. One day they were there, the next they were gone, and it was of Beth he thought as he dropped into second gear to tackle Quarry Hill, remembering passing this way in a more carefree mood one sunny May afternoon in 1920, when he had driven over to take his first peep at the twins. Howarth's enigmatic remark returned to him—'Wish I could have believed . . .' Believed in what exactly? In God? In marriages made in heaven? In Amy Crispin's lasting affection for him? Probably the first, for Howarth, although a born cynic, had never professed himself an atheist. Just one of the bewildered majority facing the fact that they had no way of knowing whether life was a planned process or a cosmic accident. It was strange, he thought, that in all their discussions, talk that had ranged over almost every conceivable topic, they had so rarely touched on faith.

*   *   *

He read the good news in Willoughby's face the moment he ran up the steps and met him in the act of lighting his cherry-wood pipe beside the receptionist's desk.

"Went like clockwork," he said, eagerly. "A boy. Seven pounds, three ounces, and yelling his head off! About an hour ago, soon after matron's phone call actually."

"Chris?"

"She's bonnie. And drunk with triumph. Never knew such a stayer. She'd absolutely made up her mind to it. She'll take me more seriously in future, I hope. I was always telling her there was absolutely nothing to stop her producing a live child."

"An hour ago, you said? Should I go in?"

Willoughby considered, drawing noisily on his pipe. "I'd leave it a bit if I were you. She's asleep. It's only three-thirty yet. Suppose you accompany me on a couple of local calls, we take a dish of tea in Glossops then pop back here about five-thirty? They can manage headless for that long, can't they?"

"Yes, but poor old Howarth is dying, Doc."

The news didn't surprise him. He said, "Amazed he lasted this long. Tough old bird." Then, shrewdly, "He talked you into letting him go back there, I imagine?"

"I don't regret it. Should I?"

"No, no. Kindest thing to do. Made it much easier on him, but you'd better go on pretending to be shocked. Some of the parents might think it wasn't quite the thing in the circumstances," but David said, "To hell with that. If Alcock could die on the premises why couldn't Howarth? He was as much a part of the place as Algy and I'm going to miss him like hell."

"Queer chap," Willoughby said. "Frankly I have always respected him without being able to like him. But you did both, didn't you?"

"I knew him much better than most people."

He found her much as he had found Beth when he had called in this same place for the same reason eighteen years before. Radiant, and extraordinarily pleased with herself, so much so that he thought, smiling, "Why the devil did she ever bother with politics? This is what she really wanted. Maybe it'll take some of the steam out of her and that can't be a bad thing. We've all got too much head of steam these days."

She said, "Have you seen him yet? He's an absolute cherub, Davy, and very much the Celt. Or will be, as soon as he loses that outraged look they all seem to start off with. Long bones and lots of dark hair. No doubt at all about him being yours," and he said, letting his hand run over her own smooth brown head, "Fine time to be telling me that. Was it as bad as you thought?" and she said, no, not as bad as the last miss, and a lot more rewarding.

He didn't stay long. He had a suspicion amounting to a certainty that Howarth would have gone by the time he got back, and it seemed a shabby thing to cloud her happiness with such dismal news. He drove back through the gathering dusk and stopped a mile or so beyond Quarry Hill, where he could just see the lights of Bamfylde winking under long, blue trailers of mist. The day had brought good news and bad, like most other days up there, and it crossed his mind that it might be an idea to marry the events by naming his son Ian, after Howarth. In a way, the crusty old chap had seemed to move on to make room for the child. Chris had wanted to call him David but he had had too much experience with duplicated initials to agree to that. In a place like Bamfylde identity mattered, and two David Powlett-Joneses about the place simply wouldn't do. He wonder how Grace would take it, a baby brother eighteen years her junior, and decided it didn't really matter much, for Grace wouldn't stay indefinitely. One or another of her swains would come asking for her in a year or so and he wondered briefly, which of them it was likely to be. His money was on Winterbourne, who made no secret of his affection for her. He remembered seeing them only last summer, strolling up towards the planty hand in hand, not the least bit interested in the match against Somerset Stragglers being fought out on the pitch.

It was curious how life seemed to weave a pattern that was not in the least haphazard, as it so often seemed to be. His own, for instance, and Keith Winterbourne's and Grace's, all linked by the fatal circumstances of that sultry day in 1925, when Winterbourne had appeared out of a blinding rain-storm and drawn him into that hideout he had beside the rushing stream.

He restarted the engine and went along the level stretch to the foot of the plateau, where a rather fussed Renshaw-Smith signalled him as he turned in at the corner of Nicolson's to head round the main buildings.

"You won't have heard about poor Howarth," he said. "He died, quite suddenly, about two hours after you left. I was going to ring the nursing home but Barnaby said you had other things to worry about. How is Mrs. Powlett-Jones, Headmaster?"

Renshaw-Smith had never been able to bring himself to use an informal mode of address and David had been obliged to accept his rectitude.

"She's fine. Just presented me with a seven-pound boy. You're the very first to know."

"I *am*? She *has*? But that's splendid! . . . Absolutely splendid! . . . Congratulations, Headmaster!"

He was so delighted that chance had chosen him for the honour of being the first Bamfeldian to hear the great news that he forgot for a moment he had been the bearer of such gloomy tidings. David said, to correct any impression Renshaw-Smith might have that he was taking Howarth's death calmly, "I saw Howarth this morning and realised then that he was critically ill. I've just been talking to Dr. Willoughby about him. I'll have to get him over right away."

He parked the car and stared up at the windows of Nicolson's, relieved in a way that old Howarth was released, but sorry he died without learning that Chris's guts and determination had been rewarded. They had always got along very well, Howarth having seen her as a fighter the day she arrived and he recalled again that it had been Howarth who urged him to put Chris to work in the Cradle.

He cut through the kitchen passage, out into the quad, then into his own house, where Rigby told him Grace was with matron, tracing laundry that had gone astray and been the subject of tiresome correspondence.

"Shall I tell her you're back, sir?"

"No, Rigby. I'll see her at dinner."

"Very well, sir. I'll be serving in twenty minutes."

He went into the study, where the day's correspondence was spread out on the right-hand side of his desk, with a note from Grace telling him which letters had been answered, which were pending. One unopened letter marked 'Personal' lay there. It had an American stamp and a Boston postmark. He opened it absentmindedly and was amazed to find it was

a letter from Julia Darbyshire, the first he had received since
that day in 1927, when she had written telling him of her
marriage to Sprockman, the restaurateur. He let his eye run
down the pages with a sense of wonder that the letter should
reach him today of all days.

It had a breezy, impersonal note, almost as though they
had been corresponding regularly all these years, and concerned her eldest son, Charles, now almost eleven. She was
asking if he would have room for him next term, when he
would be coming up to twelve. She had two other children,
both daughters, but Hiram Sprockman had died the year
before, leaving her comfortably off. She had a poor opinion, it
seemed, of the American educational system,

> You recall what an Anglophile Hiram was and he was
> determined to send the boy to an English school as soon as
> he reached his teens. He liked you, and I told him every-
> thing I remembered about Bamfylde, even the reason I
> left. That made him laugh for nearly a week. Shortly
> before he died he asked me to try and get Charles fixed up
> there as soon as he was old enough, so here goes. If there's
> no vacancy, or if you have any prejudice against Ameri-
> cans, I'll understand, but I'm sure Charles could manage
> the entrance exam. Drop me a line saying yes or no, be-
> cause if it's no I shall send him to Canada. And if you're
> wondering how I knew you were still there (and head-
> master to boot!) put it down to our business efficiency over
> here. All I did was to call our advertising agency, giving
> the name and location. They called me back in twenty
> minutes with all the details, including the fees. I hope
> you're well and happy, P.J. I've never ceased to think
> kindly of you. Affectionately, Julia Sprockman (née
> Darbyshire in case you've forgotten all about me!)

He poured himself a whisky and sat at his desk, trying to
imagine what she looked like now, what her son and daughters were like. He had no snapshot of her and could only
recall, at this distance, that she was pretty, broad-featured,
and had once had luxuriant hair, tresses she used to torment
poor Blades, down in the goyle that summer day so long ago.
Yet, although his memory of her was vague, erased perhaps

by Beth and Chris, he found the prospect of Charles Sprockman coming here a pleasing one, partly because Sprockman had seemed so English somehow, and recalling this there came to him the American's quote from one of Rupert Brooke's letters: 'There walk, as yet, no ghosts in Canadian lanes . . . at a pinch one can do without gods, but one misses the dead . . .' One did miss the dead and he wondered if he should go and look at Howarth, but he did not feel equal to it. The boys would have to be notified officially, and he supposed he would have to make an announcement in the morning, but there would be no service at Stone Cross. Howarth had left explicit instructions concerning that, and had asked to be cremated. He heard the quad door bang and Grace's footsteps on the flags and rose quickly, suddenly glad of her company.

IV

He told them at breakfast, letting the house prefects know in advance that he would ask for a moment's silence in Big Hall, so that the moment he mounted the dais every face turned to him expectantly. He said, once they had resumed their seats, "You will have heard that Mr. Howarth died yesterday. At his own request we won't be having a special service. Everyone who remembers him, before he was taken ill, will recall how much he disliked fuss and ceremony. But I should like to say a word or two about him, and how much he meant to the school. He was a very good friend to me, ever since I came here as a young man, before any of you were born. Hardly a day passed when he didn't give me the benefit of his experience, and when I became head I couldn't have managed without him. Bamfylde owes him a very great deal. He was a first-class teacher, and I suppose those of you who didn't have time to know him well were sometimes a little scared of him. I know all the new boys were, but the Upper School, and even some of the Middle School, soon realised how wonderfully kind he was. I could give you many instances of his kindness but he would have hated that. I see no reason why I shouldn't tell you, however, that he left everything he had to Bamfylde. Perhaps we should acknowledge his great love of the school by standing in silence for a moment."

The house prefects took their cue from him and stood, more or less in unison, so that upwards of four hundred heads bobbed up, and upwards of four hundred pairs of eyes studied porridge plates for what seemed to him a long sixty seconds. Then he stepped back and they sat again, subdued and a little embarrassed, so that it occurred to him that he might have chosen the wrong moment. Barnaby disposed of the doubt at once. Leaning forward he said, quietly, "Thank you, P.J. That was just right, I think. He wouldn't have approved, of course, but we owed it to him, anyway."

Immediately below, the continuous murmur rose steadily, falling short of its usual breakfast crescendo, a low buzz of conversation against a sustained rattle of china and cutlery. A very Bamfylde sound at this time of day. Some of them, he supposed, might be exchanging comments not on Howarth but on the arrival of Chris's boy at Challacombe, for that, too, would be common knowledge by now. Howarth had often voiced his respect for the speed and deadly efficiency of the Bamfylde bush-telegram. "Bulletins, I am persuaded, are issued regularly on the hot-water pipes. The way they circulate in gaol," he had said, and David, remembering this old joke, discovered to his surprise that he could already think of Howarth, not as he had seen him twenty-four hours ago, sick and ravaged, but as Bamfylde would always see him in the future, irascible, frigid and occasionally frightening, but underneath all that as soft as thistledown.

That wasn't quite the end of it, however.

At the Old Boys' Annual Dinner in London not long afterwards, Masterson, that year's president, paid a warm if jocular tribute to Howarth in his speech, making gentle fun of his acidity, and even giving an excellent imitation of one of Howarth's quiet eruptions in class. It was well received, for the three hundred assembled here recalled Howarth in his prime and not, as David's audience would remember him, as a tired, ageing man, racked by 'that bloody cough'. But Gilmour, a plump, rosy man in his mid thirties, sitting at the far end of table 'D', had a sobering surprise for everyone when he rose to reply to the last speech of the

evening. He said, half-apologetically, "The president referred to Mr. Howarth and I should like to add something
to that, something I never felt free to tell anyone until now,
for had I done so Howarth would never have forgiven me.
Back in 1923, when I was sixteen, and in the Lower Fifth, my
father died suddenly, and in tragic circumstances. I won't
bore you with details but I have to tell you this. There wasn't
much money to go round at the time, and my mother at
once gave notice that I would be withdrawn at the end of
term. Howarth wrote my mother a letter and, having heard
of his death in October, I looked it out and brought it with
me. It's short, and like all Howarth's letters, very much to the
point. Have I your permission to read it, sir?"

He had everybody's attention now and waited for the
murmur of assent to die down.

Dear Mrs. Gilmour,
I heard of your loss from the headmaster, and write at
once to express my sympathy. In the meantime I take the
liberty of expressing an opinion that you would be ill-
advised to remove your son before he qualifies to sit the
Cambridge Senior examination. In my view he has every
chance of achieving a creditable result, particularly in
English subjects, and I am given to understand, again by
Mr. Herries, that the reason you are removing him is
financial. If I am wrong, please ignore this letter. If I am
right, may I make a suggestion? I would take it very kindly
if you permitted me to contribute one half of Gilmour's
fees until he arrives in the Sixth, and I do not advance this
somewhat impertinent offer in what some people would
regard as a spirit of charity. Gilmour has ability, of the
kind that I regard as rare, at least in one respect. He can
express himself simply and clearly and if, as I understand
was your intention, he enters the Civil Service on leaving
here, that facility alone should stand him in good stead,
and benefit us all. Please let me know if this is acceptable,
    Sincerely, Ian Howarth.

The effect of this letter upon the audience reminded David
of the reception accorded Algy Herries's speech at his farewell supper. No after-dinner speech that he had heard on

these convivial occasions had been received so spontaneously and Gilmour, flushing, was obliged to wait for the clamour to subside. He concluded, "My mother accepted that offer. I stayed on another two years, and it cost Howarth three hundred pounds, or one year's assistant master's salary at that time. Like everyone here there are times when I feel I owe Bamfylde a good deal. But looking back on what happened at that time I think I owe Howarth more."

Gilmour sat down amid tremendous applause and was further embarrassed by a standing ovation, something no one had ever previously witnessed at an O.B.A. dinner, usually no more than a beery get-together. But the ovation, David realised, wasn't for Gilmour at all. It was for Howarth and, to his way of thinking, not only deserved but years overdue. As they crowded round Gilmour at the bar afterwards he remembered Barnaby's almost obligatory quotation the day after he told him he had scattered Howarth's ashes on the Bamfylde preserve at Stone Cross. Something from Horace, Livy or Plautus, he had forgotten which: 'Love is very fruitful, both of honey and gall.' Like most of Barnaby's quotations it was extraordinarily apt.

I

Prague occupied, Albania overrun. A sense everywhere of living on borrowed time and yet, for him more than anyone on the plateau that spring, there was still an inner fortress into which he could retreat, slamming the door on the babel outside with a finality never quite achieved in the tranquil days, before he was head and before Alcock walked among them. And this, he supposed, stemmed more from her and the child and Grace, than from his own convictions, or from a persistent hope that somewhere something would happen to arrest the movement of the long creeping shadow over the Western World.

There were moments when he could even see himself, half-humorously, as a Victorian paterfamilias, presiding over a complaisant household comprised of dutiful wife, young girl in the first bloom of womanhood, baby with powerful lungs and a phenomenal appetite, and creaking manservant, as though, in unspoken agreement one with the other, all five of them had agreed to enact a charade that had, as its keywords, felicity and domesticity.

The child had this effect on her, a very surprising one to any who had known her in her electioneering days, so that sometimes he wondered if she wasn't overdoing it a little, or perhaps conserving her nervous energy for some tremendous challenge that lay in the future. The question teased him so persistently that one evening, shortly after the opening of the summer term, he said, watching her powder the baby after his bath, "Am I right about you? Has that child taken over the Chris Forster of the barnstorming days?" and she threw him a saucy look over her shoulder and replied, "If he has are you complaining, Davyboy?" and he admitted cheerfully that he wasn't but that it surprised him none the less. With everybody finally convinced that Armageddon was just

over the hill he would have looked for a little crowing on her
part, or at least an occasional comment on the day's headlines.

She said, dumping a drowsy Ian into his cot, "Maybe I
am crowing inside. I've been wrong so often it's a rare
pleasure to be right for once. But don't misunderstand me.
I'm not blind to what's going on. It's just that none of us
can do a damned thing about it at this stage but sit and wait.
And hope, maybe."

"Hope?"

"That's what I said. I did my best to stir 'em up, and they
are beginning to stir a little. A possible Polish guarantee,
evacuation plans and air-raid trenches in Hyde Park
establish that, if nothing else. You've done your bit, too, in
a different way right here, on your home ground. I imagine
you'll go right ahead doing it while there's breath in your
body."

"I still don't see that as grounds for hope," he said,
remembering Christopherson II on his way to Spain.

"You will, Davy, when it happens. Read your Froude
again, that chapter on the early summer of 1588. Or read
Churchill and L.G. come to that, writing of what they call
the last summer of the old world, in June–July, 1914," but he
was not to be fobbed off so easily.

"We left it until five minutes to twelve on both those
occasions, and we had a hell of a lot of luck into the bargain.
This time it only wants about thirty seconds to midnight and
that little bastard will pick his own time, won't he?"

"Well," she said, philosophically, "it's not for me to
remind you of that old jingo nostrum about England losing
every battle but the last. You have a chat to the Sixth and
Fifth, and then come back and convince me that Hitler
and Musso are going to push us around indefinitely."

After that she wouldn't be drawn. Indeed, once a reliable
nanny had been found in the village, and she could return to
her beloved Cradle, and their halting readings of *Huckleberry
Finn*, *Treasure Island* and *Robinson Crusoe*, he did not see very
much of her, for he still had his hands very full, with a muster
of four hundred and two boys, and a record number of
thirty-eight new arrivals down for September.

He did take her advice, however, and raised the subject with the two Sixth forms and three Fifth forms. Nobody seemed to share his lack of confidence. All appeared to regard an ultimate confrontation with Hitler as a certainty, but the prospect of squaring up to his enormous army and air force, with dubious allies, and a totally inadequate armament, did not seem to daunt them. Perhaps their forefathers had won too many battles. Or perhaps, like Fleet Street, they fell for all those tales about Hitler's cardboard tanks and dummy submarines.

He was taking no chances, however, and that summer the Corps had a lively time of it, with new exercises on open warfare, Lewis gun and grenade training, and a concentrated programme of long-range shooting down at the Bamfylde Halt butts. Anything he could teach them he taught them well, and they seemed to respond to his zeal, sometimes calling him a slave-driver with the wind up, but doing their best, none the less. A young and rather foppish War Office captain, down for the Certificate 'A' pass out that year, complimented him on their keenness and turnout, saying, over a farewell gin, "Heard you were in France for four years, Headmaster. Maybe that accounts for the high morale of the chaps," and David, suddenly seeing himself as a kind of Blimp, mumbled that he had served three years in the line but left it vowing he would never be caught in khaki again.

The young officer looked a little outraged. "But you're the official C.O. of the outfit, aren't you?"

"Yes, I am," he growled, "for I've since come to the conclusion that if some of us don't make a stand soon it'll be all over bar the Sieg Heils." The War Office man, who would have been about five years old when Passchendaele was fought, raised an eyebrow. "You mean you don't think that chap's ravin' is four-fifths bluff?"

"Do you? After Munich?"

The officer shrugged. "Never meddle in politics. Just get on with the job. It's done one thing for us, I will say. The Territorials are up to strength for the first time since I left Sandhurst," and he excused himself with a nod, leaving David with the impression that Whitehall could still count on its Haigs and Robertsons.

A week later, however, he had unexpected proof of the
man's claim concerning the sudden popularity of the
Terriers. Spats Winterbourne turned up in uniform, on his
way to summer camp on Bodmin Moor, a trim, uncharac-
teristically subdued young man, who looked very smart in
his uniform, but reminded David poignantly of youngsters
like Nick Austen and Robin Barnes, his own friends and
contemporaries, killed on the Somme. He said, apologising
for what he called his fancy dress, "Had to do something,
Pow-Wow. If it does come there'll be conscription, and a
chap might as well get in on the ground floor. I'm ack-ack,
actually. Is Grace around?"

Grace was around and they went off together in Winterbourne's rakish car. Late that night he heard the car roar into
the forecourt and then Grace's hurried footsteps on the stairs,
but she didn't look in to say good night. Neither did Spats, for
the usual nightcap, a circumstance he thought little of at the
time but was to remember a few months later, when he had
occasion to put two and two together.

The term seemed to pass very quickly, with no improvement in the situation, so that he abandoned a half-formed
plan to park Ian with the Boyers for a fortnight, and take
Chris across to the Continent to make his own soundings,
and went instead on day-trips into Cornwall and South
Devon. It was as well he stayed home. News came of the
Russo-German pact, and on its heels renewed outcry about
the Polish Corridor, so that he wasn't much surprised to hear
Carter's voice on the phone one morning in late August,
suggesting they met before the new school year began and
finalised the evacuation plan, agreeing to meet in London
on Saturday, September 2nd.

In the last week of August he interviewed Howarth's
replacement, a cheerful, thirty-two-year-old Cornishman,
called Heathcott, who seemed by far the best of the bunch,
even though he had been slightly crippled in a road accident,
leaving him with a limp that reminded David of Grace's
handicap before her determination (plus Sax Hoskins'
unconventional exercises) had strengthened the damaged
muscles of her leg. Heathcott had been teaching at a grammar school in South London and wanted to get away to the

country, chiefly on account of his wife's health, for she had spent some months in a tubercular clinic. "The doctors say it will do her all the good in the world to live up here," he said, enthusiastically, as soon as he knew he had been accepted.

"They told me the same thing when I was discharged from the army in 1918," David said, "and they were right. But she might find it deadly dull after a place like Croydon."

They had dinner together and David decided he was going to like the talkative, freckled young man—he had begun to think of everyone under forty as young—and they chatted far into the night, discovering that they shared many old favourites, among them Gray, Goldsmith, the Restoration poets and even Tennyson, whom David would have thought a chap like Heathcott would regard as old hat. Heathcott was interested in history, too, and had made an amateur study of the early Plantagenets. His clear favourites were the obscure Henry III and his more popular son, Edward I. "They each gave the country something lasting," he said. "Henry built most of the best cathedrals, and I always see Edward as the real originator of our legal system."

"What did you make of Heathcott?" he asked Chris when they were going to bed, and she replied, predictably, "Liked him. If his wife is half as intelligent they're going to be assets. I had a word with him on politics when you were talking to the bursar, and discovered that he's an old-fashioned Liberal. Thinks the balloon will go up in a year or so, unless we decide to get in first, and I can't see that happening."

Heathcott was over-optimistic. He drove off to collect his wife and arrange his move, but four days later the school radios crackled with news of Hitler's onslaught on Poland. It was here again, two months short of the twenty-first anniversary of the night he and Howarth had escaped from the Armistice celebration concert in Big Hall and sat under the fives court, discussing the poet Heine.

II

It fell upon them like a cataract, days before the twin drives were jammed with cars bringing boys back for the opening term, such a coming and going as nobody at Bamfylde could recall, even at Whitsuntide reunions in the halcyon days. Carter's contingent of fifty arrived, sleeping rough in class-rooms until they could be sorted out and organised as a separate unit, with headquarters in a couple of Nissen huts erected just short of the Junior rugby pitch. Official forms arrived in a steady stream, 'a flood-tide of bumf', the over-worked bursar called it, and David sympathised with him, cowering under the Whitehall bombardment concerning rationing, blackouts and emergency regulations. And then, while they were still in a hopeless muddle, the term began, and what had seemed confusion slipped into chaos, with a new timetable to be drawn up, extra domestic staff signed on, the workshop set busy making trestle tables and forms and a miniature farmyard established down by the pig-geries, with a nucleus of a hundred White Leghorns, and a dozen ravenous Saddlebacks.

"Damn it," he complained to Chris, soon after the start of term, "it's like preparing for a siege, with the place full of peasants fleeing from the surrounding countryside," and she said that that was what it amounted to, although the anti-climax of those early autumn days did not confirm her view. Nothing seemed to be happening in the Maginot Line, so that he wondered whether there might not have been some substance in that War Office man's comment about Hitler's diatribes being bluff, and even relayed the possibility to Chris, whom he had come to regard as an oracle since the day she had appeared with little Ulrich Meyer in tow. And thinking of Meyer, he remembered to tell her that he had promoted the German boy to the rank of sergeant-major of the Corps. Ulrich was eighteen now, and in line for a pre-fecture if he stayed on.

"Can't help laughing when I think of his transformation," he told her, describing Meyer's first parade, north of the cricket pitch. "He was a weedy little beggar when you drop-ped him off but the traditional Prussian in him has begun to emerge. Adolf missed a good thing when he forced that boy into exile. There's Potsdam in his ancestry somewhere. He regards drill as poetry, and his voice, hectoring the awkward squad, carries farther than the bell. Scares the living daylights out of some of the recruits."

There were unexpected departures, as well as a flood of
new arrivals. Five of the Upper Sixth, scheduled to stay on
until March, did not return, among them, Crispin, handbell-
ringer and stealer of toffee bars. And after Crispin, Keithley,
the tiny Mancunian who had the honour of being the first
new boy David had welcomed as headmaster in January,
1932. And after that Lackaknacker Briggs, still secretive and
evasive about his alleged kidnapping. Crispin and Keithley,
both members of a gliding club, went straight into the R.A.F.
Lackaknacker took up a commission, wangled for him by an
obliging uncle at the War Office, sailing the day after he had
passed out to join Wavell's army in the Near East.

Among the newcomers that term was somebody he had
forgotten in the rush of events. Julia Darbyshire's boy,
Charles Sprockman, of whom both he and Chris instantly
approved, a tall, confident youngster, likely to be popular,
despite his transatlantic drawl, that won him the overnight
nickname of 'Clark', Clark Gable being the current favourite
among Bamfylde's many cinema addicts. Julia had sent a
letter with him, that went some way towards explaining why
she had taken the momentous step of sending her son east,
when everybody who could afford it was shipping his children out of harm's way. "He's half-English," she wrote, "and
I'm sure his father would have approved. I think he ought
to be in on anything that happens, and not dodging the
column, likes scores of Britishers I'm meeting over here, all
busy explaining they're over here on official business." He
thought it worth while to mention this eccentric approach
to young Sprockman and discovered that he had already
discussed it with his mother and endorsed her view. "I was
looking forward to coming, sir," he said, "and I can't see
what the fuss is all about. It won't last all that long, will it?"

"I don't know about that," David said, with a glance over
Sprockman's shoulder at the rehung photograph of Algy's
1913 Rugby Fifteen. "The last war was supposed to be over
by Christmas and it lasted more than four years. My guess is
we'll be lucky to settle Hitler's hash, in less." Then, as the
boy looked puzzled, "I've fought Jerry, lad, and he's tough.
Don't let anyone fool you into thinking he'll cave in quickly,
the way the Italians will, if they're crazy enough to get

mixed up in it," and the boy said, "No, sir. Guess I won't," and politely excused himself.

But then somebody appeared who succeeded in putting his manifold problems out of mind for a day or so. One wet and windy November afternoon Sax Hoskins knocked on his study door and said, with rather less than his usual assurance, "Er . . . have you time for a word, Pow-Wow? Kinder personal?"

Since taking up a professional career among musicians, and playing so much blues music, Sax had dropped into the habit of using American idioms and sounded, David thought, more American than Sprockman. He said, "You know I've always time for you, Sax. What's your problem?"

"Well, I guess it could be yours as well," Sax said, smiling uncertainly. "Grace and me . . . well, we figured on getting married before Christmas. Providing you'll wear it, that is."

David opened his mouth, closed it again, and ran his hand through his greying hair.

"Married? You and Grace? Christmas, you say?"

"You mean you didn't figure on it? Not ever?"

"Well, no . . . that is . . . I had some sort of idea that when she did marry . . . if she married, it would be you or Spats Winterbourne—I never could decide which. But good God, Sax, she's only nineteen . . ."

"She tells me her mother was nineteen when she married you, Pow-Wow."

He hardly knew what to say. He had always liked Sax, and he knew that Grace had been very devoted to him since that far-off day in 1926 when, as a lad of thirteen or so, he had marched into Havelock's and asked if he could teach Grace some of the latest dance steps, partly to boost her morale, partly to supplement the exercises she had been doing at that time. Now that he came to think about it he would have said Sax didn't stand much chance while Winterbourne was in the offing, and Spats had never ceased to be in the offing, since leaving Bamfylde almost nine years ago. Winterbourne had a lot to offer, not because he was the only son of a rich man but because he was more serious-minded than Sax, who was reckoned a bit of a gadabout, not the kind of chap likely to clutter himself with a wife, unless there were bonuses of one sort or another. He was a rover, too, here today, up north tomorrow, and playing a date in a Continental resort the day after. He just couldn't imagine Grace opting for that kind of life. She had always seemed so wedded to Exmoor.

Sax said, amiably, "If you've got any objections you'd better spill 'em, Pow-Wow. I've always had a hell of a lot of time for you, and nobody could kid me you don't top the bill with Grace. So if you put your foot down we'd wait until we could see further ahead. The point is," he continued, "it's not really as simple as that. I'm starting my A.G. course at Jurby, Isle of Man, on Monday, but there, I haven't told you I'm in the R.A.F. have I?"

"No, you haven't, and while you're at it, what the devil is an A.G. when he's at home?"

"Air Gunner. I was lucky to get signed on aircrew at my age. I'm twenty-six, Pow-Wow."

"You don't have to tell me how old you are," David said, still trying to absorb the situation, "but if you're already in the services why are you wearing civvies?"

"Oh, that? Well, my rig doesn't fit. The tunic makes me look like Joan of Arc and I'm having it tailored."

"But why is twenty-six reckoned old for flying? There must be pilots and observers older than that in the regular service?"

"Oh, there are," Sax said, "but they qualified on long, peacetime courses. Our A.G. course is only six weeks, and there are scores of kids queuing for it, some of 'em with the cradle marks still on their backside. I had to use a drop of the old palm oil with a recruiting sergeant and he put me down as twenty-three. Cost me a fiver as a matter of fact."

He gestured, hopelessly, "Look, sit down, Sax . . . give me a minute or two. Where is Grace right now? Listening outside the door, as they do in Victorian novels?" and she said, laughing, "Yes, I am," and then to Sax, "You might have closed it properly. Prefects are always using this passage as a short cut to the linen room. I had to head one off or your proposition would be all over the school by now."

She slipped inside, looking, he thought, as pretty as he had ever seen her, in her new blue two-piece, bought, he guessed, with a honeymoon in mind on her last trip to town just before term began. She said, casually, "I didn't hear every-

thing. Daddy isn't making a song and dance about it, is he?"
and Sax said, "Not really, though he has mentioned your
age, just as you said he would," and David thought, "My
God, there must have been some odd conversations in this
room over the last seventy years but never one quite like
this . . ." But then, right on cue, the bell began to clang in
the quad and he said, shutting the door, "I've no objections
at all in principle. You must know I haven't, the pair of you.
But why all the rush? I mean, you'll be home-based for
some time, won't you, even if you pass out. And talking of
passing it would be the first time you ever did pass an
examination."

"Oh, I'll walk this," Sax said. "Piece of cake. I'm genned
up on it," and years later David realised that this was the
first time he ever heard the new R.A.F. slang, that was to
pass into the language in a matter of months. Grace said,
"It's like this, Daddy. Once he's passed he gets a week's
leave, but after that he could be sent absolutely anywhere,
couldn't you, Sax? I mean, it might be years, and we couldn't
wait that long, not when we don't have to. We're in love,
Daddy, and he's too bashful to tell you. I daresay we would
have been married in the spring, anyway, if there hadn't
been a war. Isn't that so, Sax?"

The way she kept referring everything back to him robbed
her of maturity somehow, so that he saw her, not as a woman
of nineteen, but as a seven-year-old, skipping round the
Havelock parlour with the gangling Sax, to the strains of
'Bye, 'Bye, Blackbird', played on his portable gramophone.
Sax had gone red in the face, shamed by her forthrightness,
but he stood his ground, just the way he had that night in Big
School, when he owned up to finding Alcock's pipe-smashing
ceremony very funny. "It's true," he said, doggedly. "There's
never been any other Judy for me, Pow-Wow. How about it,
then?"

"Well, you'll suit yourselves, I suppose, for it's clear you've
made up your minds anyway. Coming here was a formality.
Will you be getting married in church?"

"Good Lord, yes," Sax said, as though someone had questioned his integrity. "We'd like to be married at Stone Cross.
Grace would like that, and I think it's a bit of a lark, I mean,

getting married where I've sat through so much jaw. How about the seventeenth? That's the day after I complete the course."

"And the last full day of term," Grace added, "so everyone can come who cares to."

He got out his day-book and marked the date, and as he did it struck him that Grace and Sax had almost certainly taken instruction from someone on how to play this rather old-fashioned scene. "That could only be Chris," he thought, "and they aren't going to get off scot-free and write me off as a dimwit," and he said, artfully, "Why don't we go in and get Chris up to date? She'll be so surprised she'll probably drop the baby."

He had his small revenge. They both looked a little out-faced and then Grace said, "Er . . . she won't, Daddy . . . be surprised, I mean. She might pretend to, but the fact is we talked it over with her an hour ago. She took it very calmly."

"She was flat out for it, as a matter of fact," admitted Sax, "so let's go back into the parlour and drink on it. You've got Scotch in there. You can't oil a prospective son-in-law with Old Boys' sherry."

*   *   *

They were going to bed about midnight before he made his first direct reference to the query uppermost in his mind. "I always thought it would be Spats Winterbourne if it was anyone. I would have bet on it, wouldn't you?"

She didn't answer for a moment, tugging at a knot in her hair, with her head on one side, so that he could see three aspects of her face in the three-sided mirror and reflect, idly, how young she had looked since coming home with that baby, as though she had just won first prize in the Irish sweepstake. Then she laid aside the comb, pivoted slowly on the stool and looked him over carefully and judiciously. "Your trouble is you have a surfeit of males and male psychology, Davy. No, I wasn't in the least surprised to discover it was Sax. In fact, I would have been very surprised to learn it was Winterbourne, poor devil."

"Oh, he'll get over it at his age. They all do."

"It'll take him longer than most."

"If he was so keen why didn't he put up a fight for her?"

"How do you know he didn't?"

"I don't know. He was here on a flying visit in the summer. Come to think of it he went off without saying goodbye, and hasn't been near us since."

"Well, that isn't hard to explain. That would be the day Grace told him the score."

"You mean that she was always in love with Sax?"

"Rather more, I suspect. That Sax needed her more than he did, and Grace is a woman who has to be needed. Keith Winterbourne is a sensitive, civilised human being, and he would have made her a good husband. But Grace wanted more than that. She wanted someone to spoil and that disqualifies anyone as self-sufficient as Winterbourne."

He thought about this and then about her, how wise she was in so many ways, how well endowed to operate at a far wider range than he, whose talents were confined to handling males between the age of about thirteen and eighteen. He said, "I think Grace is damned lucky. She not only had a stable to pick from when it comes to a husband, she got a Grade A stepmother for good measure."

"I don't take much credit for that. Anyone could get along with Grace."

"Anyone couldn't."

"Well, anyone you picked for her stepmother could."

She got up and moved between him and the dressing-table light, so that the lines of her figure—the figure of a girl athlete he sometimes thought it—were displayed through the flimsy material of her nightdress. It struck him then what a tremendous part she had played in keeping him young in heart, warding off the fossilisation that threatened all men in his profession after more than ten years on the job. "You don't look much older than Grace in that get-up," he said, and she replied, switching off the light, "I know a lot more about men. Notwithstanding the head-start she's had over most of her sex."

"I'm glad to hear it. It follows you probably know what I'm thinking."

"I knew before you did. Wedding talk always makes men randy. Women too, sometimes. Me, for instance."

She stood still in the darkness for a moment, out of immediate reach but close enough for him to hear the soft rustle of her nightdress as she shrugged herself out of it.

III

Twice during that winter of war that was not war the battle flared, two live coals in an otherwise dead fire. H.M.S. *Royal Oak*, at anchor in Scapa Flow, was torpedoed by a U-Boat and sank at dead of night, taking with her Lieutenant Graves-Jones, who had served in the Navy since leaving the plateau in the mid-twenties. Beth would have remembered him well, for he had been the least shy guest at her first new boys' party in 1919, acknowledging her hospitality with a Prussian heel-click when saying goodbye in the garden of the cottage. Always a bit of a ladies' man, Graves-Jones, but a credit to Bamfylde, for he was naval cadet of the year when he passed out at Dartmouth. But David recalled him for another reason, seeing him as a self-assured senior standing on the threshold of Havelock's parlour the night they buried Beth and Joan up at Stone Cross, holding a bunch of flowers he had intended laying on the grave and suggesting they went instead to Grace, lying trussed in hospital at Challacombe. "She won't see them, sir, but maybe she could smell them. The freesia has a lovely scent . . ."

He wrote his name, achievements and dates in the rearward section of his day-book, on a page that was blank save for the name of Christopherson, killed in Spain two years earlier, and as he made the entry he shuddered at the prospect of seeing the page studded with names. But records would have to be kept. Already letters were beginning to trickle in from all over the world, so that he found himself stuck with his old job of O.B.A. Secretary, a task he had cheerfully surrendered to Howarth but did not care to entrust to anyone else these days. Not even Barnaby who, with the best will in the world, would be likely to revere the dead of Thermopylae and Salamis above those doing battle in aircraft and tanks. Bamfylde's naval minority had it very much their own way that season. Letherett was aboard one of the destroyers that pursued the *Graf Spee*, and Ruby

Bickford, surely tailored for the role, was aboard *Cossack* when she intercepted the prison ship *Altmark* in such dashing style, the boarding party leaping on deck like Elizabethans capturing a Spanish treasure galleon off Panama.

Then, for the first time since any of them could recall, there was a school wedding at Stone Cross, almost a fairy-tale wedding it seemed to him, when he came in by the west door with Grace on his arm, and moved up the aisle to join Sax Hoskins, in R.A.F. uniform, with sergeant's stripes up, evidence of promotion that had astonished him until Sax explained "Aircrew get their third automatically . . . Can't have A.C. plonks flying kites, can you, Pow-Wow?" Sax was good enough to offer a free translation of this jargon for the benefit of those who did not yet speak the strange new language, a language that was already invading civilian sectors.

Algy Herries married them, and besides a full congregation of staff and boys there were one or two former cronies present, down to give Sax moral support. Massa Heilbron was one of them, the West Indian Sunsetter, over here on a gunnery course. Rowlandson was another, who might have remembered upsetting the teapot at the new boys' party, in 1924. David kept hoping to spot Winterbourne but he did not, and when he asked around nobody seemed to have news of him.

There was a lively reception back at the school, and the rowdy send-off he would expect in the forecourt as the short afternoon died, and the couple drove off to catch their train to Taunton and Paddington. The finality of the event did not strike him at the time, for so many old friends hung about the place until late that night, and there was the usual end-of-term tumult at first light the following morning.

"Have a good hols, sir . . . !" "Don't join up while we're gone, sir . . . !" and the inevitable sober note, this time from Vicary, head boy and due to join the Royal Marines in the new year—"I'll keep in touch, sir . . . Might even be handy for a spell. They tell me there's an R.M. training camp at Lympstone, just south of Exeter."

He stood on the steps and watched the last of them go, and it was then that he missed Grace most keenly, and was glad that she was likely to be back for a spell, at least until Sax found out where he was posted, and could wangle a living-out pass near the camp. He would miss her secretarial work too, for the post did not get any lighter, and Chris couldn't help him much, with her Cradle at full muster, and Ian at the toddling stage. Chad Boyer nudged him, collar turned up against the biting north-easterly and said, "How about a coffee, Pow-Wow?" in a way that suggested a confidence of some kind, so he went back into the house and told Rigby to bring coffee into the study, where a mountain of work awaited him. Chad said, when the door had shut on the old man, "Are all those letters from Old Boys overseas, Pow-Wow?"

"Most of them. Care to read some? There are several from chaps here in your time."

"Not in my present mood," Chad said, and when David asked what was amiss he said, gloomily, "I don't know. I feel out of it somehow. All the old crowd are doing something—Letherett, Dobson and even the Gosse brothers."

"A lot of the older bunch made a career of the services, Chad. It's no more than their job. Yours is right here, especially with Alison, one boy, and a second child on the way."

"Sure, sure but . . . I don't know . . . I still feel out of it. Is that so crazy?"

"I think it is. You're not much younger than I am, and from all I hear they can't cope with more men at the moment. Nothing seems to be happening, does it? Sometimes I see it as a kind of mime, a ritual squaring up to one another that will end in a compromise."

"Does Chris see it that way?"

"No. She says it'll get going in the spring, but she could be wrong. Frankly, I never imagined anything like this. The last war started off at a rare gallop. Mons was twenty days after declaration and I was in action three months later. Do you really want my advice?"

"I don't. Alison does."

"Well, for God's sake go back and tell her I said don't do any enlisting until it's absolutely necessary. For one thing I'd find it damned hard to replace you. For another you've got her and the kids to consider. But quite apart from all that, I think you'd find it difficult to land anything but a stooge job, in one or another of these new ministries. You'd be making a far better contribution here than getting bogged down at a desk."

Chad said moodily, "You were under eighteen when you signed up," and he snapped, "I was a bloody fool and lived to regret it. Besides, nobody knew a damned thing about war in those days."

He foraged among the incoming mail and found a single-sheet letter. It was from Gilbert, the Tory M.P.'s son, a contemporary of Boyer's and postmarked Tiree, in the Hebrides. "Listen to this. It illustrates my point.

Dear Pow-Wow,
    You'll note from the above address the Governor managed to get me into the R.A.F. after all. You need a lot of influence to get in, I can tell you. I tried half a dozen things off my own bat up to the end of October, but they didn't want to know. I couldn't even get into a line regiment as a ranker, and as for Cert 'A', nobody seemed to have heard of it. They probably regard it as a passout at the archery butts, or the Bamfylde certificate of proficiency for pike-drill. I was chuffed when I made it to O.C.T.U., but I might just as well have stayed put. I was failed aircrew on account of age (!) and given an admin. job up here, and I've never been so brassed off in my natural. All I do is look at the sea, sign chits for crafty weekends, and churn out daily returns that nobody reads. Believe me, it's all a big-scale hoax. Drop me a line if you've time, and tell me how my lot are making out. And tell old Barnaby, preferably in Latin, that the pen is not only mightier than the sword, it's a hell of a sight more universal in this man's army.
    Warmest regards, R. S. Gilbert."

He was relieved to look up from the letter and see Chad grinning. "You're wasted as a schoolmaster, Pow-Wow," he said. "You ought to have been one of those barristers who sit waiting for hopeless briefs handed down from the Bench. If ever I fall foul of the law I'll engage you. You'd come up with something proving I had a damned good reason for having the spoons in my pocket."

CHAPTER TWO

I

Chris was right, as usual.

In April, Chamberlain was talking about Hitler missing the bus. A fortnight later Denmark and Norway had fallen, and the summer term was less than a month old when Rotterdam was reduced to rubble and the distracted French Government had scuttled off to Bordeaux. The river of steel poured unchecked through the Low Countries, leaving in its wake a Maginot Line as obsolete as Martello towers, built to resist invasion in 1805. It was too late to do anything but run for cover, if cover was to be found.

The speed, and horrid finality of the onrush, stunned a man conditioned to think of an offensive's territorial gains in terms of yards, and those yards won at a cost of a hundred thousand casualties. It was an entirely new concept of war. He could think of no historical equivalent. The Napoleonic swoop on Ulm, culminating in Austerlitz, and the encirclement of Sedan, in 1870, were measured manoeuvres compared to this. At a stroke, huge French armies were dispersed and isolated, and the B.E.F., pushed back on three Channel ports, was reckoned lost.

*   *   *

He could not remember feeling so desolate since they brought him news of the accident on Quarry Hill. Catastrophes fell one upon the other like the subsiding storeys of a row of tall houses, overwhelmed by a hurricane. Belgium surrendered, then France, whereas over here all was confusion and dismay, even after Churchill had ousted Chamberlain, and thundered defiance in cadences that struck the ear like parodies of Henry V's oration before Harfleur. Soon long-range shells were falling on Folkestone, road blocks were set up, even down here in the wilderness, and a local

L.D.V. force, armed with rook rifles, old army Webleys and farmers' shotguns, patrolled the moors and coastal sectors. There was a sense of unreality and lack of purpose about everything one did, as if the ordinary processes of life, governed for so long by bells, by the school calendar, by arrivals and departures at the beginning and end of each new term, had lost their significance, were mere gestures in a compulsive ritual initiated long, long ago and persisted in from habit. A terrible sense of urgency, seen on the faces of adults, spread downwards to the Middle and Lower Schools, where he found himself the target of repeated questions for which he had no kind of answers.

"Will they invade, sir?"

"How about the navy, sir?"

"Is it true they're dropping paratroopers disguised as nuns, sir?"

"Will France fight in North Africa, sir?"

"Can't we join the L.D.V.s? There are rifles in the armoury, aren't there, sir?"

At least he could answer that one truthfully. There were no rifles in the armoury, not even the much-derided dummies, issued to the very youngest recruits in the Corps in their first month of training. Only a week ago a detachment of Terriers had arrived in a lorry, and carted them all away, together with what small arms ammunition was available. By now, he assumed, those same rifles, that had been humped up and down the playing fields since the days when Carter had been Corps Commander, were in the hands of half-trained men drawing army pay, awaiting the first shock waves of German invaders behind the beaches of Sussex and Hampshire, and in the hopfields of the Kentish Weald.

But then, like a blessed spate of silence after an earsplitting cacophony, came whispers of a fleet of small ships, and the lifting of 360,000 castaways from the littered beaches of Dunkirk. No more than a rumour at first, but a persistent one, that presently emerged as a fact, a kind of massive lifeboat snatch from a foundering vessel, surrounded by bobbing heads and upraised arms, and after it a vast wave of thankfulness, followed by a mood of buoyancy not unlike the first

stage of intoxication. Apparently it was not the end of everything, or not quite, so that, like everybody about him, he
plucked up heart and took up the threads of authority again,
snatching a moment here and there to collate the snippets of
news that found their way to his desk via post and telephone,
and the occasional appearance in his parlour of a harassed
parent, past or present. It seemed a miracle that, of the score
of Bamfeldians serving with the B.E.F., fourteen were already
reported safe and well, and one or two had actually rung
through while on survivors' leave. He conceived the idea
then of posting a list of them on the quad notice board,
announcing details within minutes of receiving his stream
of messages, then squinting through the window of Algy's
Mount Olympus, where he could see them crowding round
the slip of paper hanging there, relaying the news to the
outer fringes of the crowd.

More and more news filtered in, almost all of it good.
Gilbert, last heard of looking out at sea, and signing chits on
a lonely Hebridean Isle, was spirited from a French beach
by an amateur yachtsman, and confirmed as much in person, writing cheerfully from Newhaven where he was set
ashore. Kassava II, he who had clung to the guttering of the
blazing Havelock dorm until his brother knocked him
senseless, showed far more initiative at Calais, hiding in a
partially collapsed slit trench until it was dark, then making
his way along the tideline to the nearest evacuation point,
where he was taken off by the boat's crew of a destroyer.

Through the blazing summer days the list lengthened until
it ran off the page and was replaced by a larger, more comprehensive one, with notes beside every name, Daffy Jones,
Nipper Shawe, Gage and Stilts Rhodes rescued by destroyers, and set ashore at Dover; Bummy Bristow, whose elder
brother had been Bamfylde's last casualty in the First World
War, having more luck than his brother, this time off
Bordeaux, where he got off in the *Lancastria*, went down with
it, but bobbed up and was hauled aboard a trawler and
carried into Falmouth; Johnston, the indirect cause of
Winterbourne's flight in 1925 (he had told him his mother's
divorce was all over the Sunday papers) taken prisoner at
St. Malo but dodging the column (Johnston was always a bit

of a column dodger, David reflected,) and making his way to
Brest, where he caught the last refugee boat out of the harbour;
Maxton, third official bell-ringer in David's recollection,
together with Heffling and Keith Blades, rescued by the
navy at Dunkirk; Parker and Morgan-Smith carried home
on a paddle steamer that had once plied for hire from the Isle
of Wight; Cookson, whose father had once shamed him by
appearing on Sports Day in a chauffer-driven Rolls-Royce,
using more plebian transport and landing, black as the Ace
of Spades, from a collier at Newport, Monmouthshire. Some
fifteen in all, the last being Driscoe who had partnered
Beth and Phyl Irvine as the third of the three little maids in
the 1920 *Mikado*, reported safe a week after having been
listed a P.O.W. Driscoe, it seemed, had made it all the way to
Marseilles in an elderly Citroen, found by the roadside near
Abbeville, paying his way with cigarettes, looted from an
abandoned N.A.A.F.I.

And after that a lull, while David was seeking, and
getting, confirmation of their two known casualties, a sad
pair to anyone's way of thinking. For Briarley, serving as a
captain in the Calais garrison, was killed some thirty miles
from the river Lys, where his father had died in the Big
Push of 1918. Details concerning Skidmore's death were
more confused but it looked as if he had achieved a kind of
martyrdom after all. Serving in the B.E.F. as a Methodist
padre, he had remained behind to tend to the wounded and
was now reported missing, believed killed.

*   *   *

The day he got confirmation of Briarley's death he went out
across the forecourt to the big cedar beside the tennis court,
sitting near the spot where he had talked to the boy twenty-
two years before, after Ellie Herries had sent him out to offer
what comfort he could. He wondered if Briarley's mother
was still alive, and if she was, how would she take this second
blow? Bitterly, he would say, for Briarley Senior had died in
what was reckoned a war to end war, and Briarley Junior,
he recalled, was an only son.

The boy's voice seemed to speak to him over the years—
"Didn't see a great deal of him, sir . . . when I was small he

was mostly in India or Ireland . . ." and a later question, "Would it have been quick, sir? I mean, you'd know . . ."

He sat there in the blinding heat, biting his lip and silently cursing the fools who had let things drift and drift until they had reached an impasse where the only hope of a future rested on the wanton sacrifice of boys like Briarley, boys with guts and imagination, now called upon to go out and do their fathers' work all over again. The bell rang for lunch but he did not hear it and later Chris found him there, staring into the heat haze shimmering on the western slopes of Middlemoor.

She said, quietly, "What is it, Davy?" and he told her of all three Briarleys, father, thirteen-year-old son who had sat here beside him, and thirty-five-year-old regular, left behind in Calais to stop Panzers with hand grenades and a standard issue revolver.

She said, taking his hand, "All in all, we've been lucky, Davy. In two ways if you can bring yourself to see it in that light. Fifteen out of seventeen saved by a miracle, or a string of miracles. But that isn't what I mean."

"Well?"

"God knows, I've never seen you or myself as people subscribing to those platitudes about the nobility of sacrifice —*pro patria mori*, and so on. I never was entranced by Kipling, or that chap Newbolt, who wrote that slosh about the voice of the schoolboy rallying ranks. But this is different, utterly different. I think it's important you should face up to it now, for it looks to me as if there's worse to come."

"How is it different? Briarley, father and son, died in the same war, on the same ground, fighting the same enemy. What's different about it?"

"I don't think I have to go over that again. I made it clear five years ago, when I backed down on every principle I ever held. This time it isn't a question of dying for king and country, for the flag, for honour and glory and all that rubbish."

"It never was," he said, "for the chaps called upon to do it."

"But it was for the people who weren't, people like me standing on the touchline. Only now there isn't any touchline. We're all in it, right up to our necks, and that's a point in our favour, I'd say. At least, there's no more bloody hypocrisy, no more do-your-bit-son, no more white feathers and promises of homes fit for heroes to live in. This is total war, with nothing but survival as the prize-money. More muddle if we win, a living death if we don't. It's worth dying for if that much is clear. Briarley was killed at Calais, you say?"

"Left to his fate, back to the sea. Bombed from above, fired on by God knows how many tanks."

"But if it hadn't been for Calais, what would have happened up the coast at Dunkirk?"

"I'm damned if I know and I don't see how you could know."

"It so happens I do," she said, "for Bradshawe told me. He plied one of those small boats, and that's something else you should put on your little list before you draw a line under it. Don't look so outraged—Bradshawe was here and I tried to find you but you were over at Challacombe at that L.D.V. conference. He couldn't wait. He was on his way to Plymouth to join the navy."

"What exactly did Bradshawe tell you?"

"A lot they didn't print about Dunkirk. More than he's told anybody, I'd say. I have a very special relationship with Bradshawe."

She had too, beginning that day during her first term here, a month or so after they were married, when Howarth, the old fox, had persuaded her to mediate between Bradshawe, then fifteen, and his parents, plaguing him with their respective versions of the family divorce. "He picked nine out of the water, close inshore. I didn't know he was a yachtsman, did you?"

"No," he said, the weight beginning to lift from his shoulders, "but I settled years ago for learning something new about every damned one of them every day I make contact. Both during and after their time here."

He stood up. "That's not such a bad idea, either—adding Bradshawe to the list, I mean. He only left in 'thirty-eight, and there'll be quite a number here who remember him. They'll be excited to hear we had someone who took part in that crazy armada."

He made no excuse for his sudden change of mood and she watched him move with long strides across the sunlit tennis court, over the forecourt and through Big School arch to the quad. He already had his fountain pen unscrewed and she thought "He's no more than a Briarley or a Bradshawe himself some days. But, just occasionally, he's as old as God. That's the way of it in his job, I imagine . . . my job, too, now, if I'm honest with myself . . ."

She got up, smoothed her skirt and walked thoughtfully across the sunbaked lawn to the steps, meaning to pass straight through into the kitchen and warm his untouched lunch, but tempted, en route, to use his Judas window in the lavatory. She was in time to see him repin the notice and stand back to let the first quad loungers read the addendum.

II

She had promised him worse and he had learned to trust her judgment in these things, yet the summer blazed on tranquilly enough, with plenty of bustle, and a steady bombardment of officialdom certainly, but as yet no cataclysmic sequel to the epic of Dunkirk.

World War was lapping into the quadrangle, into the nooks and crannies of the old place in a less dramatic way, creeping paralysis rather than a seizure, for the very influx of boys that summer slowed them down, sometimes to a virtual standstill. Seemingly the reverse of the 1931 slump was at work in the minds of parents, particularly those living in Greater London, and the threatened south-eastern areas. Younger brothers arrived out of nowhere, often at short notice, so that the waiting-list, that had always had to be nursed, shook itself out well ahead of time as people remembered the relative immunity of the plateau.

In addition to their own swollen complement of four hundred and seventeen, there was an increase in Carter's contingent. 'Minimals' Barnaby called them, a play of their school's official name, St. Magnus, and Carter was very jealous of their identity, keeping them within their perimeter, which was just as well in view of the chronic shortage of dormitory, classroom and playing field space. There were now over sixty Minimals, living like a dependent and slightly disreputable tribe under the lee of the planty, where two more Nissen huts were erected to serve as dining-room, kitchen and communal classroom. Carter managed them with one assistant master, an elderly man called Badger, said to be an amateur archaeologist, with extravagant theories about Middlemoor being the real site of Arthur's Camelot.

They lost Molyneux towards the end of term. It seemed that he, too, heard the call of duty, in the form of a muted 'Marseillaise', played by the exiled de Gaulle. He was not a Frenchman but had many Gallic friends and one of them, a certain Capitaine d'Orley, appeared in uniform one morning and talked him into joining the nucleus of the French Resistance Group as an official interpreter.

He went off gaily, despite David's indignant protests. He had never really integrated into the school but his work was first-class, and David was reluctant to lose him. He said, by way of valediction, "I've been stuck here fifteen years, P.J. and I've never had any *fun*. I'm nearly forty now, and if I turn this down I'll marry a local peasant and grow a turnip for a head. Time I moved on, but it took a thing like this to shake me loose. Never had enough initiative, but d'Orley tells me there's a prospect of seeing the world once we get properly organised. It was that that decided me."

He was replaced, almost at once, by an elderly Belgian refugee, a Monsieur Oujardier, a name that the boys instantly converted into 'Ooojah', without waiting for Barnaby's cue. In some ways the Belgian reminded David of the long-dead Bat Ferguson, in that he was excitable and very voluble, but he showed promise of being adequate, and at least qualified as an eccentric, an honour that Molyneux had never achieved, notwithstanding his middle name, Aloysius, and that awful Australian uncle who looked like a Colonial pretending to be Bernard Shaw.

Then, in the final week of term, when he was in the throes of making arrangements to house an additional fifty boys for the holidays, on the lines of the Sunsetters, a much heavier blow fell on him. A grim-faced Boyer invited him and Chris down to the cottage for tea one baking Sunday afternoon, and announced in the momentary absence of Alison, that he was enlisting in the merchant navy as soon as their second child was born, and that it was no good trying to talk him out of it because he had been to Plymouth and signed on the previous Saturday.

In the last twenty-odd years there had been many occasions when Boyer had exasperated him but never more so than now. He said, explosively, "But that's absolutely crazy, Chad! The merchant navy! Good God, what the hell do you know about the sea? It's no more than a Quixotic gesture. Why don't you borrow a suit of armour while you're at it, and charge Man Bullivant's bloody windmill at Bamfylde Halt?"

Chris said, "Keep your voice down, Davy. Maybe he hasn't told Alison," and Boyer said, calmly, "Yes, I have, and she's behind me, odd as it may seem. Or not so odd, perhaps. Her kid brother, Hamish, went down on the *Jervis Bay* last winter. She was very fond of Hamish. He was only seventeen."

"I never heard that," said David, checked somewhat. "She kept it very much to herself, didn't she?"

"She isn't a song and dance artist, Pow-Wow, but it left a scar. I was scared of admitting how I felt about things, but when I did she saw my point of view, particularly as I've every hope of training as a gunner, although my real duties will be steward."

"Steward!" David growled, warming up again, "Steward, with a good degree and a reserved occupation!" but Chris intervened again, saying, "Do stop erupting, Davy. Let Chad explain if he wants to."

"He already has. He came to me when the phoney war was still on, mumbling about missing out, but I thought I'd talked him out of it. Damn it, I could understand it if you were in the Sixth, or still up at university. But thirty-five, with one toddler and another expected in October!"

Chad said, addressing Chris, "The trouble with Pow-Wow is that he won't accept the end product of his own gospel. He's like an apostle of the early Christian Church who gets cold feet and urges his converts to pay homage to Nero the minute he hears the lion roar," and Chris said, laughing, "That's a pretty good analogy, Chad. Go on."

"I don't know whether or not you realise it, Pow-Wow, but all these years, ever since you walked into Big School with the shakes on you before that last show ended, you've been preaching tolerance, equality of opportunity, the true essence of democracy, small 'l' liberalism, and British standards of equity and fair play. Everything, in fact, that places like Bamfylde are supposed to stand for. All that red flag flapping never fooled me, and it never fooled anyone else except that idiot Alcock. Even Sir Rufus Creighton saw through it the moment he put his glasses on and that's what got you the job. We almost nicknamed you 'Bolshie' your first term but if we had it would have been ironic. You're no more than a Tory, slightly left of centre, and as a rebel Welshman you're a damned fraud. Bamfylde took you over body and soul and did it in a matter of weeks. It beats me why you haven't admitted as much to yourself."

"I don't see what my political outlook has to do with you throwing up a responsible job and risking your life in order to bring the skipper a mug of cocoa at six bells."

"Tell him, Chad," Chris said, "you're doing fine so far."

"Well, the fact is, all your own chickens, and those you inherited from Algy, are coming home to roost. God knows we've had proof of that lately. For years and years you've been jawing about the struggle of the British tribes to hammer themselves into a unit qualified to make a contribution to real civilisation and you seem to have done a pretty good good job one way and another. On my reckoning we've already got around sixty Old Boys in the scrap, all squaring up to that bastard and his thugs, and pretty sure to make mincemeat of 'em given time and equipment. Fifteen slipped the collar at Dunkirk and lived to fight another day, and three, four if you count Christopherson, who was too quick off the mark, have already died for what you and they believe in. Well, you have to take some of the responsibility for that, and for any more chaps who go west before it's over. But would you be any more pleased with your work if nobody stepped forward? What would you have done then? Taken to recruiting, I wonder, or gone back yourself to take a second crack at Jerry? Pour him some more tea, Chris, and call up to Alison to bring Robbie down. If he sleeps any longer he'll keep us awake all night."

So there it was, his philosophy, his ultimate responsibilities, fed back to him, spoonful by spoonful, by one of his own converts, and there was no alternative but to open his mouth and swallow it. The flavour was sharp at the time. Within a month its bitterness set his teeth on edge.

*   *   *

The tempest rushed down on them again about the time a majority were leaving for the summer holiday. Radio bulletins told of massed air attacks on Channel shipping, on port installations, on fighter airfields, and finally on the Port of London itself, so that the Armageddon everyone had looked for on that clear September day almost a year ago was here now, and the more thoughtful among them began to understand why the R.A.F. had made such a modest showing over the beaches at Dunkirk. Defence squadrons had clearly been held in reserve, against just such a contingency as this.

They saw nothing of the air battles, of the twisting vapour trails in the clear blue sky to the south-east (the summer seemed endless that year) but the B.B.C. soon evolved a cricket score technique concerning the state of play, and it caught on at once, after he had installed their most powerful radio in Big School, so that no one missed any bulletins, and they could use the blackboard for a score board. Even the rump of the Cradlers, and the junior Sunsetters, were given permission to stay until the last bulletin of the day.

The damage inflicted on the attackers was astounding if true. Squadron after squadron decimated between the Normandy airfields and the Home Counties, where a junkyard of Luftwaffe hardware was said to be building up in fields and coppices of Sussex, Kent and Essex.

There was a price to pay, of course, but it seemed, to most onlookers, a modest one, again if the bulletins were true. For every Spitfire or Hurricane lost Goering had to sacrifice three aircraft, and the R.A.F., fighting over its home ground, had the advantage as regards pilots parachuting to safety.

But again, as snippets of news filtered on to his desk, he began to feel more and more like Algy Herries during the Somme and Passchendaele offensives of 1916 and 1917. The price might be modest in terms of men and machines, but it was terribly high to him, and mounting week by week, for the Junior Service seemed to have attracted a swarm of Bamfeldians, mostly the younger ones who had been here as recently as 1938 and 1939, and were now, unbelievably, among those spearheading the battle.

News had reached him via telephone in late July that Hislop had been shot down off Folkestone. Hislop, who had once stood in this very room, and told the Stoic the truth concerning his exploits as school bookmaker, and had then disappeared from their midst, to reappear more than a year later, with his sights set on a commission in the R.A.F.

Mrs. Hislop rang late one night, when he was wrestling with the September timetable. She was extraordinarily resigned, he thought, but he pitied her from the bottom of his heart when she said. "He was something of an ace, P.J. I had that from one of his squadron, who brought me the news. He shot down three M.E.s in France, and was credited with five certainties over here, one Heinkel, one Dornier and three Junkers, I think they said. I haven't told his father yet. He's away up North, attending a relative's funeral, but I had to talk to someone tonight."

David said, "He was everything I hoped in the end, Mrs. Hislop, and I'll never cease to be grateful to you for letting him return here. It turned out splendidly. He was one of the best seniors we ever had. But what comfort is that to you now?"

She said, quietly, "Some comfort. More than you'd think, maybe. I'm proud of him, and his father should be. I hope so, anyway, for it's all he'll have to hang on to. I keep telling myself that if it hadn't been for trained pilots like him we'd be finished by now. You think that too, don't you?"

"I've thought it ever since Dunkirk," he said, fervently. "The Services didn't get much of a show before the war. People thought of them as old hat I suppose, but it's a damned good job some youngsters opted for them."

"Will you pass it around among his old friends?" she concluded and he said he would, and thanked her for ringing. "Don't thank me," she said. "He 'went a bundle' as they say, on you, and on that place of yours. In spite of that silly business with Alcock. Good night, P.J."

"Good night, Mrs. Hislop."

He replaced the receiver, with no stomach to return to the madly complicated timetable. Hislop's death made four certainties in less than a year. The list was lengthening. All one could do was pray it wouldn't be as long as the one on the cross outside before they blew the Cease-Fire.

He thought about prayer for a moment. Almost nothing remained of the conventional faith of his Valley upbringing, the chapel-based certainty of a glorious resurrection, that had proved such a rock of comfort to his mother. He supposed himself an agnostic, like old Howarth, but he wasn't even sure of this. The outlines of his earthly beliefs were well-defined, but he had never exercised his mind to fill the spiritual vacuum, created by his first few weeks in the trenches. There might be something, he supposed, some vague creative force, impossible to define in words, or even contemplate in solitude. Prayer would be a help now, he imagined, but the best he could do was rally on what he thought of as the Abu Ben Adam philosophy, the substitution of faith in one's fellow man as a workaday equivalent for faith in God. Given there was a God.

He turned off the desk light and went out into the passage, passing through the door leading to Big School passage, then out on to the playing field.

A harvest moon hung over the moor. He could see the dark line of the planty all the way from the spot where it turned a right angle to run the full length of the crest as far as the cricket pitches. Below it, fifty yards or so nearer the school, was the stark silhouette of Algy's thinking post, and he bent his steps there, lighting a cigarette, leaning against its brittle bark, and remembering not only Hislop, who had once hit a stupendous six about here, but other moments he associated with this spot. It soothed him somehow, so that he could find some kind of anchorage for his confused thoughts. He was by no means sure about a God but he acknowledged the clear difference between good and evil, and according to Chris there had never been a war in which the options were so clear. That ought to help, and might, perhaps, as time went on, and you could see a pinpoint of light at the end of the tunnel. But so far evil seemed to be winning hands down, with a Continent enslaved, and Britain hanging on to the coat-tails of a few thousand boys like Hislop. There was only so much they could do and they had already achieved far more than he, and all the other anti-militarists of the 'twenties, had the right to expect. He thought, bitterly, "By God, we've got a lot to answer for—not just the politicians but all of us, Left, Right and Centre, from Versailles onwards. I saw the red light before the majority, but I wouldn't have if Chris hadn't had the moral courage to point it out, and bring me evidence in the person of that kid Meyer. It's our fault the odds are so long up there. Who the hell am I to put the responsibility for Hislop's death on politicians?"

Prayer was denied him but there was its equivalent, a mute appeal to the ageing ghosts of all those names on the memorial, and the newcomers to Valhalla, like Briarley, Christopherson, Graves-Jones, Hislop and old Preacher Skidmore, and he made that plea, now, standing in a flood of moonlight, his back against Algy's thinking post. "Get us out of this somehow. Show us the way. Give us the guts and stamina, but don't be too greedy for company . . ."

One of the planty owls hooted, perhaps with derision at his naivety, but he felt a sense of release, as though the soft night breeze, gusting down from the moor, carried the hopes of all Bamfeldians who had stood at this spot across four generations and seen below a sprawl of buildings that was something more than a seat of elementary learning, a place where, in their brief span hereabouts, they had imbibed a little of the ethos of the island, and its struggle over twenty centuries to fashion apparatus capable of accommodating free will with justice and human dignity.

He extinguished his cigarette and went down the slope to the fives court, round the promontory of the Bog and through the flagged court that led, via Outram's and the Third Forms, to the quad. Everyone was asleep but him, moonlight reflecting on the windows of the Sunsetters' dormitory, and the steep, tiled roof of the new labs. The place looked washed clean in this strong, bluish light, looked as if nobody had ever trodden the asphalt circuit about the Founder's statue, and as he passed it, on his way to his own back door, he gave it a new boy's bob. For to-night he felt more defenceless than Endsleigh Minor, youngest of last term's Cradlers.

CHAPTER THREE

I

And that was really no more than the beginning. The end of the beginning, as Churchill would later describe it.

On through an endless succession of blazing summer days the battle continued, rising to three screaming crescendos on August 13th, August 18th and September 15th, the day school reassembled for the start of another year. On that day alone, Buck Suttram, the West Indian Sunsetter, who had been keeping score, chalked up a total of fifty-six German aircraft destroyed.

On through the full month of October it continued to rage, when Suttram, reduced to keeping a private record after Big School blackboard had been restored to normal use, told David that the R.A.F. and anti-aircraft defences had accounted for just over two thousand enemy aircraft between July 10th and the last day of October. The figure was duly entered up in the records and Suttram wasn't so far out at that. Years later, when official figures were reissued after the capture of Luftwaffe documents, it was seen that, between the dates quoted, an admitted total of German planes destroyed was one thousand, seven hundred and thirty-three, with a further six hundred and forty-three damaged.

Suttram had not kept tally of R.A.F. losses but David had, in terms of lives if not machines. Of the one thousand, four hundred and ninety-five R.A.F. personnel killed, four, including Hislop, were Bamfeldians. A fifth, Crispin, was so badly burned over the Thames estuary, that he was in Halton Hospital for months and left it on crutches.

*   *   *

Alone among those who stayed on at school throughout that unforgettable seven weeks, David was unable to share the Test Match excitement prevailing in Big School around the Sunsetters' radio. How could he? The impersonal announcements, relevant to the cost of victory, were translated, figure by figure, into a sombre parade of faces recalled over recent years, all linked in his mind to some quirk, nickname or exploit, attaching itself to every boy who had mooched about the quad, or added his quota to the changing-room cacophony attending the end of every rugby game.

News of Towers's death, for instance, received the same week as that informing him of Crispin's terrible injuries, touched him almost as deeply as the loss of Hislop and Briarley. For he saw it as an ironic adjustment in the balance sheet of life, recalling how once—long ago it seemed now—Crispin, alone and friendless, had worshipped Towers from afar, and had stolen a bar of Mackintosh's toffee from the village shop simply in order to register with his hero. Now they were level pegs, or almost so. Towers, shot down over Maidstone, was dead. Crispin, trapped in blazing debris at a satellite field in Sussex, was half-dead, 'cooked' they would say, in their pitiless new slang, and in the hands of the skin-grafters for months to come.

He wrote to both boys' parents and Crispin's mother replied at once, promising to keep him informed on her son's progress. But then, for a brief spell, his attention was switched to more personal concerns. Grace, who had been living with them since she returned from her honeymoon, was whisked away at a day's notice by Sax Hoskins, now commissioned and stationed in Yorkshire, on a basis that enabled him to live out of camp.

He had a few minutes' garbled conversation with his son-in-law, due to begin yet another course the following day, and nervous of missing his connection if the London termini were blitzed. Sax was developing a variety of new skills in his wartime profession, even showing marked proficiency in maths, something that would have astounded his Bamfylde mentors. Gunnery was behind him now and he was moving on to qualify as a navigator.

"Will it keep you out of harm's way for a few months?" David asked anxiously, and Sax replied gaily that it would, for the R.A.F. did not yet possess the means to mount a sizeable bombing offensive on Germany.

"We won't start dishing it out on their scale for a year or so," he said, "but when we do, oh boy! Hamburg, here I come!" David gathered there was a certain amount of rivalry between the men who flew bombers and those who flew fighter aircraft. Sax said, "So far the Spits and Hurrys have had all the glam but the war won't be won by the Brylcreem boys. We've got to go over and sort 'em out on their own ground, and we've got some real beauts on the assembly lines." Then, less breezily, "You don't mind me taking Grace off your hands, do you? The way I see it we might as well spend what time we can together. It won't be all that much, with me genning up like a bloody boffin."

He said his next farewell, in early November, to Boyer, off on the first stage of his Quixotic odyssey, an odyssey that was to take him, in the next few years, all over the world. Chad's second child, a daughter, had been born in early October, and his place at the little cottage had been filled, to some extent, by a landgirl who lodged there. "I was chuffed to get her," Chad said, "for she's another Scots girl, and will be great company for Alison. But you'll keep an eye on her, won't you, Pow-Wow? And I'll keep in touch wherever I am, whatever I'm doing."

Everybody but himself, it seemed, was either dying or tearing about the country in a prodigious hurry, and his very rootedness made him feel his age. Boyer, had he stayed on, would have become housemaster of Nicolson's in place of Howarth. As it was, he made do with the new man, Heathcott, and judged himself lucky to have him, for Heathcott, like his wife, was not strong and unlikely to disappear into the blue like so many others. He came to like Mrs. Heathcott, whose health improved as soon as she settled on the plateau, so that Heathcott said, "Gladys and I are a couple of creaking doors, I'm afraid, P.J., but these days that's insurance."

It was at that, as he found himself thinking when he had final confirmation of two more casualties, Churchill and Keithley, both reported missing earlier in the term. He thought of them as hardly more than babies. Churchill had been one of the very earliest Cradlers, whose name had occurred to him when he and Chris were motoring back

from their honeymoon in 1934, and had stopped to picnic
near the spot where the Duke of Monmouth was hauled from
a ditch and carted off to London to die on Tower Hill. It
was Chris who reminded him of this when he relayed the
dismal news. "I always thought of Churchill as my trum-
peter," she said, sadly. "It was mention of his name that
made you suggest I started the Cradle. How old would that
make him, Davy?" and he said Churchill was still under
twenty, for he had only left them at the end of the Lent
term, in 1939.

He had even more poignant memories of Keithley,
remembering him as the tiny, heavily mufflered figure,
mousing his way into the parlour carrying an attaché case
and a plaid rug, the very first new boy he had ever greeted as
headmaster. Keithley, he recalled, had been very scared at
the time, but had plucked up heart when he had con-
gratulated him on travelling all the way from Manchester
unaccompanied. "Change at Bristol," Keithley had piped
on that occasion, before Grace whisked him away to warm
himself and have tea, and try as he might, David could not
see Keithley as more than twelve, although his records
told him he would be coming up to his twenty-first birthday.

But not all the news was depressing. Word came from
Venn, serving with a New Zealand contingent in Ethiopia,
telling of a surprise encounter in an Eritrean camp with old
Lackaknacker Briggs, who had just been recommended for
a gong, as they called decorations these days. Briggs, it
appeared, was still a loner and had put up a sensational
one-man show near Adowa, bluffing a column of about
seventy Italians into surrender, and somehow persuading
them to lay down their arms and accompany him back to
base.

And then, towards the end of a cheerless term, Chris told
him she was pregnant again, and it gave the usual upward
twist to her spirits, for she had been saying lately that it
was time Ian had some competition before he was spoiled
by everyone about the place. "Not many children are as
unspoilable as Grace," she said, "and this time I hope it's a
girl. Something has to be done about the frightful imbalance
of the sexes up here."

He had never admired her more than he did these days. She shared his personal grief over the sacrifice of the Churchills and Keithleys, but her sense of mission, that had carried her through the entire holocaust since the end of the phoney war, buoyed her up in a way he envied. More and more she saw the war as a crusade against unspeakable barbarism, and everyone actively engaged in it as a crusader. He did not doubt her courage or her sincerity but he wondered, sometimes, if her faith would have sustained her to the same degree if she had been subjected to nonstop air attack, in the way Londoners were, or had her son been old enough to take his place among the elite. Perhaps, he thought, but then, unlike him she had not suffered the disenchantment of the years following the armistice and neither, for that matter, had any of them, except a few old war-horses like Barnaby, Carter and Algy Herries, now seldom seen this side of the moor, for he was getting feeble and transport was difficult.

He stood on the steps as usual the last morning of term and saw them off, only a very few departing in cars this time, for petrol was strictly rationed, but in other respects it did not seem to differ much from the tri-annual exodus of earlier years. The war had not blighted their spirits, as it had his, and there were the same old quips and promises as they shook hands.

"Have a good hols, sir! . . ." "I'll keep in touch, sir! . . ." "Don't forget that live wire in the Christmas tree decorations, sir . . ." and so on, until the last of them were lost to sight in the grey trailers of morning mist eddying about the trunks of the beech trees lining the east drive.

II

The bulk of the Christmas mail was late arriving, owing to iced-up roads down by Bamfylde Bridge Halt, and on both westerly approaches. But on the last day of the old year a bumper delivery appeared, two dozen welcome food parcels for the Sunsetters, and a shoal of Christmas cards and overseas mail.

He took his into the study while Chris and Mrs. Heathcott, Barnaby and others were superintending the second stage of an uproarious New Year's Eve party, staged by the Sun-setters in Big Hall, where the blackouts were manageable owing to the narrowness of the windows.

There was a good deal of Old Boys' news, cheerful for a change. Briggy's son, Major Cooper, was now a lieutenant-colonel. Lackaknacker wrote in his own account of his Roman triumph, with his seventy Eyetie prisoners in tow, but played it down, Bamfylde fashion, saying it was all a bit of a spoof really, for the Eyeties were 'brassed off and bloody well starving, and flocked round me as if they expected me to go through the loaves-and-fishes routine'.

There was a long-overdue letter from Spats Winterbourne, serving in a Scottish infantry regiment, and about to start a commando course in the Highlands. He made an oblique reference to Grace's wedding, asking for Sax Hoskins' latest address, so that he could write about a belated wedding present, but this must have nerved him to be more explicit for he concluded:

I never did bring myself to wire them congratulations, Pow-Wow, but at least I went out and bought a present. It's still at my mother's old place in town (if it hasn't gone up in smoke), and if Sax or Grace are in London any time they could call in for it, for I don't expect to come south for several months.

That was all, except to ask for any Bamfylde news and David, reading between the lines, concluded that the loss of Grace had hit him terribly hard and he was still, after a year, trying to adjust to it.

The last letter in the pile was a thick, much-franked package, postmarked 'Santa Barbara, Calif.', and he recognised the hand-writing of Julia Sprockman. He opened it reluctantly, for it occurred to him that she was having second thoughts about exposing her son to the bombing and was sending instructions to put him on the first available ship for the States. But when he opened the envelope he found it enclosed another, addressed to himself, with an under-scored note in block capitals, reading, "In the event of this not reaching David Powlett-Jones personally return unopened to the address below." The address was that of a firm of attorneys-at-law, in Los Angeles.

He slit the letter carefully and drew out several sheets, written in what looked like a laboured hand. Automatically he glanced up at the address and was shocked to find it was the Galilean Hospital, in a coastal town north of Los Angeles. He settled back in his chair and read.

My Dearest David,

This is probably the last letter you will receive from me and the last I will write unless, by what could be a miracle, I come through the next op. and get my reprieve. In that unlikely event I'll write to Charles myself. I was in here just over a year ago for breast cancer, and they thought they had caught it in time, but they were wrong. Doctors are even more fallible than your lot when it comes to the crunch. Well, it's tough at forty-odd, I guess, but I'm not bitching. I've had it pretty good since I came over here, and the kids won't have any financial worries from here on. I should have liked to have seen Charles again, and the old country too, although I've had far more luck here than I ever had there, except running into two nice men, you and Hiram. Three, if you count Keith Blades, whom I've never forgotten, or regretted for that matter.

However, writing isn't all that easy in these circumstances, so I'd best come to the point, or rather points, of this mysterious letter. First, if what I expect to happen does happen, I've arranged with my attorney to notify you at once, and you'll be saddled with the job of telling Charles. I'm sorry about that, David, but it can't be helped, and I imagine you've had to do that kind of thing before in your time and done it very tactfully. In any event, though, as soon as you can bring yourself to do it, will you drop him the hint and prepare him in some way, so that it will prove less of a shock for a lad of his age. I realise that this is putting a lot on you but I've a right to ask. Which brings me to my next point.

He put the letter down there, leaning forward on his elbows and reassessing her courage and fortitude, characteristics he had noticed at their first encounter, when he had

marched up into her room over the quad arch to discuss
Blades, demanding an explanation for that extraordinary
scene he had witnessed in the goyle behind the planty. In her
way, he thought, she was as singular as Beth and Chris, and
it was a privilege to have held her in his arms all that time
ago. And yet, acknowledging this, and even remembering
it vividly, the next paragraph had the power to shock him
as he had never been shocked.

I've had a long, long debate with myself about the
wisdom or unwisdom of telling you this, particularly as you
seem to have made another happy marriage after all,
and taking into consideration the fact that Charles is well
provided for, and you don't owe him anything in the
material sense. But the truth is, of course, he's your boy,
and the real reason why I married Hiram in such a rush
that time. It wasn't that I gave a damn at the time—for
myself that is—but I had an absolute conviction that it
would land you in a series of complications, both emotional
and practical. It wouldn't have most men—they would
have thought themselves off the hook—but not you, with
that Celtic conscience you're lumbered with. So I took
Hiram up on his standing offer and I don't regret that
either for I'm confident he never once suspected Charles
wasn't his son. He was always very proud of him, and they
had a nice relationship from the very beginning.

I could see you in Charles to some extent when he began
to shoot up, and he has at least two of your characteristics,
namely patience, and a rare disposition to stand on his
own feet, and take a crack at things. Maybe you've already noticed this. I kind of gathered as much, from your
latest school report.

The point is, I see no advantage at all in telling him and
for his sake more than yours. Your wife can't very well
hold it against you, for it all happened years before you
met her, but adolescents have enough problems these
days without adding to them by presenting them with a
choice of loyalties. In the final instance, I leave it to you,
of course, whether you tell your wife or not, but the best
course would seem to be to leave it right where it is and

just—well, keep a fatherly eye on him, something that will come naturally to you, David. That's about it except to say goodbye and good luck always. I still think I did the right thing in refusing to marry you. You never would have made it, David, with me in tow. I'm not the domestic type, and I would have vegetated down there and might even have degenerated into a nag, but that isn't to say I haven't thought of you often, and always, *always*, with great affection. My love to you both, Julia.

He sat there a long time with her letter held lightly in his hand, thinking of the dark, slender boy, at this moment joining in popular choruses with all the other Sunsetters in Big Hall, trying hard to see him as something more personal than a unit in the long, long procession of youngsters who had passed through his hands in the last twenty-two years. He found himself quite unable to do this, although, now that he came to think of it, the boy had always had something of the look of his brother Huw about him, the seventeen-year-old who had gone down the pit with his father and elder brother that May morning in 1913, and never surfaced again. But his immediate concern was not with young Sprockman but with the woman who lay dying—was probably dead by now—six thousand miles away, across an ocean and a continent, and he saw her as he recalled her that morning when she had awakened him with a breakfast tray in her Camden Town flat, a final courtesy after what he had never ceased to regard as a gesture of rare generosity. He had a curious sense then, of being almost the last survivor of his generation, a stubborn piece of flotsam that had somehow managed to weather the nonstop buffeting of the years, embracing as they had two World Wars, linked by a long period of slump and uncertainty. He knew he would follow her advice, leaving both Charles and Chris in ignorance of the relationship. It would do the boy no good, and although Chris would almost surely take a tolerant view of it, she might see it as a circumstance that down-graded her own son, the boy she had been at such pains to have, and largely, he suspected, on his account.

He got up and went into the quad, then down the draughty

stone passage to Big Hall, where the concert was still in full swing. Buck Suttram, inheritor of the Sax Hoskins mantle, was leading community singing with what his cronies called Buck's squeeze-box, an ungainly piano accordion. They were singing, 'Roll out the Barrel' at the tops of their voices, and he caught a sidelong glimpse of Chris, joining in the chorus and smiling up at the stage. Then, as the song came to an end, somebody shouted, 'There'll Always be an England', and there was an immediate howl of dissent. He was glad about that. Like him they would consider that a blushmaking number, out of tune with the national mood that was now, thank God, one of stark realism. Somebody else shouted, "Get Clark! Get Clark and his banjo!" and it was not until Charles Sprockman was pushed forward that he remembered 'Clark' was the nickname they applied to his own son, turned thirteen now, and tall for his age.

He had not known until then that Charles Sprockman was a dab hand with the banjo, specialising in Western ballads. He mounted the dais with an engaging grin and began to strum 'Oh, Susannah', a ditty they all seemed to know.

He withdrew to the passage, pausing a moment to listen to the rollicking chorus:

> *Oh, Susannah!*
> *Don't you cry for me,*
> *I'm going back to the Oregon*
> *With the banjo on my knee . . .*

His eyes pricked a little, standing there in the strong draught, and he gathered his gown about him and sought the solitude of the quad, finding that a sickle moon had come out from behind the belt of blue black clouds, and was riding high across Middlemoor. There was just enough light to make his way round past Outram's and the fives court, then diagonally across the field to his compulsive anchorage, Algy's thinking post.

In the flare of a match he saw that it wanted ninety minutes to midnight when the year, surely the most momentous year in history, would be dead and done with, except for the history books. He was glad to see it go. It had brought a reprieve certainly, but at what he could never cease to regard as a prohibitive price, with a lot more owing, he wouldn't wonder. But that was the way of things, even up here, where the setting never changed and the stream of life flowed on and on, over rapids and through occasional green pastures.

The moon clouded over momentarily and he waited, drawing on a cigarette, until it rode out again, clear and white above the indistinct blur of the planty.

Improbably, in this subdued light, it recalled the winter landscape of 1916–17 in Flanders when the future, as now, had seemed dismal and unpredictable. They wouldn't invade now, he supposed, and that might mean they had missed the bus after all, but that, in itself, decided nothing. Sooner or later they would have to be invaded, thrown down and flattened, and how was this possible, with jackboots already planted from the Pyrenees to the Carpathians, from Narvik to Benghazi? It wasn't, or not in the foreseeable future, and yet . . . could such an obscene tyranny endure indefinitely, with one offshore island holding out under a nonstop bombardment?

This time he looked back across the centuries for his sign, ranging eras as far distant as those of Alfred, Hereward the Wake and the bloody chaos of Stephen's reign. Things must have seemed pretty hopeless then for those holding the short end of the stick, for the poor and landless, for what Masefield would call the men hemmed in by spears. But something gainful had emerged from it. Magna Carta; Simon de Montfort's so-called Parliament; centralised government, and a rule of law under Edward I and later Henry VII. Nothing much, perhaps, or not until Cromwell and his successors won a constitution from their overlords, and city merchants held backsliding kings to ransom. It was always a long, pitiless haul, with any number of backward lurches, but finally, inch by inch, democracy had been dragged on-ward and upward, and he wondered, fitfully, who did most of the heaving when it came down to bedrock. It wasn't the privileged and the wealthy, and it wasn't the masses, thrust-ing upward from below, for almost all their efforts had been swiftly neutralised by reaction. If he was asked to name a class to which most of the credit was due it would be that

section of the community he had once affected to despise, the
petty bourgeoisie, and who were the petty bourgeoisie when
you thought about it—thought about it really hard? They
were the kind of Englishmen, Scotsmen and Welshmen who
were neither rich nor poor, intellectual nor illiterate, well-
endowed or down-and-out, the section who sent their sons
here, to a place like Bamfylde, to acquire, through books,
example and, above all, a mingling and sharing of ideas, a
creed of common sense and tolerance. They were the end
products of all the Briarleys, the Christophersons, the His-
lops, the Winterbournes and that long-shanked, open-faced
stripling, playing 'Oh, Susannah', in Big Hall at this very
moment, himself the product of a few minutes' exchange of
affection between a rather gallant woman like Julia Sprockman, and a three-hundred-a-year schoolmaster, both in
search of a momentary escape from loneliness.

*   *   *

The temperature was hovering a degree or two above
freezing but he did not feel cold. He seldom did up here, for
in peace-time the scatter of friendly lights lower down the
slope had warmed his heart, a fire to go home to whenever
he needed one. He had need of it now for suddenly, out here
in the frosted silence, he felt not cold but frightened. The
moonlight held on long enough for him to stride down to
within ten yards of the fives court and then, just as it clouded
over again, he saw Chris, muffled to the ears, move into the
fleeting patch of light. She called, "Davy? Is that you,
Davy?" and, when he answered, "Anything wrong?"

"No," he said, "just popped out to blow the cobwebs
away," and sought her hand.

"I told them you wouldn't mind them staying up to see
the New Year in. Is that all right?"

"Yes, it's fine. They'll do it anyway, and we might as well
join them. But how about some tea first?"

"I'll make some." Then, as they moved round the bulk of
the new wing to the forecourt, "You'll be glad to wave
goodbye to this one, Davy. The next can only be for the
better can't it?"

"Yes," he said, with certainty, "it'll be that all right."

He spun her round as she went up the two steps and kissed her mouth, finding her lips as warm and reassuring as her hand.

"This won't do at all, sir," she said, laughing. "Not in front of the children," and steered him into the hall, slamming the door before she reached for the light switch. "It's okay," she said, offhandedly, "I saw to the blackout on the way through," but somewhere, probably in old Rigby's kitchen, there was a window open for faintly, carried on the downdraught in that funnel of a passage, came the sound of the Sunsetters, singing to Buck's accordion. He was leading them in an old community favourite, 'Shenandoah', and the sound had within it comfort and continuity.

III

It was inconceivable as well as unforgivable that he had completely forgotten his appointment with Earnshaw at eleven on New Year's Day.

He had just popped down to the cottage to wish Alison a happy new year and was walking back when he spied Buck Suttram scudding across the rimed football pitch towards the field gate. Buck gestured urgently, and changed direction, arriving out of breath, and saying, "Someone waiting, sir—been waiting half an hour. Said he had an appointment. Mrs. Powlett-Jones said I was to find you and tell you to hurry."

He remembered then. Earnshaw was a twenty-four-year-old, whom he was interviewing as a possible replacement for Boyer, and he bent his steps to the forecourt where Chris was standing on the steps, looking a little fussed. "He seemed put out you weren't here, Davy. Said the agency told him you fixed the appointment yourself."

"So I did," he said, "but it completely slipped my memory. I must be going senile," and he hurried into the study, Chris calling after him to say the visitor had been given coffee on arrival.

He had expected a very different kind of man. The agency had described him as keen, ex-service, and interested in games, so that he had pictured an extrovert like Irvine. The youngster sitting on the window-seat was small-boned, haggard and emaciated, as though he had walked here on short rations, and his blue suit looked, not soiled exactly, but threadbare, as though it had been pressed and cleaned for the interview. In spite of this, however, the unsmiling face that glanced up as he entered was at odds with Earnshaw's general appearance. It was an intense face, with strong features that were emphasised, if anything, by a broad expanse of scar tissue, reaching from the right temple all the way down to the long jawline. The eyes were blue, deeply socketed, unwavering and a little challenging, as though the mind behind them was acclimatised to rebuffs. David said, shaking hands, "I'm most terribly sorry. I do apologise. I've been swamped in work this holiday and your appointment got buried under an avalanche of forms and correspondence. At least, that's the only excuse I can offer. Please sit down. You've had coffee, I understand," and surprisingly the eyes smiled, softening the rather grim expression, and the small, taut body relaxed as Earnshaw said, "Mrs. Powlett-Jones was very kind, Headmaster. She seemed to think you were on the premises somewhere. Please don't apologise. I'm sure you're busy."

"I oughtn't to be too busy to remember an appointment with someone who has come all the way from town. You are a Londoner, I believe?"

"No, but I've been based there since I got my ticket. I'm Lancastrian. Burnley."

"And ex-service. The infantry, wasn't it?"

"Ordnance Corps. I was invalided in early November. I'd only been in just over a year."

It was the word 'invalided' that did the trick. He had a curious sensation then of looking at himself in a time mirror, a jittery twenty-one-year-old, fighting the battle of his life to stave off a fit of the shakes in this same room half a lifetime ago, with Algy Herries prowling about behind this same desk searching for a means to put him at ease. He said, "You got knocked about pretty badly, Earnshaw?" and Earnshaw said, flatly. "A Stuka dive-bombed the lorry I was driving, south of Lille. I was sprayed with petrol. I don't remember a damned thing about it until I came round on the

Red Cross ferry. They were still running then. It was less than a week after the breakthrough. But I'm fit now. Or fit enough."

It was very curious, the speed with which he assembled the bridge between them, almost as though the agency had given him all the facts in advance and he had pondered them overnight. He said, "I was going to treat myself to something to keep the cold out. You'll join me?" and without waiting waiting for an answer he rose and opened the door, calling to Rigby to bring two glasses, the whisky decanter and the siphon.

When he turned back Earnshaw was smiling. "You didn't have to do that, Headmaster. I'm nervous right enough, but it's nothing to do with this," and he raised his right hand to the scar. "I would have been nervous in any case. An inferiority complex, they'd call it, I imagine. The fact is, I've only read about places like this. I'd never visited one, much less worked in one."

"That puts us on a level footing. When I came here, straight from hospital in March, 1918, I thought of all schools like this as a cross between Eton and Borstal. An upper-crust Borstal," and he was relieved to see Earnshaw's smile widen, embracing the reluctant part of his face that a grafter, somewhere, probably thought of as the best of a bad job. It encouraged him to add, "As a matter of fact, you've got the edge on me. Your application says you had a year's pupil teaching before the war. I'd never faced a class in my life."

The news must have surprised Earnshaw for he blinked rapidly and began, "But surely . . ." and then Rigby doddered in with the whisky and he subsided until the butler had gone and David was busy with the drinks. "You're saying you worked for your degree *after* coming here?"

"Years after. They were so short of manpower in 1918 they had to put up with it. I got an external degree. Not a very brilliant one, either."

"But Bamfylde is a big school. And quite well known, isn't it?"

"It's big, but it's always been second grade. Academically and socially, that is. Not in any other way."

It served to banish the last trace of Earnshaw's nervousness. He said, "That makes it a lot easier. I'd intended working for a degree anyway. There never was much chance of a varsity place. My father works in a mill when there's work about, and my mother keeps a corner shop to help out. I got a scholarship in 'thirty-seven but I couldn't take it up. There was no way of making up the grant, so I took a course at a teachers' training college and a year's practical. I was going to complete the course when war broke out and would have qualified by now but I couldn't have hoped for anything like this. Frankly I was amazed when the agency put me up. They must be pretty hard pressed."

He took the whisky but didn't sip it.

"What attracted you to teaching in the first place?" and Earnshaw replied, after a moment's hesitation, "The subject itself. History. I could never get enough of it. I've hardly read anything but history since I was a kid."

"Were you going to specialise in any period?"

"Eventually, or so I hoped. Military history. But I'm not so sure now. The real thing dulls the appetite, doesn't it?"

"No, you only think it does. Then you read and talk yourself to the point where you're convinced you could win a war on your own if they gave you the chance and why not? We couldn't make a worse botch of it than your lot or mine, could we?"

"You won yours eventually."

"We don't seem to have." Then, impulsively, "You were there when it happened. How does it look now?"

Earnshaw took his time answering. Then he said, with conviction, "A lot better than it looked then."

"Because of the Battle of Britain?"

"Not entirely. Mainly for quite another reason. We're on our own now. It's up to us, all of us, not a gaggle of generals, who don't seem to have learned much since your show. And not cluttered by Allies either. That always affords a better field of fire. You're a history man, aren't you, Headmaster?" and when David nodded, "I keep making comparisons. The performances we put up against even bigger odds at places like Crecy and Agincourt. And later against Spain, in the sixteenth century. Allies slow us down, somehow.

Politics keep coming into it and we lose unity, sense of purpose and direction. We'll win all right. Handsomely, I'd
say."

He realised he had taken an immense liking to the boy—
he could only think of him as someone a little senior to, say,
Boyer about the time he had beguiled the Lower Fourth with
his fit, or Winterbourne, when he appeared out of the storm
to steer him down to that cave beside the torrent. There was
real substance here, plus a quiet, deadly kind of confidence
in himself and his world, and it had a tremendously bracing
effect on the spirit. "We'll win all right . . ."; he had heard it,
or its equivalent, so often in the last few months, but the
expression of confidence had never carried Earnshaw's
quiet conviction, a conviction based, he assumed, on experience rather than yesterday's newspaper headlines. It
was a tonic, too, at such a time, with so much confusion and
rumour and propaganda lapping across the country.

He heard himself say, echoing old Algy Herries, "No need
to go back if you don't have to . . . we can put you up in the
President's room . . . we always keep a room for the Old
Boys' President, that's his privilege . . . I can lend you some
pyjamas and we'll root out a toothbrush . . ." an old, old
record, playing a tune that was able to inject him with
confidence of a kind he had never been able to find in this
room, not even in his most tranquil days, when Armageddon
was only a dire possibility.

He jumped up and called through to Chris, "Mr. Earnshaw will be staying to lunch and dinner, Chris. Will you tell
Rigby? He's out front somewhere . . ."

And then, like the final touch of an artist's brush completing the picture, the bell began to clang as Gibson, depu-
tising for Killerton, the official bell-ringer in term time,
summoned the Sunsetters to lunch, and they came clattering
down from the library where they were having what Buck
Suttram called 'a jam session'. The scrape of their boots
passing along the quad arcade reminded him of the touchline supporters who had witnessed Nicolson's surprise
victory in the 1918 house final. Out of the corner of his eye
he saw Earnshaw's surprised look and thought, "I daresay
he's wondering what the hell he has let himself in for but

he'll soon find out, and live to thank his stars maybe, as I did once, but had stopped doing lately . . ."

The President's room was still on the top storey of the head's house, above the old sanatorium, and he left Earnshaw there, telling him he would call up the stairwell when lunch was ready.

It was some time since he had been up here and he stopped on the landing to take in the south-eastern aspects of the moor, glittering under hoar frost as far as the copses climbing the western slopes above Bamfylde Bridge. It was a view he remembered from his very earliest days, the short end of the Lent term, 1918. It framed the sense of renewal and continuity Earnshaw had stimulated.

Almost everything that he had experienced over the last twenty-two years was compressed into the scene. The early runs, whipping in laggards like Dobson, Letherett and Driscoe; the coming of Beth and the twins; that tiny blur of white under Stone Cross that was Boyer's cottage; state funerals of veterans like Bat Ferguson and Judy Cordwainer; the materialisation of Chris, with Ulrich Meyer in tow; the Sunday pilgrimages of a thousand gourmets to Ma Midden's window for pies and pasties; and away to the left, where the smooth fold of the hillside narrowed to the goyle, that idyllic scene played by Blades and a woman who had brought him a son he could never acknowledge, save in his heart.

Peace, of a kind that had eluded him for sixteen dismal months, stole over him, ironing out the stresses of wartime turmoil, easing the smart of wounds caused by the sacrifice of boys like Briarley, Skidmore, Christopherson, Graves-Jones, Hislop, Churchill and little Keithley. The winter sun, red as a cider apple, set the plateau aglow, picking up the quartz in the scatter of boulders up there, full of muted promise somehow, that the new year would be different, more positive, signposting a road back to sanity and ultimate fulfilment.

He drank it all in thankfully, his thinning hair lifting in the strong draught that searched these landings at this time of year. Then, turning back to the stairhead, he stepped briskly down to ground level, remembering that sixteen days from now the unnatural quiet of the sprawl of buildings would be shattered by the clamour of his enormous family, drawn back to him from what he had come to think of, in his years up here, as the ends of the earth.